The Allenby Bridge

Theodore Ponticelli

PUBLISH AMERICA

PublishAmerica
Baltimore

First printing

Hardcover 978-1-4512-3617-0
Softcover 978-1-4512-3618-7
PUBLISHED BY PUBLISHAMERICA, LLLP
www.publishamerica.com
Baltimore

Printed in the United States of America

DEDICATION

To My brothers, Lou and Bob

Table of Contents

CHAPTER 1
A VISIT TO TEL AVIV

The Ben-Gurion Airport terminal was empty with the exception of Flight 882 passengers arriving from New York.

Richard Bridges glanced at his watch, it was four in the afternoon, Tel Aviv time. Surprisingly, he felt rested after a hectic flight from New York. The glare from the sun shining through the windows of the terminal obstructed his vision for a few moments as he avoided getting run over by a group of noisy school children obviously on their way to Jerusalem and other religious places.

Bridges followed the other passengers to the Customs Counters. He noticed the terminal hadn't changed since his last trip to Tel Aviv. The Israeli women were still attractive but a bit more Americanized. He thought one would think the Iraq and Gulf War would have brought changes of improvement, at least with all the money the United State paid to keep the Israelis out the war against Iraq.

Remodeling the terminal would have been a pleasant change, at least attract the tourists trade.

While passing through Israeli Customs, Richard Bridges received a smile from an Israeli Customs Agent whose appearance was striking and more American. Bridges detected a slight accent in her English when she requested his passport. As the woman examined and stamped his passport, she looked directly past Bridges and spoke Hebrew to a man standing just behind him. Bridges turned, glanced at the stranger and felt the man looked vaguely familiar. He was slightly over weight, dark complected, and obviously needed his hair trimmed. As the Custom Agent spoke, Richard understood his own name being used. On previous trips, he usually met his contacts either at the rental car counter or in front of the terminal. Suspecting that the man was his contact, he wondered perhaps this time something was wrong. Richard glanced at his watch again, the Custom's Agent looked at him once again as she conversed with the man behind Bridges. She interrupted herself to instruct Bridges to close his bags, with a wide smile handed him his passport and wished him a pleasant stay in Tel Aviv.

As Richard zippered his bags, the man standing behind to his left immediately approached him and spoke American with an Eastern accent, as though he was from Delaware or Pennsylvania or some other place in that vicinity. Bridges thought the voice didn't match the image. The man appeared to be an Israeli official, maybe Mossad. It was obvious his suit was tailored, possibly Italian.

The man introduced himself, "Mr. Bridges, I'm Charles Goldberg, my American name. I changed it to David Halim when I became an Israeli citizen but I still go by the name of Charlie, the name I was called at school in North Philadelphia…I always respond to Charlie."

Bridges shook hands with the man, noting his handshake indicated he was sincere and sure of himself. Bridges teaches body language and physical characteristics in many of his classes while lecturing to law enforcement students as well as those wishing to become intelligence agents.

As both men walked to the black American made car parked next to the curb, a dark.complected young man in his teens, possibly Arab, ran past them attempting to snatch one of the bags from Bridges' hand. Charlie immediately took the bags from Bridges and placed them in the trunk of the car. Bridges asked Charlie what the incident was all about. It was obvious Charlie down played it and briefly explained. "Just a thief." Then Charlie smiled.

Bridges was pleasantly surprised to find an attractive young woman would be their driver. She made no comment as both men entered the rear seat of the Lincoln Town-car. The conversation was at a minimum as they traveled to downtown Tel Aviv, he thought perhaps the driver wasn't cleared for access to information Bridges was expected to discuss.

Realizing the driver spoke English and she was possibly American, Bridges attempted to be witty, "What is a nice girl like you doing in Israel?" The young woman smiled, recognizing Bridges' feeble attempt to make conversation with her, "I was born in California, I grew-up in Newport Beach and left after completing undergraduate studies at USC. After graduation I wanted to visit Israel before my father packed me off to graduate-school, and that was almost four years ago. I love Israel and what the Israeli people are doing to build this country. I want to be part of it. My mother, of course, is so upset that I've stayed here. She thinks with all the trouble in the Middle East, and Israel with it's boarder problems, I'm going to get hurt or killed." She smiled at Bridges as they made eye contact in the driver's rear view mirror.

Bridges found her refreshing, amusing and thought she was about twenty-seven. She had long blond hair, which she conveniently braided into a single braid. Her deep tan and smile revealed perfect white teeth. She was a pretty girl Bridges thought, and friendly enough.

The young woman seemed uninhibited about talking about herself, "I'll return to California next year and enter graduate school. I haven't decided what my studies will be, but working and living here has given me insight".

Bridges turned to Charlie asking about his background as the car moved toward downtown Tel Aviv. "I grew up in North Philadelphia and attended Temple University. After receiving a degree in sociology, I felt compelled to visit Israel." He sighed and took a breath. "I became so involved with political interests and how it affects the Israeli people and the free world. Then I enlisted in the Army and after basic training I was considered for the rank of Captain. I expressed an interest in the intelligence field and they transferred me to the training facility for Mossad agents…the rest is history."

Charlie went on to explain that it took him ten-years to learn Hebrew, "I've been told that I speak Hebrew with a Philly accent." Both men smiled at the comment.

They arrived at the Basel Hotel located on the Mediterranean seashore at the center of the nightlife of Tel Aviv. The driver stopped next to the main entrance. Charlie and Bridges got out of the car, Bridges removed his bags and brief case from the trunk. The driver informed Charlie she would return in thirty-minutes.

They entered the lobby of the hotel, Bridges noticed the hotel had been renovated and felt good to be inside an air-conditioned building. Charlie headed for the lounge, "Meet me in here after you check in my-friend, I need a drink…its been a long day."

Bridges looked around the lobby and discovered the check in desk had been moved during renovation. He approached the desk and asked for his reservations. The desk clerk smiled and handed Bridges a registration form. She informed Bridges he had a message waiting. Bridges was surprised. Only a few people knew his itinerary. The message read: Call Billy-Ray at 517-4338. The number was a local Tel Aviv exchange. Bridges thanked the desk clerk, and as he turned to leave, the clerk reminded Bridges his room number was 333, and not to forget as the key is not engraved with the number. Again Bridges thanked her and headed for the lounge. The place was full of young people most of them appeared American.

Bridges found Charlie seated in a booth near the entrance of the lounge. He joined him as Charlie ordered him a beer. Thirty minutes passed and the driver returned and joined them in the lounge. She changed into a light blue jump-suit complementary to her bodily attributes and gave a certain sexual appeal. Bridges complimented her as she sheepishly smiled and ordered mineral water.

Bridges finished his beer and excused himself promising to return after he changed his clothes. He took the elevator to the third floor, remembering his room number was "333". He amused himself at the thought of how serious the desk clerk was when she reminded him of the number. As he entered his room he turned the lights on and discovered the phone on the bed-stand. He was curious then dialed the local number listed on the message. A voice on the other end bellowed, "United States Embassy," Bridges smiled to himself, "This is Richard Bridges, I'd like to speak to Billy Ray."

"One moment SIR." The Marine responded. After a short time a voice was heard, "Billy Ray here." Bridges responded, "Listen shit-head, what do you want?" Billy-Ray was sarcastic when he realized it was Bridges, "Dicky-boy, why didn't you check in with us?"

Bridges became annoyed and in a caustic voice, "I'm on contract to the AID program. You know...United States Agency for International Development. My mission has nothing to do with your employer's business, so back off."

Billy-Ray was indignant and shot back, "Dicky-whenever you get involved with something, to include teaching a pretty young woman the art of playing tennis, you always find yourself in the middle of an international incident and I want to be there...that's all."

Bridges smiled to himself, then answered, "Thanks for the concern, I'll be at the Country-.Club for the next few days. Maybe we can meet for lunch or something. By the way, did you arrange for one of those sand-niggars to harass me at the airport?"

Billy-Ray answered sneeringly, "Who-me?" Then agreed to meet and discuss old times. "You know, down south, El Salvador my man...Central America you remember?"

Bridges spoke, "I remember, the old time's in Central America almost got me killed. I'm not sure I need to remember 'old-times.' Bridges said goodbye and hung up.

He sat on the edge of the bed and thought that as long as he had known Billy Ray, he never learned his real name. Then he recalled that most everyone knew him only as Billy-Ray. Again he recalled his mission into Central America—El Salvador and the problems he had. Billy-Ray and his communications team supposedly saved his ass along with the Salvadorian team. Bridges never felt comfortable about his rescue. It seemed so long ago and he knew Billy-Ray could only mean trouble. Surely he was up to something. In due time it was sure to reveal itself.

Bridges quickly showered and changed into casual clothes, khaki pants, dark blue poplin shirt with military style epaulets, chukka boots. The standard attire for the region. A give-away as having Agency connection in Central America and Vietnam many years before. It had been the so-called uniform of the day. While looking at himself in the mirror as he combed his now thinning hair, he couldn't help noticing his mustache was turning grey although his hair was still dark brown and showing little of his age except for the touch of grey on the sideburns.

Bridges met Charlie and the young woman in the lounge, "Sorry for the delay. I needed to return a call to those clowns at the Embassy."

Charlie acknowledged he clearly understood.

The young woman was busy reading a paperback love story. The lounge was crowded and lighting dim, Bridges tried his wit one more time, "I'll bet the ending is sweet—she lived happily ever after." Bridges teased Becky.

The young woman sighed and looked at Bridges then smiled. She blushed slightly. Charlie laughed as he watched Bridges tease her.

Bridges suggested they leave for the "Country-Club…" a term used to describe the Mossad Training Academy. American agents having business there agree the building from a distance resembled a country-club. The true reference was: "Midrasha".

They traveled north leaving the busy section of Tel Aviv, with Bridges seated in the rear and Charlie up front with the driver. "Its beginning to get dark." Charlie broke the silence. "We'll be in time for the evening meal. Whenever an American visits, the chef prepares a spread enjoyed by everyone." The driver responded, "Charlie likes to eat, its his hobby." She laughed in a soft girlish manner and then commented that she was starved and hadn't eaten all-day. Charlie teased her, "How can anyone forget to eat?"

Bridges joined in, "The young lady wants to keep her figure."

As they arrived at the Midrasha, a white building that sat on a small hill which provided observation to all four sides, Bridges grabbed his briefcase, an old brown leather looking type he carried since his tour in Vietnam back in 1969.

Charlie noticed and remarked, "The U.S. Government could at least issue you a new brief-case." He smiled

Bridges liked the brief-case. He used it whenever he went into the 'bush', "It brings me good luck." He satisfied himself with the remark, although agreed the brief case looks like hell.

Charlie agreed, "I'll bet it does—it looks like something you would find in a museum."

The driver told Bridges not to pay attention to what Charlie said, "He's pulling your leg," Becky smiled.

As Charlie and Bridges entered the building through the front door adjacent to the guest parking area, Bridges glanced at the driver as she removed three automatic weapons from the trunk. What a gutsy woman he thought. Both men entered the building. As they walked down the hallway, Bridges said hello to several employees that were busy and glanced at them as they walked to the office of the Course Commander. The door was open and Charlie approached first casually announcing that Richard Bridges was with him. The older gentleman, slightly over-weight and had a heavy bushy gray mustache, smiled when he recognized Bridges. He extended his hand to shake and impulsively hugged Bridges.

"You haven't aged a day since Operation-Sphinx in eighty-one." Bridges smiled happy to see his old friend then reminded him of the nick-name given to him when they met at the U.S. Defense Department Institute in the late sixties.

The older man smiled and said "LOU". Charlie was standing in the door-way and appeared puzzled over Moshe Cohen's nick-name. Bridges recognized the puzzled look on Charlie's face and explained. "When Moshe attended the course in Washington he often watched American TV, a recommendation by the Director of Foreign Students. It enabled the student to learn English, in addition to the formal classes. Whenever I visited Moshe, I found him glued to the TV watching LOU COSTELLO movies. Moshe liked them to the point of getting up at three-in-the morning to watch the old movies until his roommate started calling him 'Lou'. During the training program, Moshe was called the nick-name...by fellow students as well as instructors. For some reason it stuck. Come to think of it, you look a lot like Costello with a mustache." The three men roared with laughter which could be heard down the corridor. Moshe added, "We have a collection of the same movies on video upstairs in our TV studio. They're used to teach students to speak American-English. It really works well, plus the student gets a laugh while learning.". "Oh well, whatever works." Bridges responded as the Commander of the Midrasha passed Moshe's office, Moshe directed Charlie and Bridges to the conference room next to the kitchen.

In the conference room, Bridges noticed the tables were set for the evening meal. The room smelled of fresh cooked food which reminded him he hadn't eaten since the meal on his flight from New York, then suddenly felt hungry. As Bridges was directed to a chair at the table, the young woman driver hurried to be seated next to him on his left. He was flattered, then remembered the Israelis never do anything without being directed. Moshe Cohen seated himself to Bridges right saying nothing to him. The mood seemed to change when Bridges was introduced to members of the teaching staff, guest instructors from the field, administrative staff, students in their advanced phase of training, and to the Commander of the Midrasha, "Aharon Risken". The Commander was tall, a well built man in his fifties with thinning gray hair and bushy eyebrows. Bridges was sure they had met before, maybe during 'Operation Sphinx'. As Moshe completed the introductions, the Commander was seated across the table and asked Bridges about his flight from Washington to Tel Aviv. Bridges felt uneasy. As often as he's been to Israel and worked with the Mossad, he felt like one of them, at least that's the way they made him feel. He sensed something needed to be discussed, however, those seated did not speak with exception of Charlie and the Commander. Bridges was served his meal. The food needed seasoning but he ate it anyway. After the meal, everyone excused themselves with exception of Moshe Cohen, Charlie, the Commander and Bridges. Commander Risken spoke in perfect English as the room cleared, he asked Bridges if he had been contacted by anyone from the American Embassy.

Bridges informed Risken that upon arrival at the hotel he had a message waiting from Billy Ray. The message was to call him. Bridges indicated that he didn't know Billy—Ray's true name, however, he is a communication specialist and a long time employee of the CIA. They had worked the same project in Central America during the late eighties.

Risken inquired as to the nature of the phone call. "I assume you returned the telephone call to the Embassy with great deal of suspicion, and of course, caution?"

Bridges thought at first the Commander's questioning was unusual and became suspicious, then responded showing the utmost respect, "Yes Sir, I called him and he wanted to be made aware of my activities in Tel Aviv." The Commander was indignant, "I know you are here on a State Department contract. Isn't your contract actually a USAID project? No intelligence work required? Your contract specifically outlined your duties as an instructor to teach our recruits methods of interviewing and interrogation, nothing more. Why the hell does the CIA want to monitor your activities?"

Bridges felt uncomfortable and didn't want to offend the Commander anymore. He was hoping Risken wouldn't think he had a hidden agenda. Bridges responded to Risken that he wasn't sure and he also thought it was strange, and further told him he agreed to meet him while in Tel Aviv. The time and place had not been agreed upon.

"Commander, if I recall, Billy-Ray is somewhat a 'hot-dog', that's an American term for someone who gets carried away with their importance. I'm sure this is why he remains a communications specialist and never went operational or became a Station Chief."

Risken didn't buy Bridges' explanation and fired back, "I believe this Billy-Ray is dangerous. He could compromise our mission with your Country in the Middle-East."

"Should I be concerned?" Bridges asked the Commander.

Commander Risken lowered his voice, narrowed his eyes,

"What I am about to tell you is of grave concern. Not only to Israel, but our closest friend, the United States." Risken continued, "we do not have all the facts, details, or operation layout, but we have enough information that will upset you, cause you great concern, frustrate you, and give you the feeling of helplessness. I know of what I speak."

Bridges sat and listened with alarming concern. His mind was cluttered with crazy thoughts. He gazed into the grey eyes of Commander Risken sensing he was about to reveal information Bridges didn't think he wanted to hear, at least not now. He thought his trip to Israel was going to be smooth teaching recruits at the Midrasha. Perhaps a little social time with his old friends, and maybe a side trip to Jordan to see the Arabian horses at Jordan's National Stud-.stables. His interest in Arabian horses began many years ago when he bought his wife her first bay-mare for her birthday. Bridges often thought of his wife when ever he was around horses, thoughts which brought on mixed emotions as he was reminded of the tragic accident which took her life several years ago, leaving him with their daughter and a stable of horses.

His attention was focused once again on the conversation with Risken. The Commander's voice was low and cautious as he explained a plot to assassinate the President of the United States, "This plan is not clear, Richard."

"We are in receipt of information that members of your Congress are involved, possibly those close to the President."

At this point in the conversation, Bridges smiled nervously looking at Risken, "Every time the liberals control things including the damn White House, there seems to be a mood the economy in my country is doomed and headed for socialization. Is this what you're talking about?"

Risken became upset with Bridges for his lack of comprehension thinking he wasn't taking him serious. He became impatient and asked for Bridges' attention. Bridges glared at Risken in contempt but trying not to show disrespect. He was trying to convey that he knew his Government and it's players.

The Commander directed Charlie and Moshe to leave the conference room. The kitchen staff cleared the tables. Now alone, Risken sat himself closer to Bridges, and continued his conversation. "I want you to listen to me Richard. We have serious concerns. Again I will repeat, we have substantial information from sources in Washington and other locations in your country that there is a plot to overthrow your government by unsuspecting factions. Who...we do not know at this point. We, at the Mossad, feel you are one of the few who can be trusted. Our experience with you supports our opinions and we stand ready to render assistance should you need us. I feel certain you will. A situation like this could disrupt our progress in the Middle-East, not to mention what it will do to your country."

Bridges couldn't believe what he had just heard. He knew the Israelis were a serious people and that the Mossad worked hard, they are good at what they do. But Bridges was having problems comprehending just what it was Risken wanted him to do in order to counteract a plot.

As Bridges tried to digest the information, Risken continued, "Our information is enigmatic and lacks specific details but is solid and reliable. Our source wants to talk to you...only you, I hope that you will confide in us once you learn the specific details."

Bridges expressed disbelief but reluctantly agreed to meet the source. He looked around the room and realized the room was empty except for him and the Commander. He experienced a lonely feeling and wanted to remind the Commander he no longer was an operational intelligence agent.

Commander Risken quickly explained a meeting had already been arranged, "You must limit who you share information with or who you may consult for advice. You can trust David Halim...Charlie to you, and of course your old friend Moshe Cohen. There are others, but for now limit your contact."

"I would like to talk of this person you refer to as Billy-Ray, the communication specialist at the Embassy. We have a profile on him. His true name is William Randolph Smyth, a graduate of Georgia Tech. He started working for your government after he completed college. Then he worked in Central America on USAID projects where he was recruited by the CIA. Smyth seems to appear in every hot-spot in the world, either just before it happens, or shortly there after. We know he was in Panama prior to that action. We know he is a communications expert and a computer engineer, but we don't know what this actually means in terms of intelligence activities. He is a mystery to some, and an over-zealous employee to others."

"Do you have reason to believe Billy-Ray, or should I say Smyth, is on the side of the Black-Hats? That's a term used in our western movies to identify the bad-guys." Bridges asked, trying not to sound patronizing.

Risken smiled with understanding and agreed the term was well defined. "We are uncertain as to what part Smyth plays in events about to happen. Our Mossad agents who know him, do not trust him, socially or professionally."

Bridges whistled in response, "When you people black-ball someone, that's the end, no redemption, a sort of kiss of death.". Commander Risken had a sober expression then asked Bridges, "Is this the image we demonstrate to our friends in the intelligence community?" Risken laughed out-loud as if he had just made his own joke. Bridges joined in breaking tension of the moment. Risken poured Bridges some Hebrew wine, and then both men sat in silence, a tasting ritual until Risken spoke again, "Once we learn what side Smyth is on, and if its not our side, the Mossad will handle the details with little or no effort, trust me my friend."

Bridges remarked, "Spoken like an elderly Rabbi."

Bridges glanced at Risken when he made the remark about the disposal of Smyth, "You have to be certain that he is a black-hat before such a task would be accomplished, I hope."

Risken smiled, "Listen Richard, if Smyth is a good-guy, a white-hat as you would put it, we will just see what he's up to, I'm convinced he's dirty, even without evidence, you Americans need evidence. This is where we differ. Now relax. Maybe you should sky-dive with our team this week, or are you too old?"

Bridges sighed as he thought of his friends at the Agency and what they would think if they were in receipt of the information, "I need more information about the plot before I can move in any direction. We've never worked together." Risken interrupted him, "Listen Richard…I have enough of a profile on you that I felt I knew you before we met this evening. Allow me to continue—you are a former U.S. Marine with awards of valor, you were recruited by the CIA during the Bay-of-Pigs operation, you were an aerial-photo interpreter, intelligence data analyst, field operative, and not to over-look an advisor and instructor of human behavior. Your education includes graduate studies in human behavior. You are six-feet tall, weigh about 195, you like to eat, seldom drink, love dark haired women. Unfortunately your wife was killed in an auto accident several years ago, need I continue? Oh yes, a master parachutist, skills used in Vietnam in 1966, you are no longer an employee of the CIA, but are now a contractor, a hired gun, need I say more?"

Bridges resented the part about 'hired-gun' he was sure the Commander meant it as a compliment.

Risken looked at Bridges, satisfied he was getting through to him, "Why did you become bitter over the information I provided? Save your energy for when you receive hard facts and details, remember my-friend, the fall of the Roman-Empire came about by internal corruption so what makes you think the United States is any different?"

"Commander, when do I meet the source?" Bridges impatiently asked.

"I would like you to meet the source tomorrow, however I want you to first meet with Smyth in the morning, very early, bate him. See what he has or what direction he is heading then a meeting will be arranged for you to meet the source at the Allenby Bridge tomorrow afternoon."

Richard Bridges agreed to the plan, assuring the Commander he would meet Smyth early in the morning and perhaps have breakfast at the hotel. Bridges telephoned the American Embassy from the Midrasha, hoping it wasn't too late to reach Billy-Ray. The phone rang, and then answered, "Embassy, Sergeant Oliver." Bridges identified himself and requested to speak to Billy-Ray.

The marine responded "Yes Sir," after a few moments a voice was heard, "Billy-Ray."

"Let's meet at my hotel for breakfast, say around seven, is that too early? I'm at the Basel as you know."

Billy-Ray gave a smart ass response, "Dicky-boy, I'll be there, might even buy your breakfast, meet you in the restaurant."

They hung up, Bridges sat in silence for a moment, thinking that the situation could get out of hand. Then informed Risken of the meeting at the Basel Hotel in the morning. Risken alerted Bridges that they would be under surveillance. Bridges smiled and thanked Risken then requested transportation to his hotel. Risken instructed Charlie to arrange for transportation. Bridges shook the Commander's hand, and once again thanked him. Charlie arrived at the conference room, Bridges noticed he was carrying a black case containing what Bridges suspected to be an nine-millimeter UZI. Charlie started to speak, but Bridges interrupted, "Nothing has changed in this area after dark."

Charlie took a deep breath, "Nothing is different as long as the PLO wants recognition. The Arabs want us to die and blow away in the desert-wind. We will always have to defend ourselves and of course our friends." Bridges picked up his brief case and followed Charlie out the door to the parking area. He was surprised to discover the driver was the same woman who drove him from Ben-Gurion Airport.

As they got into the car, Bridges remarked that by night they traveled first-class, meaning the car was American made, bullet-proof or armored plated.

The driver laughed and stated, "It was Charlie's idea, I guess he wants you to be safe." Charlie and Bridges laughed at the driver's comment.

During the trip to the hotel, Charlie inquired if Bridges enjoyed his chat with the Commander.

"He's a tough man. He got his point across without mixing words," Bridges responded.

You could hear the driver give a chuckle and a sigh in agreement.

As they traveled in silence, Bridges realized he failed to consult the training schedule to determine when he would be teaching the recruits.

Charlie broke the silence, "Everything is under control. Moshe is Course Commander and is aware you have business with Risken and others tomorrow. You are scheduled to teach the day after tomorrow. I mean the day following our holiday."

Bridges thanked Charlie for the information, then asked where Moshe had gone. Charlie responded, “Moshe went home after he discovered you and Commander Risken were involved in deep discussions. You will see him after your breakfast meeting.”

Bridges suddenly realized that he didn’t know the drivers name, “Young lady…I’m sorry…I don’t know your name.”

“My name is Rebecca.” She answered. “I go by Becky.”

“Will you be driving me tomorrow Becky?” Bridges inquired.

“Yes, as a matter of fact I’m assigned to you while you’re here.”

They arrived at the hotel, Bridges and Charlie got out of the car. Charlie walked him to the elevator. Bridges thanked him for his assistance and reminded him about his meeting with Billy-Ray at seven at the hotel restaurant. Charlie indicated that he remembered and would have transportation waiting for him after the meeting.

As Charlie began to walk away, Bridges called after him that he didn’t need the VIP treatment. “I’m just following orders, that’s all.” Charlie remarked, stopping to look back at Bridges.

“I understand.” Bridges responded. “I’ve been to Israel many times, I’ve worked with the Israeli government on several projects, there is no need to treat me like a diplomat.”

“Well my friend, when you worked as an agent, you were not treated special. Now that you are a contractor, you have become a VIP, that’s it.” Charlie smiled and wished Bridges a good night.

As he unlocked his hotel room door, Bridges couldn’t help thinking about the room number—333. For some reason the number kept going through his mind. As he entered the room and discovered a basket of fruit on the dressing stand. He smiled to himself and recalled receiving a fruit basket from an unknown source the last time he stayed in the hotel. He never discovered who sent it. Bridges noticed the message light was on and immediately contacted the front desk. The message was from Billy-Ray reminding him of their breakfast meeting in the morning. He thought it was damn strange Billy-Ray was anxious to meet with him.

After he showered and got into bed, Bridges couldn’t help thinking about his conversation with Risken. It was ever-lasting in his mind. He drifted off to sleep with thoughts of Becky, the driver. What a nice young woman. Then his thoughts turned to Charlie, a totally committed American-Israeli who was dedicated to the cause of Israel and enjoyed every minute of his career. Bridges drifted into deep sleep.

The telephone rang several times before Bridges answered.

"Hello", the voice on the other end sounded like an American woman, "Time to get up Mr. Bridges."

"Thank you very much, what time is it?" Bridges asked.

The caller informed Bridges it was six AM, Bridges thanked her, got up and prepared for the day. He dressed in the usual freshly washed and pressed Khaki trousers, a light blue shirt with epaulets and starch in the collar, and of course chukka-boots.

As Bridges glanced at the basket of fruit, he couldn't help wondering who sent it, maybe the hotel provided it, he thought he would ask when he approached the hotel front desk.

He looked at his watch, it was almost seven. He grabbed his old brown brief-case and headed for the elevator. As he waited he noticed a professional looking Israeli man waiting for the same elevator. Bridges thought he looked familiar, however, when he greeted him, the man returned the greeting with some effort. They both enter the elevator and went to the lobby. Both headed for the hotel restaurant.

Bridges spotted Billy-Ray in the corner of the restaurant, walked over to him and shook hands. Bridges thought his hand shake was weak with a sense reluctance, similar to a criminal suspect about to be interrogated. He seated himself, at which point the waitress arrived at the table and took their order. Bridges ordered, "One toasted bagel…cream-cheese…a cup of hot tea, no cream or milk, thank-you."

Bridges looked at Billy-Ray, who was obviously out of shape and over-weight. He had sandy hair, almost red, which needed a cut. His clothes were neat, tan trousers, military cut shirt, the typical CIA dress for the desert.

Billy-Ray inquired as to who the friend was that entered the restaurant with Bridges.

"He's no friend. I met him briefly getting on the elevator on my floor. He said hello, nothing else. Billy you seem a little hinky or is it

Agency paranoia setting in when one is up to no good?" Bridges laughed.

Billy-Ray got right to the point, "What is the damn Mossad up to? Why are you really here, and don't give me that shit about an AID contract. We both know AID is used as an Agency cover."

Bridges stared at Billy-Ray thinking he was about to lose it, or maybe because he is being forced to retire soon and had no place to go. The poor bastard he thought, Bridges spoke, "My friend, I use that sparingly, I'm on an AID contract, you can believe it or not. I don't know who the fuck you think you're talking to. I think you better cool it. As for the Mossad, I have no idea what they are up-to. They are my friends, however, they hardly confide in me, especially about matters that do not concern the United States."

Billy-Ray backed off and in a deep Southern accent, "Dicky-boy, you know what I mean, the Mossad is different than the CIA, or the average Israeli Army Officer. Members of the Mossad have often played two-ends against the middle. The Pollard matter will not be forgotten."

"Isn't that the way the Agency operates?" Bridges stated a matter of fact.

"We operate with integrity and never, I repeat, never double deal our allies as they do." Billy-Ray remarked belligerently.

"Listen numb-nuts, I didn't agree to meet you to debate the integrity of the Mossad, it sounds like you have some dislike for them, almost mistrusting them." Bridges answered with a smile which seemed to upset Billy-Ray.

Billy Ray was serious, and in a low voice, "I trust them as much as they trust me."

"I rest my case, now what do you want from me? Why was it so damn important we meet?" Bridges demanded. "I might as well get down to business. I know from reliable sources that Moshe Cohen, your old friend, is feeding you information concerning trouble back in Washington

Listen…it's bull-shit, it's nothing Dicky-boy, nothing at all, just politics, politics as usual. The Democrats against the Republicans, no more. I agree the American people become victims to the power struggle."

As Billy-Ray spoke, Bridges thought about what Risken told him. It now appeared Billy-.Ray was attempting to defuse the seriousness of the information. Then he became concerned about where Billy-Ray obtained his information. He wondered if there was a leak at the Mossad, or was information deliberately leaked to test reaction? He thought it was the latter, a common intell-trick to test reaction. Bridges felt a deep dislike for Billy-Ray. "Even thought he was an American and working for the same team." He just had an uneasy feeling about him.

Billy-Ray spoke slowly and in a low voice commanding Bridges attention, "Listen…we have been to many hot-spots in the world. We have shared some serious moments, we even survived the worst of it, need I mention that we are both former Marines? That should speak for its-self. Take my advise, stay out of this. Remember you are on State Department business, an AID contract as you say, that's all. Deliver your message to the recruits, collect your pay, and go home."

Bridges stared at Billy-Ray in total contempt, his warning was familiar he thought. What did he know? If its not bate issued by the Mossad, then how much did he know? Is he involved to some degree? Bridges continued in his thoughts. Perhaps there is a leak at the Midrasha. Can't be, they are damn tight, they don't have egos to feed like some American agents. This has to be discussed with the Commander.

"Billy, you're right, we've shared many of the same experiences in various hot-spots throughout the world, we worked the same projects, and oh-yes, we are both former Marines. However, I'm from the Old-Corps, that's the difference with our Marine Corps experience." They both laughed, a common joke among former Marines. "As a matter of fact Billy, a Parris Island Marine, that makes a big difference, you Texas boys went to boot-camp in San Diego, I'll forgive you." Richard smiled.

As he took a bite of the bagel, Bridges thought if he tipped his hand, it may compromise anything he may be able to do. If he denied any knowledge, Billy-Ray wouldn't buy it. He decided to deny knowledge and exercise his wild card with friends at Langley. He hoped he could trust the Station Chief in Tel Aviv if he had to, Bridges then responded,

"Billy, I agree, politics in Washington often raises it's ugly neck. But I have no knowledge of what you're telling me. You can take it or leave it."

"Do you mean to tell me that your friends at the Country-Club have not informed you as to the Washington caper, my friend? I can't believe it, you…super-agent, and they have not informed you. It's hard to believe. You spent most of the evening with the elite Mossad members and they never mentioned a thing? It's possible I guess or maybe they are waiting to tell you at a later date. If so, I would like to be informed."

Bridges was sarcastic and wanted to punch him-out,

"Should I tell your Station Chief at the Embassy first?"

Billy-Ray appeared to get upset, his face turned red, and then made a statement, "You probably had dinner last night with your Mossad friends. They usually discuss many important things while feeding their faces. If you tell me that you have no knowledge of anything brewing in Washington, then I'll have to accept your word and leave with that in mind."

Bridges laughed, "Listen my friend, I'm no longer working for the Agency. You know it as well as anyone. From time to time I pick-up a contract or two, and collect my pay. Why then should the Mossad or any member of Israeli Intelligence trust serious information to me? I'm powerless. Thanks for the compliment Billy but I have no information. Now, answer my question, if I receive information at a later date, should I pass it on to your Station Chief?"

Billy-Ray was sarcastic again, "Have your way. You may get hurt along with some of the others you hold in high regard. Take my advice, if you have plans, forget them. If I'm wrong, then I over estimated you and your Mossad friends, also, stay out of Jordan for your own safety."

Bridges felt certain Billy Ray was bluffing. He avoided answering his question concerning the Station Chief, which alerted Bridges that Billy-Ray was a rogue. He wants to play hard ball and he's going to strike out. But why is Billy so concerned about cautioning him not to go to Jordan? Bridges was amused and responded, "I plan a side trip to Jordan to see some Arabian horses. They are well trained and perform at the King's stud-stables. You're invited if you're interested in horses.

I don't know too many Texans who don't care for horses. I encourage you to come along, maybe we can get to know each other better."

Billy-Ray indicated that he had to go and Bridges agreed, "Thanks for the tea and bagel Billy, my treat next time, I'll call you before I return to the States, or if you are interested, before I leave for Jordan."

Bridges parted company and as he left the restaurant he noticed the same Israeli leaving at the same time. As Bridges walked to the main entrance of the hotel, the man followed him out the door. Bridges asked Becky where Charlie was, "He sent me. We will all meet at the Midrasha. How was your meeting?"

"It was alright, I hate talking to people who are arrogant and pretend to have knowledge when in fact they don't."

"Don't be concerned. We've got the entire conversation on tape." Bridges suspected as much, of course the Mossad would record the meeting between him and Billy Ray. Bridges now knew the Israeli on the elevator was Mossad. Probably from Moshe Cohen's staff. But why was he so obvious? Maybe to make Billy-Ray uneasy.

"I'll bet my friend Billy-Ray recorded our conversation as well. After all, he's a communication whiz." Bridges smiled.

They drove through Tel Aviv in silence until Becky asked Bridges if she could meet with him on a later date to discuss a personal matter. "It has nothing to do with work. You are older and I value your wisdom, I just need to talk."

"I would be delighted and I must admit that I'm flattered you would seek my advice." Bridges remarked. Becky smiled and thanked Bridges, "We can set a time later when I drive you to the Allenby Bridge this afternoon."

"I had no idea that we were going to the Allenby Bridge so soon. Seems the Commander mentioned it, well…yes we can discuss your situation whenever you wish." Bridges appeared surprised.

Becky informed him that the Commander would tell him the plan this morning, "I've been assigned to drive you there or any other place you need to go."

"What about Charlie? Has he been assigned to me while I'm here?"

"Yes, as a matter of fact, he requested the assignment. You should be flattered, Charlie is the assistant to your friend Moshe Cohen. He is the one who keeps the recruits moving during surveillance exercises in Tel Aviv. He is responsible for the physical training we go through. Charlie is respected by everyone, however, because he is American, I personally believe he will be limited in how far he will go unless he becomes involved in Israeli politics."

"Is Charlie interested in politics?"

Becky laughed out-loud, "Charlie hates politics with a passion, that's why he will get involved one day, I'm sure."

Bridges took the liberty to discuss his friend Moshe Cohen, "What about my long time friend, Moshe Cohen? Do you think he would like to get involved in Israeli government affairs?"

"Moshe Cohen is a super person and very family oriented. He is tired and it is my bet he would like to retire and settle somewhere in the States. He has relatives in the Miami area."

"How would that settle with the Israeli government? Moshe moving to the States after retirement?"

Becky responded, "I don't know, a lot of high ranking Mossad take vacations in the States, I don't think Moshe Cohen would be alone when it comes to retiring in Florida. With the PLO and Israel signing a peace agreement, a lot of conservatives don't like the idea of Israel paying recognition to Yasser Arafat and his band of criminals."

"Well, I have to agree Becky, the PLO stands for no-good. I'm certain there will be no peace between Israel and the PLO factions, no matter what's signed."

"What's your position in the Mossad? Bridges wanted to ask Becky when he learned she was American.

"I'm called Bat-Leveyha, roughly translated into English means a female escort, not for sex, rather an assistant Mossad Agent charged with responsibilities of supporting whatever agent I'm assigned. I like the job and I do more than just drive VIPs around. I work on gathering information for the course Commander, draft lesson plans, and see to it they are typed and filed under proper code."

"When you decide to return to the States, how will that settle with the Mossad leaders?" Bridges asked pointedly.

"They know my plans to return to school in the States. They just don't want me to write a book about the Mossad in hopes of getting rich at their expense, that's all. They would like me to return to Israel after graduate school but I don't know. Who knows, I may meet my knight on a white horse and end up getting married.".

They arrived at the Midrasha and Becky drove the car into the guest parking area. Bridges walked in the main entrance, then headed for Moshe Cohen's office after a few security procedures. As Bridges approached Moshe's office, Charlie met him in the passageway and alerted him the Commander wanted a conference with him in the upstairs conference-room.

"I'd like to talk to Moshe for a moment."

Charlie informed Bridges that Moshe would not be in until the next day. "He had personal business in Tel Aviv, you know, since the so-called peace agreement with the PLO, things are uneasy."

"Thanks for the info…Charlie."

Both went up stairs to the conference-room. In a few moments, Commander Risken arrived. Becky entered briefly, made sure the door was secured, then left the room.

As the three-men sat around the conference table, an employee from the kitchen entered the room with cool drinks and coffee. Bridges helped himself to a cup of coffee and returned to his seat. Charlie had a large glass of orange juice and the Commander settled for a cup of black-coffee in his favorite mug he received as a gift from someone in Washington. It has the U. S. Seal and his name on the opposite side. Risken seemed proud of the cup.

Bridges spoke first, "I met with Smyth this morning, as you know."

Risken answered, "Yes my friend I know. After listening to the tape recording I couldn't help thinking how could this man have survived as long as he has with your CIA? It is my opinion that he has no factual knowledge. His information did not come from anyone inside the Mossad. Maybe it was from sources in Washington. It sounded as though he expected you to fill in the details Richard. I think you handled it well, you left him holding his balls."

"Commander, what do you make of his comment about Jordan?"

"I think it was a joke, he doesn't know a thing. He does know that after the peace accord with the PLO, Jordan will want to talk to us. Cautioning you is Smyth's way of telling you he is connected and has information."

Bridges held on to something the Commander said that Smyth knows nothing about Jordan. "Then does he mean Jordan has something to do with the conspiracy?" He decided not to question this point. In due time he would learn the chain of events.

Charlie spoke, "I agree, Smyth is fishing and he thinks that by you being here, there may be a connection. Like the Commander said, it didn't come from us or anyone inside our organization. Anything we have is limited, that's why you're to meet the source this afternoon at the Allenby Bridge. You will know a great deal more at that time."

"Smyth is a cool person and his information is limited. He's what we call a 'hot-dog' in the.States. That translates into dangerous. He's been with the Agency for almost twenty-.years. I don't know his GS rating but I do know he's never been assigned to a key or supervisory position, that is, since I've known him. He continues to try to make a name for himself." Bridges smiled.

The Commander responded to Bridges, "We agree, he has some information. I really don't think he is involved with the plot. It's a case of him wanting to gain a reputation inside your Agency."

"I can check on him in due time without tipping my hand. Now what is this about meeting the source today at the Allenby Bridge?" Bridges surprisingly asked

"Becky and Charlie will take you to the Allenby Bridge this afternoon after lunch. You will make contact. We don't want you to reveal the identity to anyone, although I know the person well." Commander Risken answered as though he was issuing an order.

Richard Bridges nodded as he stared out the window facing the flowered atrium

CHAPTER 2
THE ALLENBY BRIDGE

In the classroom next to the video studio at the Midrasha, Bridges presented his introduction class to twelve Mossad recruits on the topic of human behavior. A prelude to the interrogation course he was contracted to teach. After a light lunch served in the conference room, Becky loaded the car with essentials of extra ammunition and automatic weapons. Richard smiled but said nothing when he witnessed Becky putting three US M16 rifles in the trunk.

Charlie and Bridges informed the Commander they were leaving for the Allenby Bridge. Risken was concerned, "Take it slow Richard. If the information is limited, more will be available later. I don't know if you are familiar with the area around the bridge and the element crossing the Dead Sea but I must warn you of the danger. It doesn't matter who you are or what side you're on…I caution you to be careful. Charlie and Becky know what I mean. Richard, do as you're told and all will go well."

Bridges in a wry smile, thanked the Commander and the three of them departed in the armor-plated black American car.

As they traveled in the direction of Jerusalem, Bridges couldn't help thinking he was getting too old to be involved in incidents of international consequence. He thought of the danger the Commander warned him of, but felt capable of handling himself. He wondered however, if any conflicts would be necessary while on the trip.

Charlie was seated up front with the driver who was vivacious as usual. Bridges couldn't help but notice she was wearing another jump-suit, a pale blue, which was complimentary to her deep golden tan.

Charlie handed Bridges a nine-millimeter Beretta semiautomatic, instructing him to conceal it. Bridges checked the weapon and discovered it contained a 15 round clip in place. He put the pistol in his waist band, then remarked to Charlie, "It's been a long time since I had to carry a weapon, matter of fact, I haven't been to a firing range in over a year."

Charlie explained the precautions, "Richard, I know we seem a bit over precautions, and I'm aware you are not on an intelligence mission, however, my boss doesn't want a former CIA agent to get killed on his watch. Please follow our directions and all will go well."

Bridges acknowledged Charlie's comment, then turned his attention to Becky,...Becky smiled indicating she had a rough night, quiet today Becky "I couldn't sleep, I got up about five and did my usual two mile jog. Then I came to work after taking a cold shower. When the weather changes, I have a hard time sleeping. Maybe it isn't the weather, maybe I'm home-sick, who knows,"

"What do you know about the source, Charlie?" Bridges asked.

"I know as much as you. I understand the source has traveled from Amman. My instructions are to transport you to the bridge and introduce you to the Military Commander." Charlie looked out the side window and continued. "The source will seek you out. We are not to monitor or solicit information concerning your liaison. I like it that way. Makes my job a lot easier." Charlie smiled. "All we have to do is keep you under surveillance and not allow you to get hurt."

Becky smiled, glanced over at Charlie and attempted to lighten up the conversation. "Don't be so grim Charlie. As often as we've made this trip there's been little or no activity."

Charlie reminded Becky of the peace-accord between the PLO and Israel, "There are many, including the Jordanian factions who don't want the PLO to be recognized. Who knows what they'll do or how they'll react."

"How far is the bridge?" Bridges asked trying to change the subject.

"About seventy-klicks…fifty-miles—have you ever been there?" Charlie inquired as Becky increased speed while passing a bus of high-school students on their way to Jerusalem.

"I've been to Amman several times. A few times overland but I don't recall crossing a bridge, at least the Allenby Bridge but then most of the trips were at night.". "You'll know it when you see it." Charlie stated. "With all the people in the middle of the desert, one wonders what the attraction is. Our trip will take us through Jerusalem but we want to avoid the city. Come to think of it, if you traveled overland to Amman, you had to take this route unless you traveled by armored tank across the desert."

For some reason Charlie thought he said something funny and laughed, but then Becky and Bridges joined in laughing, mostly at Charlie. As they got closer to Jerusalem, Bridges realized he had traveled the road before, most likely he crossed the Allenby Bridge into Jordan.

Charlie alerted them they needed to make a brief stop on the other side of Jerusalem at a place near Al-Quds, a small Military outpost. An inconsequential spot on the map, but an important military settlement. "It won't take long and we can stretch our legs and make a contribution to the desert." Charlie smiled, Becky looked at him in disgust.

Once at the stop, Charlie conducted his business while Becky and Bridges used the rest-rooms and then met at the car. Becky had a smile on her face, "It never fails, when ever Israeli soldiers discover I'm American they flirt and turn on the charm." Becky said, obviously enjoying the attention.

"I have a great deal of respect for the Israeli Army, however, as often as I've worked with them, I can't understand why their commanders don't require them to get hair cuts like the American military. It's cooler and looks neater, not to mention healthier." Bridges expressed his observation.

Charlie responded, "I never thought of it that way but I have to agree with you-if nothing else, they would look a hell-of-a lot better. Oh well, it's not to reason why."

They continued on to the Allenby Bridge. Bridges was silent, taking in the scenery of barren desert until Becky inquired as to his comfort.

Bridges replied, "Great ride…bumpy…maybe you would like one of us to take over the driving?"

"What would I do?" Becky answered as though something was being taken away from her.

Bridges liked teasing Becky, "You can continue reading your love-novel."Bridges looked at Becky in the rear view mirror, he could see she was embarrassed over the reminder of love-novel.

Becky responded in a half whisper, "I finished it. I haven't received my monthly installment from the States, so I'll have to suffer until my next book arrives. It's my adult education, you know." She giggled like a young girl.

Bridges couldn't help from making one more remark, "I'll bet it is."

Charlie could see no humor in the play between Bridges and Becky, he turned the conversation back to business. "We could have used a helicopter but it would have brought attention to us. We thought of flying a chopper to the outpost near Al-Quds, pick-up a car, but again, this may have alerted the curious or the factions, so we decided to drive. Becky would have had to drive to the out-post so it wasn't an option."

"I don't mind driving, but alone is much too boring." She laughed, "Then there was a chance of me getting into trouble with the soldiers at the outpost." She teased again.

Bridges announced he was going to catch a little shut-eye and Charlie agreed it would do him good. He thought the trip from Kennedy to Tel Aviv was catching up with him.

As they approached the bridge area, Becky directed her conversation to Bridges in the back seat, hoping to wake him, "Do you know you snore? Matter of fact, you snore loud."

Becky's remark woke Bridges from a deep sleep. "I don't, its just your imagination."

Becky offered a reply, "My father said the same thing whenever my mother complained of his snoring. I think it's cute, my mother takes it serious and sleeps in the guest room. This of course makes my father furious and his feelings are hurt."

They arrived at the location of the bridge. Becky parked next to a Military Police vehicle. The soldiers were alerted as they recognized the car as being from the Israeli Government. Richard remarked to Charlie. "Did you know the Israeli Army Military Police are trained in the States by the Americas, they used to go to Fort Gordon , in Georgia, now I think Fort Jackson, in South Carolina."

"I didn't know that, interesting." Charlie remarked. Then informed Bridges they had thirty-minutes before the source made contact with the area Military Commander. They got out of the car. Charlie spoke Hebrew to one of the soldiers.

Bridges asked Becky what Charlie was saying.

Becky laughed, "Something about women in the region, something to do with prostitutes visiting the bridge area…he's making small talk.". "Do you speak and understand Hebrew Becky?"

"I learned fast. I've been speaking Hebrew for two-years, lot of people say I speak well, not like Charlie with his Philadelphia accent." Bridges smiled at what Becky said and clearly understood.

Becky's tone turned serious as she directed her question to Bridges, "Do you mind if I called you Richard?"

"Not at all, Becky, as long as you don't call me Dick." He smiled at her.

"Richard, are you concerned with what you've learned about the mess in our country?"

"When I learn specific details which can be substantiated, I might become overly concerned and want to slay the dragon."

"This is serious Richard. It could hurt the progress of Israel and other countries depending on the United States for moral and financial support." Becky articulated her point well.

Bridges realized Becky's deep concern, "You're right…if what I've learned from Moshe and your Commander and any information provided by the source, then I'll have to lock myself in a room, maybe the Mossad's think-tank, and plan what has to be done. It's a lonely feeling, Becky."

Bridges continued, "I can't over-react, maybe there isn't much time, I feel anxious. I'm sure most people in my situation would feel the same, if not worse."

Becky looked at Bridges, she wasn't laughing or teasing, she was quite serious, "It's my country too, also Israel is my country, I have duel citizenship. I haven't told my mother about my duel citizenship, my father knows, it's not a big problem. In order for me to work for the cause of Israel, I had to apply for dual citizenship." Becky explained.

"I understand, Becky. Now where the-hell did Charlie go?"

"He's over there talking to the Military Commander…now they're walking this way."

Charlie and the Military Commander approached and Charlie introduced Bridges to the Army Major, as a visitor from the United States. They exchanged hand shakes and common remarks military people are known for. The Major invited Bridges to a temporary modular building often used for classrooms. A woman followed them into the building. She was dressed in American clothes, a tailored dark blue pant-suit. She had dark hair almost jet black and very tanned. She appeared to be in her mid-thirties, maybe older. Bridges found her very attractive; she walked with pride and self-confidence.

The three of them entered the building and once inside, the woman finally introduced herself to Bridges, "Hello, I'm Adriana Myers. As you may have guessed, I'm an American. I'm currently visiting a relative in Amman."

Bridges was amused with the woman, "I'm Richard Bridges. I assume you know all about me, at least the important part that allows you to trust me."

The Military Commander left them alone, Adriana turned to Bridges, "Mr. Bridges…Israeli Intelligence holds you in high regard. They have recommended that upon your arrival in Tel Aviv, I should meet you and relinquish certain information to you. In addition, I've spoken to other people about you, those connected with the American intelligence community, I hope you don't mind."

"I don't mind. You should know I have domestic enemies…based primarily on professional jealousy." Bridges said, not wanting to sound like he was defending himself but at the same time letting Adriana know there were those who didn't care for him.

"Before we get into the details I want us to enter into an agreement that we will work together on this project. Any information I have can be substantiated." Adriana responded. "Do we have an agreement Mr. Bridges?"

"I don't understand what the agreement means. What am I agreeing to?" Bridges asked feeling somewhat confused.

"I want us to work together, as partners, I have contacts like you do. I'm sure we could get a great deal accomplished by working as a team. Do you have problems with this arrangement Mr. Bridges?"

Adriana Myers suggested they be seated and asked Bridges not to take any notes, "The building is clean, I have the word of the top Mossad Commander that we will not be interrupted or monitored. Mr. Bridges, as I said, I know a great deal about your background, and I like what I hear. Please listen…there are many people in government who would sell their mother's souls to get ahead, do you agree?"

"Please call me Richard…as I listen to you, I was trying to recall some of personalities you may be referring. I have to analyze whatever you have. I don't have vast experience in domestic intelligence…remember, it was outlawed. I'm thinking of those we can trust, should this project get off the ground."

"Does that mean we have an agreement, Richard?" This was the first time Adriana used Bridges' first name and she wanted to experience how it felt.

"Yes, but first I must hear some details in order to charge…my…batteries…so to speak." Bridges said as he prepared himself for the details of what was ahead.

"Thank-you Richard, I'm sure I can recruit those we can trusting individuals inside the CIA and FBI. I don't think the military has been contaminated yet. Most of our generals are unhappy with the present administration, if not the President's inability to govern. We will then need to rely on the military should this situation get out of control."

"As Americans, we have two problems. One of course, is the conspiracy to assassinate the President. The other is our relationship with the Israeli Government. Of course our immediate problem is with our country. " Adriana looked around the room, sighed, and continued. "The rest will fall into place as you know. Whatever we do, or cause to be done, the Israelis must not be identified. If they are, then we become conspirators. I don't like that image." Adriana lectured.

Adriana continued, "I know the Israelis are counting on us with the PLO Peace Accord. I know what you are thinking Richard, the PLO is not important, but they are, at least for the Israeli economy and world opinion. Without the support of the United States, all will be lost. I believe coming to the Israelis first was the best approach in the disposal of our problem." She took a breath then went on. "Our present administration isn't behind Israel, that is sad, Israel is our trusted and best friends in the region."

"I am aware of the situation…I have many friends here."

"Richard, this situation is as dangerous for me as it is for you. If we fail, we could be in serious trouble. I know your reputation and that's why I want your help and understanding."

Bridges was professional as he addressed Adriana, "You sound like a lawyer, I'm trying to understand as much as I can. I don't object to working with you, or to you directing me in certain domestic situations, however…young lady, I don't know who the hell you are, or what you stand for. Further more…I don't mind working with you as long as we share information and not withhold any facts from each other that may be essential to the investigation." Bridges making Adriana aware of the ground-rules.

Adriana was taken back with Bridges' remarks, "Richard…I'm sorry, I neglected to provide you with my background and any information which would assure you that I'm sincere. As I mentioned, I'm visiting a relative in Amman, Jordan. My sister is married to the King of Jordan. I'm not telling you to impress you but rather to let you know that I have reliable information. I sense you are upset with me. Maybe we should meet on a later date, say tomorrow…in Tel Aviv? I promise I will share everything."

"I don't feel comfortable talking to you here. I trust the Israelis but we are out here in the middle of the desert protected by Israeli Military, I have an uneasy feelings. " Adrianna remarked.

Bridges starred at Adrianna, then put on a mock smile.

" Tomorrow I will lay out every detail. But right now all I can tell you is that the President is in danger. I know he's not of your political party, however, he is our President. Another assassination of a United States President would cause the free-world to mistrust us and our allies such as Israel, Great Britain, and other countries who have allegiance. This is dangerous. There has never been a military take-over in the United States and this could be the straw that broke the camel's back."

Bridges stared deeply at Adriana, thinking either Adriana Myers was crazy, or brilliant and intelligent. He couldn't help thinking how attractive she was, with her dark hair, olive skin from a tan no doubt, and her small mouth. She had green eyes and her hair was pulled back exposing her small ears. She was perfect in every way. He remembered it had been a long time since he had been emotionally involved with a woman. Maybe she would be too intelligent to work with, this alone could be a conflict as to who would be calling the shots, or who was to direct an inquiry or an investigation, or may be emotion might get in the way.

Bridges looked at Adriana, "Do you know how many threats the Secret Service receives monthly? Threats on the President's life…what makes this situation any different?"

"I know Richard, I'm aware of the many threats and they are from unhappy Americans, kooks, as well as left and right wing factions. But this is different. All I will say at this point is the threat is being generated by those in high places…a machine. Adriana took a breath, then sighed, "Can we meet in Tel Aviv tomorrow? I must return to Amman before dark. I know you have a rough trip back. I'm sure you'd feel better if your return trip was in daylight also."

Frustrated, Bridges agreed, "I will meet you in Tel Aviv tomorrow. You set the time and place."

Adriana was satisfied and informed Bridges she would telephone him with details, "I know you're staying at the Basel Hotel, I'll call you tonight."

"By the way Richard, were you contacted by a Mr. Smyth from the American Embassy in Tel Aviv?"

"Yes…why do you ask?" Bridges was surprised Adriana would ask.

"Richard, don't trust him. As a matter of fact, stay away from him, he could compromise our plans and should be considered dangerous."

"Adriana…do you believe Smyth is involved?"

"I'm not sure…however he gets carried away even with little information he learns. He has a tendency to embellish facts to suit his own needs. It's hard to believe he works for the CIA. He's not stupid…just reckless. Please don't mention to him that we've met. He may be able to piece things together."

"Adriana…how well are you known inside the belt-way?"

Adriana was surprised at the question, then responded to Bridges, "Too well, I'm afraid I know many Senators and members of the House. I hope you're not upset with me Richard, the little information I've provided you would frustrate anyone, however, I will complete the details when we meet in Tel Aviv."

"Richard, when I call, I'll use my first name should I have to leave a message."

They left the building at the same time. Bridges walked to the car and Becky was already seated behind the wheel. Charlie was talking to the Military Commander and excused himself when saw Bridges.

Bridges watched Adriana as she walked to her waiting white Mercedes, no doubt on loan from her sister. He couldn't help admiring the way she walked, like a lady…very proud. His thoughts were interrupted when he observed Adriana stop and talk to an Arab looking man. He was well dressed, probably American clothes. He could see she her smile as she shook hands with the man. They spoke briefly and appeared friendly…as though they knew each other. They parted company after a short conversation.

Adriana got into her car. Bridges couldn't help but wonder what the meeting with the Arab man was about.

Adriana's chauffeured car drove away. The Arab man, Adriana briefly spoke to was immediately apprehended by two Israeli Military Police. It appeared he had an object in his hand which resembled a camera. It was seized upon his arrest. Bridges' curiosity was stimulated with what he just witnessed.

Charlie approached Bridges, "How did it go my friend?"

"I don't know. She didn't give me much information to sink my teeth into. We agreed to a meeting in Tel Aviv tomorrow, I hope."

Charlie put his hand on Bridges shoulder, "Don't get pissed at her, she's got to be as cautious as we do. I'm sure she trusts you Richard. She may have been tight on time."

Bridges agreed with Charlie and explained that Adriana wanted to return to Amman before it became dark.

"Charlie, why did the Military Police arrest that Arab after he spoke to the source?" Bridges asked as they got into the car with Becky.

Charlie looked out the window of the car before turning to Bridges, as to avoid having to answer the question. "It's not our concern, trust me…friend. I believe he was carrying a camera, which alone would cause anyone from the Jordan side to be detained and the camera seized."

Bridges sat back as they drove off. He wasn't satisfied with Charlie's answer. As they traveled toward the Military outpost, Charlie contacted the outpost by car phone for any messages. He became angry with the person on the other end of the phone, "We will be there shortly and we will handle the situation." Charlie continued the conversation in Hebrew.

Becky laughed but Bridges became curious to why Charlie broke into Hebrew. Becky translated, "Charlie told the military liaison officer that he is an idiot; that he should use his head besides just to put a hat on." Becky laughed again.

Charlie completed the call, leaned over the seat, "Richard the Arab arrested at the bridge would like to talk to you. I don't think it's a good idea, you can if you wish, but we don't have much day-light left. I want to be close to Tel Aviv when it gets dark, if you know what I mean."

Bridges thought for a moment then looked at Charlie, "Charlie, I'd like you to be in the room when I talk to the Arab."

Charlie repeated himself, "I don't know if it's a good idea for you to talk to the Arab, or whoever he is. He is being detained at the outpost. If you want, I'll sit in with you but I'm sure whatever he has to say will only add to your frustration. I'm only guessing."

Upon arrival at the Military outpost, Charlie instructed Bridges to leave his weapon in the car.

Once inside the office of the outpost, Becky headed for the restroom. Charlie and Bridges made contact with the Military Liaison Officer at which time the sergeant escorted Charlie and Bridges to a room resembling an interrogation room, similar to those found at any police department in the States.

Upon entering the room they found the Arab seated at the table. As the man lifted up his head, he recognized Bridges. In perfect American English, he greeted both men as though they had met before.

Bridges asked the Arab if they had met before, to which the Arab responded, "My name is not important. If we met before, it was by accident. I just want you to know that the woman you met with today is in great danger. If you get involved with her, your life will also be in danger."

Bridges asked the Arab how reliable his information was.

The Arab remarked, "As reliable as you knowing a person you call Billy-Ray."

Charlie asked the Arab if he knew Billy-Ray, "I know of him, and his reputation. I know from reliable sources that he has been involved in the deaths of people employed by the Israeli government as well as Jordanian Security Forces."

Bridges impatiently asked the Arab the obvious question, "What business do you have with the woman I met with today?"

"I have no business with her. I know she is the sister to a woman in high places in Jordan. I know her name is Adriana Myers and she's an important lady. My purpose in meeting her at the Allenby Bridge was to warn her." The Arab looked worried. "I never got a chance because she was in a hurry to return to Amman. I then thought the best way to get a message to her was through you gentlemen. That's why I exposed my camera, I knew I would be arrested for the infraction."

Bridges asked the Arab if he knew who they were or anything about the meeting with Adriana Myers.

The Arab responded, "I know Adriana met with you; that you are American and you must be important because of the manner the military officer treated you and allowing the use of his office. I have no idea what you do but it must be important."

"If your information is solid, then it's important you tell us who you are. I'm told you posses an American passport." Charlie replied with little patience.

"I'm a citizen of the United States. My family being Christian, left Amman Jordan when I was a small child. I grew up in the Washington area, near Reston Virginia. I attended college in California, University of California at Berkeley, and my major studies were in economics."

The Arab continued, "My name is American. My family decided to change the family name once we settled in the United States. Our family name is Myers, my brother was married to Adriana. That is when they attended Georgetown University. My brother was killed in a traffic accident shortly after being employed by the State Department. The family has always felt the incident was not an accident; we believe it was a planned."

"Adriana took it real hard, matter of fact…she has never been seen with any man in public outside of business since my brother's death, that was over ten-years ago. I'm not sure she would discuss it openly." The Arab continued.

Bridges looked at Charlie, "Why are you here in the Middle East?". "I came to visit relatives and visit my birth place, something I've always wanted to do. I had no idea Adriana was here but I thought I saw her at the Tel Aviv Airport last week. Then I heard from my relatives that she was visiting her sister at the Palace."

Bridges sighed, took a deep breath then asked the Arab another question which bothered him the most, "What do you know about Billy Ray?"

The Arab appeared nervous for a moment then answered,

"The person I know as Billy-Ray works for the CIA or maybe the National Security Agency. I believe he is CIA, although he spends a great deal of time at NSA. I have friends who are communication specialists at NSA. They have a strong dislike for Billy-Ray, as a matter of fact, they believe that anything of importance hc is involved in, someone always ends up dead. A few of my friends were in El Salvador during 1988, and Billy-Ray was there at the same time. They feel strong about him being dangerous."

"Do you believe that Billy-Ray knew of the meeting between Adriana and myself?" Bridges asked the Arab, Michael Myers.

Michael Myers answered in a nervous manner, "I don't know. He's assigned to the American Consulate in Tel Aviv, an assignment that was not a reward or promotion but rather a punishment for something he did which violated policy, that's all I know."

Charlie excused himself from the room, Bridges continued asking questions, "What kind of work do you do?"

Michael responded, "I was an economist with the Treasury Department. Under the new administration I was forced to leave. I was a political appointee under the Bush administration. Now I'm a consultant to various firms in and around Washington." Charlie returned with the Michael's passport, "Your passport indicates you are Michael Myers, is that the name you work under?"

"Please, my name is Michael Myers, that's all, I will never use my Jordanian name again. I'm an American. I love the United States and my family has a great deal of respect for our country and enjoys the American way of life."

"Do you belong to any political factions in the United States?" Charlie asked abrasively.

"I don't know what you mean by POLITICAL—FACTIONS, I'm Republican and vote Republican. I once belonged to the Young Republicans but I no longer have time for that sort of social life."

Bridges smiled at the man, "That isn't what Charlie was searching for. But I appreciate your answer."

"If we made arrangements, would you come to Tel Aviv to discuss the Billy-Ray topic?" Charlie asked.

Michael Myers responded, "I would like to help, I don't know how much more I can provide, however, you be the judge of that."

Charlie inquired as to where Michael was staying, Michael responded that he could be reached at the Hilton in Amman.

Charlie returned the passport to Michael Myers, then instructed a military driver to return him to the Allenby Bridge.

"Do you have transportation from the bridge to Amman, Michael?" Bridges asked with sincere concern.

"Yes, I have a rental car parked at the bridge, that is if it hadn't been stolen." A remarked that caused them to laugh.

As they left the outpost, Charlie placed his hand on Bridges' shoulder and asked, "Do you believe him?"

"I feel good about his sincerity Charlie, I believe what he said, however, he may be giving Billy Ray too much credit. Then again…maybe not…we must find out before I return to the States and get myself involved in a bag-of-worms."

Charlie provided his opinion, "I believe him, but I think he may be holding back something. I also believe he has no idea what he's getting himself involved in. We have to formally check him out before your meeting with him and the source."

Bridges agreed. They tried to relax during the ride back to tel Aviv.

Charlie offered to drive but Becky was glad to have something to do, "What will I do, it's too dark to read even if I had something to read, besides I enjoy driving even if the road is bumpy."

Bridges agreed with Charlie that they should brief the Commander before calling it a day.

When they returned to the Midrasha, Bridges and Charlie got out of the car, while Becky parked it in the rear of the building. They entered the building through the game-room and found two-recruits playing ping-pong. Both men climbed the stairs and met Commander Risken in the passageway. They assembled in the video studio. Risken was handed a message which he first read in Hebrew and then out loud in English, "Michael Myers checked out…he's solid…he's who he says he is…if he wasn't Jordanian by birth we could use him here." Bridges was relieved and they laughed about the Commander's comment. "He was valuable to us awhile back." Risken didn't elaborate.

Bridges felt better about his meetings with Adriana Myers and Michael. He couldn't help thinking there was more to Michael Myers—something that he hadn't revealed. He thought of what the Commander had said, then assured himself he would find out later. Both men briefed the Commander with details of the meeting at the Allenby Bridge and their discussion with Michael Myers. They offered opinions as to strategy to be employed when dealing with Adriana and the recruitment of Michael Myers.

Risken agreed, however, offered a suggestion, "Richard, you should talk to Michael Myers again before you meet with the source, if that is possible."

Bridges asked, "What about Smyth—Billy Ray?"

Risken informed Bridges they would decide what to do with Smyth, "He has to be seriously dealt with. He can't be allowed to interfere with this ongoing investigation, whatever his motives are. Before we do anything about Smyth, I would like to coordinate things with his Station Chief, who you know very well, Richard. If he had been responsible for any deaths of Israeli government personnel, then he becomes our responsibility."

Charlie agreed with the Commander, then added, "We should receive reliable information concerning Smyth's activities first thing in the morning."

"Let's have something to eat, some dinner." Risken suggested as they walked downstairs to the conference room next to the kitchen.

Becky seated herself next to Bridges and informed him that she received her monthly supply of love-novels from the States. They laughed as though they had a private joke between them.

Moshe Cohen arrived late. He sat next to the Commander and informed Bridges that he was scheduled for a four hour class starting at nine in the morning. Bridges thanked Moshe for the information and requested Charlie's assistance.

Charlie nodded his head., "It would be a pleasure, this is a good bunch in this class, a little young and some-what liberal in their thinking but we can turn that around before we turn them out into the cold-world."

"They seem to be better educated. Several of them attended Universities in the States and speak good English. They feel strong about Israel and it's image throughout the world." Commander Risken added to the conversation.

Bridges hesitated about asking a question on a subject that most members of the Mossad didn't like to discuss, or even be reminded, "Quite often I'm asked by American intell-candidates, questions about the Pollard affair. Jonathan Pollard attempted to seek political asylum at the Israeli Embassy in Washington. Should the recruits solicit my opinions, how would you like me to answer them...Commander?"

Risken chuckled before he answered, "I doubt if any recruits dare ask you questions concerning the Pollard incident. I'm sure they would like to hear your opinion however, they have already received a class on the subject, that should be enough."

Moshe agreed and informed Bridges that he will be impressed with the Class, "If one of them asks you off-the-record, so to speak, you certainly will answer as an authority. Israel has no intelligence gathering operations in the United States. As a matter of fact, many Mossad agents use various passports from other countries. The passport that's never issued is from the United States. That's the rule from the highest level of Israeli Government. There has been exceptions during joint operations with the CIA. In those cases there is always tight control of passports."

Embarrassed that he brought-up the Pollard incident, Bridges extended his appreciation for the information.

After dinner Moshe Cohen offered Bridges a drink but Bridges declined, "I'd like a drink, but I'm tired and have to prepare for class in the morning. It's been a long day. I'm sure you agree. I've got a lot of information to digest which I've been burdened with. I promise before my return to the States we'll have many drinks together. I think I'll need them by then."

Becky drove Bridges to the hotel and asked to meet him at seven for breakfast.

Bridges remembered she wanted to discuss a personal matter. They arrived at the hotel and as Bridges got out of the car, he bid Becky good-night and assured her he would meet her at in the morning.

Bridges entered the hotel and as he walked to the elevators he noticed the same Israeli man he met earlier. Bridges nodded…good evening but the Israeli man barely answered a hello in a thick broken English, almost German accent. They both got off the elevator on the same floor. Bridges walked to his room, noticing the Israeli entered room 335. Bridges became suspicious, but he was tired and didn't think about it anymore.

Bridges entered his room and noticed the message light. He immediately contacted the desk and received his messages—three in all, one from Adriana, the other two were from Billy Ray.

Adriana's message said she would call him early in the morning. Billy-Ray's were the same…call him at the Embassy.

Bridges decided he would ignore Billy-Ray's calls, at least until he could plan his next move. Bridges showered and went over the day's activities in his mind. He was curious as to what Becky wanted to talk about, then his thoughts turned to beautiful Adriana Myers. He smiled to himself as he thought she was either a woman of courage or she was going-off half cocked, time would tell. If her information was valid, there would be a great deal to accomplish before returning to Washington.

As Bridges thoughts drifted and became tangled, he recalled his last assignment to Central America. He remembered how corrupt the Military had been and how his team was forced to produce misinformation just to stay ahead of the factions who wanted to assume power, but at the same time, keep their hand-out for United States financial aid.

Bridges remembered a Lieutenant he had befriended in El Salvador. He was in the Salvadorian Army for 15 years and assigned to a Special Investigative Unit. The mission of the unit was to put-down activities of the insurgents and over-see intelligence gathering operations. By night, the Lieutenant led a death squad against the religious factions sympathetic to anti-government causes. He recalled having mixed emotions when he discovered his friend was instrumental in many of the killings. His friend believed he was right in the name of democracy. It was wrong because it got out of hand.

Bridges had difficulty falling asleep and continued to think that the situation in El Salvador wasn't any different than the situations which existed in other small countries throughout the world. Then he thought; to assassinate another President would send a message to the rest of the world that we were no more civilized then they are. He wasn't surprised with what Adriana mentioned, however, he was sure there was more she hadn't explained.

He tried to sleep. After all he has a four hour class in the morning and Adriana was going to call early. He wanted to be alert when he spoke to her. The breakfast with Becky…finally he drifted off to sleep. After a few hours, his sleep was interrupted by a noise. He kept very still when he realized that he was able to see an opening in the door and realized that someone was leaving his room. Whoever it was closed the door carefully not to disturb him, so it appeared. Bridges immediately sat up in the bed. He was certain he saw a silhouette of a large man just for a few seconds. The image was clear in his mind. He got out of bed and looked around. Then doubled locked the door. He smiled to himself for double locking the door after the intruder left, sort of like closing the barn door after the horses got out. He felt foolish for a moment, then he wondered if he had a dream. He glanced at his old beat up brief case which was wide open and was sure it was closed when he went to bed. Bridges examined it and discovered the contents had been disturbed but nothing was missing. As Bridges sat an the edge of the bed, he was convinced he wasn't dreaming. Someone had been in his room and went through the brief case. He thought for a moment, then turned on other lights for a better look inside the brief-case. There was nothing of value he thought. Reference material, lesson plans, passport, and a copy of USAID contract which revealed nothing other than details of the contract, nothing else.

Then he thought of the strange Israeli he met on the elevator. Bridges felt compelled to consult Moshe Cohen in the morning.

Bridges tried to return to sleep. He glanced at the clock, it was three-thirty. He thought he had to get at least two-hours sleep in order to function in the morning. Finally he drifted off until the telephone rang. He answered on the second ring, he looked at the clock, it was six. It was Becky informing him she would be fifteen-minutes late. Just as he put the receiver down, the telephone range again. It was a woman's voice but Bridges recognized it wasn't Adriana's voice. The caller was American. She informed Bridges that the person he met yesterday would not be calling until later that day. She wished him a pleasant day then the line went dead.

Bridges felt uneasy. He went over the details of the brief message he received, then spoke to himself out-loud.

"What the hell is going on?" He asked himself, there must be a damn good reason Adriana didn't make the call herself, he thought.

Bridges hurried to get ready. He hated to shave, threatening many times to grow a beard. He got dressed in his Palm-Beach poplin suit, blue dress shirt and conservative paisley tie. He left his room after putting his brief case in order, then went directly to the lobby. He found the hotel restaurant and looked at the wall clock, it was five minutes after seven and remembered Becky would be late, but then he was surprised to see that Becky had already been seated and reading one of the paper-back novels. He approached her and in a seductive voice, "Have you got to the juicy part yet?"

Becky looked up and gave Bridges a big smile. She was excited to see him. She blushed, "Richard, you look adorable."

Bridges remarked, "Adorable? Since when do men look adorable?"

Becky laughed, then asked if he had a good night sleep.

Bridges revealed his annoyance and answered, "No, I'll explain later. I didn't get a bit of sleep…well maybe a few hours. I feel hung-over only without the benefit of drinking, that is if drinking provides a benefit." Becky was concerned, "I'm sorry, you should have called me when you couldn't sleep. I would have read to you over the phone, I'm sure you would have fallen asleep.". Bridges smiled glancing up at her, "Oh well…are you flirting with me young lady?". "What's wrong with a woman flirting with an older man—a man with obvious class?" Becky continued, " Women have fantasies too when it comes to love and sex."

Bridges felt his ears getting red and tried to maintain his composure. "I'm flattered young lady. I find you attractive, but we're friends…without complications."

Becky pretended to pout, "I can't stand rejection Mr. Bridges." She smiled. "I'm sure many women, find you attractive…"

"Thank-you, is this the reason we met this morning? To discuss me, or do you have something else you wish to talk about?"

Becky looked at Bridges trying to appear more serious, "Is the young-lady routine a barrier in an attempt to cool me down? If it is, you're wasting words. I can't be cooled off that easy."

Bridges sighed, trying to maintain patience, "Becky, sweety—I agreed to meet for breakfast but lets eat and discuss your situation, the one you related as being of personal nature."

The waitress took their order of fruit, coffee and a bagel.

Becky felt she was trying Bridges' patience, "Richard, I don't have a serious problem. I just don't want to go to graduate-school. I want to stay here but at the same time I want to return to the States. Someday I would like to get married to a professional man, have a child or two. I know I won't marry an Israeli man. They're too demanding, they tend to put women down. I don't mean to stereo-type them but even an American who becomes an Israeli citizen seems to take on that attitude. What should I do?"

Bridges was relieved that her problem was so simple, "Becky, you are an attractive, intelligent woman. I believe two years in graduate school will help you make up your mind. Should you return to Israel, you know you're limited in what you can do in your present employment."

"I thought about going to work for your former employer, that's if they would have me."

"It would be a great career but without a graduate degree you'll be limited. You're an outdoors girl. If you work for the Agency with your present experience and education they'll assign you to a training facility or assign you to the Office of Security. The internal investigation arm of the organization, with a VIP Detail thrown in. I'm sure this wouldn't settle with you. You might be assigned to an operational position but again, you could be limited. My suggestion to you would be the State Department. They have research and intelligence, they like women, many of them have key positions through-out the world." Bridges hoped he was helpful to Becky. He like her and she reminded him of his daughter.

"You're right Richard. I need excitement. Although I could stay here in Tel Aviv, work in the Hakirya district for the Migdel Insurance Company and earn a large salary. Can you see me in a highly charged insurance company jumping through my ass to compete with the rest of the world." Becky sneeringly remarked.

Bridges laughed, "What's the difference, business is business no matter what the commodity may be, paper or people."

"You're no help, I sense you're making fun of me."

"I'm not making fun of you Becky. I think you are a super person. You seem to have control of things, maybe a little distracted by your family. I really believe you can do anything you set out to do, and you will be a success."

Becky thanked Bridges and suggested they better get going, "You have a class to teach at-nine. I know you want to meet with the Commander and Moshe before you start."

"Where is Charlie this morning?" Bridges asked.

"He's got business in Tel Aviv, he'll be in later."

Bridges couldn't help thinking about Adriana Myers and the woman caller this morning. The caller had been perfectly calm when she delivered the message concerning Adriana. He was curious as to who the caller was and what she knew. Then he wondered if the caller was Adriana's sister, the King's wife, he smiled to himself.

Becky interrupted his thoughts, "Richard, why didn't you take me serious when I flirted with you at breakfast?"

"I'm sorry Becky, it's just that while I find you attractive, I have a daughter almost your age. It's hard for me to look at you in any other way except as a professional and a friend. I'm the same age as your father no doubt."

Becky was frustrated, "Listen Richard, I don't think of you as an older man. Besides what's wrong with a woman my age getting involved with a man your age?"

"Thanks Becky, you are good for my ego. This is not the time or place, if we were in the States and met at a social event, maybe, just maybe—there would be sparks. I don't need a reputation with the Israeli Government that I sleep with their women. Don't get me wrong, I find you sexually attractive and very desirable, but I don't see a future for you in a relationship with me."

"Well thank-you Mr. Bridges" Becky said sarcastically.

Bridges looked over at Becky as she increased speed and stared straight ahead while she drove through the traffic and headed north to the Midrasha.

Becky finally settled down, glanced at Bridges with a smile, "Richard, we could make wild-fire together, I bet."

"You never give up. Lets put it to rest and remain friends…who knows what will be." Becky pouted, "Richard, I'm sorry for placing you in this situation. I'll back off."

As they arrived at the Midrasha, Security Officers greeted Bridges, then he met Moshe Cohen in his office.

Moshe asked Bridges how the meeting went with the source, the phone rang. Moshe answered then handed the phone to Bridges. There was a familiar woman's voice, "Richard I'm sorry I was unable to talk to you this morning. My sister called you—can we talk this afternoon or maybe this evening at your hotel?"

Bridges smiled and looked at Moshe while on the phone with Adriana, "I understand, yes…this evening will be fine, will you call me or do you plan to be in Tel Aviv?"

"I plan to be at your hotel whenever you say Richard."

Bridges looked at Moshe, he nodded his head, and answered, "Six my time will-be-.fine, will you be staying at the hotel?"

"Yes, I'm planning to stay until we accomplish our business, with your approval of course."

"Fine with me, I'm anxious to get started with this. What should we call it, a project?" Bridges asked.

Adriana answered, "A project will be fine. See you this evening.".

CHAPTER 3
THE SOURCE

Bridges woke to a knock on the door. He dozed off for a few minutes. As he glanced at the clock on the bed-stand it was six-thirty and Adriana was late. Cautiously he opened the door as if he wasn't quite sure the caller was Adriana. To his surprise she was there dressed in a casual navy-blue jump-suit with a white collar which revealed an almost perfect curvature of a woman's body. Bridges couldn't help thinking how attractive she looked and he felt Adriana knew it.

Bridges greeted her and invited her into his room. He couldn't help feeling excitement as he shook her hand and realized she had self assurance. He guessed she was strong willed, maybe fearless. His instincts and training made him apprehensive. He offered her a drink which she declined as she seated herself on the lounge as she slowly crossed her legs.

"I apologize for being late. I had difficulty using my cell—phone where I didn't have an audience. I had a telephone in the guest room, however I had to go through the palace operator to place a call to you. Making a call to Israel is not something a Jordanian would do. I asked my sister to call you since her phone is direct and one doesn't need to use the operator. I just let her think you were a good friend or my lover—which she found exciting."

Bridges understood the situation and explained the ground rules they should follow during the planning of coming events.

"Richard, I'm not planning to return to Amman until we decide what action we should take."

Bridges put a fingers to his lips jesting to Adriana to be quiet as he turned the television on high volume. He leaned over and whispered, "We've got to find a place to talk without fear of being monitored. I'm not concerned with my friends at the country-club, however, someone was in my room early this morning. I was able to see his silhouette when the door opened and he left. He was big or heavy and I discovered my brief case had been ransacked. I'm sure someone was trying to send a message to me. If, whoever it was, wanted into my brief case or any of my other belongings, they could have entered my room anytime when I wasn't here. If I didn't know better, I would say it was a training exercise for a Mossad recruit, I doubt it."

"Did you tell your friends?" Adriana inquired.

"Not until I had a chance to talk to you, I'm positive my room is being monitored but not by the Israelis."

"Who do you think is responsible, Richard?"

Bridges smiled, "Who else but our dear friend Billy Ray?"

Adriana sighed, "It figures, he's up to something, no good I would imagine. Do you think he's the one that entered your room…I can't stand him?"

"My friends will take care of him. If it wasn't him who entered my room, it was some off duty Marine he bull-shitted into doing it for him. They don't know any better especially when they know he's CIA, a young Marine would jump through hoops for the excitement." Bridges whispered.

Adriana stared at Bridges, "Sounds serious. As you well know, we can't get involved with any Israeli activities."

Bridges nodded in agreement, "We don't need distractions."

Bridges stood and took Adriana's hand, "Let's have dinner, I'm hungry. I know of an Italian restaurant with a hint of Hebrew flavor not far from here, is that alright?"

"Yes lets get out of this room so we can talk, maybe you should have your friends check it for bugs." Adriana suggested.

Bridges used a phone in the lobby of the hotel to make a special request to clean the room of any monitoring devices. He felt better when he was informed it would be accomplished within the hour.

Adriana had a rental car waiting and suggested she drive. "Is the restaurant far?" She asked.

"No…do you know your way around Tel Aviv?"

Adriana, unsure of herself answered, "I'm familiar with the Hakirya District but point me to Derah Petha Tikvab, then I can find anything in this city."

Bridges smiled "It's near here, I'll know it when I see it. I didn't know you spoke Hebrew, Adriana?"

"I don't. I just made it a point to learn how to pronounce land sights or places. I had you fooled for a minute." She looked at Bridges and smiled.

As Adriana drove, Bridges alerted her they were being followed.

Adriana laughed then responded, "It's my sister's idea. She hired someone in Tel Aviv, maybe a local private investigator, to look after me. We can lose him if you wish."

"We don't need an escort." Bridges remarked.

"It's a done deal. Hold on." Adriana increased speed, changed directions and managed to lose the other car.

"It may have been Billy-Ray, I didn't answer his last two-calls."

"I don't think so, I'm sure your friends are occupying his time this evening."

Bridges looked over again at Adriana. He was amazed at some of her comments including the one about Billy-Ray. "I hope you're right. We don't need to run into him this evening."

"To be honest Richard, your friends knew we were meeting, they were sure to distract Billy Ray."

They arrived at the restaurant and greeted by a young Israeli woman. She seated them in a dark corner. thinking they were lovers. Bridges counted at least twenty people eating and talking business. The cigarette smoke was heavy. Bridges asked Adriana if the smoke bothered her.

"A little, I can handle it sitting back here. You know the Israelis keep the American cigarette companies in business, everyone smokes."

Bridges smiled at Adriana and she smiled back. She found Bridges intriguing and was anxious to know him better.

The waitress approached their table and they both ordered pasta, salad and a bottle of red-wine.

Bridges became serious and reminded Adriana that tomorrow was Rosh Hashanah. "Most of the businesses will be closed as well as the government offices. What do you haveplanned?"

"We can accomplish a great deal tomorrow without the distractions." Adriana said encouragingly.

"I agree. Now...I know little about you. I'd like to get to know you better. When I spoke to your brother-in-law, I'm sure my friends filled you in on our meeting, he provided me with fragments of information concerning you and the death of your husband. I'm sorry...is this upsetting you?"

"I'll tell you anything you need to know, after all, I know a great deal about you...you lost your wife to an accident as well, I'm sorry for you, it must be lonely."

Bridges was surprised Adriana knew so much, he then responded. "I don't have time to be lonely. My daughter keeps me busy and of course, I have happy memories. It was a terrible loss but we've managed to continue with our lives. I do admit I get angry when I think of all things we never had a chance to do. My daughter was young when her mother died, and I often catch her talking about her as though she were alive." Bridges sounded melancholy as he recalled the tragedy of his wife's death.

"I hadn't been married to my husband too long when he died in an accident. We met in college, both of us attended Georgetown University. I went to Yale Law School after we were married, and we were both successful in getting a job with the State Department. As you may know, he had an accident in his new car. The brakes failed...he only had the car less than a week. I have reason to believe it wasn't an accident. I think the brakes were tampered with, but, it was never proven. The insurance company paid off and of course I received a large amount from the manufacture of the car after a long law-suit."

Bridges reminded Adriana that Michael had only given him minor details of her husband's accidents.

"Michael is a good person. I feel bad I haven't kept in contact with the family after all these years. They are originally from Jordan. They changed their family name when they decided to become American citizens. The entire family loves the United States. As far as they're concerned, there is no other place on earth."

"I was impressed with Michael. He seems worried about your welfare, as a matter of fact, he warned me that you were in danger and cautioned me that should we work together, I would be in the same danger."

"Michael is a serious person." Adriana said convincingly. "He's always been cautious. When I arrived in Tel Aviv, I thought I saw him at the air terminal but I didn't want to engage in conversation at the time. After all, I haven't talked to members of my husband's family in several years. If I recall, Michael worked at the Treasury Department. I don't know if he's still there." Adriana briefly explained.

"As I understand it, he was an appointee during the Bush administration but he was let go during the present administration. Is that correct?"

"I should have known that." Adriana remarked. "Richard, I work for the President's wife. I took a sabbatical and came to the Middle East."

Bridges was surprised. "What do you mean you work for the President's wife, are you talking about Mrs. Bush?"

"No Richard, Mrs. Banks, or should I say Heidi Jefferson Banks, as she prefers to be called. She is a descendant of Thomas Jefferson, you know Jefferson's slaves fathered several of his children, at least that's the word around the belt-way. "

"I can't believe it." Bridges remarked, "You are not from the same political persuasion. Why wasn't that an issue in the media?"

"I worked for her as a researcher on many of her high priority projects. When you graduate from Yale Law School, for some reason your name appears on a list that's passed around, not only in Washington but other places throughout the country. My name was on the list and I had a reputation of being a damn good researcher. I was hired before the election. This was when her husband was Governor of Virginia.

Richard said, "amazing…you are incredible"

"When he won the Presidency to my surprise, I moved into Heidi Bank's office at the White House." She smiled. " Richard, I gained a great deal of information while I was there, most of which is relevant to the topic I'm about to tell you about."

Bridges was eager to hear the rest of Adriana's story. Their dinners were served with red-wine, tossed green salad European style, Jewish-Italian bread. Bridges poured the wine and thought to himself that Adriana was so close to the flag-pole. "Why did you take a sabbatical, Adriana?"

"I thought about resigning but I'm still on the payroll. Heidi knew I needed a rest. She suggested it and I accepted. She needs my input on a project. To be honest, I can't subscribe to this administration's way of thinking. It has nothing to do with my politics, it's just that they are so damn disorganized. They have no idea where they're taking the country. During daily activities I uncovered something which is the reason I'm here."

"I'm following you with some difficulty Adriana, are you saying the administration is corrupt?" Bridges eagerly asked, waiting to hear what she had to say.

"You're right. It's corruption involving certain members of congress and the Vice President. And God knows whoever else. Richard, I don't believe it's political differences. I believe it's motivated by power hungry, greedy, whore-loving bastards."

"Those are strong opinions you're expressing, Adriana. Are your feelings getting in the way of facts which only appear corrupt?"

"Listen Richard, I've been around Washington and inside the beltway for many years. I know my politics. I also know that most of us have strong moral convictions and a strong sense of what is right or wrong. I'm not a school girl, I didn't just arrive in town with stars in my eyes. After my husband died, I grew up fast."

Adriana continued and Bridges listened intently. He wanted to ask a lot of questions but felt the restaurant wasn't the place. Bridges looked around to see if anyone was listening to them. People were busy eating and talking in Hebrew or some other language other than English.

"I'm worried this plot, for lack of a better description, could gain momentum in a very short time. That is, if the players can agree to the object…the target is obvious."

Bridges waited for Adriana to pause, then asked, "Do you know the identities of the major players? I mean, who is the driving force behind this plot?"

"I know there are at least two Senators, a member of the House, the Vice President and of course your highness, the First-Lady. The one to gain the most is the First-Lady." Adriana explained with bitterness in her voice.

"Do you believe the First Lady, Heidi Banks, excuse me Heidi Jefferson Banks is the actual driving force above everyone else you mentioned?" Bridges asked, eager for her answer.

With an immediate response and in a laudable whisper, Adriana responded,

"Richard, I have damn good reason to believe the entire idea and plan was hers. She cunningly recruited power hungry participants and with the utmost control. She is the queen-bee."

Bridges broke into a boyish grin and looked into Adriana's green eyes, immediately changing the subject. "Do you know you're beautiful when you get angry? I mean there is a certain sensuous expression in your face." Bridges couldn't help noticing.

Bridges apologized for interrupting and Adriana smiled. Both were relieved of the tension, if only for a few moments.

"I know we need to take a break Richard. I get so involved with this I can't think of anything else."

"Who knows about this besides you?"

"No one, I'm sure, except your friends at the country-club. I had to consult them in order to meet you. I trust them, after all, they have an interest in this also." Adriana was quiet for a moment then continued. "The interesting point is that the major players don't know what I know. They're being used and love every minute of it."

"Why do you hate her, I mean, oh you know who I mean."

Adriana explained., "I don't hate her but she makes me sick, she is half black and half white, and wants to be white."

"I have one questions which needs to be answered, Adriana."

"Ask me anything you wish, I'll try to provide the proper answer."

"Why me? Why have you selected me to assist in this project?" Bridges needed to know her answer and hoped she was straight.

Adriana smiled and looked away, then she looked at Richard, "Every contact I have at the FBI and CIA recommended you, but I've told them nothing of the plot. They recommended you as a person of high integrity and knowledge. You're what I needed to help bring this plot down."

"I'm flattered. Do you believe the people at the FBI and the Agency are involved in some way?"

"To my knowledge, NO. At least not anyone under the new appointed FBI Director. I know the military is not happy with the administration and the people at Langley were unhappy with the election results. But I'm sure you knew that."

"Yes, I know the feelings, we need help from law enforcement and the intelligence community. The Israelis will only assist from a distance. They don't need another incident like the Pollard fiasco. We need to build a case but it may take time to gather any substantial evidence and then find a tribunal to present the evidence. Do you agree, Adriana?"

"I don't know how much time we have. The administration is in it's second year and approaching the third. My feelings are that the assassination will be attempted soon. Then again, they may wait until the last year, then they'll assume power." Adriana was skeptical. She knew more about the time-table but was hesitant to share the information with Bridges at this time.

"You haven't finished your dinner, I thought you were hungry? Do you want to order something else?" Bridges asked.

"Thank you Richard, I guess I wasn't hungry after all, let's leave and return to the hotel. We can continue our discussion there. I'm sure your friends had enough time to sweep the room."

"Tomorrow is the Yiddish holiday. Do you have any commitments?" Adriana anxiously asked.

Bridges thought for a minute, "No, I should make a trip to the country club to check on a few things. I'm sure there's no classes scheduled. We can have the entire day to discuss the situation. I'm still having problems understanding this entire mess. It's not you Adriana, it's so damn bold and the consequences bother me." He took in a deep breath and waited,

"I know I should be concerned for the President's life, but I think of the ramifications. Members of Congress are no surprise to me."

"Richard, let's get an early nights sleep. Tomorrow will be another day. We should be able to cover a lot."

As they left the restaurant, Bridges noticed the familiar face of an Israeli he believed was assigned by the Midrasha. He decided not to tell Adriana at this time. Once they arrived at the hotel, Bridges finally asked Adriana if she had noticed they had an escort.

Adriana looked at Bridges puzzled, "You mean you were not going to tell me? I understand you didn't want to alarm me, but I can handle things like this, remember I've been around. I don't panic, I'm not helpless. I'm sure he was assigned by your friends."

"It's strange, he want's us to notice him. I would have objected had they informed me of assigned security. Adriana, whenever I'm around women or work with them, I become protective, I guess I'm a born big-brother." Richard smiled.

Adriana also smiled, then she laughed, "I understand Richard, you're from the old school but I'm not implying you're old."

"Oh but I am old, at least I feel that I'm getting old, I can't compete with the young upstarts."

Adriana suggested they have a night-cap in her room.

Bridges flirtatiously smiled, "Do you think people will talk?" He smiled at Adriana and they both laughed at the comment.

As they entered the hotel Bridges noticed the lobby was full with people. He glanced at his watch noticing it was past ten, it was party time. The next day was the Hebrew New Year. It seems they picked up the celebrating of the New Year by emulating the Americans. He spoke softly to Adriana, "Do you want to participate in the celebration of the Jewish New Year?"

"I'm afraid not, I don't like to be around people who are intoxicated. I resent being in the same room with them, besides, I was told you like Cognac, I have a bottle I smuggled in from France." Adriana laughed.

"Should I conclude from that remark that you were certain you would meet me, or is Cognac your drink as well?" Bridges enjoyed teasing and Adriana seemed to like the attention as the elevator door opened on the third floor.

Adriana remarked she was in room 332.

"How did you manage to get a room next to me?"

"I didn't have to arrange anything. The room was assigned to me when I checked in."

They entered Adriana's room and Bridges remarked that he always suspected his friends at the country-club owned the hotel or a least managed it. "I'm sure they arranged for the adjoining room. I don't mind." Bridges remarked as he looked around the outer room of the suite.

Adriana smiled at Bridges. "I don't mind either, it's exciting, I feel like I'm doing something I'm not suppose to.do."

Adriana kicked off her shoes and walked over to the wet-bar where she proceeded to pour the Cognac into two-snifters. Bridges watched her. She turned and handed him a glass and they toasted to the success of their project.

They sat in silence for a few moments listening to the people out in the halls celebrating the Jewish New Year. It reminded them of New Years Eve in the States.

"I guess we won't get much sleep tonight with all the celebrating." Adriana said as she tasted the cognac and they listened to the festivities outside of the room. Bridges turned up the volume of the television. He was careful even though his friends check the room for monitoring devices, especially if they had arranged for Adriana to be next to him. "I know they swept the rooms, but I want to be certain no one hears our conversation."

Richard and Adriana settled into lounge chairs facing each other. They both began to speak at the same time causing them to laugh. Bridges asked Adriana, "What kind of woman is the First-Lady? Is she as far out to the left as the news media portrays her, or is that a distortion of her true character?"

Adriana looked down and glanced into her drink then looked up at Bridges. "She's a bitch. Vicious and power hungry. As a matter of fact, she believes she's running the country." Andriana took a sip. "You know they are not sleeping together and they haven't slept in the same bed since they moved into the White House. Her power hungry drive is the root of her evil which has generated to a plain old murder idea, or call it what you want, the assassination of a President or the killing of a husband."

Richard responded, "Then you think she's the driving force behind the entire plot? Are you sure of what you're saying?"

"Listen Richard, she controls ranking members of Congress, at least those from her own political party, and members of the Cabinet, specifically the Secretary of Labor and Treasury. She has problems with the Defense and State. They, of course, are of the same party but dislike her immensely." She looked at Richard to see his expression. "She does not like being half black. I don't know why they dislike her but I'm certain they don't know what I know. "

Richard smiled when he heard Adriana say that Heidi didn't like being black and brags about being a great great granddaughter to Thomas Jefferson.

"We should consider them when we put our plan in motion, that is, when we're looking for allies in the President's party. There's a funny story Richard, I laugh about it often. The President is fucking a pretty young black woman who works at the White House." Adriana smiled. "She is assigned to house-keeping duties in the First family's living quarters. One evening while I was working late, Heidi was out-of-town on one of her save-the-world campaigns. The President came out of his bedroom half-dressed and a young black woman left the room shortly after him." Adriana smiled. "She appeared scared to death when she noticed I had seen her. Since then the young woman is at my beckon call, she can't please me enough. I recently realized since the incident her hours were changed to the early morning shift. He's fucking her replacement, no doubt." Adriana laughed out loud. "I haven't told a sole other than you and I'm positive the First Lady is unaware of her husband's liaisons. Heidi's great-great-grandfather, Thomas Jefferson, had White House affairs. History suggests he had a few children by his the maids."

Bridges was surprised at Adriana's choice of words, but he was glad she could feel comfortable with him. "It doesn't surprise me Adriana, but we can't under estimate the First Lady."

"Well she's no dummy, but her desire for power has interfered with her rational. I've seen her become enraged over the slightest thing when it comes to the President, or Rob, as she calls him. If she had any idea he was fucking the maids, she would castrate him, not out of jealousy, but for distorting the office of the President, like Kennedy and Clinton.".

Bridges asked for a clear view of the situation. "Are you saying she's plotting to kill the President for the sake of power?"

"She's too damn smart to allow herself to be placed in the point-position, as you military-type might say. She's recruiting without them realizing what the goal might be. I know a great deal about her, her moves, the people she talks to throughout the day, and I have access to her daily activities. Please don't misunderstand me Richard, she didn't sit me down and tell me she was plotting to kill her husband, she didn't have to." Adriana sipped her drink again and continued. "She has communicated with people who could perform the act for her; people who are so far removed it would be difficult for the average police-investigator to connect her in a plot." Again she paused and sipped her drink. "That's where we come in. I hope I don't sound like an arm-chair detective Richard, but that's the only way I can explain Heidi's moves."

Bridges whistled softly, then responded, "This is heavy Adriana. Our work is cut out for us. Michael may be right, if too many people know about this we could be in danger. Do you think Billy-Ray is working for Heidi in some way?"

"I don't think so. I think Billy-Ray is just a self serving bastard who wants to be the hero in any war. He thinks your trip to this part of the world was for a dual purpose. The USAID contract was your ticket to travel and meet with your friends at the Mossad. Seriously though, I think he wants to be part of whatever you're doing, which may make him a hero in his own eyes as well as his employer."

"I agree, Billy-Ray is an accident on it's way to happen. He doesn't get along in Washington circles. He likes to shoot off his mouth about being from the Agency. He's not liked at NSA, but he's got a few friends there who use him." Bridges explained in simple terms. There was more he could have told her but held back until he felt comfortable with her.

Adriana nodded in agreement as she sat and listened to Bridges while admiring him.

"He openly tells anyone who will listens that he's from the CIA, that alone is grounds for dismissal. Not too many professionals take him serious. He could cause us some grief. To ignore him would be a mistake. Adriana do you agree?"

"You're absolutely right and as I mentioned earlier, I'm sure your friends found work for him to do to keep him out of our way, at least until we could discuss strategy."

Adriana noticed Bridges had finished his cognac and asked if he would like another.

"No thanks, I should get some sleep. I'm sure you're tired as well. Funny thing, the noise in the halls has subsided, it must be past mid-night."

Adriana was tired but was glad to get to know Richard.

"Richard, thank you for listening. You're easy to talk to. Your friends at the country-club and in Washington assured me you were an understanding person."

"Please Adriana, I'm flattered, but I'm sure you could have found a few people in Washington who would disagree with my methods of operation, and in gathering information. I guess one has to make a few professional enemies, but I've learned to live with it. I'm a little surprised you found anyone at the FBI who paid me compliments. When It comes to handling domestic intelligence the FBI resents people like me."

"I spoke to a few who were not admirers of you, but it was off set by those who respect you. We don't have time for people like that."

Bridges glanced at his watch, "I think we better call it a night. I'll leave the adjoining door unlocked. Early in the morning I'll be leaving for the country-club and when I return, we can meet here at the hotel for breakfast."

"Sounds good. But right now I'm going to take a warm shower and go to bed…good night Richard." Adriana was feeling the effects of the cognac and was ready to call it a day.

***

Bridges returned to his room and noticed the message light on. He contacted the desk for messages. There was a message from Becky, "Call her when you can." Bridges was relieved that it hadn't been an urgent message. Her call had brought on a smile.

Bridges undressed and decided to take a shower. There was so much to think about. He was curious as to what Becky wanted…then…there was Adriana. She was different, very attractive…even striking. He thought of Billy-Ray, then tried to dismiss the image from his mind. And then there was Michael Myers. Michael could be helpful back in Washington, he thought. He finished his shower and thinking of mysterious Adriana in the next room. No, he couldn't get involved with her, he thought…at least during the project. It would complicate matters. Finally Bridges drifted into a deep sleep, his last thoughts being of Adriana.

Suddenly, Bridges woke to sounds in his room. Hung over from sleep, he could hear a woman's voice, the voice sounded familiar…then he recognized it was Adriana.

“Richard…Richard…wake up…wake up please, I need to talk to you.”

Bridges instinctively jumped from bed, realizing he wasn’t dreaming. He could barely see the silhouette of Adriana from the only available light shining through the window. She was wearing a white night gown, her long hair over her shoulders.

“What’s wrong, Adriana?”

“Nothing is wrong, Richard. I just received a call from Michael. He’s terribly upset and said my life is in danger. He’s returning to Washington tomorrow and wants me to return with him.”

“What did you tell him?” Bridges impatiently asked.

“I explained I had unfinished business in Tel Aviv, I let him think I was doing business for the President’s wife. I also told him that I didn’t know when I would return to Washington.”

Bridges was annoyed, “What do you think Michael meant when he said your life was in danger, is he aware of anything?”

“He has friends at NSA and over at Treasury. Many of them are old college friends who work in the DC area. I’m sure he doesn’t know a anything. He knows I work for the President’s wife, that’s it. I believe his trip to Jordan was just pleasure, he always wanted to visit his birth place, but I could be wrong. He was young when the family moved to the United States.”

“Where the hell did he get the idea your life was in danger?” Bridges asked as he become upset trying to understand the significance of Michael’s call.

“I’m not sure, he didn’t say. He wants me to meet him at the airport tomorrow. You should be there, he may want to reveal something and I’d like you to be present. I’m sure he suspects we are involved in serious business but I don’t believe he’s unaware of your Agency connections.”

“Yes, of course Adriana, I’ll be there during your meeting with Michael. First, I have to contact my friends and let them know the latest. They won’t want any harm to come to you. Am I to understand that Michael will be leaving from Tel Aviv and not Amman?”

"Yes…he leaves on a flight heading for JFK. I asked Michael to be at the air-terminal at least two hours before his flight departs."

"Adriana, how the hell did he find you here at the Basel Hotel, did you tell him?" Bridges asked impulsively.

"No, I never told him that I was leaving Amman or anything to do with my plans. I'm concerned now."

"What time is it?"

"Just past three."

"I don't think I can return to sleep. Do you have any more Cognac?"

"Of course, I'll be right back with the bottle and glasses."

Bridges put on some pants and an undershirt just as Adriana returned with the Cognac. She smiled as she caught a glimpse of him putting on his pants. Bridges was slightly embarrassed. Just then, she asked if legends put their pants on the same as ordinary men, she laughed as she handed Bridges a glass of Cognac.

"And just what will the Washington elite say when they learn you were in a strange man's room at three in the morning?" He was entertained by her presence, after-all…it had been a long time since he had a woman in a room at that hour.

Adriana looked at Bridges, it was obvious she was upset by Michael's call. "I'm not worried or afraid of Michael's warning but what concerns me is where he got his information and why hasn't someone alerted me before now."

"Michael seems to be a conservative person, I'm sure Michael is concerned for your safety, but you're right, we have to find out how reliable is his information.

"Richard, he may feel reluctant to reveal the identity of his source of information unless he has some idea what we are doing together."

"We can't tell Michael anything until I feel comfortable with him. If he were to work with us, he has to give us total commitment, understand Adriana?"

"Yes, however, I must be honest, I'm suspicious of Michael. That's what caused me to react and wake you. I want to trust him, but I don't know where he's been or what he's been doing since my husband died. I hate to think he would be disloyal to our country, however he could be involved with people in the consulting business. They may be using him as a source of information well knowing I work for the President's wife. He hasn't attempted to contact me since my husband died so why now? He leaves around three-thirty tomorrow afternoon, let's plan to meet him around one-thirty. I'll treat for lunch."

"Thank you Adriana, I haven't had a woman buy my lunch in some time. Do you think Michael has business connections in New York? The reason I'm asking is that you mentioned his flight is to JFK, the flight terminates at Dullas International, why would he get off in New York unless he had business?"

"I don't know Richard, that's a good point. He didn't mention any business connections in New York, however, I suppose it's a possibility. He did say he would take the AMTRAK from New York to Washington…now I'm curious."

"Sitting here speculating isn't going to give us any answers. We may want to ask him in a subtle way so we don't appear to be prying into his personal life. You never mentioned if he was married Adriana, is he?"

"I recall Michael dating a young woman who we all thought he was serious about. I don't know what happened. I'm sure, if he married her I would have been invited to the wedding, his mother would have seen to it. I must say, Michael is a private person. I don't know if he would confide in me."

"You're tired. Why don't you get some sleep? I'll call you before I leave for the country-club. I shouldn't be long…is seven okay?"

"Seven will be fine. That will give me a chance to clean up and catch up on some other business."

Bridges was awaken by the demanding ring of the phone. He glanced at his watch…it's was five-thirty. He wondered who it could be. He picked up the phone, "Hello," the caller identified himself. "Hello Mr. Bridges, this is Michael Myers, I'm sorry if I disturbed your sleep. I called to invite you to meet with me at the airport this afternoon. I'm returning to the States, Adriana will be there. Why don't both of you come together, that is if you can make it. I'd like to talk to you both."

"I'll be there Michael. Are you taking the Flight to JFK? I believe it departs at three-thirty?"

"Yes, that's correct, ISRAIR, please meet me at ISRAIR terminal ticket counter, one-thirty will be fine. We'll find someplace to talk."

"Good, we'll be there Michael."

Bridges tried to return to sleep and for some reason dreamed of his daughter and the horses. He promised her that he would take photographs of the Arabian horses in the Jordanian Royal Stud. The horses were trained for the Royal Guard. He recalled the stables were located across from the Royal Palace and remembered that was where Adriana stayed when she visited her sister in Amman.

Bridges woke at six-thirty to the ringing of the phone again. This time it was a wake-up call from the front desk. He showered and called Adriana reminding her of his itinerary. He got dressed then called for his transportation to the Midrasha.

Bridges arrived at the Midrasha and was surprised at the number of cars in the parking area. It was a holiday and no one was expected to be there except the agents on duty. His driver was a young Israeli man who probably one of the recruits. Bridges entered the building through the main entrance and was greeted by Charlie. They immediately went upstairs to the conference room. Commander Risken entered and greeted them.

Bridges expressed his surprise at seeing them there on the holiday.

The Commander explained, "We are on alert since the peace agreement was signed between Israel and the PLO. There are factions who would like to cause problems and disrupt the peace accord."

Bridges understood and inquired as to the number of reported incidents since the signing of the agreement.

"None of any consequence, but the day is young and we must be cautious. What is the latest on your project?"

Bridges brought the Commander up to date on his discussions with Adriana, "We have a preliminary plan. I find her intelligent and strong willed, and...very attractive."

Commander Risken found Bridges' comment amusing but decided to keep matters at business, "I understand our man we assigned to you has annoyed you. I'm sorry but it's for your safety even though you think it isn't necessary."

Bridges responded, "You should know I had an intruder in my room. Of course I don't think it was your man. I'm certain it wasn't Mossad, I'm suggesting it may have been Smyth or someone working for him."

The Commander assured Bridges the intruder wasn't Mossad.

Bridges continued to explain, "The intruder didn't take anything, he just went through my brief case. What's the latest on Smyth?"

"We sent him on a...how do you Americans say...a wild goose chase. He won't be returning to Tel Aviv for a long time." The Commander smiled and appeared amused at his own cleverness. Charlie laughed, then Bridges joined in at the thought of some clever tactical joke played on Billy-Ray.

Bridges, then inquired, "Commander, what else do you know about Michael Myers? As you know he was born in Jordan and is an American citizen."

"Michael Myers was an informant for us during the Pollard incident...he's non-political. His information was relied upon by both us and your Justice Department. We have nothing but praise for him. We also know your source was married to Michael Myers' brother and that the brother was killed in an accident, or should I say...a contracted assassination."

"Commander, do you think my source knows the entire story of how her husband met his death? She has suspicions you know?"

"She's unaware of what we know. Besides this is a different story all together. That was ten years ago. Richard you have to trust your source. She's well connected and many important people in your country respect her from both political parties. And I might add, she has limitations, after all, she's a woman." A complement made by Commander Risken, typical of how most Israeli men look at their woman as being limited, neglecting to recall Israel was led by a woman when the country became more than an idea.

Bridges thanked the Commander. The Commander's comment reminded him that Israeli men don't permit their woman to succeed beyond most man, but there are exceptions, he thought.

Commander Risken assured Bridges the Mossad was ready to render assistance if needed, however, insisted Israel must never become embarrassed as it could destroy relationships with the United States.

During their discussion Charlie suggested coffee, however, Commander Risken declined and politely excused himself indicating he had work to do and left the conference room. Bridges accepted thinking it would be a good time to talk to Charlie. "As long as it's American and not something the Italians or Israelis call coffee."

Charlie smiled and informed Bridges the coffee was right from the American Consulate Embassy commissary. "Remember Richard, I'm still American, I'm reminded whenever I try to eat camel-food."

Both men went downstairs to the kitchen which was closed but they were able to brew a fresh pot of coffee.

As they sat at the small table in the kitchen, Charlie inquired, "Richard, how are you getting along with the source?"

Bridges smiled, "Great. She's an intelligent woman, a good sense of direction but a little strange at times. She tells it as she see's it. If she doesn't like something, she'll let you know."

Charlie felt it was a good time to give Bridges a piece of advice, "You have to take control of this project...a bit of advice from my boss. You have the ability to put a plan in motion but you need to start setting the rules of operation and engagement."

"Thanks for the advice, the Israelis are always one step ahead of a situation. I'll take the Commander's advice as well but I hope it's not because I'm working with a woman. Of course I'll direct things that have to be accomplished and Adriana knows it, however I need to know what I'm up against. Thanks again Charlie for your input. You know we're meeting this afternoon with Michael Myers. He's returning to Washington on the three-thirty flight. I'd like the meeting to take place at the air-terminal if at all possible.

"We didn't know he was here in Tel Aviv, that is unless the Commander knew and didn't share the information. I'll arrange for a room at the terminal if that's where you plan to meet."

"Thanks again Charlie, that's a big help."

Charlie looked at Bridges, almost staring and explained, "I'll also be there, Richard, I'll keep my distance. I'm leaving for Washington on the same flight. I have business at the Israeli Embassy and will return to Tel Aviv next week. Becky is assigned to you while I'm gone. Please, for security reasons follow her directions....We expect problems from the PLO over the Peace Accord, as you well know."

"Thanks, I'll do as Becky directs." Bridges was amused with the idea that Becky would be in charge of his safety.

Bridges checked in at the Course Director's office. He discovered he was scheduled to teach several classes with the recruits. As he recorded the times and dates in his small note-book, he found a page with writing already on it. It wasn't his handwriting and he was curious as to how it got there. His note-book was useless to anyone else, he thought, especially for any intelligence purposes. It only contained memos concerning things he had to do for his daughter. One page contained a grocery list for a dinner party he hosted several weeks prior. It appeared brief and partly cryptic, although he could read a line or two that amounted to nothing. Bridges turned to a blank page, finished writing his teaching schedule, then turned back to the page with the cryptic writing and wondered what it meant. He returned to the conference room upstairs. Charlie was packing his brief case and seemed startled to see Bridges. "What's up friend?" Charlie asked.

"I'd like to consult you on a matter. I discovered an entry in my notebook...in someone else's handwriting."

Charlie took the notebook, examined it, smiled and then laughed, "This looks like child's writing, or someone who was in a hurry. Can't figure what it means. Who had access, Richard?"

"No one other than that intruder could have gone through my the brief case. I discovered it open, like someone had gone through it. I thought is might have been Smyth, you know Billy-Ray. The Commander also thought is was Smyth or someone working for him. The Marines at the Embassy will do anything for the CIA, you know. They'll jump through their ass for anyone from the Agency."

Charlie agreed and made a suggestion, "I think we should have it checked at the our lab. Maybe we can determine the origin of ink…maybe the author, male or female if we're lucky. We'll be able to tell if it was written by an American of someone with European education.".

"Good idea Charlie." They left for the research lab located in the government district of Tel Aviv.

They met with the document examiner and Bridges learned the expert was trained at the Los Angeles Police Department, and also worked at the Treasury Department in Washington before he relocated to Israel.

The examiner quickly looked at the page and commented, "There is good reason to believe the ink came from an American made ball-point pen, an inexpensive model. Some of the handwriting is cryptic and spurious. My guess is that it was written by a male with an American education. The entry says nothing, probably to stimulate curiosity if nothing else. There's enough letters to compare if we had a known standard."

Bridges sighed, "Thank you for your time. If we could get a sample of Billy-Ray's handwriting we may have a comparison."

The document examiner asked if Billy-Ray worked at the American Embassy. Charlie answered, "Yes. His true name is Smyth."

"I have his sample in the files. We've done some work for him or the Embassy in the past and his signature and printed handwriting is part of our records. It will serve as a good exemplar for comparison. It will take a few hours, I'll call Charlie with the results."

"Thank you for the prompt service." Bridges responded with sincere appreciation.

The document examiner smiled for a moment, "I have no choice. When Charlie makes a request, it receives priority, besides I enjoy doing it."

Charlie spoke to the document examiner off to one side of the room. Bridges didn't care to hear their conversation but he imagined it involved the request and an urgent need for the results.

They left the building where Charlie dismissed the driver, then he personally drove Bridges to the Basel Hotel. Once they arrived, Bridges remarked, "I may see you in Washington, if so, let's have dinner?" A day at my farm may be a restful time, you will be certain to enjoy it." Bridges suggested.

"I'd love to, however, I don't think we should be seen in public, especially Washington." Charlie responded, causing more curiosity.

Bridges was hesitant but then agreed with Charlie, "Then let's meet when I return to Tel Aviv? Thank-you for all your help, you're a true friend. By the way, how will I get the handwriting comparison results?"

"Becky will have the results for you later today, I've instructed the examiner to contact her."

"Have a safe trip, enjoy your visit to Washington, I'm sure you'll visit friends and relatives in Philly."

"I'm afraid not, I have no reason to return to my birth place. My mother and father have passed away and my only sister lives in California. I'll conduct my business and stay close to the Embassy. Good luck Richard, it was my pleasure."

Bridges shook Charlie's hand, "Thanks again."

Bridges went inside the hotel and took the elevator to the third floor. He entered his room noting the message light was on. He contacted the desk. The message was from his daughter Jennifer. She left a phone number but Bridges recognized it wasn't the home number. He thought she probably needed something, maybe money, or maybe she had a new boyfriend at school.

Bridges smiled to himself thinking her call could wait…after-all she didn't indicate it was urgent. She was twenty years old and capable of handling herself…he could call later.

Bridges dialed Adriana's room and couldn't help thinking of Charlie. He felt an uneasiness when they parted.

Adriana answered, interrupting his thoughts, "Adriana…Richard here, what time would you like to leave for the airport? Remember, you offered to buy lunch."

"I'm ready now, you offered to buy breakfast and yes, I'm buying, we can have lunch at the terminal. But first a cup of American coffee would help. I'll meet you in the restaurant in ten minutes. First I need to call my sister in Ammen. It won't take long."

Since Bridges had an extra few minutes he decided to call the caretaker of his farm. Perhaps he would know the nature of Jennifer's call, since she never calls him when he's away unless it's an emergency. He was relieved to find out that Jennifer was okay and wanted to buy another horse, an Arabian yearling colt. But first she wanted to discuss the matter with him. Bridges thanked the caretaker. He smiled to himself...he should have known the matter had something to do with horses. No sooner had he hung up, the phone rang. No one was on the other end, perhaps the desk rang the wrong room. The call bothered him. He couldn't help but wonder of someone wanted to find out if he was in his room. He dismissed the idea...he thought he was getting paranoid. He removed a small notebook from his briefcase and left the room to meet Adriana.

Bridges greeted Adriana in the hotel restaurant entrance. He couldn't help but notice how attractive she looked in her tan-colored jumpsuit. The top two buttons were open revealing her cleavage.

Adriana smiled and instinctively knew Bridges found her appealing. Impulsively she wanted to hug him then changed her mind and extended her hand.

Bridges felt tension at the moment. He sensed Adriana was going to hug him and felt embarrassed when she extended her hand.

They were seated and ordered coffee. Bridges complemented Adriana. She thanked him with a shrewd look on her face which told him she had dressed to attract his attention. They finished their coffee, left the hotel and had the valet bring the car around to the front. Bridges drove to the Ben Gurion International Airport. The traffic was light and Bridges remembered it was a holiday and most people were home.

Bridges spoke of his daughter and told Adriana that she was crazy about horses. Adriana provide little response over his comment.

The silence between Adriana and Bridges left him to wonder if he had offended her in anyway. Then he recalled the advice Charlie gave him about taking charge of the project.

They arrived at the airport, parked the car and walked to the terminal. Bridges reminded Adriana the VIP lounge served international food. She agreed and they were seated to the rear next to the wall. They were able to observe the travelers as they scurried to their destination.

"There seems to be many travelers today." Bridges remarked attempting to start a conversation.

Adriana nodded, "I believe we've got just enough time to have lunch and meet Michael. Maybe we should have had lunch with Michael. Where do you think we should talk to him?"

"My friends arranged for us to use an office next to Customs."

Bridges was in the middle of answering Adriana's question when he suddenly noticed Charlie walking with a familiar person, it was Billy-Ray. They appeared to be traveling together. Bridges knew the Mossad was clever shrewd and well calculated. But he couldn't help feeling uncomfortable over the sight of the two together. He recalled how Charlie did not want to meet at the Airport or to be seen together in Washington. He decided to share his information with Adriana and explained his meeting with Charlie earlier.

Adriana didn't seem surprised although appeared preoccupied then paid for the lunch. They left the lounge and walked to the TWA ticket counter where they found Michael waiting. He was dressed in a light olive green Palm Beach suit, blue oxford button-down shirt, and a silk print tie. He looked very American.

Adriana hugged Michael and kissed him on the cheek. He smiled and extended his hand to Bridges, "It's good to see you Mr. Bridges, and you Adriana. How are you? I wish you would call my mother and father when you return to the States."

Adriana promised she would. They started walking in the direction of the Customs Office where they met Becky who escorted them to a private office. She smiled at Bridges and whispered to him, "Is that my competition?" Before Bridges could answer, she reported the handwriting was similar to Billy-Ray's, then she left them alone.

Michael excused himself to go to the rest-room.

"Adriana smiled and looked at Bridges, "Is that young woman one of your fans?

Bridges smiled his face becoming flush, "Adriana, that young woman is assigned to me while I'm here. She's a bright young woman."

When I was looking for you, I learned from reliable sources that you earned a title, or should I say a nick-name. There are those at CIA and FBI use it and they cautioned me about you. What's the story behind the name?"She tried not to laugh, as she teased Bridges

As they sat waiting for Michael to return, Bridges smiled and remarked, "Its too long of a story to explain, I promise to fill in the details later when time permits."

Adriana was disappointed but pursued the topic, "Richard, the Highwayman? It makes no sense without the story." She giggled like a teenage girl.

CHAPTER 4
REVELATION

Michael returned from the rest room and noticed Adriana smiling as she talked to Bridges. He over-heard Adriana ask Bridges about a nick-name. At this point they both noticed Michael and became serious.

Acting like an older sister and showing concern Adriana wanted to offer Michael advice but he was bent on telling her she was in danger. "Michael are you anxious to return home?"

Michael responded with a long face and deep concern. "Adriana and also you Mr. Bridges, I'm concerned for your safety—can we speak without being over-heard?"

Bridges remarked. "I'm sure anything we discuss will not be over-heard by third parties, I've been assured of that."

Well as I said, you both are in danger. I have many friends in the Washington area, many work at the Pentagon and the National Security Agency. Several in important places. be certain I'm told there is a situation brewing that may affect our government and the balance of power. Many at the Defense Department dislike the President and the way he's handling foreign affairs. There are many that also dislike the President's wife. People inside the belt-way think she is running the country. She's rude to people in public, as you know Adriana, many have reason to think she is up to something , something radical, am I right Adriana?"

Adriana responded. "You are right Michael, I'm aware of her attitude behind the scene as well. I constantly remind her of her problems, it's as if she wanted to rule the country, she presents an image of…no one can touch her, it leaves me cold."

Bridges asked Michael the question that was instrumental in the meeting. "Michael, you've cautioned us of the danger, what is it you know that causes you to believe we're in danger?"

"Mr. Bridges, I fear for Adriana's life because of what happened to my brother several years ago. You recall that Adriana was married to my brother, well…Adriana has been bitter over the situation all these years, isn't that right Adriana?"

Adriana wanted to explain her bitterness but she didn't think it was the time and place. "Yes that's right. I've never gotten over Bill's death. I've always believed someone was responsible for the accident, that's if you want to call it an accident, I'm sure it wasn't."

Michael remarked. "Well…many believe being close to Mrs. Banks places you in a dangerous situation. It's no secret you work for her and that I'm you're late husband's brother."

Adriana became impatient. "I understand Michael, however what factual information do you have, what do you know that's important?"

Bridges nudged her under the table as to calm her.

Michael hesitated, then provided them with information in a calm manner concerning his purpose for the trip to Jordan. "To tell the truth Adriana, I had advance knowledge that you were going to visit your sister in Amman. I always wanted to visit my birth place. I decided to make the trip in hopes we would meet and have time to talk."

Adriana being curious and in an excited voice, asked Michael the pointed question. "How did you know of my travel plans? No one besides Mrs. Banks and the White House travel office had knowledge."

"Adriana, I mentioned I had friends at NSA, they handle the communications at the White House as you well know. My former room mate monitored installation of new telephone lines. He over heard your plans to visit Amman and related the information to me. I'm sorry if it offends you, at the same time he related that the President's wife talks to people over the telephone, people that have no business with her or the country. You know she speaks Spanish like a native. She was overheard talking in Spanish to people in Central America. The conversation is on tape, however from what I understand it hasn't been translated."

Adriana hid her feelings and felt frustrated that she couldn't spend more time with Michael. "Michael, what else do you know?"

"Well…I understand they, that is my former room mate monitored your conversations from Mrs. Banks's office. You were talking to some people in Central America. I knew you also spoke Spanish, however I didn't know you were that proficient. Believe me, my friend was not monitoring you, just the calls made from Mrs. Banks White House office phone."

Adriana wanted to remind him that his friend could get into serious trouble if anyone were to find out about the recordings. "Michael you understand that I often make telephone calls for Mrs. Banks, many to other countries. My calls to Central America involved projects that we are working on."

Michael interrupted Adriana. "The calls you made were to a number in the city of San Salvador, a number assigned to people that were involved in assassinations in El Salvador during the late eighties…did you know that Adriana?"

Adriana answered as she glanced over at Bridges. "I made the calls at the direction of Mrs. Banks. Has my calls been translated?"

"Not that I can determine, however my friend suggested that Mr. Bridges and other members of the CIA know the people you and Mrs. Banks called."

Bridges answered. "I'm sure I do, I worked with a special unit when I was in El Salvador, later found out they were involved in assassinations of those they believed were against the democratic government. I recall the team was made up of several women, one of which lives in Los Angeles at this time."

Bridges continued. "I'm sure the Agency has a handle on her. Her name escapes me at this time, I'm sure I'll recall it before the day is over. The rest of the people have either been killed or faded off into the landscape after President Duarte died. They shouldn't be hard to locate, my guess is that they live in Los Angeles or some where else in California with the rest of the Hispanic population."

Adriana quickly responded. "What else do you know, that is what else did your friend tell you?"

"I know that you spoke to an old classmate of your that was in your wedding. I can't recall her name, however I've been told you shared with her your feelings of dislike for the President's wife. The reason for this information is you used the telephone my friend monitored. I've been assured that it's not a routine thing, he became curious, that's all. Most of my friends know who you are Adriana, they seem to like you, I'm certain they mean no harm. I took advantage of the information so as to meet you in Amman." Michael expressed himself well but in a nervous manner.

Adriana acting as though her privacy was invaded and she didn't care about anything else, she had to find out before Michael left for the States. "Michael you haven't told me much about being in a dangerous situation."

Bridges joined in. "Michael what makes you think Adriana is in danger?"

"The fact my friend has reason to think the President's wife is going to arrange for the President to be assassinated. He's troubled with the information. He thinks that Adriana is on some type of hit list if Mrs. Banks knew Adriana disliked her."

Adriana in a calm voice responded by asking a question Bridges planned to ask. "Michael do you think your friend would be willing to talk to us, this of course when we return to Washington?"

"Adriana I'm sure he will, however it has to be somewhere away from the Washington area, he's got his job to worry about. If it got out that he monitored the President's wife, his ass will be grass, I'm sure you know what I mean." Michael remarked.

Bridges changed the subject in an attempt get a handle on Michael. "Michael what are your plans when you arrive in New York, do you have business there?"

"No I plan to take the AMTRAK from New York to Baltimore. I have a girlfriend that lives in Germantown. Outside of Baltimore, she teaches at the University of Maryland. I have a few days before I return to my job in Washington."

Bridges hoped Adriana would shut her mouth and allow Michael to talk. Obviously he had more to say and is interrupted ever time Adriana asks a new question

"When will you be seeing your parents?" Adriana asked in hopes to maintain a closeness and being concerned.

"I plan to see them Sunday before returning to work. My mother wants to cook for me. She likes to cook our native food. No one can cook like my mother." Michael smiled as he answered.

Recalling that Michael was planning to meet a girlfriend in Baltimore, she wanted to know if Michael was serious and had been planning to marry her. Michael hesitantly answered that the plans were set for June of next year. "A church wedding, she's catholic as I am and she has a large family. As you know Adriana, my mother wouldn't have it any other way.

Bridges looked at the clock on the wall, it was almost three. He thought Michael's plane departed around three-thirty, then he spoke. "Michael there are many things we should discuss, your plane leaves at three-thirty. I want you know we will say goodbye here, I don't think it's a good idea to walk you to the departure gate. There are people we should avoid. I might add, they are on your flight. I'm sure will not discuss this information with anyone. Don't solicit any further information from your friend. I understand you are no longer room-mates?"

Michael answered. "Yes, he got married and has a little girl…a daughter, we remain friends, good friends. I work out with him at the club. Sometime we play tennis in the warmer weather. I've taken up golf, my girlfriend is a damn good lady golfer, that should interest you Adriana, I recall you play golf."

Adriana ignored Michael's remark about playing golf, she anxiously asked him a question. "Would your friend be willing to provide us the tapes, that is if he still has them?"

Michael answered. We anticipated you would ask, he has them in a safety deposit box at his bank, they are copies on cassettes. The originals were reel to reel and I'm sure destroyed.

"Does your friend know Billy Ray?" Bridges asked in a bold expression.

Michael laughed, then answered. "Yes…everyone knows Billy Ray, that is, over at NSA. He is a constant visitor there he has some friends there, the kind that think it's neat to someone from CIA, most mistrust Billy Ray, or just dislike him."

Bridges asked another question. Michael do you think Billy Ray has access to the tapes of the first lady and Adriana's telephone conversations?"

"I doubt it, however we can't be certain, if he had access, he didn't get it from my friend."

"Michael you better be going. Do you mind if I call you when we return to Washington, that is Adriana will call you, and we can meet somewhere away from the D.C. area.

Michael thought for a minute and then responded. "I would like that, in the mean time please don't take any chances. Will you be returning to Amman Adriana?"

"Yes, we plan a brief trip. I'll visit my sister and Richard wanted to photograph the Arabian horses at the Royal Stud. This of course will be shortly before we return to the states. Goodbye Michael, have a safe trip." Adriana hugged him, Bridges shook hands and wished him well.

As Michael left the office, Adriana watched him walk to the ISRAIR gate, she observed Billy Ray in line waiting to board the flight to JFK. Adriana backed into the office and informed Bridges she spotted Billy Ray.

Bridges suggested they stay put until the flight loaded, and recommended they take a ride to the beach later and continue their discussion.

During the trip back to Tel Aviv, Bridges asked Adriana what she thought of the conversation with Michael.

"I think he's afraid, I sincerely believe he knows more than what he revealed, my telephone calls to San Salvador were harmless. They were follow-up calls for Mrs. Banks. She has a project going with the President's wife of El Salvador, nothing more I'm sure. I'm the one that stimulated her interest with the project, something started with Mrs. Bush and relinquished to who-ever was in the White House."

Bridges in deep thought felt strong that Michael's life may also in danger. He recalled Michael had been an informant for the FBI and Mossad during the Pollard mess. He shared his thoughts with Adriana. Adriana conveyed her knowledge of Michael expressing that he's always been a cautious person in everything he did.

Bridges thought of his planed trip to Amman, for a moment thought he should cancel the trip, then thought of Jennifer and didn't want to disappoint her.

"I'd like to make the trip to Amman the first of the week, after I finish my project at the Midrasha. I of course expect you to make the trip with me. Is there a problem with that?"

"No Richard, I'd planned to go with you, however I wanted to be invited. I'll arrange for your visit to the Royal Stud, also we can use a think-tank in Amman if you wish, I can make those arrangements also."

Bridges assured Adriana that he would arrange for the trip. He had to stop by the hotel to check his messages. He was expecting to hear from his daughter

Bridges agreed to meet Adriana in the lounge. As.Bridges entered his room, he noticed a fresh basket of fruit, he thought maybe Adriana arranged for the delivery of the basket. He thought that he must remember to ask her when they meet in the lounge. He noticed the message light on, immediately he contacted the desk. The desk clerk related he had one message from Becky, instructions to call her at the office. Bridges thanked the desk clerk, then dialed the operator for a call to his daughter Jennifer. The phone rang several times until someone answered, it was the caretaker of the farm. Bridges thought that he answered the phone in the barn or the phones in the tack room.

"Hello William, this is Richard, is Jennifer there?"

"No Richard, she left for town, something to do with getting a new blanket for the colt."

Bridges responded to William's comment. "You mean she bought the colt?"

"Yes...she brought it home this morning...she's crazy about him, I must agree, he's a damn good looking horse."

"William, what can I say...please tell her I called, I'll try to call her tomorrow, I'm going to Amman, Jordan next week, tell her I'll take photos of the Royal Stud when I'm there. She's alright? Is she eating and taking care of herself?"

"Don't worry, she's fine, believe me, she eats more than I do, I can't figure how she stays thin, oh well, she'll slow down someday I'm sure, she's fine, don't worry. My wife Beth is taken care of her, they get along fine as you know, I'll give her your message, you take care of yourself Richard. It's not like before and your not young anymore. Bridges said goodbye to the caretaker, sat on the edge of the bed, thought for a moment, called Becky at the Midrasha. "Hello Becky, Richard here, what's up?"

"Richard, the writing belongs to Billy Ray, you know your pal, he's such an ass-hole, you know what I mean, how did the airport visit go?"

"It went okay, I noticed Charlie left with Billy Ray, I'd like to hear more about that when I see you." Bridges remarked.

Becky laughed. "The commander arranged for that situation, they sent Billy Ray on a special mission, if you get my drift, I'll explain later."

Bridges responded by laughing, then spoke. "Becky, I plan to go to Amman early next week, would you make arrangements for me, also include arrangements for my associate as well."

A brief silence on the other end of the phone, then Becky wanted to know if Adriana was her competition, realizing she sounded like a school girl, Becky agreed that she would make the arrangements for Bridges' trip to Amman. She reminded him that because she was a Baldar-Bat Leveyha she was certain not to go. It was obvious that the government of Jordan would have a field day if Becky was found in their country. She sounded jealous and Bridges didn't know how to resolve the situation. He thought for the moment, he would ignore Becky's jealous attitude although he didn't want it to over-flow onto their project. Both woman would be in trouble with Commander Riskin.

Bridges smiled to himself, then explained in a stern voice that they would be gone over night, two nights at the most, and assured her that Adriana's plans to stay at the Palace with her sister and he would stay at his hotel in Amman. The purpose of the visit was personal, he didn't think Becky believed him. He explained once again that the trip was for his daughter. Bridges reassured Becky that there was nothing between he and Adriana. A relationship would muddy the water and make things difficult for their project. Becky seemed to come around to accepting what Bridges was saying. They laughed together.

As Bridges hung the phone up, he couldn't help thinking about Becky being so damn jealous, then he thought of his daughter's new colt.

***

Bridges left the room and met Adriana in the lounge, she was reading an American newspaper when he approached her, she looked up and smiled, put the paper down and took a sip of her drink, then spoke. "Richard, there's talk about Jordan signing a peace accord with Israel, similar to the one the PLO signed, what are your thoughts?"

Bridges responded to the question. "I've always felt that once Israel made friends with it's neighbors, trade would increase and the economy of Israel would start moving in the direction of true capitalism. PLO isn't that important, however it served as a message to the rest of the world that Israel is willing to be reasonable and friendly and willing to open up trade venues with other countries including it's neighbors. The Israeli people are strong, they have good ideas, they remain obsessed with the holocaust, they should put it away, get on with building their country and developing their lands."

Adriana looked at Bridges and remarked. "Richard you sound like a politician."

Richard smiled, then responded. "Not really, I've had many talks with my Israeli friends about their economy and mending fences with their neighbors. Often I attempted to point out the problems they are having with world trade. I enjoy the Israeli people , sometimes they get a little narrow minded, once you realized it, you can cope with them."

Adriana smiled and reminded Bridges that he hadn't ordered a drink, as she sipped on her own.

Bridges ordered a beer and went on discussing his brief conversation with the caretaker concerning his daughter. "My daughter has another horse, I should say a colt, I can't figure why she wants to raise another stallion, we have two excellent breeds, they are magnificent producers."

Adriana looked at Bridges and responded. "You are into horses emotionally as you are financially, isn't that right Richard?"

"Yes Adriana, my daughter loves them as my wife did, I love an early Sunday morning ride in the countryside, it gives me a great feeling of being at peace with myself. Virginia is beautiful this time of the year, the trees are of brilliant colors and the air brisk, perfect for riding. The horses love it as well. When we return, I'd like you to be a guest at my place in Virginia. Have you ridden very much?"

"Yes, many times, never an Arabian, my experience has been either Thoroughbreds or Quarter horses. I'm not sure I can handle the Arabian."

"Ridiculous Adriana, Arabians are no different when it comes to riding, that is if they were trained properly. If my history is correct, George Washington rode an Arabian. They are intelligent and loving. I have a gray mare you will love, her name is Hearts of Fire, I call her Fire or Cracker, as in fire cracker. She is a pleasure to ride, trust me."

"Spoken like a true Rabbi, with that trust me bit." Adriana remarked. Then she laughed like a young girl.

"Oh well, being around the Israelis as much as I have, one tends to emulate them, I'm sure you understand." Bridges reminded Adriana that it's getting late, they should go down to the beach, maybe have dinner and discuss what comes natural.

As they walked to the beach area from the hotel, they decided to have dinner at a small restaurant nearby. During their meal, neither spoke of the project. The conversation continued along the lines as to their likes and dislikes, as one would do during an acquaintance date.

After dinner they walked back to the Basel Hotel. Bridges noticed they were being followed and he cautiously mentioned it to Adriana.

Adriana assured Bridges that it wasn't someone her sister arranged. "It's probably someone your friends assigned to watch over us. Didn't you say they had someone watching over us?"

Richard in a serious tone looking over his shoulder responded. "I'm sure you're right, Charlie left for Washington, Becky has been assigned to me and I'm sure it's the big guy I ran into at the hotel."

They arrived at the hotel, entered and walked over to the elevators. While waiting, the Israeli assigned to Bridges arrived, he smiled at Adriana and said hello to them both. They entered the elevator briefly discussed the New Years holiday, nothing of any consequence. They got off the elevator on the third floor. Adriana and Bridges walked directly to Adriana's room. The Israeli entered another room, not the one he had used on the previous day. Bridges thought it was strange, then decided to call Becky to check on it.

As soon as they entered Adriana's room, Bridges dialed Becky's number at her apartment, she answered on the first ring. "Hello Becky…Richard. How are you this evening?"

Becky answered. "Richard, what a pleasant surprise, what's up?"

"Becky, this guy assigned to watch over me, why is it that he has a different room than yesterday?"

Becky laughed. "To be truthful Richard, I don't know. Is the guy a big one, your know big and round as well as tall, speaks like maybe he is German?"

"Yes, that's him." Bridges remarked.

"I'll check on it and call you back. Are you at the hotel?"

"Yes, just call my room, 333, I'll be waiting to hear. By the way, did your office sweep my room today?"

"Yes, I'm sure they did."

"Let me get back with you shortly." Becky hung the phone up.

Bridges suggested they go over to his room and wait for Becky to call.

Shortly, Becky called and informed Bridges that his room was clean of electronic bugs and the agent moved to another room for his own comfort, the bed was larger.

Bridges thanked Becky and agreed to meet at seven in the morning.

The Basel Hotel is at the seashore overlooking the Mediterranean Sea. As Bridges stared out the window, Adriana spoke. "How about some coffee?"

Bridges turned to face Adriana and smiled. "As long as it isn't Italian or Israeli coffee, one in the same, I'd love a cup, maybe with some of your smuggled cognac would be great."

Adriana smiled, then spoke. I'll call for service and have the coffee sent up, American style, right?"

Bridges continued looking out the hotel window toward the setting sun. Then spoke. "I always feel comfort when I watch the sun go down across the Mediterranean, it's a sight to remember. It adds to my visit to Tel Aviv. Often I sense there is no bad in the world when I watch this scene. Then of course I come to my senses and realize that every time I come here, there is an enemy out there. Oh well, where's the coffee Adriana?"

Adriana pleasantly smiled as she sat at the edge of the bed. "Richard, what bothers you the most about this situation?"

"Adriana, we don't need another President, assassinated. I don't care who likes or dislikes him. The fact remains that we are a strong nation. To resolve our problems through the use of force and violence troubled me. " Richard shook his head. " I've seen a great deal in my day. Countries of Central America struggle with their civil wars. Useless killing of people over power and corruption. I've seen the trouble here in the Middle-East, now this same thing may be happening in our country."

Adriana looked up at Bridges and spoke in a soft voice. "Richard we can stop it without the American people knowing, that is if we get the cooperation from your connections."

"Yes Adriana, however in order to defuse it, we have to light back fires, that is…we need to create incidents that will distract the people and of course the News Media, if you know what I mean. I've always believed the Watergate scandal was embellished by the Press. What ever Nixon did was accomplished by others before him, it didn't make it right. Look at the Kennedy administration, he was corrupt to say the least, not to mention incompetent to govern. I'm sure this had a lot to do with his assassination. I don't care what the so-called experts said, it made him a hero in the eyes of the world. If Kennedy was a presidential candidate today, he never would have made it." Richard realized that he was getting political. "Hell, Ted Kennedy is gone, I get sick thinking that he could have been president."

Adriana responded. "You have strong feelings Richard, I thought I felt strong concerning my dislikes for this administration, maybe you top me."

"If we don't watch out, we'll become radical Adriana. The present administration has it's problems. Many are self inflicted, the American people deserve what they got, after all, they elected the him President. Then again, it would appear to a political scientist that the people were deceived, I believe it." Richard smiled and thought he was on a soap box. "Hell, this administration seems socialistic, do you agree?"

A knock at the door interrupted the conversation and Adriana answered, it was Room Service with the coffee.

Adriana using the adjoining doors, went to her room for the cognac. She returned and handed the bottle of cognac to Bridges, as she passed the bottle, their hands touched, Bridges looked into Adriana's eyes, she smiled like a school girl. Bridges poured cognac into his coffee cup, Adriana waved at him indicating she didn't want any.

As they sat facing each other, the room was dim the one light next to the television set illuminated a small portion of the room, Bridges became serious and inquired if Michael read and spoke Spanish. Adriana hesitated and answered with uncertain knowledge. Many things have happened since her husband died and that if Michael studied Spanish in college, she was certain.

With curiosity, Adriana wanted to know the purpose of Bridges question. As Bridges answered, she recalled that the tape recordings Michael spoke about were in Spanish.

Bridges was concerned over the contents of the tapes, if Michael understood Spanish, he thought out loud, he would have complete knowledge of conversations with the people in El Salvador, specifically, Rosa Correa, the reason for his apprehension and fear that Adriana was in danger. Then again, if Michael's friend understood Spanish as he said, then the information was translated and left up to the interpretation of the contents, never the less, the words were recorded and Michael felt helpless and thought he should warn Adriana by traveling to the Middle East. Bridges felt certain Michael knew the contents and was able to listen with understanding.

Adriana didn't feel comfortable knowing there were tape recordings of her and Heidi talking to suspected assassins in Central America. What ever Heidi said in the tapes, had to be obvious to anyone she was up to no good, although there's always the interpretation, as anyone knows.

Adriana expounded on the translation or better still, the interpretation of the conversation to anyone that doesn't know the language fluently. As she looked at Bridges, she sensed he was curious as to why she would come to the defense of the Spanish spoken tapes. Then he stated in a gentle voice that it sounds defensive, causing Adriana to be lost for words and she explained that often a translated language can be misinterpreted, depending on the person's knowledge or lack of knowledge of the spoken language. At this point Bridges was willing to give Adriana the benefit of the doubt.

Richard gulped his coffee and poured some more cognac into the cup, he then looked over at Adriana and asked a question that he wanted to know when they first discussed Central America. "Where did Heidi Jefferson Banks learn Spanish?"

"She worked for the State Department after completing college. Her first assignment was the Central American desk in Washington. Then she went to Central America, assigned to the Embassy in Honduras, or maybe Guatemala. In order to work in those countries, she had to learn

Spanish. She learned it so well that many say she spoke Spanish like a native. I speak it, however not as well. I spent some time at the Embassy in Mexico several years ago. First I went to Guatemala, actually the city of Antiqua to learn Spanish. After six weeks I had a good command of the language. It was a one-on-one learning experience. I then learned to read and write Spanish. I've visited the Embassy in San Salvador right after the earth quake. Why have I told you this, you've spent a great deal of time in Central America as well as the Middle-east."

"Adriana, your got that right, however my Spanish isn't as accomplished as it should. I can speak Spanish with an American accent. Often I need a dictionary or a Spanish translator."

Adriana became serious. She conveyed her suspicions that Michael always wanted to work for the CIA. She was certain after receiving word that during the recent war with Iraq, he wanted to be part of it in some way. His job at Treasury wasn't rewarding. " Adriana explained the information came from a third party that knew the family. In the middle of her explanation, Adriana reminded Bridges that her late husband worked for the State Department, assigned to the Central American desk the same time Heidi Jefferson was assigned to the Embassy in Central America.

Bridges agreed that the information provided by Michael was an excellent start, especially the tape recordings of Heidi's conversation with a person believed to be Rosa Correa. He continued to expound on the difficult job they had once returning to Washington.

Adriana brought up her curiosity as to why Michael would fly from Tel Aviv to New York and then take the AMTRAK to Baltimore. She offered the better solution that Michael could fly into Dullas, rent a car if his wasn't there, and then drive to Baltimore with little difficulty.

Bridges didn't find Michael's reason suspicious at first, then he thought about it and agreed it didn't make sense. Adriana was also curious if Michael was...Agency or working for some other government organization.

Bridges agreed that maybe he's a contractor or is working as a paid informant for the government.

They couldn't be certain until Bridges checked it out with his source back at Langley.

Adriana reminded Bridges that Michael has friends at NSA and he went to college with most of them, that his major was in economics.

Bridges was curious if Michael was into computers or computer programming. If he was, he explained, then maybe Michael is Agency, and went on to explain that there should be a paper trail, although difficult determine from Tel Aviv.

Bridges suggested he call a friend in Washington, at least, it would get the ball rolling. The suggestion was to start at Treasury Department, Michael's date of birth and Social Security number should be known.

Adriana responded. "That's easy, his birthday is the same as mine, however several years later."Bridges planned to call the contacts at the Midrasha tomorrow. He felt the best they could hope for is a paper trail from the time Michael left Treasury. If Micahel made application to any of the government agency, they would be able to pick up on what he was doing. Bridges explained to Adriana that they would a more difficult time if he was a multi contractor, his payment would come through the vouchers system. The CIA on many occasions pays contractors cash, therefore, it's difficult to trace unless the project was known.

Adriana was interested to learn about political assassination and out of the blue and without warning, she asked Bridges

"Richard what do you know about political assassinations? What are the procedures involved, if you can tell me without violating your former position?".Bridges looked at Adriana for a few moments, he then smiled as though had a secret and didn't know if he should go into detail when he answered Adriana's provocative question. "Well…if we are going to work together, then I have to educate you, are you prepared? I mean emotionally. I don't mean to imply that you can't handle information, rather I'm seeing a lady that has class, style and has worked inside the belt-way for some time, never to be exposed to the nasty side of life, that is if I'm reading you right."

"Richard, the revelations of life and all the short comings don't shock me. After my husband died I grew up fast to say the least.

Anything you tell me will be digested and considered a learning experience. Please feel free to explain in anyway you wish. I'm a big girl, I can take it."

Bridges provided the basic concept that all assassination are not motivated by politics, even though the target is a public figure., big or small.

"Do you mean in the case of Kennedy, was it political?"

"No Adriana, the Kennedy assassination was political in many ways, to cover the bottom line or motivation would be difficult. You first must understand that all political assassinations are either subjective or objective. In many cases covert. The actual person that commits the assassination is not connected to the persons responsible for the plot." Richard thought maybe he was moving too fast. " This was the suggestion in the Kennedy assassination, believed an objective procedure. The subjective assassination is accomplished by the socio-pathic personality, as an example, the attempt on President Reagan's life. The target makes it political, regardless who accomplishes the act. Remember, it may not be political at all. No political assassination is defined without the determination and classification, Objective or subjective, clandestine an covert. Setting aside the nut that attempted to take out Governor Wallace of Alabama and the Reagan attempt. In order to expand on this topic it would take some time. A little bit of knowledge will get your juices flowing if they aren't already."

"Richard I'm beginning to understand, however in our case, what is the category? Would it be clandestine or covert?"

"Adriana, a little bit of both with the limited knowledge, if you have more please relate it."

Adriana responded. "I may have more to say, however let's talk about it tomorrow. I'd like to hear more about the procedures and what we are up against."

"A planned assassination, which this situation seems to be the case, the action is formulated by an outline or plan. The target is of course determined, the object or desired effect, what is expected after the nasty deed is done. " He sighed, then continued. "Technical procedures, who and when, and of course the weapons to be used, the cost and source of finance, requirements of support, who will set it up and implement the plan of action. Many times, it is performed by someone or group outside the country of the intended target. Then damage assessment should the assassination fail. The group of conspirators need to be covered and identities never known."

"Richard, then what you are saying is that if the President's wife is behind the plot, she has to recruit several people in order to accomplish the assassination. She has to conceal her identity in case it fails or even succeeds?"

"Not exactly. She has to make one contact, then who ever is the broker for lack of a better term, has the responsibility of assembling a team. The money has to be from a source that can't be traced."

"Okay, if members of congress are involved, they know nothing other than provide funds for a worthy cause so to speak?"

"An assassination of this magnitude is either simple or has long term plans, recruiting the hit-man or woman from another country, maybe a renegade intelligence agent that left his agency under a cloud. I know who you're thinking about, Billy Ray."

Richard smiled. "No he's not the caliber. He's too much of a hot-dog, besides he doesn't fit the image, although he could be a broker, he could set things up. There are several renegade Mossad agents that have been known to offer their services." Richard looked at Adrianna to see if she was offended. "As you know, the Mossad would never acknowledge that they were members or former members. The CIA is no different. If an agent or former agent went south or decided to wear a black-hat, the agency would never admit knowing the person. I'm sure under this administration the procedure is the same".

"Richard, that's interesting, I'm sure there's more, how would someone like yourself accomplish an assassination of a political figure, say this situation, the President?"

"Adriana, this is a low level opinion, nothing more. If I were to plan it, it would be accomplished when the President was jogging around the streets of Washington, near the White House., or playing basketball on the outside court." Richard thought he said too much. "The assassin would have to operate from a distance with a weapon designed for snipping. That's the simple way. Another procedure is when he leaves Washington and visits a state where there are gang activities. The assassination would have to be confused with the local crime activity. These are just ideas, based on a quick thought and my knowledge, not experience." Bridges laughed nervously thinking that Adriana caught him off guard.

Adriana finished her coffee and suggested they retire for the night. Bridges reminded her that he had classes all day at the Midrasha.

Adriana smiled and remarked that she would sleep in late.

"I wish I could, duty calls. I'm looking forward to working with this new group of Mossad recruits." Bridges remarked.

Adriana returned to her room through the adjoining doors. Bridges wishing her a pleasant nights sleep

The telephone buzzed at least three times before Bridges answered it. He looked at the night-stand clock and discovered it was only three, he thought for a moment he had been dreaming, then brought into focus by the voice on the phone. "Richard…this is Adriana, sorry to wake you. I can't sleep. With all that you told me, caused me to think about something I need to discuss with you."

Bridges was curious however he was more interested in getting some sleep. He tried to persuade her to tell him over the phone, he became cautious, then invited her to his room.

Adriana repeated herself and then agreed to the invitation. While slipping his trousers on he managed to turn one of the night-stand lamps on to bright, realizing it hurt his eyes, he dimmed lamp to low. Adriana entered his room through the adjoining doors. She was in a dark colored robe, for some reason she looked made up, her face looked fresh and clear. Bridges sat at the edge of the bed and stared at her. "Well…young lady, what's so important that couldn't wait until morning, you interrupted my beauty rest?"

Adriana sat herself on a straight back chair while Bridges remained on the edge of the bed. In a clear voice, she proceeded to tell Bridges she may have done something to aid Heidi in setting up the assassination.

Bridges perked up, he's awake now, he feels self-conscious sitting with mo shirt on. His hairy chest and back has always made him conscious of his image. He late wife always teased him about being too hairy. As he sat waiting to hear what Adriana had to say, he caught her staring at his chest. He folded his arms across his chest and Adriana sensing that he was self conscious, started the conversation.

"I flew to Los Angeles to meet with a woman from El Salvador, her name is Rosa Correa. She spoke good English, very attractive in a way that most men would want to have an affair with. I met with her at the Hyatt Hotel near the Los Angeles Airport. We had a conversation about her working on a project for Mrs. Banks. She informed me she would have to return to El Salvador in order to accomplish the project. In exchange, she and her daughter would receive citizenship in the United States without any questions asked. It would be granted without complications. I didn't at first think there was anything wrong with that, it happens all the time, where some Congressman with the stroke of a pen, the person becomes a citizen."

Bridges responded by asking the obvious question. "What's the project, what did she have you do?"

"That's just it, I don't know, my instructions from Mrs. Banks was to meet the woman, treat her nice and request she work on Mrs. Banks project. The woman acted as though she knew what the project was. The remainder of the message was that Mrs. Banks would contact her when she arrived at her home in San Salvador…all expenses paid."

"You said her name was Rosa Correa?"

"Yes, or something like that, I don't have my notes, they are in my desk at the White House."

"Adriana are you sure or almost sure of the woman's name?"

"Richard I feel certain that's her name, a very intelligent woman, educated, a neat dresser, however her clothes were cheaply made. She was staying with an aunt in South Central Los Angeles, Our visit was just before the riots. Why do you ask…you look so serious…do you think you know her?"

"I'm sure I know her, as a matter of fact she was assigned to the special investigative unit. I had responsibility for many of their operations. They were involved in political assassinations in El Salvador, nothing I had been responsible for. You recall I briefly mentioned it. I'm confused, didn't she ask you about the project or anything about the President's wife?"

"No, it was as though she knew why I was there, she appeared cautious not to ask questions. It was as though she was looking forward to my visit, I might add, I gave her an envelope containing a large amount of cash."

"Adriana, why the hell didn't you tell me about this before?"

"I'd planned to tell you when we went to Amman, I didn't think it was relevant until you gave me a crash course on assassinations. This caused me to think and recall the meeting. At first I thought it may be related, then I dismissed it. I thought it may be part of many projects Mrs. Banks was involved in."

"What then made you think she was plotting to have the President assassinated?"

"Richard she has spoken to people all over the country, some in New York, Miami and even San Francisco. Organized crime type, not Italian types, or street gang type. I mean some are connected to the labor unions and organized crime dealing in dope, gambling, prostitution, many areas that involves violations of the RICO Act."

"Anything else Adriana, anything that we can use to map out our plans?" I hope we agree, I think our first object is to prevent the assassination at the same time identify the players. It doesn't matter if they have knowledge of the actual plans or not. We need evidence to convince the right people, you being a lawyer should be the first to recognize that."

"Richard, I do, there is so damn much to discuss. Heidi has a hatred for her husband, it's really deep, but yet she wants to preserve his memory as a potentially good president, at the same time, distance herself from the actual assassination, sort of what you mentioned. I don't think a day passes that she makes remarks to me behind closed doors that she thinks he's an incompetent fool. Adriana's eyes widened. "I've never asked her to elaborate, rather go about my work. It isn't as wife not being happy with her husband, she thinks she would have made a better President, but knows the time has not come for the women. That's her thoughts. She feels that if he died in office, she could control the person that would take his place."

"What about the Vice President, does he fit in, or the Speaker of the House?"

"Richard I have good reason to believe he is part of it, I'm not sure, but Heidi talks to him often."

"Do you know what they talk about?"

"They talk about things such as the Central American projects, various other projects that she cooked up, things that gives the appearance of social reform, forcing the American people to live by the numbers with government controls and regulations. She even wants to tame the press, not radio and television, just the press, big newspapers."

"Is the health care proposal part of her scheme?"

"That's a joke, I mean it sounds good to the people of our country, it's just a way for her to gain recognition. I think if the American people had enough sympathy for her, that is after the President is removed, then she may have a chance for being president. That is if she convinced the Vice President to resign, or wait until the term expires. Then she will set herself up as the first woman candidate, gaining the sympathy vote. You recall how the American people felt about Mrs. Kennedy after John Kennedy was assassinated."

Bridges reluctantly answered. He didn't want to say too much until he had a chance to evaluate the information. "Sure the people that elected her husband plus, would elect her. She sure would gain more sympathy than Jackie ever had."

"Richard, yeah his color...she will stop at nothing, can you see she is keeping herself in the public eye. She sends messages out that she wants to help the people. Seeing it from a distance makes sense, do you agree?"

"Adriana, I agree with the scenario, but how much of it is fact?"

"All of it Richard, the only thing is I didn't figure the Central American contact as being relevant to the plot. Now that you educated me, It's clear. What do you know about the woman I met in Los Angeles?"

"I know a great deal, I knew her husband as well. He got killed when I was there. I know she is militant and I know she loves money. Money to her is the root to good even if it was for evil. She's a charmer and often get's her way. She's dedicated to her daughter and fears harm may come to her because of the many enemies she made in El Salvador. I'll bet she returned to San Salvador, and left her daughter in Los Angeles."

"You are right, that's was the issue she brought up when I met with her, she wanted a guaranty that her daughter would be cared for. She enrolled her in a Catholic school, clothes and enough money to sustain her until the woman returned from El Salvador."

"Well it's starting to make some sense Adriana, however there are things missing about the woman in El Salvador. When did she return to her Central America?"

"Right after we met in Los Angeles, three weeks ago. I made the arrangements myself. Yes, the arrangements were made by using Heidi's telephone. I'm sure Michael's friend has it on tape. Where do we go from here?"

CHAPTER 5
TRIP TO AMMAN

As Bridges prepared for his class at the Midrasha, he couldn't help think of his conversation with Adriana the night before. She wanted to know where they were heading. Simple, he thought, he didn't know, he could only take one step at a time. He was still a little angry with Adriana for not informing him of her meeting with the woman from El Salvador. Of course he had information about this woman which he hadn't shared with her, information which was pertinent to their project. He just wasn't sure how Adriana would react when he told her the woman belonged to a hit-squad and should be considered extremely dangerous. He knew from the woman's background and file that she enjoyed killing…showed no remorse at all.

The phone rang and his thoughts were temporarily interrupted. It was Becky telling him she would be at the hotel in thirty minutes and she would meet him in the lobby.

Bridges finished getting ready and headed down to the lobby. Becky smiled as he approached her, "Why do older men look so damn good in the morning? Maybe it's the shave lotion." She giggled to herself trying to make light of her comment, but deep inside she couldn't help being attracted to Richard. He was older, more knowledgeable, more worldly…and handsome.

Bridges put his arm around her shoulders in a fatherly gesture as the two of them walked through the lobby to the main entrance. The hotel appeared to be filling up with visitors, mostly Americans. "This is more like it, Richard", she said as she snuggled close to him like a little girl. "You could really turn me on." Richard smiled and couldn't help the chance to tease her, "I'm afraid you are suffering from a common disease which afflicts most young women, my dear,an abundance of hormones."

"Oh…Richard," she said, "I was serious."

As they got to where the car was parked, Bridges dropped his arm from Becky's shoulders and tried to ignore any further conversation about the matter. He didn't want to be caught in this female flirting trap with her.

They sat in silence until they arrived at the guest parking area of the Midrasha. "Would you mind if I sit in on your class, Richard?"

Bridges smiled and sighed, how could he say no, "Only if you behave yourself and keep quiet like a little mouse. But then again I wouldn't want to distract you from your duties."

"Richard, you are my assigned duty as long as you're in Israel." Becky was proud of herself that she had managed to sit in on the class instead of waiting for Richard in some office or the car. She was going to jump at any chance to be near him.

Becky parked and secured the car as Bridges headed for the main entrance of the Midrasha. The early morning sun was already hot and he paused for a moment, taking in the view below. The Midrasha sat high on a bluff overlooking the desert floor and the city of Tel Aviv. It was a long sprawling white stucco building with a second floor at one end. There were a few trees and shrubs covering the well landscaped yard beyond the parking lot. It might easily be mistaken for a governor's mansion if not for tight security. There were many Israeli people who thought the Midrasha was the Prime Minister's summer residence, at least this is what they are led to believe.

Bridges greeted the security personnel who were already briefed to his visit and headed directly to the Course Commander's Office which he had been to many times on previous visits. After a brief greeting with Moshe Cohen, both men went upstairs to Bridges' assigned classroom. Moshe assured Bridges that Becky would be available should he need anything in the way of supplies.

The new Mossad recruits stood at attention as Moshe and Bridges entered the classroom and Moshe introduced Richard, after the introduction, quickly he left the classroom.

Bridges always opened his class by getting acquainted with the recruits, asking them several questions about themselves and their backgrounds. It usually made an intense situation comfortable and everyone relaxed. Today, they would discuss 'Human Behavior', a topic Bridges was fond of teaching.

Bridges was quick to notice a large heavy set man in the back of the classroom. He recalled the man was assigned to servile Bridges' activities. He seemed embarrassed when asked to participate with the recruits in the getting acquainted process.

Bridges glanced at the clock on the wall above the chalk board. It was registering almost noon and he wasn't surprised that four hours had passed so quickly. He hadn't even noticed Becky as she slipped into the back of the classroom. It was a good time to stop for the noon break and Bridges dismissed the Mossad recruits. As the men were leaving, Becky headed towards the front of the classroom informing Richard that the chef had prepared an American dish for lunch. "Hamburgers…Kosher style. Just for you, Richard." She laughed.

"I'm starved, didn't realize it until you mentioned food." Bridges said.

"I love listening to you lecture. It's very interesting and the way you relate to real examples of life…well, I'm sure they are enjoying your class." Becky was full of compliments as usual. "Why, thank you Rebecca, I needed that."

"Damn it, Richard, please don't call me that. You would think I was some school girl. I hate the name, it's just not me." Becky became upset with Richard always treating her like a young girl. She wanted him to think of her as an equal…well, maybe not an equal, but as a woman, and she wanted him to see her as a woman.

After lunch, Richard used Moshe's office to call the hotel to see if he had any messages. There were none. He also had the operator ring Adriana's room. He was actually surprised when she answered the phone, thinking perhaps she wasn't back from her shopping trip. Adriana sounded glad to hear from him.

"I'll be finished with the class at four. I hope you don't mind, but I've invited Becky to have dinner with us."

Adriana didn't mind, "Of course, Richard, see you later."

Bridges had no sooner hung up the phone than Becky knocked softly on the door. She came in without waiting for Bridges invitation. "What was that about?" she said, as if she had overheard the whole conversation.

"I just informed Adriana that you would be having dinner with us tonight…is that okay with you?"

"I wish it was just you and me…but thank you." Becky had a silly little smile on her face and the tone of her voice told Bridges that she was a little jealous that Adriana would be there.

"Rebecca…I need to get back to the classroom. I might add, you are sounding more like a Jewish American Princess every time you pout and can't get your way."

Becky didn't say a word. She didn't like Bridges scolding her, but she couldn't help what she said.

After the class that afternoon, Bridges informed Becky that he would meet her in Moshe's office after he finished writing a brief report. He also took a few moments to consult the next day's schedule, recording the information in his note pad. Moshe Cohen entered his office. He retrieved a file from his file cabinet and mumbled something about leaving for Tel Aviv. He barely said goodbye to Bridges. Just then Becky arrived after almost bumping into Moshe as he was leaving. "What's with Moshe?" she said.

"I'm not sure but he's obviously preoccupied with something. Oh well, whatever it is, I'm sure he'll work it out on his own."

Becky and Bridges left the Midrasha for the day and she drove him to his hotel. On the way Bridges explained that he planned to go to Amman the first part of the following week and hoped that his teaching program was completed by then. Becky was in a world of her own with thoughts of what she should wear for dinner that night. Then realizing what Richard was talking about, she said, "I'll take care of the schedule for you. When you return from Amman, you'll have only one eight hour class left and that will complete the program. There is no problem."

"Becky, I assume you will drive Adriana and I to the Allenby Bridge…we can't fly."

"Richard, I'd love to drive you to Amman but that wouldn't settle too well with the Jordanian Government, they know I work for the Mossad."

Bridges expressed his optimism that maybe in the not too distant future, Jordan and Israel would become diplomatic friends.

Becky smiled, then sarcastically, "Don't hold your breath. Israel and Jordan can sign documents all night long, shake hands, slap each other on the back, but they will never be true friends as long as Israel occupies the land around the Mediterranean Sea and other choice real-.estate."

Bridges was surprised Becky had such strong feelings about the matter. As they drove to Tel Aviv, Becky expressed her concern for Charlie. Again, he was surprised Becky was so concerned, "He's in Washington. Why the concern? Unless you know something I don't".

"It's just that he is with Smyth. The wrong people may get the idea Charlie works for the Agency and Smyth's bad reputation may put Charlie in danger. His trip is a simple one, little politics and a liaison with the boys at Langley. You know the trip with Smyth was planned between the Mossad and the Station Chief at the Embassy here in Tel Aviv. They don't think too highly of Smyth."

"Charlie made it clear that when I return to the D.C. area, he and I should not meet. I thought that was a little odd but dismissed it. You've got me curious not." Richard said.

"I'm still concerned. He's good at his job but sometimes he is too damn trusting. Just remember, you did not hear any of this from me and don't ask me anymore questions, I've said too much already. Just file it somewhere, Smyth-Charlie-Iraq."

"What are you trying to tell me, Becky?"

"I can't say anymore, please don't ask me." Becky said, realizing she had said too much to even Richard. Her job required her to remain silent and to never repeat anything she overheard, especially if it came from the Mossad.

Becky pulled up in front of the Basel Hotel and as Richard got out of the car, he suggested they meet later at seven for drinks in the hotel lounge. Becky smiled in agreement and drove off.

As Bridges went into the hotel, he couldn't help notice a heavy built man, about his age, a familiar face, who seemed to be following him to the elevator.

While they were waiting for the next car, the man looked at Bridges and spoke, "Richard, it's been a long time, hasn't it?"

"Well I'll be damned, Roy Gannon, is that you? I haven't seen you since we worked at the Embassy in El Salvador. What the hell are you doing here, or are you still active?"

Both men vigorously shook hands genuinely glad to see each other, then Roy answered, "Well, they've got me assigned to the office in Jerusalem, sort of my last assignment. I don't think it anything big, just working with a few Israelis from the 'Country Club', sort of a watch-dog assignment keeping track of who's coming and going over the Allenby Bridge. Seems I caught a glimpse of you with the Mossad's best, last week." Then before Richard could answer, "I need to talk to you Richard, perhaps your room?" Bridges realized that his old friend was there specifically to talk to him.

Both men went up to Bridges' room where they had room service bring up cold American beer.

"Okay, what's up Roy?"

"It's about that ass-hole, Billy-Ray. With the help of the boys at the Country Club and my Station Chief, we cooked up this project and sent the hot-dog to Washington.Seems we all had the same thing in mind. Anyway, we think Billy-Ray is up to some bad shit. When he arrives in Washington, he'll be placed under surveillance."

"What's he up to, Roy?" Bridges asked deeply concerned.

"We're not sure. All we know is that he is running errands for people who are not too friendly to us. He's been bad-mouthing you too. By the way, I see you have a new lady friend, Adriana Myers. She's a powerful woman and I might add, quite a catch. Of course you are aware she works for the President's wife and her sister is married to the King of Jordan?" Roy was sure Bridges was aware of this but it was his way of letting him know that he knew everything that was going on.

"Okay Roy, what do you guys think that ass-hole Billy-Ray is up to…level with me?" Bridges let Roy know that he made his point.

"I'm sure your friends at the Country Club keep your room clean so let me tell you what we know. We think he is building a retirement fund by dating the boys from Iraq." Roy spelled it out in language the two understood.

"He's a gutless bastard Roy, you know that. Remember that incident in Honduras where he claims he saved my ass, well…I think it was actually designed to be my demise. You know he's a computer nut and specializes in communications. How is he courting the Iraqis?"

"We believe he is feeding them information on arms-for-sale and might be acting as a broker for many of the deals. We can't connect him with the North Koreans yet, but we think he's testing the water with them too."

"That son-of-a-bitch!" Bridges was pissed.

"Let me tell you Richard, he thinks you are going to get in the way here in the Middle East, that's why he doesn't trust you."

"I wondered why the Israelis didn't fill me in, maybe they were waiting for the right time."

"We think so. We didn't take them serious at first then it started to come together. We're trying to get a handle on his bank account, probably German or Swiss. We arranged to send him back to Washington with the help of the Israelis. Now, once he's back in Washington, I'm sure he'll be busted. The Station Chief here in Tel Aviv is on it."

Roy and Richard finished their beer, reliving old times. Bridges felt some comfort at the thought of BillyRay being bagged when he got to Washington. Roy Gannon had to leave to return to Jerusalem but he paused to complement Richard on his choice of women. Richard wasn't quite sure if Roy was aware of the business between he and

Adriana, but he wasn't ready to recruit anyone else for their project. He thought best not to elaborate on any conversation concerning Adriana Myers

"There is something you could do for me, Roy. Could you please check out a Michael Myers for me?" Bridges was certain that whatever information was found would not surprise him. Gannon agreed and promised to contact Bridges through the Midrasha. He then left and promised they would get together when he finished his assignment in Israeli next year

Bridges met Adriana and Becky in the lounge at seven. They socialized for a short time then ordered dinner. Their conversations revolved mostly around Arabian horses and Becky's passion for love stories. It wasn't until the dessert portion of their dinner that they discussed the upcoming trip to Amman. It was agreed that Becky would drive Richard and Adriana to the Allenby Bridge or at least as far as the Military Outpost. Adriana's sister would then send a car for Richard and Adriana for the remainder of the trip. Bridges was to stay at the Hilton and Adriana would, of course, stay with her sister at the Palace. A jealous Becky was relieved that the two would not be staying at the hotel together, although Adriana did remark that she was not fond of staying with her sister because of the demands that were placed on her.

Leaving for Tel Aviv Monday would place them in Amman before sunset. Bridges reminded the two women that the desert was a dangerous place after dark.

Becky had suggested that they leave for Amman over the weekend but Bridges had promised his daughter, Jennifer, that he would visit the Royal Stud and a weekend would be crowded, something he had hoped to avoid.

They finished their dinner agreeing to leave for Amman Monday morning, and that the weekend would be spent shopping for a french-cut swimsuit for Adriana and lying on the beach. Becky was quick to volunteer for the shopping expedition with Adriana. It was at that point that Adriana excused herself for the evening and went to her room.

Becky suggested they have one last drink in the lounge. After they were seated, she relayed a message to Bridges from the Agency Office in Jerusalem. The message was only that Michael Myers had, at one time, been an applicant for the CIA. This didn't surprise Bridges in the least.

"Richard, when I drop you two off at the Allenby Bridge on Monday, you will be on your own. I won't have any control over anything that might happen. That area is extremely dangerous, so please...please be careful." Becky was deeply concerned and Bridges sensed it.

"Becky...I know you have a responsibility to me, but it's going to be a fast trip, just overnight...two nights at the most. I promised my daughter I would visit the Royal Stud and take pictures."

"Damn it, Richard...this is not personal, it's not that I'm jealous. I just think Adriana is hiding something, I'm uncomfortable with her. I can't put my finger on it yet, but I will."

Bridges explained to Becky that Adriana had lost her husband ten years prior and that she had suspicions of wrong doing, that he may have been killed. Perhaps it was this bitterness she was detecting.

"Becky...with all these Israeli studs around, how come you haven't found someone you could be close too?" Bridges asked thinking that perhaps it was Becky who was bitter or jealous.

"There are a lot of them out there. I just prefer older men...like you for instance, Richard. Damn it, can't you see you turn me on?" Becky's eyes met Richards and for a moment neither said anything.

"Becky...if I took you to my room right now, I'm sure we would have a great time. But the Commander and the others would learn of it and I would be shit in their book. Don't you see, the Israelis respect me and they know that I have never compromised myself over a woman." Richard knew this wasn't the only reason but he tried to persuade Becky through logic.

"Sounds great, Richard. I'll be sure that you receive the award for being the straight arrow among the intelligence community." Becky retaliated, feeling Bridges was putting her off.

"You don't understand, Becky."

"No, Richard, you don't understand. Don't you see how I feel about you? You could seduce me…no strings attached…no demands…it's simple." Becky whispered almost pleading.

"Boy, you don't pull any punches. I'm flattered, really flattered, Becky. You bring out a desire in me, a fire I haven't felt since…but let's don't and pretend we did."

"No…let's go to my place and we can have the memory forever." She whispered again the words, trying to reach him.

"I'm tempted…but no, I'm sorry. And we need to leave here, a few more drinks and I wouldn't be able to contain myself young lady. Besides, I have a class tomorrow. "

Deep inside, Richard yearned to make love to her…he could eat her up in a minute. But he couldn't let her know that. He was much older and it would never work out, let alone all the trouble it might cause.

Becky was disappointed, "You don't know what you're missing, Richard. You're going to let me go home and take a cold shower, how could you?"

"You drive a hard bargain, and a tempting one, but I need my sleep. Let's just meet for breakfast in the morning before we go to the Country Club?" Richard said as he tried to change the conversation.

"No…I'm not leaving until I have seduced you." Becky teasingly although she meant to see how far she could push Bridges.

"Becky, I can't promise you anything. When we meet in the states, I might take you up on the offer, but right now…"

Becky was briefly embarrassed and her face flushed. She wanted to hurt Bridges for putting her down, either that or the drinks were having an effect on her at the moment. "That's bullshit and you know it. The pat on the head like a little girl, that shit doesn't cut it with me. Don't you understand my feelings, I need you, and I want you or am I turning you off?"

Before Bridges answered, he became awsare of the people in the lounge and cautioned Becky to lower her voice. He assured himself that whatever he said would be remembered and that he better be cautious about hurting Becky's feelings. "Hell no Becky, it turns me on. The thought of being with you is flattering and exciting. I'm not rejecting you, just postponing this situation until later. Besides, what would the Commander say?"

Becky took in a deep breath then, as if to defy him she said, "I don't think he gives a damn. In fact, he may think more of you, it's not like you were sleeping with the enemy. Anyway, you can't get out of it that easy. Besides, Israeli men think differently than American men."

Bridges searched for more reasons why he shouldn't go to bed with Becky and it was becoming increasingly difficult. But he couldn't put his reputation on the line, not after all these years. And the Mossad trusted him. "I think we'd better be going. If Adriana calls my room and discovers I'm not there, she'll know I'm with you and I don't need that."

Becky smiled as she thought to herself that those were her sentiments exactly. "She can think whatever she likes. I know by seeing you both together tonight, that she finds you as appealing as I do. I'm sure you recognized it yourself, Richard. Besides, if you were to sleep with herthat would be a compromise in everyone's book as well. Right Mr. Spyman?" She said in a snippy voice.

Bridges felt as though he was in a no-win situation. Becky was wise and witty and determined to get him in bed. "Becky, walk me to the elevator. Seriously, I need to get some sleep and you're not making things easy for me. In the old Marine Corps days, I would have never said no to someone like you but things are different. Please respect my wishes. You are a beautiful woman, a little fast for this ole' dude. I'm sure you could compensate for that."

"Oh Richard, what are you every bit of forty-nine or fifty?"

They were waiting for the elevator and Bridges tried to ignore answering Becky. He had hoped that he could say goodnight to her without having to hurt her feelings anymore. Just then the elevator arrived and Becky entered along with Bridges.

They were the only two passengers and it seemed to Bridges like the car would never reach the third floor. He was about to kiss Becky goodnight on the forehead when all of a sudden she reached for him and with one arm around his neck she drew her body close to his, putting her wet moist mouth to his. She pressed tight and inserted her tongue and for an instant, he responded. At that point, the elevator doors opened and Richard quickly backed out waving goodnight to her and then the doors closed but before she blew him a kiss and said "It's a start, Richard. See you at seven."

Bridges was relieved to get to his room. At one point in his life, he would have jumped at a chance for a situation like this, but now, he was more concerned about h is reputation and what others might think. He placed his keys and wallet on the bureau and went directly to the shower. It was only afterwards that he noticed his message light was on. It had been his daughter Jennifer returning his earlier call. He would have to call her in the morning.

Sometime during the night, Bridges woke to the sound of the phone ringing. "Hello…Oh, Becky, what's the matter?" he asked half asleep.

"Nothing Richard…I loved that kiss. It's what I wanted, a long sweet kiss. Now, I have a memory and I'm looking for more. Do you want to know what I am thinking right now?"

Bridges knew he was going to hear from her again, but it was two in the morning. Boy, she never gives up he thought.

"Listen, I'll see you in the hotel coffee shop at seven but right now I need sleep. Don't mean to be rude, but goodnight, Rebecca."

Bridges knew he had hurt her feelings again but at that hour in the morning, he didn't care. Besides, he didn't like Becky acting like some young high school girl. Women like that were definitely not his type. He turned off the light and went back to sleep until he was again woke by his six o'clock wake-up call.

After another shower, Bridges dressed and then dialed Adriana's room to remind her of the daily activities. She was happy he kept her abreast of his daily routine and thanked him for the call. She would was going shopping later in the morning and would see him later.

Becky met Bridges at seven as planned and she drove him directly to the Midrasha for his class. They greeted each other with in tones barely above whispers. She, embarrassed at her behavior and Bridges, for allowing the situation to get somewhat out of hand.

Bridges' class was going as expected until he realized that one of the recruits was missing from class. He was particularly concerned until he was informed by the class leader that the amir (agent) was on a temporary assignment or special project. Bridges gave it no further thought.

At the end of the day, Bridges met Becky in Moshe's office. He asked her about her silence but she chose to ignore him and explained to Bridges that the amir who was missing from his class was on assignment and would return in a few days. Bridges thanked her and then mentioned that he had noticed she did not sit in on his class today. Becky was quick to let him know that her feelings were hurt.

Bridges left his guard down and for a moment, he felt sorry for Becky. He reached over and hugged her like a father would if his little girl and hurt herself. As he held her, he thought how easy it would be to love her. He already had affection for her, she amused him. On the otherhand, he couldn't weaken or let his guard down. Maybe Becky was looking for a hormone release, but he wasn't.

"Let's go to the hotel and have an early dinner with Adriana."

That was alright with Becky, but she wasn't sure she wanted to share any part of Richard with Adriana. At any rate, it gave her a second chance to redeem herself in Richard's eyes after making a fool of herself the night before by acting so childish.

They met Adriana in the lounge. She was sipping on a tall glass of ginger ale and was delighted when she spotted the two. "How are you two working people doing?" she asked teasing both of them, and quite unaware of their experience the evening before.

Becky was quick to ask Adriana how her shopping spree went and if she had found a bathing suit.

"Why, yes, as a matter of fact. Wait until you see it, you'll love it." Adriana sounded pleased with herself that she had found the right suit but she was also aware that Becky would find it out of style, or not in keeping with the times.

It was Adriana who suggested a quiet dinner away from the hotel. Bridges went to get Adriana's rental car and on the way to the beach he could feel the tense feelings between both Adriana and Becky. He couldn't be sure, but he was getting the feeling that he was the target of their frustrations and jealously. Why, he hadn't felt like this since his own high school days.

Dinner was quiet with little conversation and Bridges was almost relieved when it was suggested they return to the hotel for a quick nightcap. This time, he would be careful not to get into any compromising situations with Becky. Bridges found it amusing that in spite of the rivalry between the women, Becky had agreed to go to the beach with Adriana in the morning. Bridges announced he would stay in his room and catch up on some phone calls and paper work.

***

On Monday, Becky met Bridges and Adriana in the coffee shop of the hotel. With Becky was the Amir, the same Amir who had been assigned to Bridges earlier. It was obvious Becky was trying to out do Adriana by wearing a pale blue jump-suit with the zipper conveniently lowered just enough to show off a well tanned cleavage. Adriana was wearing a conservative white dress, but of course, that is what she would be expected to wear since she would be entering Jordan and she was well aware that her brother-in-law, the King, was not accustomed to women wearing any type of pants or slacks. Nevertheless, both women were very attractive and Bridges was content to be in their company.

They had a light breakfast and it was five thirty when Bridges suggested they leave for the Allenby Bridge. Adriana assured Bridges they would be met at thre bridge by car her sister sent. The Amir sat in the front with Becky while Adriana and Bridges were comfortable in the back seat of the American armored plated car. Adriana was concerned about the Uzi in the front seat until Becky informed her that were more in the trunk. The Amir remained silent and only spoke when spoken to. After a brief stop at the military outpost, they continued on to the bridge. When they arrived, they had to wait until the army check point guards checked the bus in front of them. Bridges and Adriana got out of the car while Becky informed them that she would wait until she was sure they were safe in the care of the Jordanian government officials. No sooner had they neared the dirty white stucco building of the check point, than an Arab man with a very beautiful Jordanian woman approached them. Becky waited and observed all she could.

Adriana introduced the man and woman as employees of her sister's. They were escorted to a white Mercedes limousine which had been waiting. After a brief conversation with the Arab man, it was obvious to Bridges that he was educated in the United States and that he spoke perfect English. It was confirmed with the man explained that he grew up in Los Angeles and returned to Jordan when he had completed school.

Adriana appeared concerned for Becky and asked Richard what she would do once she returned to the States.

Bridges smiled. He knew Adriana was thinking of her rival. "Becky's a bright young woman. After she finishes graduate school, I suggested she go to the State Department."

The tinted windows of the limo shielded Adriana's face as she looked beyond the desert floor while listening to Bridges.

"She's torn between Israel and her parents. Loves her job but she knows she's limited." he continued.

"You are almost all she spoke of while we were at the beach yesterday. I believe she's extremely fond of you, Richard." Adriana smiled as she teased Bridges. Perhaps hoping he might reveal himself or his feelings.

Bridges was uncomfortable the topic of conversation but wanted to qualify his position before moving to another topic, "I'm old enough to be her father for heaven's sake. You know how these young girls get these silly infatuations. I'm sure that's all it is."

Adriana was quite willing to change the subject, but her personal feelings towards Bridges wouldn't allow her to. She needed to know how Bridges actually felt about Becky and decided to pursue the subject.

"I might agree with you Richard, if it weren't for the fact that she made it perfectly clear to me that you were her property and I was to keep my business with you strictly on a business level."

"Our relationship is professional. That's it, Adriana. I only hope you were able to handle her." Bridges felt now he made it clear and set the record straight.

"You are an attractive man, Richard. Intelligent, wise and not hard to look at." Adriana laughed at her own words. "It's just that Becky sees me as some sort of rival and I don't want to do anything to fuel the fire. I'm sure you don't either." With those words, she felt that she made her point.

There was a long silence before Adriana spoke again. "I would like to introduce you to Princess Alia, the King's daughter from a previous marriage. She's a wonderful young woman, educated in the United States and she's in charge of the Royal Stables and the Arabian Horse Registry. You'll like her Richard. She is well organized and keeps the horses in fine condition. I think you find that she seems more American than Jordanian."

Bridges was relieved to change the subject. "I would love to meet her. I only wish my daughter, Jennifer, was here. I hope the Princess won't mind if I take some pictures for Jennifer. Maybe the Princess herself with one of her stallions. Afterall, this trip to the Royal Stud is only for Jennifer." Adriana detected pride in Richard's voice as he spoke of his daughter and was sure there wasn't anything Richard wouldn't do for her even though he was pretending he was going out of his way.

***

After arriving in Amman, Adriana directed the driver to the Hilton Hotel where Bridges had reservations. They planned to meet for dinner later in the day. Bridges had been eager to discuss the woman from El Salvador with Adriana but that would have to wait, now.

Bridges was puzzled with the fact that Adriana seemed in a hurry to leave. She was quite anxious to see her sister at the Palace. He dismissed his thoughts as being only in his imagination.

Once in his room, Bridges laid back on the bed attempting to catch some shut-eye when the phone rang. It was probably Adriana he thought, although the Mossad knew how to reach him if necessary. Then, it might be his daughter…he picked up the receiver, "Hello." There was silence and he repeated himself twice more. He was annoyed and hung up.

The phone rang again and this time it was Adriana. He asked if she had just called and she explained that she did, however, there must have been a bad connection so she had the Palace operator try again. "I'm sorry for interrupting you, Richard. My sister would like to meet you. I'm not sure it's a good idea in light of the situation we're involved in…then again, I think she feels we're more than just friends. She's fascinated with the idea I'm traveling with a man. After all, she hasn't known me to be with a man since my husband died ten years ago. If you don't agree to meet her tonight, she'll only find some other reason to meet you tomorrow."

Richard sat back and listened as Adriana rambled on.

"I'm concerned about the Jordanian press…they find everything that goes on in the Palace news worthy. Even though the King controls the press, if my sister thinks something should be published, it's published. I just don't want the American press to get the idea we are courting the Jordanians and then later find out what we are up to. Do you get my point?" Adriana finally gave Bridges room to comment.

The more Adriana explained, the more Bridges became uneasy. "Adriana, are you on a safe phone?" He laughed at his own words as he realized his own CIA training had told him that no phone was safe.

He suggested to Adriana that she tell her sister that he was married and any press would compromise his position. She agreed.

"She will want to meet you anyway, Richard." Adriana continued. "Please don't be angry, but I told her you were good in bed…just girl talk, you understand." She laughed.

Bridges wasn't satisfied with Adriana's explanations but agreed to the charade. This was h is first glimpse at Adriana's cunningness and realized how shrewd she could be.

He dozed off to sleep once more only to be awaken some time later by a knock at the door.

When he opened the door, he was surprised to see Adriana. She was dressed in a pale yellow dress which showed off her deep tan. Her dark brown hair was swept back behind her ears and she was truly a lovely sight.

How could he be mad at her? Afterall, she had to tip toe around as well…she worked for the President's wife. Any press release at all would be misinterpreted around the world.

"I'm sorry, please come in. I dozed off again…anyway, it will only take me a moment to shower."

Adriana didn't mind waiting. She poured herself a glass of Hennessey Cognac from a bottle she had brought with her from the Palace. Her eyes glanced around the room. It had been a long time since she had been in a man's room feeling the way she does. His things scattered about…the smell of his cologne…she missed the feel of a man's body and the security of having someone to lean on. Richard finished dressing after a quick shower and was ready for dinner. His presence had interrupted her thoughts.

They ate in the hotel restaurant and afterwards, Richard invited her back up to his room.

Once inside, Adriana kicked off her shoes poured a cognac for herself and Bridges and found a comfortable spot on the sofa.

Richard was struggling with trying to figure out the right moment to bring up the woman from El Salvador.

"I know her. She was a member of the hit squad." he said.

"Who are you talking about?" Adriana asked, surprised at his comment.

"The woman from El Salvador. She's an assassin. She belonged to a hit squad and they assassinated several people in Central America they believed were against democracy and reform that the United States was attempting to implement in those Central American countries. She was part of the team who killed those nuns and priests in the last big anti-government operation down in El Salvador."

"My God, Richard." This was all Adriana could muster as she listened.

"They thought they were justified because the Catholic Church in El Salvador was protecting the guerrilla factions, an act of treason. This same woman worked with me during the day and was assigned to my unit. Our mission was to track guerrilla activity, collect data and pass it on to the Salvadorian Army. I didn't discover her involvement until after President Duarte died." Richard paused for a moment. "The woman didn't kill the Nuns, they were killed by idiots from the Salvadorian Army."

"I had no way of knowing." Adriana said as she sipped her cognac.

"I realize that. How could you know this woman's past. But, I'm sure the First Lady had information when she sent you to Los Angeles to arrange for the woman's return to El Salvador. And I might add…provide her with a fat cash down payment." Bridges was angry at the thought.

Adriana was silent as her thoughts raced back to her visit with the woman. She had been impressed with her but their seemed to be something the woman knew, and it was as though the woman wasn't sure how much Adriana knew, either.

"Richard, there was something elusive about her that bothered me. I just gave her the cash thinking it was for her to sustain her stay in El Salvador. I was led to believe that she was working on a some project to educate women. They were taking young women out of the fields and training them so that when and if American industry located to the area, they would be able to go to work. I must say the program looked great on paper and the Salvadorian government was all for it." Richard now seated, allowed her to continue. " We pumped a million dollars a day into that country to help the economy. After a short period of time, they would not have had to rely on USAID money. I had no idea this woman was political. I just had my suspicions. When I returned to Washington, Heidi wanted to be briefed. All I could tell her was that I managed to get the woman to return to El Salvador and that she had left her daughter in the Los Angeles area with relatives."

Bridges listened to Adriana explain but he had to be blunt with her.

"As I said, I knew the woman. The real issue is that if Heidi hired Rosa, then her name is Rosa Carrea Gonzales and we've got a big problem. I know that she lives with an Army Colonel, Jose Gonzalez-Gonzalez, when she's in El Salvador. He was never suspected of directing the hit squad but he may look the other way. If I'm not mistaken, he would like to move to the States and begin a business. Damn it…we have to return to Washington next week…maybe the end of this week. We've got to get things rolling. Damn...I feel so helpless when I'm away from Langley."

Adriana realized Bridges was shifting into second gear and assuming a leadership roll. She had to tell Richard everything.

"Richard, I have to explain before you find out from someone. I have a passionate dislike for the President and his wife. But at least I know where Heidi is coming from. With your help, we'll be able to put the entire plot down, I'm confident." Adriana paused a moment.

"Is there something else you should be telling me?" Bridges asked.

"When Banks was Governor of Virginia, I attended a political function where he was in attendance. That son-of-a-bitch assumed I would go to bed with him. That's not why I despise him, but it adds to it. He had one of his flunky aids approach me like I was some piece of meat just waiting to jump in bed with him. I ignored the aid and walked right up to Banks and told him off in front of everyone within ear shot. I told him not to under estimate me. He couldn't wait to get me alone and apologize. When Heidi hired me as her research secretary, there wasn't much he could do since it was our little secret. Even though I was Republican, I knew my way around and Heidi felt she needed me. You know the rest. A Yale Law School graduate cuts a lot of red-tape. So you see, Richard, I too, could be a good candidate to assassinate the son-of-a-bitch. I wouldn't shoot him though, I'd cut his balls off and watch him bleed to death.

"That would be one for the history books, wouldn't it?" Adriana laughed at the thought of such a sight and even brought a smile to Bridges.

Adriana's bitterness had no boundaries and Bridges was relieved she had chosen to confide in him. He hadn't wanted to be suspicious of her and a lot of his questions were answered and she recanted her stories.

There was something else she hadn't told Bridges yet, but now was probably a perfect time. She only hoped it wouldn't shut him off to the project.

"Richard...please listen to what else I have to say. When my husband died, Heidi was working for the State Department. I believed then, and I believe now, that she had something to do with his death. She was assigned to an Embassy in Central America. At the time, my husband worked on the Central American desks in Washington. I'm sure there was a connection." Adriana paused for a moment to sip her cognac. At times, when she spoke of her husband, it was difficult to relive the memories

"I'm sorry…so sorry, Adriana. But why do you think Heidi was involved." Richard's curiosity was aroused now.

"Well, I don't think it was political in a sense…not Republicans versus Democrats…it was deeper, socialistic. Heidi had this idea of forming a National Police Force because of the rise of street violence. Government projects would eventually control our lives, the way we live. My husband was adamantly against Heidi's ideas and spoke out against her and the idea of forming a National Police Force."

"What you are saying is that her ideas were very socialistic. But neither of them had any power." Richard said.

"There were many people at the time who believed Heidi should never be in charge of any Judicial Reform projects because of her socialist views. My husband never missed his chance to tell anyone at the State Department. Many of them strongly agreed with him."

"So how does all this tie into your husband's death?" Richard asked.

"Heidi came back to Washington. Since she was powerless, she set out to marry Banks It was shortly after their marriage that my husband died. I haven't put it all together, maybe I never will. But nevertheless, I'm sure Heidi had something to do with Bill's death." Adriana sighed, shrugged her shoulders, and looked up at Bridges.

"So how did you happen to go to work for her?" Bridges asked.

"After she became the First Lady, I applied for a position on her staff. She was quick to put it together that Bill Myers was my husband. Bill was Jordanian, you know. Anyway, she hired me with no questions asked. I assume she thought I didn't share my husband's feelings about any of her projects."

Bridges watched Adriana, this was the first time she mentioned her late husband's first name. He listened to the anger in her voice as she spoke of Heidi. There was a sound of revenge, something militant. He wondered if she might have a hidden agenda, or perhaps there was something else she hadn't shared with him. He would have to be sure she wasn't using him for her own selfish motives. But for now, he had to put it aside and plan their return to Washington.

He continued to listen to Adriana. He knew the present administration in Washington was the worst in the history of the country. Even though Shepherd was President, his wife was running the country, trying to put through all her socialistic ideas. It would be a sad time in American history if the American people believed such foolish policies would work in this country.

"Adriana, am I seeing another side of you, I mean, you are so wrapped up in your hatred for the Banks I have to ask you why you wouldn't want to save the President from an assassin's bullet?"

Adriana was surprised at Richard's question, almost feeling insulted. Of course she thought Banks should be removed from office, but she didn't want him elevated to a Saint. Presidential…

"Don't you see, if the bastard is assassinated, the American Press will elevate him to Sainthood like they did with Kennedy. Besides, I'm not sure if the United States could stand another presidential assassination." she paused.

"Then there's Heidi. She would run for her husband's vacated seat and I think she would get a large sympathy vote. And she could do it, making her the first woman President in American history. No…Richard, she has to be stopped." Adriana's hatred had no boundaries.

Bridges listened as his mind raced back and forth. There seemed to be a contradiction to Adriana. She appeared to him at first as a lovely sensitive creature, and now he was seeing this callous militant side of her erupt. Besidesher beauty, she was intelligent, even perhaps a little cunning.

Bridges knew that if the President was assassinated, the Vice President would take over. Perhaps Heidi would convince him not to run, opening the door for her. Maybe that was the plan. If they were successful in preventing the assassination, then they would certainly have to expose Heidi as the one behind the conspiracy. At any rate, they had to be careful.

"There are only a few people we can trust and we can't go to the military until we have significant evidence to present our case." Richard told her. "Besides, the few people at Langley that I might ordinarily trust would want to immediately make the investigation official and we can't do that until we knew who is behind this."

Richard poured Adriana another cognac and the two sat in silence for a moment. He suggested they talk to an old friend of his, a Marine Corps buddy, who had a powerful position within the government. He had been a hell-of-a prosecutor and U.S. Attorney and now he sat on the Supreme Court. But just before Bridges said his name, Adriana looked over at Richard.

"Paul Castilli..." She whispered as she looked over and smiled at Bridges sitting next to her on the sofa

Bridges was surprised at the fact that Adriana knew who he was about to mention.

"That's right. How do you know him?" a curious Bridges asked.

"Well, I attended a few social functions with him after his wife died...just as friends. He just never got over his wife's death. Seems they had gone to Europe and when they returned, she came down with hepatitis. He still lives in the same house with all the memories they shared, and I keep in touch with him periodically. He was appointed to the Supreme Court by President Reagan...he's a brilliant attorney and judge."

Bridges was intrigued with the fact that Adriana knew many of the same people as he did, and found it amusing that their paths had never crossed. He had to agree with her though, about Paul, he was an excellent attorney and judge. But he and Paul had personal problems dating back many years.

Bridges went on to explain that he and Paul had gone to Officer's Candidate School at Quantico, Virginia many years ago.

"There is another person I would like to talk to, someone I know we can trust with our lives, and that's Tom Moore at the D.C. Metropolitan

Police." Richard said.

"Doesn't he hold a high-level position...a Captain or something? It seems I remember his wife being involved in one of those children's charitable organizations." Adriana asked.

"That's him. He's a good family man and honest, and he was an ole' Marine Corps buddy as well. What I find amusing is that you and I have never met before." Bridges was still intrigued with the acquaintances they had in common.

Adriana wasn't sure if she should confide in Richard. She ran the risk of insulting him or hurting his feelings but then she decided to explain.

"Richard, since I've been a widow, my friends have tried to introduce me to various men and get me out to social functions. They have meant well, and most of the time I will follow through and go out. It was during one of these times that your name came up. When I was told that you worked at Langley, well...that sort of put the damper on things. I knew you were a widower, but it was the Langley part that wasn't for me." Adriana seemed relieved that her and Richard were finally getting to know each other. It would be easier on both of them.

"I guess you must know everyone around Washington then."

Adriana explained to him that she didn't know everyone and there were certainly a lot of people she never cared to meet. And even some whom she wished she had never met.

Bridges noticed a change in Adriana. She appeared more relaxed...maybe it was the cognac. Nevertheless, it was good to finally drop the formalities and get to know her. He was even amused by his feelings of jealously as she spoke of Paul Castilli. It was the way she spoke of Paul which made him realize that Adriana wasn't aware of Paul's eye for the ladies, even before his wife died. There was one more thing he needed to know from her, and now was as good a time to ask.

"Adriana, I would like to know how deep this hatred for the Banks goes? What I'm really asking, is your hatred going to get in the way of this project?"

Embarrassed by the question, Adriana and wasn't quite sure how to answer. She knew Bridges was concerned and perhaps she should explain her feelings.

"I'm not sure hate is the proper word. I can get along with Heidi on a daily basis and she even has a fun side to her when her guard is down. I think when she realizes she's having a little fun, she puts on her other face. She's confided in me about her husband. While in the White House, she threw a Lincoln era vase at him and just barely missed him. What a scandal that would have been. Anyway, to answer your question, I hate her when she's playing the role and manipulating people, and that's the majority of the time."

Bridges was satisfied with her explanation. For the project's sake though, he didn't want Adriana to become contemptible with Heidi.

"She must continue to trust you, Adriana. We need the information, especially the movements of the woman in Central America."

"Actually, Richard, Shepard's a wimp…even thinks he's a ladies man. He knows nothing about foreign policy or running the country. He's a disgrace to the American people."

Adriana's explanations about her feelings towards the Banks seemed simple enough, but there was still a part that left Bridges suspicious. There would be no room for her to lose control of herself once the project was rolling. He liked Adriana, she was intelligent, extremely attractive and desirable. He could easily become involved with her, and he wanted desperately to trust her. The thought of her body stimulated him. No…no, he put the idea in the back of his mind and reminded himself the project must come first.

Bridges had been so deep in thought that for a moment he hadn't realized Adriana was speaking to him and suggesting they have breakfast in the morning before they go over to the Royal Stud.

"My sister and Princes Alia expect to meet you tomorrow. Princess Alia already knew that you and Jennifer raise Arabian horses in Virginia. She said she had read an article about your farm in the Arabian Horse World. And I was told that you may take all the photos you like. In fact, Princess Alia would like your daughter to come over and visit as her personal guest." Adriana turned and smiled at Bridges.

"That's very generous of her. Jennifer would be extactic over such an invitation, especially to be the guest of the Princess." Bridges was excited at the thought.

"And…thank you, Adriana. I'm sure you had a lot to do with that. I shall always be indebted to you, my dear." Richard teased. Then, as if driven by some deep feeling, he winked and smiled at her, causing Adriana to blush.

For the moment, Bridges decided not to pursue any flirtations with Adriana. He focused on the project and told her that sources had provided him with information that Michael had made application to the Agency but had never followed through, at least as far as they knew.

Of course Bridges knew that it was also typical of the CIA to deliberately reject an application but then contract the person for a specific project somewhere else in the world. Such could be the case with Michael. Afterall, he spoke fluent Arabic and English and he was a mathematical genius. He reminded himself of the conversation he had with Commander Risken who informed him that Michael Myers had assisted with the Pollard affair. In light of the World Trade Center bombingsand growing terrorist activities in the world, Michael would certainly be of help to the Agency, even the FBI.

Adriana didn't seem surprised. Afterall, it was no secret Michael loved the United States more than his country of birth.

Just then Adriana softly smiled and turned to Bridges. It was her turn to ask questions. "I'm very curious, Richard, how did you get the nick name the 'Highwayman'? I've run into a few people who smile whenever they call you that."

Bridges really didn't want to explain. He knew exactly where the information originated from and it wasn't from Billy-Ray. Either someone at the State Department or the Agency assigned to the project in El Salvador had related this to Adriana. "I'll tell you later, Adriana. Although it's clear to me now that the Highwayman and this project have something in common. I promise I will fill you in at some later time."

***

The next morning Adriana and Bridges met for an early breakfast. He wasn't at all surprised to see her dressed for the occasion in English riding clothes. Tan riding breeches, black knee-high boots, and a white sleeveless blouse. Even though the weather was too warm for a coat, she had a brown checked worsted wool riding jacket in her hand. She was truly lovely and Bridges was not surprised she knew exactly how to dress. He, too, wore riding breeches just in case an opportunity was extended to go for a short ride.

When they arrived at the Royal Stud, they found Princess Alia instructing a small class of young girls mounted on Arabian horses. She seemed to be teaching them proper use of holding a riding crop. When she noticed Adriana and Richard, she turned her class over to another young woman and walked to the edge of the arena.

The Princess spoke perfect English and explained she had been educated at Smith College in Massachusetts. She was dressed like Adriana although her own riding boots showed wearing on the inside of her calves. It was obvious she spent a great deal of time in the saddle. As she shook Bridges' hand, she looked him directly in the eyes and smiled softly. She invited the two to a table in the shade and ordered a member of her staff to bring cold drinks.

From the table under the umbrella, they could view the class of young girls. The Princess was interested in Bridges' farm and his horses and Adriana sat patiently in silence as she listened to him explain the blood lines in great detail. Princess Alia provided a captivating audience as she listened to Bridges rattle off name after name of various horses. It wasn't long before the Princess had invited Bridges' daughter, Jennifer, to be her guest. Just as Adriana had said.

Bridges was greatful and indicated he would pass on the invitation to Jennifer. They sat for awhile until they finished their drinks and then the Princess took them on a brief tour of the Stud. Bridges noticed the ground and horses were kept immaculate and the horses were truly beautiful.

"I see you are dressed for a ride." Princess Alia said. "Would you like to go out?"

"That would be wonderful, thank you." Bridges remarked.

The Princess selected a grey stallion for Bridges and a bay mare for Adriana. They would go out under an Army escort which was a relief to Bridges and made him feel more comfortable. As the horses were being prepared and saddled, the Princess invited them to watch an exhibition by the Mounted Palace Guards. Adriana and Bridges were truly impressed as they watched the horses go through their various dressage drills.

"Such discipline and precision." He remarked as he snapped picture after picture.

After the drill, two Mounted Palace Guards brought up the horses which had been chosen for their ride. The two women were assisted, however, Bridges mounted on his own. In Jordanian culture, it was considered an embarrassment for a man to be helped in the saddle.

The group left the Stud followed by three Mounted Palace Guards with three additional armed guards behind them. They headed for the ancient City of Jerash and the Dead Sea Valley where Bridges again took several photos. After few hours, they returned to the Royal Stud where they dismounted and the grooms took their horses. It had been a most memorable trip for Bridges and he was anxious to tell Jennifer all about.

No sooner had they dismounted and headed for the table under the shade for a cool drink, than Bridges was handed a an invitation for his daughter, her name in gold leaf. The open invitation was an honor and the invitation itself was a collector's item. He thanked the Princess. Only when they were leaving did Adriana receive a message from her sister that she would not be able to be in attendance and apologized.

***

Bridges and Adriana returned to the Hilton. They would meet for dinner after Adriana freshened up and Richard phoned Jennifer. He had just hung up the phone after a lengthy conversation when there was a knock on the door.

"Am I too early, Richard?"

"Not at all. I guess I was on the phone longer than I thought. Jennifer was thrilled with the invitation. Make yourself comfortable and I'll shower quickly. Why don't you call room service and order a couple of drinks…I'll have a martini straight up."

Bridges finished his shower and dressed quickly returning to the sitting room of his suite. Adriana handed him his martini and explained why she was early.

"I can't stay at the Palace too long, it drives me nuts. You know, all those servants and stuff…so, I thought I would join you a little earlier than you expected me. Besides, my sister was still taking care of some business that she hadn't finished earlier in the day. That's why she couldn't meet us. You know, Princess Alia was very impressed with you. I guess it's because you both raise Arabian horses. I guess you have that charismatic personality that just wins over women."

With that remark, Adriana leaned over and kissed Bridges gently on the mouth. Bridges returned the kiss. After a moment or two, Adriana smiled softly and said. "I guess it was the idea of a freshly showered man that made me do it."

Richard took a sip of his martini as he look into Adriana's eyes. She kissed him once again, this time longer and more passionately. He didn't resist and participated with his whole being.

It was Bridges who didn't want the moment to go any further. Not now, not as long as they were involved with the project to foil the attempted assassination of the President. Somehow, Adriana sensed he was holding back and she understood. He held her for a moment that told both of them this was not the right time. It was Adriana who finally spoke.

"Richard, there is something I should explain, I don't quite know where to start. Probably at the beginning would be good." She said as Bridges became highly suspicious.

"After my husband was killed I was very lonely not quite knowing what I should do. I became romantically involved with a married man…the Senator from Massachusetts.not Kennedy…another bleeding liberal, although it didn't seem to make a difference at the time."

Bridges listened as he sat on the lounge sipping his martini trying not to show any emotion until she was quite finished. He knew she was waiting to see if he showed any signs of emotion and she paused several times to allow him to speak but he didn't. Finally, he couldn't stand to see her struggle anymore. "Adriana, just go on and tell me everything.

We need to know if your involvement with him is affecting our project or our feelings for each other."

"Thank you, Richard. Well…my friends tried to warn me but I didn't listen. It seems I wasn't the only one he was romancing. Even Heidi had an affair with him when her husband was Governor of Virginia. Anyway, it didn't last between us. I'm not sure about Heidi and I don't even know if the President knew. I can't see where it would matter since he has his black maids and he and Heidi haven't slept together for years. Maybe its the Senator who's behind the plot." Adriana said, trying to be brief about her involvement with the Senator.

"It wouldn't surprise me in the least. Afterall, if Heidi was having an affair with this…Senator, then who knows?"

"Does it bother you knowing I had an affair with him?" she asked.

"Listen, we're human. Whatever you did back then has molded your character today. But beating yourself up for having an affair with someone you now dislike is a form of self-punishment. You need to let it go, or has it compromised you in some way?"

"No, not at all." Adriana said

"So what part does this slime-ball Senator play in this dirty game?" Richard sounded harsh but he was pissed at the thought of the bastard taking advantage of such a lovely woman.

"That's just it, I don't know. Sometimes I think he might be the one behind it all. Then again, maybe Heidi is using him as a source of information, I just don't know."

Bridges thought for a moment. "This playboy Senator is a complete idiot. I know DIA had him under surveillance at one time. I can't believe he would allow himself to be used for information. He's too smart for that. He's just got a lot of people bullshitted."

"Are you offended that I kissed you, Richard?" Adriana hadn't wanted to offend him…but it had been a long time since she had been with a man and the moment was just right…

"I believe I kissed you, don't you remember?" But before she could answer, Bridges took her hand in his and kissed her fingertips. "Adriana, we can't compromise our position. We've got to be disciplined." He had hoped she would understand but even he was having a difficult time believing his own words. How long could he continue to look into her beautiful face, smell the sweetness of her, or even touch her before he would want to take her off to bed?

Adriana wanted Bridges more than anything. She was quivering inside as he held her hand and she nodded in agreement to his words. She didn't believe for one moment that Richard had any intention of keeping disciplined as he had put it, even though he might not know it now

"I need to confirm our arrival time at the Allenby Bridge tomorrow. Then plan our trip to Washington."

CHAPTER 6
RETURN TO WASHINGTON

Bridges received a message from Becky that Commander Riskin requested they meet before he left for Washington. The class was over and several of the students surrounded Bridges with their personal questions and extended their appreciation for being patient with them and pointing out important human behavior matters that are unique and important to the intelligence community. The big man that served as Bridges' watch-dog was last to thank him. bridges shook his hand and wish him well.

During the meeting, Commander Riskin thanked him for an excellent program and conveyed the sentiments of the recruits that they enjoyed his program. The Commander cautioned Bridges not to contact Charlie while in Washington. He insisted he maintain contact with him should he need the assistance of the Mossad. The topic concerning Billy-Ray, is a done deal and that he will no longer be a bother to anyone. Bridges was glad to hear the good news about Billy-Ray, although wondered if the Commander meant that he was taken out. Immediately Bridges thought about what Roy Gannon shared with him about Billy-Ray being involved with the Iraqis. He thought he's got enough to contend with and expressed his feelings to Commander Riskin. After their meeting, Bridges went to Moshe Cohen's office and said goodbye. Once again both men embraced each other as brothers.

Bridges invited Moshe to his farm in Virginia. moshe in a soft voice related that he would and informed B.ridges he was about to retire and settle in Florida.

Becky drove Bridges to the hotel in silence. He attempted to engage in a meaningful conversation but Becky's answers were short. At the hotel, Becky agreed to be available in the morning for the transportation to Ben-Gurion Airport. She reminded Bridges that his flight left at six-thirty in the morning and handed him a large manila-envelope. Bridges was curious as to the contents, and thought he shouldn't ask, especially now that he sensed Becky was feeling sad. Becky reminded him that his flight was 883, departing at 640 from Tel Aviv to Kennedy, arriving in New York at two in the afternoon, connecting flight to Dullas.

Before Bridges left Becky to enter the hotel, she finally inquired if anything happened between him and Adriana when they were in Amman. Bridges smiled and assured her that nothing happened and provided Becky with his home telephone number and address in Virginia, and further extended an open invitation to visit. Bridges was anxious to enter the hotel, although it was obvious Becky was expecting an invitation. Bridges suggested that she not over-look Georgetown University for her graduate-work. Becky with certain demeanor, informed Bridges that she is seriously considering Yale. He agreed it was a wise choice, he then hugged and kissed her. As he walked to the entrance to the hotel, he looked back and she reminded him that she would be there at five-thirty in the morning. Bridges waved in acknowledgment.

In the hotel room, bridges sat in silence. He didn't want to call Adriana just yet, he wanted to think things out. His first curiosity was what Adriana told him about the woman from El Salvador. Something didn't ring true, Adriana didn't suspect the woman until he provided a crash course on political assassins. Then he thought that the plot to assassinate the President had to be put down. If Adriana has told him everything she knows, which is much, then they had a big job ahead of them. Bridges thought of who could assist him without getting too nosey. Then he thought that he had to trust someone, someone with power and authority. The curiosity of Adriana not making the connection between the plot and the woman from El Salvador bothered him. Adriana is a bright woman, he thought. She certainly would have put it together, although maybe he was being to hard on her, after all, not too many people deal with assassins on a daily bases, he smiled at the thought.

Bridges lay his head back while he sat on the lounge in his room, he quickly dozed off. The phone range, he answered, there was no-one at the other end. He thought he had to call Adriana's room, then decided to wait.

Immediately he thought about the death of Adriana's husband almost ten years ago. They all worked for the State Department and even then Heidi Jefferson was a power hungry woman fresh out of college. The fact that she could trace her heritage back to Thomas Jefferson was a mind trip of it's own. If she was responsible for the death of Adriana's husband, then why did she hire Adriana as a research secretary, a constant reminder, our is the woman a cold-blooded bitch with one thing on her mind…power. Bridges recalled Commander Riskin sharing suspicions that Adriana's husband was killed and didn't die as result of an auto-accident. The other side of the scenario is that Adriana arrange for the husband's death and collected a large sum of insurance money. Bridges quickly dismissed the idea. He felt embarrassed that such a thought came to mind.

Bridges dialed Adriana's room. She obviously had been napping. Immediately recognizing Bridges, she came alive and suggested they have dinner and that she would invite Becky

. ***

At the hotel lounge, Adriana and Bridges had a drink, while waiting for Becky. Bridges had a martini on the rocks and Adriana had a tall vodka-tonic with lime. As they sat talking, Becky arrived dressed in a tan jump suite, the zipper was low enough to reveal her cleavage. Her hair was drawn back and she had make-up on, something the Mossad doesn't want their woman to use, at least on duty. Adriana also had a light blue jump-suite on, her tan skin brought out her natural beauty. Both women were looking great, Bridges thought, he was proud to be with both of them and wondered if he was the envy of the male hotel guests.

Adriana became quiet after Becky arrived. They finished their drinks and went into the formal restaurant for dinner. During their meal, Bridges asked Adriana if she was feeling alright. She responded that she was fine, although she was becoming up-tight about returning to Washington. Then she explained that she had to return to the White House the following Monday, which she dreaded.

"I don't mind the job, but Heidi is so full of herself, I have problems tolerating her." After Adriana expounded on her feelings, she then provided Becky with her home address and telephone number. She extended an open invitation as well to visit her when ever she was in the DC area. Becky was surprised at the same time happy that Adriana extended an invitation to her.

After dinner, Adriana excused herself and provided an excuse that she wanted to pack her bags and get ready for the return trip to Washington.After Adriana left, they had coffee as the waiter cleared the table. Becky started to cry. "What's wrong Becky, why the tears?"

"Shut up Richard, shut up…I'm not crying…there's something in my eye." They laughed at the same time Bridges put his hand on top of her's.

"I'll miss you Richard, damn it…I love my job here. I enjoyed your visit and I heard the recruits talking about your classes, they were really impressed. Please for me Richard, please be my friend always. You are a special person, I mean it. I've heard stories about you from the old timers at the Midrasha. They all say the same thing, you are a loyal friend, once betrayed, you are a holly-terror. I believe it, you are a special kind of person, I mean one who cares. Your daughter is lucky to have you as her father. I'm lucky to have met you, now I'm getting mushy, forgive me, I can't help it.".

"Becky as I said before, you're an intelligent-bright woman with a great future…I'll always be your friend."

"Damn it Richard, you always put a damper on things when it comes to us. Why?"

"Listen I can't begin to tell you how sexually attractive you are, I'd make love to you in a heart beat. Let's put it on hold, who knows what the future will bring. Please promise to visit me in DC."

"I promise, now hear me, don't be surprised if you see me very soon.

"You and Charlie are special, I only wish I could see him when I get back to the DC area."

"If I know Charlie, he'll find reason to call you, I'm not sure he'll meet with you…but he'll call."

"Becky, you and Charlie are special. Please thank him for me. I'll visit Tel Aviv again I'm sure. I may come when my daughter decides to visit Princes Alia. I need you to accomplish something for me, please contact Roy Gannon in the Agency's office in Jerusalem, also thank him and explain I had to return to Washington. I'd call him myself, but he'll want to get together and have a few drinks and talk about old times, I don't have time for that."

Becky agreed to give the message to Roy Gannon and informed Bridges that Mr. Gannon has been to the Midrasha many times. Becky didn't miss a chance to comment that he was an attractive middle age man with sensuous appeal. Becky felt mushy and thanked Bridges for being her friend. She kissed him on the cheek and reminded him she would see him at five in the morning.

Bridges returned to his room, packed his bags, left the shaving gear out and a fresh suit of clothes out. He planned to travel in a business and thought the weather was getting cool back in DC.

The phone rang exactly at four, it was Adriana giving him a wake up call. Bridges thought she sounded distant, they agreed to meet in the lobby at five. After he hung the phone up, he became concerned over Adriana's change in mood. it had to be something more that returning to work at the White House. They met in the lobby, she presented a masked cheerful smile. Bridges immediately asked her reasons for the mood change.

Adriana explained that the project is becoming a reality, and that she realizes it's a serious matter and a heavy responsibility. She thought that if they turned it over to the FBI and Secret Service, both agencies would be interested, but they would step on each other in attempting to gather evidence. Eventually they would lose interest and the investigation would be filed away. The only thing it would do is change the date and time of the assassination She reassured herself that she was doing the right thing in recruiting Richard Bridges and plot the entire project even though it was a mess. Adriana being in a deep thought, became conscious and aware of her surroundings. She immediately asked Bridges if he had transportation at the Airport, assuming that he left for Tel Aviv out of Dullas International Airport. Bridges smiled and felt that Adriana was back-to life so to speak, and answered that his car is at Reagan International Airport. Adriana suggested she drive him to pickup his car. Bridges was glad she offered, he was feeling like he wanted to be around her more. He then thought better, but remained in the sentimental mood and realized he was experiencing feelings for her. He embarrassed himself with the thoughts of Adriana

Becky arrived and transported them to the Ben-Gurion Airport in the same car they traveled to the Allenby Bridge the first time he met Adriana. Upon arrival at the airport, Becky parked the car in the VIP government parking spot, which made it obvious to Bridges she wasn't going to wait for them to leave. Bridges kissed Becky as a father would to a daughter, she hugged him as though she didn't want to let go. Then she hugged Adriana and promised both that she would visit them when she returned to the states. At six-fifteen they boarded American Flight 881. final destination Dullas International Airport. They were seated in first-class. While the plane lifted off the ground, it became obvious to Bridges that Adriana was silent, immediately Bridges noticed she was holding on to the arms of the seat and her knuckles were white. He wanted to ask her if she was apprehensive when she flew, but thought better, it was obvious. As the plane leveled off, Adriana relaxed as the flight-attendants served breakfast. After they had breakfast and two Bloody-Maries and several cups of coffee, Adriana appeared completely relaxed. They had light conversation and Adriana wanted to discuss their plans, but thought better. Bridges recalled seeing a familiar face boarding the plane when they did. He was certain the man was Mossad or at least had something to do with the intelligence community. With that in mind, Bridges whispered to Adriana not to discuss the project unless she spoke in cryptic terms and not to use names. Adriana clearly agreed and asked if he would be visiting Paul soon after they arrived. Bridges knew exactly who Adriana was talking about and answered a simple “yes.”

Their conversation continued throughout the flight until Adriana fell asleep. Several hours later the Flight Attendants served a light lunch of salad small portions of roast-beef, potatoes and carrots that Bridges thought was like eating rubber. They both ordered Bloody-Maries, doubles. Adriana returned to sleep. Bridges read or at least looked at the pictures in the magazines in first-class. Their stop at Heathrow Airport was a short delay, unloading and loading passengers. Several hours later, Adriana woke as the Flight Attendant announced they were arriving at JFK. The delay in new York was no more than forty-five minutes. Adriana was becoming anxious to arrive in Washington. Bridges shared the feelings. He noticed the familiar man was still seated behind them. Bridges thought he would stretch his legs and strike up a conversation with him. Then he thought better after he stood and had difficulty getting the man’s attention. Bridges noticed the man was dressed in an American made suit, light weight worsted wool, fresh white shirt and a color coordinated tie. Next to him was a vacant seat, on the seat was a brief case similar to the one Charlie carried, a dead ringer for an Israeli official. The man got out of his seat, avoided eye contact with Bridges as he walked past him on his way to the restroom in first-class section. Bridges thought, when the man returned he would at least say hello, hoping to determine if he had an European accent. Shortly, the man returned and Bridges satisfied his curiosity and said hello. The man returned the greeting in Hebrew, avoiding eye contact. Bridges returned to his isle seat after he used the restroom.

Adriana couldn’t help noticing what Bridges was doing and became entertained with his coolness. She also thought the man appeared familiar and shared her opinion with Bridges. They both agreed to ignore the gentleman and go about their business which was sitting waiting for the flight to end.

Adriana sat back in her seat and thought of Paul Castilli, an important man now that he's a member of the Supreme Court. She wondered if she should tell Bridges that she dated him briefly shortly after his wife died, then recalled she may already told him, but didn't know if Bridges thought it was a whirl-wind romance. Adriana felt she had to tell him it was casual and nothing serious. She was glad Bridges was planning to consult Paul on the matter in chief.

Their flight finally landed at Dullas International Airport. Adriana and Bridges were one of the first passengers to exit the plain. As they walked in the direction of the exit to the terminal, they were approached by two men dressed in suites. Bridges recognized one of the men as being from the FBI field office in local Virginia, the other man identified himself as Secret Service.

Adriana grabbed Bridges arm as the men greeted and introduced themselves. The taller of the two men spoke with authority by informing them they were there to assist them. Bridges quickly thought that both men were there in connection with the plot Adriana had informed him about. Jokingly, Bridges explained he was a big-boy and didn't need assistance. The FBI Special Agent smiled and attempted to renew their acquaintance, at the same time the Secret Service Agent pulled Adriana aside and was talking to her. Bridges looked over at her, she was smiling as was talking to the agent, then looked over at Bridges and nodded her head, indicating everything was alright.

At this point, Bridges interrupted the conversation and requested Adriana's telephone number. She immediately opened her purse and retrieved a business card, wrote the number on the reverse side, then handed it to Bridges. At the same time the FBI agent informed Bridges that he wanted to talk in private and that he would transport him over to Reagan to get his car. Before he could object, Adriana said it was alright. It seemed as though Adriana understood the situation. As they parted, Adriana walked away with the Secret Service agent, told Bridges to be sure to call her as soon he arrived home. Angry with the situation, Bridges felt tempted to make a scene in the terminal and demand to know what the situation was about. He didn't think Adriana was in danger, he then agreed to allow the FBI agent to drive him to pick-up his car at National.

En route e to the Reagan International Airport, the FBI agent asked Bridges if he knew Michael Meyers. This question alone stopped Bridges in his tracks. Bridges wasn't going to lie, but then he had to know why the agent was asking the question. Before Bridges could challenge the agent, he told him that Michael Meyers was found shot to death in his car at Union Station.

As Bridges sat in silence, he peered out the car window at the light rain, then requested from the agent what the connection was, attempting to avoid directly answering the question as to knowing Michael Meyers. The agent immediately followed up with the fact that Bridges' name and telephone number was discovered in the dead man's wallet.

Bridges wasn't going to say much until he had more of the facts concerning Michael. He wondered if by now Adriana knew, at least she didn't know when they parted. The FBI agent spoke again, interrupting Bridges train of thought, and if he knew Michael Meyers well. Bridges thought better to play cat and mouse with the agent, he then admitted meeting Michael Meyers in Tel Aviv and that he knew he had been Adriana's brother in law. Bridges decided that he wouldn't say anymore, at least until he could talk to Adriana and think the situation out. He thought if Michael was killed at Union Station, then Washington DC Metropolitan Police would have jurisdiction or at least they had charge of the preliminary investigation, depending what was the motive. Bridges took a chance and asked the agent for further details of the Michael Meyers shooting. The agent didn't hesitate to inform Bridges of the details as known to the FBI. Something the FBI doesn't do, they're always tight lipped even when an investigation was collateral to another law enforcement agency. The details shared by the agent was that Michael was shot in the back of the head with a 9mm, the expended cartridge was never found. They suspected his assailant was hiding in the rear seat of the car and the shooting was accomplished shortly after Michael arrived at Union Station yesterday. In his suit pocket were AMTRAK ticket stub and an unused AMTRAK tickets to new York from Baltimore. In addition were his Israeli flight ticket receipt from JFK to Amman, Jordan and return trip to New York by way of Tel Aviv.

Bridges couldn't believe what he was hearing, he hesitated to say anything that would tip the agent to his involvement in a project with Adriana. He hopped they thought he and Adriana were lovers. As they traveled along the Potomac River, Bridges thought of his wife and her accident that occurred on a similar day, light rain and the afternoon traffic heavy in places, although they were traveling at a fast pace. The agent informed Bridges that the Secret Service agent would inform Adriana Meyers of the details, with the exception to the investigative facts. The agent went on to explain that why they separated Bridges and Adriana, with the simple reason being, she worked for the President's wife. Bridges felt bitter and didn't like the idea he was met at Dullas by the FBI and Secret Service. He wanted to challenge the agent but he seemed to be a pleasant person doing his job and furnishing information that Bridges felt wasn't the truth, or at least he thought as much. As they arrived at Reagan Airport, the agent requested Bridges to call their office in the morning and handed him his card. He let Bridges out of the car in front of the terminal. Bridges agreed to call him in the morning but couldn't provide a time because of other commitments.

***

As Bridges arrived at his farm, he discovered his daughter Jennifer wasn't home. He discovered a note from her indicating she would return shortly. Bridges smiled and thought when ever Jennifer was less than specific in her notes, she was up to something and would seek approval later.

Bridges entered his study, not a neat place since his wife died. He thought when she was alive she always kept his hide-away neat and free of trash in the basket and dusted. As for now, the room was a mess and forbid the cleaning woman to touch a thing. He sat behind his desk in silence, he could hear the horses in the barn and remembered it was feeding time. Bridges found Adriana's card and punched her phone number. The phone range sever times, as he thought it was several times, in reality it rang three times before answered. "Hello"

"Adriana, are you alright?"

"Yes…I was just going to call you, then I realized I didn't have your home phone number."

"Did the agent fill you in?"

"I can't believe it, I'm in shock…I need to call Michael's mother but I'm apprehensive, but I know I will call her. She's probably in deep depression over losing another son. What's your thoughts on this?"

"I won't know anything else until tomorrow. I find it unusual that the FBI has the case, or at least, have an interest in Michael's death. I think I told you Michael made application to the Agency right after he left Treasury. I was told he never completed the procedure. I wonder if Michael was a contractor for the Agency and the incomplete application was his cover, or at least stopped the paper trail."

"Do you think Michael was working for the CIA?"

"I don't think we should use the phones to communicate until I'm sure both lines are clean. But it's common knowledge that Michael was an informant during the Pollard case. Maybe there's a connection, but I doubt it."

"Richard, allow me to clean up and let's meet someplace near your place?"

They agreed to meet at a small establishment owned by another one of Bridges Marine Corps buddies. It was no more than a converted rode-house and they served beer and wine.

Bridges arrived at the establishment before Adriana, he renewed acquaintance with the owner. Shortly, Adriana arrived and they sat in a booth in the dark corner away from the jukebox. The place was nearly empty, except those at the bar that stopped for a drink after work

Adriana started the conversation by informing Bridges that she wasn't aware of Michael's involvement with the Pollard affair, although she had a vague recollection of the incident. Bridges reminded her that Pollard was a Special Agent with the Naval Investigative Services. "He and his wife provided American classified material to the Israelis. The Mossad wasn't involved, although many think they had been. The truth of the matter was those involved were from either military intelligence or from the Prime Minister's group."

Bridges strongly suggested they have to locate Michael's former room mate, the one that works at NSA.

Adriana explained that she had to call Michael's mother in the morning. She explained that she seemed to have taken the news well, not as expected. Adriana had to attend the funeral, and she informed Bridges the casket is closed.

Bridges immediately became suspicious. He was told that Michael was shot with a single shot from a 9mm, probably a parabellum round. If this were true, maybe the wound would dictate the casket being closed. Bridges was curious to know if a member of the family identified the body. Adriana explained that Michael's father did, although Michael's face had been damaged beyond recognition.

"I don't think we will have a problem locating Michael's former room mate. I'll find that information tonight, if it isn't too late."

"Be cautious Adriana, who ever this guy is he'll be apprehensive now the word is out Michael is dead."

"Do you believe the room-mate has something to do with the shooting of Michael?" Adriana anxiously asked as her eyes darted around the darkened room. The place was filling up with people and the waitresses were busy serving the customers. Bridges apologized for not offering Adriana a drink. She smiled and said a white wine of any kind was all she wanted. Bridges attracted the waitress and ordered their drinks. Shortly, the waitress served Adriana a white wine and Bridges a draft beer.

Bridges answered Adriana's question concerning the room-mate. "I don't know Adriana, if anything, he may have information that we can use. Here we are in the middle of an investigation of a murder when we are suppose to be attempting to prevent another's murder. It's too early for me to know anything, but for sure, I've got to contact my old buddy, Tom Moore at Metro Police. They and the FBI have the case. If your asking or about to ask if I think there's a connection, I can say, maybe. I don't want us to over react right now, I'd like to sit back in my favorite chair and think things out. I could start looking into what we planned and Michael's death right now, I don't want others to get the impression I'm involved in something relevant to Michael's death."

Adriana agreed with Bridges and related that when she arrived home, there were no messages on her phone message recorder, something out the ordinary, she went on to explain that usually she receives calls from her hair dresser or the girl that does her nails, but nothing other than two, or maybe three hang-ups. It's almost like someone erased any messages she had."

Bridges informed Adriana that he was requested to be at the FBI office in the morning. The topic was to be about the shooting of Michael. He then assured her that any information he received, would come from the Agency and the State Department, not the FBI.

Adriana sounded off about how she felt sorry for Michael and the family, and that the person responsible for his death had to be found. Bridges cautioned her to slow down. Recognizing she was sincerely upset over Michael's death Bridges decided to call it a night. It was getting late and Bridges hadn't seen his daughter yet, she's very important to him.

As they were leaving, Bridges noticed a few guys from Langley. They waived, and continued talking to the group at their table. When they got outside, Adriana commented again about Michael. "Poor Michael, he really was a genuine person and then I think how his family loved the United States by comparison to their native country, Jordan."

"Damn you, Adriana, quit beating yourself over the head, get some sleep, I'll call you after I'm done at the FBI office."

This comment embarrassed Adriana. "I have to check in at the White House. I"m sure they know I'm back, but I'll make it official."

Bridges cautioned Adriana and informed her he would call her in the morning. At nine-thirty the next morning, Bridges arrived at the Resident Office of the FBI. He asked for the agent who met him at Dullas the day before. he was escorted to a room by the receptionist, he was soon joined by two agents, one being the agent that met him the previous day. Bridges ask point blank why they were investigating the shooting of Michael Meyers and further wanted to know if Michael had been an informant for their domestic terrorist activity. The agent in charge of the case attempted to change the subject and requested further information as to why Michael had been in the Middle East, and the purpose of their meeting. Bridges tried to be friendly and demonstrate diplomacy, but he couldn't restrain himself. They knew all about him but yet they were treating him as an outsider. Bridges stood and informed both agents that he had nothing further to say and left their office. As he was leaving the building shortly after ten, he noticed a man that he was sure he had seen on the flight from Tel Aviv. He couldn't make up his mind if the man was Israeli, although Bridges recalled that the man spoke Hebrew. Bridges watch him and he entered the same office of the FBI as where Bridges had just left. This caused suspicion and Bridges was certain there had to be some connection to the death of Michael and Adriana's trip to the Middle East.

Bridges got into his Jeep Cherokee, sat there for a few minutes. he thought he saw Adriana enter the same building. At this point he became angry and thought that if she had an appointment with the FBI clowns, why didn't she tell him. Bridges drove over to the CIA office at McLean. While at the Office of Security, he spoke to old friends. They provided Bridges with some unclassified information as to what the clowns at the Bureau were doing with this Michael Meyers murder investigation.

Bridges learned that Michael had been an informant for the Bureau and he was responsible for gathering information concerning militant Arabs in the Maryland-Virginia area. Bridges thanked his friends for the information and agreed to safeguard what he learned and offered them lunch one afternoon.

Bridges felt hungry, he thought of Tom Moore at Metro Police. He's always available for a late morning breakfast or lunch. He'd planned on talking to Tom Moore concerning the murder of Michael and thought this was a good time. He entered the front entrance of the Metropolitan Police headquarters. As he entered, he was greeted by an attractive black officer that Bridges thought, looks alone made her a credit to the department. Bridges requested to see Tom Moore, the young woman smiled and then laughed, not insulting but Bridges thought that the woman was probably teased by Tom. Inside the offices bridges was greeted by Tom Moore in the long corridor.

"Tommy…how the hell are you?"

"Well if it isn't my old spook friend…what's new in the spook business Dick, oh I'm sorry…Richard?"

"That's why I'm here…no one in this entire DC area knows what you know, so here I am seeking information. I just left the assholes at the Bureau…they are full of shit as always. I need some answers to the Michael Meyers murder which I hear you Metro guys are working with the Bureau."

"I knew you wanted something, but what do you have to trade?"

"How about a late breakfast or early lunch?"

"You're on, I won't think of it as a bribe, rather exchange of information."

Tom Moore is a Captain in charge of Criminal Intelligence. He should retire because of his age but being a cop is his life, take it away and he wouldn't know what to do. Being an old marine Corps buddy, he and Bridges have maintained a friendship over the many years. Especially around the holidays. The sad part of the relationship was that Tom was responsible for informing Bridges that his wife was killed in an auto accident. Over the years they've hunted together and their families shared summer vacation times together. When ever Bridges went fishing, Tom was the first to be invited. Secretly Bridges thought Tom was a terrible duck shooter.

They went to a local to a favorite eating place for cops. They took a table in the rear of the place, although Tom was known by everyone, they left him alone when he was conducting business. "Richard, I know what's on your mind. The Bureau people were at my officer yesterday asking questions about you and this kid that got whacked. The Meyers kid. They said he was working for you and your spook friends. I didn't give them shit, I never share a thing with them, but yet they keep coming back. I have to tell you the kid worked for us sometimes, he had a handle on the Arab bad boys in the DC area. I hear he was born in one of those Arab countries and came here when he was a baby?"

"Lets get the record straight…Michael Meyers didn't work for me, as far as I know didn't turn info for the Agency. I may be wrong there. I recently met him in Tel Aviv, he's was the brother in law of a friend, Adriana Meyers."

"Holy shit, that's the chick that is a power broker in this town. She works for the President's wife to boot. I didn't know she was one of your lady friends. She's a knockout, no dirt on her other than she has control over many of those shit-heads on the Hill."

"Tommy…who killed the kid, what's your thoughts? Why is the Bureau conducting the investigation, I know he was their informant…what do you think?"

"You know Rich…the Bureau want's it to look like he was whacked by Arabs, but you known as well as me…the Arabs would have blown his shit away in his car or in a public place. Not a single gunshot to the heart."

"Wait, you said he was shot in the heart?"

"Well from behind…a nice neat shot through his back and lodged in the heart' a surgical shot, clean and neat."

"The family, I'm told was informed he had been shot in the head and that was the reason the casket was closed. It sounds like a hired gun or someone from special weapons."

"I'll pretend I didn't hear you say that…but I agree with you…someone with knowledge of the human body."

"Tommy I didn't mean your special weapons unit, I meant the famous FBI."

As both men had breakfast, Tom Moore suggested they return to the office and go over the case as it stands.

Bridges didn't want to wait until they returned to the office. he decided to ask Tom about Adriana Meyers.

"I was wondering when you would get around to her, well I told you, she's powerful, no enemies that I know, she is a Republican and works for the liberals, that should tell you a bunch."

"What can you tell me about her husband's accident about ten years ago?"

"That was long ago, as I remember it was strange set of circumstances. I recall he picked up his new car on a Monday and then Tuesday afternoon he plows into the back of an 18 wheeler on the beltway. I understand he smelled like hell when they transported him to the hospital. He smelled as though he had been drinking all day. The autopsy found no alcohol in the blood, wait Richard, this guys was the kid's older brother, holly shit…bingo, a connection.

"Sounds like it Tommy."

"I'll pull the old traffic accident reports, we didn't cover it but for some reason it was a collateral investigation, we assisted. I think because he was a government employee. I wonder if those clowns at the Bureau realized it may be a connection. I'm not going to tell them shit. I don't tell them a thing unless I want them to chase their tails, which they are good at."

"Tommy you mentioned they were asking about me…what's that all about?"

"They said you knew the dead man…nothing else, I pretended it didn't mean shit to me. I'm sure they talked to your old employer over at Langley. Plain and simple my friend, they are looking to plug some holes in the dike. The kid was their informant, turns up dead, they got egg-on-their-face because they didn't have a handle on him, they found out he went to Jordan without telling them, their pissed over that, I'm sure."

"What's the lab say?"

"Let me call and get them to bring the file down."

Inside of ten-minutes, a young woman delivered a over-stuffed file to Captain Moore's office. He thanked her and started flipping through the pages the file folder contained.

"Our crime scene people didn't find an expended cartridge, but they are saying it was a twenty-two…long, at close range, one shot through the back as I said, entered the heart and stayed there. We're not sure if he died instantly. The FBI have it figured that the shooter was in the back seat waiting for the kid. My guys are saying that the poor bastard was hit somewhere else and put in the car within an hour from the shooting. No blood to speak of."

"Wait a fucken minute, you said twenty-two long, the fucken FBI told me 9mm, why?"

"They're fucken with your head...they didn't think you would follow up on the case. There suggesting the Meyers kid was killed by the Arab community, we say if the fucken Arabs did it, he would have been blown up in the car. Make of car where the body was found is US, a small one of those Buicks."

"What was found on him?"

"Amtrak Tickets...New York to Baltimore, never used, his wallet containing credit cards and various business cards, and a slip of paper with your name on it. He was dressed in a summer suit and tie. Oh ya, a receipt from the Hilton in Amman, Jordan and his American Airlines plane ticket receipt, JFK to Amman, Jordan and return by way of Tel Aviv, Israel."

"Tommy, I met him in Tel Aviv, actually at a place called the Allenby Bridge, he wanted to meet me, that's another story. Then we met again the day he was departing to return to the States."

"A secret no doubt?"

"Hell no, he wanted to alert Adriana that her life was in danger, but couldn't be specific. I'm involved in something heavy...Tommy, I'll need help, that is, I'll need your help. I can't trust too many people on this one."

"What ever it is, let us hope the FBI doesn't have word on it, or it will be fucked up, as always. You know Rich...say what you will about Hoover, but when he was alive, the Bureau had respect and they didn't violate the average citizen's rights. Hoover lied for the Bureau, but the agent in the field wasn't allowed to. The only thing that's the same is that State, County and City police agencies still can't trust the word of the Bureau."

"Any photo of the body?"

"Sure plenty, I got an envelope full of them, that is if you want to look at dead people."

As Tom Moore opened the manila envelope containing crime scene photos and close up photos of the body including the autopsy photographs of the entry wound. He handed the photos to Bridges. He looked through the photographs by quickly flipping one after the other until he came to the close-up photo of the victim, he stopped and stared at the picture. Bridges thought the suit and tie was the same as Michael was wearing when he left Tel Aviv over a week ago. Then he asked Tom Moore a question. "Tommy, who identified the body?"

"I'm told no one, Meyers mother and father came down to the morgue, the mother was in no condition to observe the body. The father entered the slab room, he couldn't look or wouldn't look, which ever was the case…then it was assumed the body was that of Michael Meyers. The deduction made by personal belongings being on him when he found, why do you ask?"

Bridges looked at his long time friend…hesitated then made a profound statement. "Tom, this is not Michael Meyers, at least this is not the Michael Meyers I met."

"Are you sure?"

"I'm damn sure, I'm damn sure my friend."

"The Bureau run the fingerprints for us and concluded that the body found was Michael Meyers, but I'm beginning to see the Bureau is concealing something or want us to think that Meyers is dead. Didn't you see the Post, it had a write up about Michael Moore and what an upstanding person he was, an appointee to the Treasury department by the Bush administration. That's not the usual publication of the Post.

Bridges explained that the clothes on the body was the same suit of clothes Michael Meyers had been wearing when we met last week in Tel Aviv.

"Let's see, we find a victim in a car at Union Station, we are led to believe it's Michael Meyers…you claim the body is not…the Bureau's report to us in writing that the fingerprints matched Meyers. Then you insist it's not the Meyers kid. Now what?"

Bridges asks Tom Moore to read the inventory list of items found on the body. Tom Moore arrived at the point of the wallet containing various credit cards. Bridges insisted he read each and every item.

"Rich, it doesn't break it down as to each item, our guys fucked up, sorry."

"No, don't apologize my friend, the one item most everyone carries is a driver's license, where is it?"

As Tom flips through the copies of each item found on the body and hands them to Bridges, he can't find a copy of a driver's license. Bridges smiled as he handed the copies back to Tom Moore. "Something strange Tom, who ever did it didn't have time to doctor this thing up, to make it to be Michael Meyers. It's not an amateur job, time wasn't on their side, that's all."

"Then if the body isn't Meyers, then who?"

"I got a strong hunch, but I'm not ready to say."

"Richard don't get tired of this shit, I mean this spy shit, or are you like me, it's in the blood."

"You said it Tom, do you ever think of the old days in the Corps, if I remember you were horse-shit with the troops."

In an Irish brogue, Tom Moore spoke. "That I was…that I was…laddie. We had a good time in the Corps, isn't that right Rich…I'm sorry…Captain." They laughed at the Captain bit. Tom Moore was a buck sergeant, Bridges made Captain before he got out of the Marine Corps, and their friend, now on the Supreme Court was also a Captain. For some reason they all became friends.

Tom Moore reminded Bridges that he's in his middle fifties and thinks different now, than he did when he was a squad leader in the Corps. Both men spoke of their children, Bridges having a daughter in College and Tom reminded Bridges of his two sons, one is an attorney working for the Justice department and the youngest son was undergoing Navy flight training with hopes of becoming a Marine aviator. Tom Moore became sad at the thought that Bridges lost his wife a few years ago and decided to change the topic. Bridges asked about Tom's wife.

"Richard, if you got something going with this woman, Adriana Meyers, let's have dinner some night. My wife would be happy to meet her, after all, she's big around town, she's always in the society pages of the Times and sometimes the Post."

"You know Tommy, I've never heard of her until we met in Tel Aviv. But then I don't follow the social climate inside the Beltway.

Your on, let's have dinner at your wife's favorite place. If you're fishing for information about a romance with Adriana, it isn't there yet, maybe I'll get lucky."

"You don't need luck my man, just patience."

"Tommy…need a favor, I need one of the most trusted communications specialist you have to sweep my house and Adriana's place."

"It's a done deal Rich, how soon?"

"How about as soon as he can get there, you got the address."

"It won't be a HE, it's a young woman…the best and most trusted. She'll meet you there."

"I thank you my man, but I need to run it past Adriana before we can do her place, but I want my place checked."

***

As Bridges drove to his farm, he seemed entertained by the meeting with his long time friend, Tom Moore. The information he had was valuable to the project. When he arrived at the farm, his daughter Jennifer was just leaving and threw him a kiss at the same time yelled to him she would return shortly.

Bridges telephone Adriana from his study, the housekeeper begged him to allow her to at least pick-up the room and make it look neat. Bridges told her no, she then asked if he wanted lunch, he shook his head "no" as the telephone rang at Adriana's, she answered on the third ring. She was happy to hear that the caller was Bridges. He asked if she had been at the FBI office that morning, she, hesitated, then immediately told him, she was, and apologized for not telling him before. Bridges held back his annoyance and instructed her, that if they were going to be partners, they have to learn to trust one another. Adriana explained that the FBI agent specifically asked her not to tell him of their meeting until later.

"What did you learn if anything Adriana?"

"Damn it Richard…excuse my language, the FBI is full of shit, they tried to convince me that Michael was some kind of a terrorist, that's not true, is it? They said the people he associates with are involved in a group that may have been involved with the World Trade Center bombing, I can't believe it. Who do they think I am an idiot?"

"Slow down, are you telling me they said Michael was involved in terrorist activities?"

"That's right...Michael loves the United States, if he had one regret, it was that he wasn't born here."

They're baiting you in order to learn something, don't talk to them again unless they can tell you the truth. Relax, I have to talk to you, however not over the telephone. The FBI doesn't know anything about what Michael was up to, I'll be specific later. I don't think our phones are bugged, unless the White House ordered it, but I'd like to meet with you this afternoon."

"The White House wouldn't dare put a tap on my phone, besides this administration isn't into that sort of activity, I'm sure. Can we meet at the same place as last night, I can be there in less than a half hour."

"Good idea...if I'm not there when you arrive, please wait at the bar, don't sit out in your car. Strike up a conversation with one of the barmaids."

Just as Bridges hung the phone up. Jennifer returned at the same time the woman communication specialist arrived. Jennifer wanted to talk to her father but realized he had business, so she went out to the barn after she had a quick lunch with the housekeeper. The telephone lines were checked as well as the entire house. The specialist informed Bridges the place was clean. He asked that she sweep another place, and provided the address, although explained that she would have to get a key from the owner. He instructed the woman to follow him to the Road-house.

At the Road-house, Adriana provide the woman officer with a key to her place. Bridges informed Adriana that his house was clean of monitoring devices. Hopefully her house...would be the same. He apologized for being late and explained that it took a time for the officer to sweep the house. Bridges was curious to know if Adriana contacted Michael's family. Adriana answered that they wanted to meet Bridges once Adriana led them to believe Bridges was her friend. "She provided me with the address and telephone number of Michael's former room-mate. The funeral will be tomorrow, I must attend. Michael's mother is taking his death better than I thought, although the father is in deep depression. They think Michael was working on an important matter for the government, that's why he was killed. Again I must say, both of them are comparing my late husband's death to Michael's, they are intelligent people."

"Give it a rest for now, you're uptight yourself. They have a good point, I now think there's a connection, where I don't know. As for Michael being a terrorist, that is pure FBI bullshit."

"Richard, when will you come over to my place?"

"Maybe this evening."

"I'll provide directions."

"It isn't necessary, I know a few people that worked at Langley who live in the same townhouse complex."

"Then you'll be there?"

"Of course, see you around eight, is that okay?

Adriana agreed that the time was okay and she offered to cook dinner for Bridges. As she drove off in her grey Mercedes 450SL, Bridges couldn't help noticing her license plate was a personal one baring a message, "SOCIAL", he thought as conservative as she was, the message was inconsistent with her personality. Then he thought of his daughter Jennifer's personal license plate, it was the name of her favorite mare, "GEM".

Bridges returned to the farm, before he entered the house, he went into the barn to see the new colt Jennifer bought with his money. He was impressed with the little fellow. He noticed he wasn't shy and came right over to him. The grey mare nickered and Bridges recalled that any baby, she thinks belongs to her. As he was leaving the barn, Jennifer entered and asked her father how he liked the colt. Bridges hugged her and told her he couldn't have selected a better one. "Later Jennifer let me see the papers, I'm curious as to the blood line, not that I don't think you know your breeding, but just to satisfy my curiosity."

Bridges returned to the house, he checked his messages, discovering there were none, immediately called Tom at home. He thanked him for the first class service. They talked about their next fishing trip until

Bridges informed him that he had a date with the lady. Tom hurried off the phone and wished him well.

After a long shower, Bridges dressed in casual clothes and let Jennifer know he was leaving on a date. Jennifer thought it was unusual for her father to tell her he was going on a date. She acted cheerful, but still had loyalty to her mother's memory and felt jealous that her father would date, then she reminded herself that it's been over three years since the accident

***

Bridges arrived at Adriana's townhouse at eight, he rang the charm-bell, Adriana came to the door dressed in casual dark blue slacks and a attractive white silk blouse.

Immediately Adriana handed Bridges a vodka martini. He smiled as if to say that she read his mind. He proceeded to install devices on her telephones. He explained that if there was an lien on the line while she was talking, the small red light will go dim and then bright and start blinking. "The devices are old, but they work, for how long I don't know. I was told your place is clean but I think we both should take precautions."

Bridges asked Adriana what else Michael's mother said that would lead them to a solution. Adriana responded that the mother didn't say much only that she was proud of him. As a member of the family, Adriana had an obligation to attend the funeral, although felt that Bridges shouldn't even though many may think Bridges was a boyfriend of Adriana.

Bridges felt confused, if he knew for sure the body at Union Station wasn't Michael, he had an obligation to inform the Meyers family. However if he did put a stop to the funeral, it would be risky and their project may be jeopardized. He thought there was someone out there that wanted it to appear Michael was dead. Where is Michael if he's not dead he thought, and then wondered if his trip to Jordan had something to do with the present situation

Adriana complemented Bridges as to his appearance and that he appeared rested. Bridges smiled and thanked her.

She went on to say that she recalled something else the FBI agent said that indicated Michael was working for Bridges as well as being involved with a terrorist group.

Bridges responded in anger, without missing a second on the clock. "The FBI is chasing their tails, if it wasn't for local city and county law enforcement, their record of cases solved would be zip…zero." Then he thought he had to share the information he had about Michael not being dead. He suggested they take a ride. As they rode through the Virginia country side, Bridges revealed he thought Michael was still alive. Adriana at first didn't understand, then asked him to explain himself. Bridges related to the details of his conversation with Tom Moore and seeing the photographs of the body. He further told her the body found, had been wearing Michael's clothes, at least the suit and tie he was wearing when they saw him off in Tel Aviv.

Bridges stopped and parked the car over near a large tree, it was dark and little or no traffic was on the road. In the distance they could see lights from a farm house and the moon seemed become bright all of a sudden. Bridges went on to say that the FBI report indicated the fingerprints of the body matched Michael Meyers. "You know Michael was an informant for the FBI, I believe I already told you, he was an informant during the Pollard spy case. "You see, Michael is not a terrorist of any type. He did hang-out with various Arab groups, that's how he was able to provide the FBI with information on the World Trade Center bombing. I don't really think he's done any work for the CIA, although he may have. If Michael is alive, the persons setting this thing up didn't have much time. In Michael's belongings were everything but his Maryland drivers license. The FBI told the family the body was in such a mess that the casket had to be closed, although Michael's father was suppose to provide an identification at the morgue, he was so distraught, he couldn't look at the body. I suspect they may have presented a body that was distorted or even decomposed, that no one could recognize who it was. So we have a problem Adriana, do we put ourselves in a dangerous situation and stop the funeral and blow the whistle, or do we allow it to continue and when and if we find Michael, the family will be grateful. What are your views, how do you feel about this situation?"

As Adriana sat in silence listening to Bridges, she became dumbfounded and had difficulty comprehending exactly what he was saying, she heard the words, but she has never heard of a situation where a body was buried and someone at the funeral knew it wasn't the person. Her mind went to a family of a Vietnam MIA, the family wasn't satisfied that the contents of the casket was their relative. She didn't know if she was strong enough to go along with it, before she answered, she had to run it through her mind again. Then, in a fragile voice filled with emotion answered.

"Richard, I can't believe what I'm hearing. The family has gone through a lot. I think we better allow the funeral to continue, and as you said, if Michael is found, they can only be happy that he's alive."

Bridges realizing he dropped a huge emotional bomb on Adriana, apologized for not preparing her better. He felt careless and couldn't find words to comfort her, although her answer revealed in spite of her emotional attitude, she was able to see the logic in going forward with the funeral. He was certain, deep inside, she wanted to tell the family the truth in order to save them grief.

They returned to Adriana's townhouse. Adriana had prepared dinner but she wasn't hungry, neither was Bridges. As she fixed him another martini, he hugged her from behind.She slowly turned and looked up at him, she had tears in her eyes. She asked Bridges if he thought their visit with Michael caused the situation. Bridges responded that he was unsure and went on to inform Adriana that the man they noticed on their flight from Tel Aviv was seen by him at the FBI Field Office. Adriana instantly related seeing a familiar face at the FBI office as well. "I thought I recognized the man, but wasn't sure. You know those pompous bastards, the more I think of the FBI agents that spoke to me, the more I feel they were only patronizing me."
Bridges inquired as to what the Secret Service Agent said the afternoon they were met at Dullas. "He was pleasant, after he told me that Michael was found dead, he changed the subject until I arrived at my car. He advised me to be careful and then he left once I started the car."

Adriana became silent and moved close to Bridges again. She wanted him to comfort and protect her. Bridges kissed her and she returned a long sweet kiss. Still holding her, Bridges kissed her once again and whispered that they could get into trouble if they continued. Adriana responded that she didn't care, she needed to be hugged and feel a sense of security. Then she admitted to Bridges she wasn't as tough as she pretends. This made Bridges laugh causing Adriana to push him away. Bridges wanted very much to take her to bed, but felt it wasn't the right time no matter what Adriana thought.

Seeing that Adriana was back to herself, Bridges felt comfortable asking a question that may have upset her awhile ago. "Do you think there is a remote connection between your husband's death and the Michael situation?"

"Richard, I've thought of that, but I doubt ten years ago we had Arab activity in this country as we do now. But then who am I to know. I know only what I see now. Thinking back, while at Georgetown University, there were many Arabs, I never paid attention to them. My husband wasn't ashamed of being from Jordan, he'd rather be recognized as Italian, as many took him for. When we first met, he led me to believe he was Italian without actually saying it. I found out when I first met his family. I didn't mind, they are sweet people, I'm sure if they were not Christian, they may have been different. I'm not discriminating against any other religion, but some religions feel threatened by an outsider, such as me coming from a Catholic background. It may be news if the Washington press suggests Michael's death was suspicious and connected with my husband's, remember I work the White House, and I can't say I haven't been in the news from time to time."

"I've heard from a reliable source you are often in the society page of the Washington Times and the Post. I'm sorry Adriana, I've never heard of you until we met at the Allenby Bridge. Living here for as long as I have, one would think I had noticed such an attractive woman."

"Why thank you Richard, but I haven't been in the newspaper that often, just a few time before I went to work for Heidi when her husband was Governor and then when they took over the White House. I've been photographed by the press at social functions, but I always felt the press was using me as a news worthy model."

"I must admit, I'm the closest to the President's wife besides her personal secretary, they like to keep me pumped up because of Heidi, but you know I have many friends at both papers, I think they are a sick bunch in the name of journalism. They brought Nixon down and they get a president elected. The American people have to wake up and stop being influenced by the newspapers and television news. I guess my politics are showing. I can' help it Richard."

"I may agree with most of what you said, but in government service we don't and can't speak out or it may be our job."

"I'm sorry we didn't have the dinner I prepared, maybe tomorrow night. I'll have to check in with the White House tomorrow. I will after the funeral."

"I can't say for sure, I haven't spent much time with Jennifer since we returned from Tel Aviv. I haven't filled her in on Princes Alia yet. I think I better leave and let you get some sleep. I do plan to contact Paul Castilli in the morning, maybe we can meet. I'll let you know."

It started to rain when Bridges unlocked the car door, he noticed a car parked up the street with a male figure silhouetted behind the wheel. At first it didn't concern him until he noticed the car pulled out behind him and slowly followed him to the on-ramp of I-95. Bridges drove on to I-95 and the suspicious vehicle followed, as he increased speed, the car did the same, keeping the head lights in Bridges rear view mirror. He decided to change lanes, the car followed, and then Bridges slowed down to provide the impression he would pull over or take the exit to Alexandria. The car increased his speed and passed, Bridges wasn't able to see the person but noticed he was large and was driving a government car.

Bridges arrived home. Puzzled as to who had followed him. As he drove up the house he noticed a light on in the barn and Jennifer's Jeep Rangler parked next to the large door. He entered and discovered Jennifer inside the stall with the colt. She was happy to see her father. Bridges knew that when ever Jennifer spends a great amount of time with one of the horses, she is feeling lonesome and misses her mother very much. He entered the stall, the colt immediately stood up, Jennifer hugged her father and Bridges kissed her on the top of her head. She started to cry, Bridges comforted her and suggested he make her a cup of hot chocolate. Jennifer nodded her head as she whimpered and grabbed her father's hand as they walked out of the stall and over to the house. They had hot chocolate together and he told her of his trip to Jordan and meeting Princes Alia. He also told her that the Princes was serious when she extended an invitation for Jennifer to visit her. Jennifer, acting like a small girl, smiled displaying dried tears on her cheeks and hugged her father as she cleaned the breakfast counter and placed the used chocolate cups in the dishwasher. Before Jennifer got ready for bed, Bridges promised to have breakfast with her.

It was getting late, Bridges wanted to call his old time friend Paul Castilli. He dialed the number, immediately the housekeeper answered. She was polite and indicated she recognized Bridges and indicated the Judge was sleeping. As she was to hang the phone up, Paul Castilli came on the line and said hello in a grumpy voice. Bridges smiled and remembered Paul always acted tough, but had a heart of gold, especially for his old friends that knew him well. "Hello Paul, I'm sure I interrupted your sleep, but I'd like to visit with you tomorrow. I hear you guys and gals over at the Supreme Court don't do much every day because of your ass-kissing staff needs the experience and credentials in order to function as an attorney in this cruel world."

"What's on you mind Marine?" A term often used by former Marines.

"I just need to visit with you tomorrow afternoon, maybe lunch."

"Rich, lunch is out…dinner at my place will be just great, an early dinner, say seven, I'm hungry after spending a day at the office." They both laughed. Bridges was glad to hear that Paul was in a good mood. Word has it that the job went to his head and he thinks he's above it all. The brief phone call didn't reveal the attitude, but after all Bridges knew Paul in the Corps when they shared the shithouse.

After the call to Paul Castilli, Bridges telephoned Adriana. She was glad Bridges called her, and indicated she was planning to call him to see if he returned home alright

"Adriana, I can't get to see Paul until tomorrow evening for dinner. I was followed from your place to the Alexandria exit off I-95. The asshole was driving a government car and as much as I could see, he was a big man."

They talked for a few minutes and said good-night. Bridges, in spite of the late hour, he called Tom Moore at home. "Tom I need to ask you something."

"Fire away, by the way, my wife wants to meet that classy woman of your's."

"Tell her will have dinner one night soon. Listen, when I left Adriana's house tonight around nine, maybe later, I was followed by some big looking guy driving a government car or a plane clothes detective car."

"It probably was those gum shoes from the Bureau, cool it Rich, they think they got something with you seeing the woman, what a bunch of shit birds."

"I guess you're right, it probably was the Bureau."

"I'm glad you called, we got good news, we took the case over from the FBI, they just want to be kept informed at the progress, I guess now that the body will be buried tomorrow."

"Tom when do you plan to retire?"

"Never Richard. I'm having too much fun. Alice wants me to retire, what will I do, write a book…I can't do that, I have problems with my spelling, even using spell-check." Both men laughed.

"Why do you ask Rich?"

"Well…I got a heavy situation that I'd like to discuss with you, maybe involve you in, but being a Metro-Cop, it may be a conflict, but then again it may not."

"Spook stuiff Rich?"

"Not exactly Tom. I'd like to see you tomorrow, but if I get jammed up, I'll be at you're office the following day."

"Can't you give me a hint, you got me thinking, my people cleaned your phone, didn't they, but then again we should wait. It's better to be safe.

"I can't say much, but it's right down your alley Tom, you'll enjoy hearing about it. Say hello to Alice for me."

***

Bridges got up early the next morning, he allowed Jennifer to sleep in before she had to go to school. He walked out to the barn after he put his riding boots on, saddled his favorite mare, and after warming her up by lunging, Bridges went for a ride into the Virginia country side. As he rode, he couldn't help thinking about who it may be in the casket of Michael. he wondered where Michael was and he got the strange feeling that Adriana may know more than what she's revealed. His feelings were in conflict, he liked Adriana almost to the point having a relationship, but he, for some resasn felt she hadn't been totally honest with him about something, what he couldn't figure. When Bridges returned from his ride, he discovered Jennifer in the barn. She wasn't happy about something.

"Sweet...why are you down?"

"Daddy, I hate men, damn it, why do they always lie?"

"Oh...I see, men problems."

"It's not a big thing, I'll get over it. I do better in school when I'm not in a relationship."

"What else is on your mind?"

"Daddy, you almost can read my mind...I got the feeling I'm being followed. I've noticed the same car following me...did you arrange for someone to look over me?"

"No...tell me more."

"When I leave school to go to work over at the State Departmnt, this car follows me, it's happened at least three times."

"What's the car look like...what's the person look like?"

"He looks like an Arab...or maybe Indian from India."

"Have you experienced any other incidents like this?"

"No, just from school to my work."

"Get the license number of th e car and I'll turn it over to Tom Moore, he'll get his detectives to look into it."

"I know for sure it's a Virginia license."

Bridges assured his daughter that it'll be taken care of and reminded her to get the license number. After breakfast with Jennifer, Bridges got ready to meet with Tome Moore. He also wanted to see Adriana, but Michael's funeral was that morning and she would be helping the family prepare.

He arrived at the Metro Police Headquarters. Bridges was recognized by woman office who directed him to Captain Moore's office.

"Damn it Richard, you got my curiosity up…what's up? Let's have breakfast?"

"Thanks, I had breakfast with Jennifer, can we use one of you private interview rooms?"

Inside the small room which contained a two-way mirror, two chairs and a table. Bridges seated himself in front of the mirror and agreed to a cup of coffee when offered by Tom.

"Tom this is heavy, believe it…let me first tell you a summary of events."

Bridges proceeded to explain that Adriana uncovered a plot to assassinate the President. He went on to insist that it must be kept under wraps until time to disclose all and prevent the assassination. Tom assured Bridges that no action will be taken until he gave the word and went on to reveal his personal feelings that the plot wasn't a surprise to him.

"Richard, in my political mind…the President is a dip-shit, taken him out by who ever, will make things worse for the country."

Bridges agreed, but for some reason he was surprised that Tom didn't ask about who was involved. He went on to tell him about the First Lady and good reason to believe to suspect she's behind the entire plot with a hand full of congressional members of the same party. The only thing, the bumpkins from Congress don't have a clue as to an assassination plot, just that Mrs. Banks had to raise untraceable funds for a special program. Something typical of her.

Tom Moore responded. "Holly shit, that is heavy, it sounds like the bitch…what she got in mind to run in the next election after her husband is dead and the country has sympathy for her, sort of like the Kennedy mess."

"Tommy do you think Michael Meyers' so called death may be connected?"

"It may…it very well may, but then it may not, I've got to think this over. As to your question, it's better that I don't retire to help you, I can do it from here."

"Very convincing Tom, I agree, stay here, it will help."

Bridges felt comfortable with Tom and revealed that there are tapes of the First Lady calling El Salvador and covertly arranging for a woman assassin. The tapes were made by Michael Meyers' former room-mate, he works at NSA and was in charge of the communication systems at the time the President assumed office.

Tom Moore sat back in his straight back chair, and sipped his coffee which he realized it was cold. Bridges hadn't touch his coffee, however Tom could detect was angry over the mess.

Bridges interrupted Tom's thought and ask him to run a license tag and went on to explain that some Arab looking kid is stocking his daughter. He pointed out that there was nothing serious at this time, it sounds as though some Arab has a fixation on Jennifer. On the other hand, it may have something to do with the project I'm involved with. "I'll have the tag number the next time Jennifer works at the State Department."

Captain Moore asked Bridges if he should assign a surveillance team on Jennifer. Bridges replied that it wasn't necessary unless this thing gets out of control. He further requested to review the Meyers' file again. After looking at the file and photographs, Bridges was convinced that the body wasn't Michael's and the neck tie was tied in a "V" knot, Michael tied his tie in an over-hand knot, very neat. It's obvious the suite was a tight fit and pointed out the man was shot without the coat on, no hole in the coat but definitely in the shirt.

CHAPTER 7
THOUSAND WORDS

After Bridges met with Tom Moore at Metropolitan Police Headquarters and briefly reviewed the investigative report involving Michael, he telephoned Adriana at her townhouse. She answered after the third ring. The sound of annoyance in her voice easily detected as she prepared to attend the bogus funeral for Michael. Adding to her feelings, Bridges without sensitivity informed her he was certain Michael wasn't the person in the casket. In an attempt to bring her into focus, he revealed his suspicions. "I have reason to believe the FBI is involved in the coverup…after all, didn't they tell Michael's parents the casket would be closed because of the condition of the body?"

"You're right Richard…I'm and so damn upset, but I'll go to the funeral and play the game." In the back of my mind she hoped Michael was still alive and one day he'll appear and his parents will rejoice. Something she could never reveal to them.

Bridges suggested after the funeral they meet for lunch. Still annoyed, she explained the need to return to Michael's parents home and assist in receiving people that attended the funeral. Bridges then suggested a later lunch and instructed her to leave a message on his message machine as to time and place.

He had concerns and thought he should explain to Adriana, that if Michael is missing, it could be he's assigned to a covert operation. A perfect set-up for making him dispensable. He changed his mind and thought it would be cruel to bring it up now. He'd share the thought with her when she wasn't up-tight. They said goodbye.

While Adriana was at the funeral, Bridges returned to Tom's office to reexamine the investigative file. It was his opportunity to look at the crime scene photos again and interpret the autopsy findings.

When he arrived, the reception area was crowded with people conducting business, either bailing someone out of jail or visiting someone in jail. He had difficulty attracting an officer's attention. As he waited, Tom entered the reception area looking for him. He apologized for the zoo type atmosphere. They both laughed as they got a cup of coffee on the way to his office at the end of the long corridor. Tom's office was in the older part of the building.

The file pertaining to Michael Myers was on the desk. As Bridges opened the file, he examined the photographs of the body again and then read the autopsy report. He asked Tom for copies of the photos, especially the head shots. Tom provided the file photos and explained he would have the lab make a new batch for the file. It was obvious to Tom that Bridges wanted to use the photos for identification purposes and he agreed to follow-up on locating the former roommate of Michael Myers. Bridges quickly and with confidence explained his hunch was the casket contained the body of the roommate. Tom didn't act surprised. Bridges thought, after all, he's been a Cop for thirty years and he's heard it all.

Bridges expressed his appreciation for the help and explained he felt certain the FBI was involved. The identity switch was to allow Michael to go undercover. "If something went wrong, they wouldn't be concerned because Michael is in an expendable position, a cruel way of looking at it."

As he explained his hunch to Tom, he wondered why the roommate was used as a substitute. Perhaps he thought, they were working together and the roommate ran into bad luck. The roommate was bilingual, according to Michael and didn't think he was Arabic.

This was a good time to reveal to Tom the contents of certain tapes of the President's wife talking to known assassin in Central America.

Bridges explained further. "The body identification switch served two purposes. Get rid of the only person that had evidence the First Lady spoke with known assassins in El Salvador, and send Michael Myers so far undercover in the Arab community that he'll never come out alive. I don't think they're connected by design, rather, it happened that way and one fed off the other and who-ever, capitalized on the situation."

Tom reminded Bridges of the same scenario often used by DEA when they want to get rid of confidential informants. Bridges agreed and immediately defended the CIA and deliberately avoided further discussion about their methods, not because of loyalty, rather, it was a gruesome thought. He further thought, that if the activity involved domestic terrorist activities in the United States, then the FBI is at least covering the facts that an anti-terrorist operation went south and the obvious reason for the sealed casket. He convinced himself the FBI was the culprit and Tom agreed with his rationale, not out of politeness, rather, it made sense and the body in the casket was the first casualty.

Another problem Bridges shared with Tom involved his mistrust for Adriana, specifically her lack of reaction when she was informed by an FBI agent that Michael was found shot to death. Then concealing information that she had an appointment with Bureau agents the following day after they returned to DC.

"I confronted her and her explanation was the FBI wanted her not to tell me."

Tom smiled and suggested maybe he was becoming paranoid. He assured Bridges that Adriana is a respected woman inside the beltway and she wanted to do what was right when the FBI boobs made the request.

Bridges, not wanting to argue the point, changed the topic of Adriana to the case in general. Tom reminded Bridges that the case was a simple homicide until the FBI entered the picture. He continued to explain that his investigators are unaware that the victim wasn't Michael Myers.

As Bridges handed the case file to Tom, a fingerprint card fell to the floor. As he picked it up, he realized the card contained fingerprints of the decedent. He looked at Tom, and before he could speak, Bridges suggested they run the prints and not depend on the Bureau. Tom was surprised and explained that the FBI took the dead man's prints to their own lab. "It's obvious Richard, my guys made two sets of prints for some reason, it's not a departmental policy, unless necessary. I'll have them run right now."

Bridges smiled and reminded Tom that it was his hunch the body was that of the roommate. A thought also came to mind that the body didn't have a college ring on the right hand. According to the photographs the body found had a ring tan mark on the left hand suggesting the absence of a wedding band, Michael Myers wasn't married, or at least hadn't been wearing a ring on his left hand the last time Bridges saw him in Tel Aviv a week ago.

Informatively, Tom mentioned the absence of a ring couldn't be relied upon because paramedics have been known to relieve bodies of jewelry. "The tan mark is important in making the point." He further suggested.

Concerning Tom's last statement, Bridges smiled and thought to himself, "once a homicide detective, always a homicide detective."

The ringing of the phone interrupted their conversation. Tom excused himself as Bridges continued to examine the photographs again. When Tom completed the call, he invited Bridges to lunch. He expressed his appreciation and informed Tom he had a lunch date with none other than Adriana Myers.

Before Bridges left Tom's office, he informed Bridges that he sent two investigators to Michael Myers' funeral. One of the investigators was to discreetly take photos of the people in attendance.

Bridges expressed his appreciation and agreed, the funeral photos will come in handy at a later time.

While using the phone in Tom's office, Bridges telephoned his residence to retrieve his messages. The first message was from Adriana providing the restaurant name and time they would meet. Another message was from Charlie. The message was simple and to the point. "Charlie here…don't call me…chuckle…I'll get back with you later."

Bridges remembered Becky told him Charlie would call. He wasn't surprised but happy to hear from him. The message frustrated him especially that he couldn't return the call.

Bridges arrived at Café Du Parc a restaurant close to the White House...surprisingly most of the people waiting for a table were government workers, he suspected.

As he searched the crowd for Adriana, he acknowledged familiar faces by saying hello. His eyes focused on a familiar woman talking to an older man at the entrance to the lounge. He suddenly realized it was Adriana.

He was pleasantly surprised to see her dressed in a tailored grey tweed suit with black velvet collar and an attractive white silk shell. It was obvious she changed clothes after the funeral. As he approached her, the older man was just saying goodbye. Adriana smiled as she recognized Bridges and impulsively hugged him as he kissed on the cheek. She signaled for a table, providing Bridges a glimpse of her power in and around the Capital. After they were seated, both ordered a glass of California Chardonay with a Caesar salad. Adriana was eager to learn the latest concerning the investigation of Michael's purported death.

Bridges contemplated showing the photographs to Adriana. Before their salad was served, he removed the one photograph that depicted a fully attired man with his hands exposed. She immediately responded that the photo was not Michael and then focused on the clothes. Agreeing the man had been wearing Michael's clothes. Bridges pointed to the hands. Adriana again was quick to discover the absence of a college ring which she remembered Michael nervously played with the ring as they spoke at the air terminal in Tel Aviv.

Bridges looked around the restaurant, he recognized an Agency employee that he was certain worked for the Office of Information Services. Someone he had known for years although he was busy romancing a young woman obviously new to the DC area. As he leaned closer to Adriana and feeling comfortable he wouldn't be overheard, he whispered before she asked, "I suspect the dead man was Michael's former college roommate". She looked at Bridges with a blank stare, then she put on a superficial smile in the event they were being watched and over heard. Bridges revealed another photo depicting the body with a front view. Adriana made no comment.

Their lunch was served and Adriana ate in silence with the exception of politely saying hello to various people she vaguely knew that greeted her as they passed their table and were leaving the restaurant. Upon finishing lunch, Adriana insisted the treat was hers. Without bringing attention to them Richard agreed with the promise she wouldn't make it a habit.

While they waited for the valet to bring Adriana's car around, she impatiently asked if Bridges knew the name of the former roommate. Bridges assured her that the information would be available that afternoon and revealed to her that photographs were taken of the people attending Michael's funeral.

At first, she resented hearing that they were spied on at the funeral, then she realized the reason. "Richard, there were many people at the funeral, people that I've been told either attended college or worked over at Treasury with Michael."

"Were many of them Arab-Americans?"

With the question, she thought quickly and then provided an expected answer. "Come to think of it, many were Arabs or I should say Jordanian that either knew the family or Michael knew as casual friends, at least that's what Michael's mother told me."

Bridges uttered that he "thought so" without further explanation. He then inquired if Adriana had ever met the former roommate. Adriana was quick to respond that she didn't recognize the photograph, however she explained that he may have attended her wedding, Michael and his friends were in High School at the time. They finished lunch and left the restaurant.

When the valet arrived with Adriana's car, Bridges suggested they go over to Union Station and become familiar. Bridges needed time to be alone with Adriana and bounce his theory off her. Obviously she didn't mind and felt comfortable and safe whenever they were together.

"Adriana, my theory is a simple one...Michael I suspect is undercover for the FBI, I believe for the ongoing terrorist investigations. They had a body, maybe it was the roommate and they deliberately made it appear as though Michael was dead in order to put him deeper into the terrorist movement either in New York or the Jersey area. I don't believe the FBI was responsible for the death of the young man, although, it made things convenient. They set it up to convince everyone concerned, including the family, that he was dead, allowing him to have freedom of movement. As for the body you all buried today, if it was the roommate, then his death is a clear connection to our project."

"Why Richard that's brilliant.seriously it makes sense, what then?"

Bridges went on to explain the need to identify the body and then they'll take it from there. He was surprised that Adriana didn't react to the possibility that the body buried in Michael's place was connected to their project. He decided to leave it alone and not inquire. The parking facility at Union Station was full, Bridges relied on his memory, recalling from the sketches he observed in the investigative reports where Michael's car was parked when the body was discovered.

As they drove in and around the vicinity of where Michael's car was found, bridges admitted the idea was fruitless and decided to leave Union Station. As they left the parking area, Adriana informed Bridges that she met Michael's girlfriend at the funeral. She described the young woman as very intelligent and attractive. Of course saddened by Michael's purported death. "She invited me to visit with her at her apartment over in Germantown near the University."

Bridges acknowledged the information and immediately pointed out the young woman may have information that will be helpful to the shooting investigation and their project. He suggested they go over to the Metro Police Headquarters and talk to Tom Moore.

By this time, he mentioned, Tom would have information needed to continue with their project. Bridges reminded her that they needed to locate the tapes Michael spoke about and that it wouldn't be a bad idea to get a fix on the location where the woman from El Salvador is. As they traveled in silence, Bridges thought of Charlie and his recent phone call and how he would like to talk to him but was advised against it.

At the Metropolitan Police Headquarters, they were escorted to Captain Moore's office. Tom acted like a movie fan when he met Adriana. He impressed upon her that his wife Alice would be pleased to meet her. Feeling flattered at the same time embarrassed, acknowledged Tom by shaking hands and took a seat in front of his desk as he offered.

Bridges winked at her as he was seated. They started serious conversation. Tom informed them that the body was that of James Allen, an employee of the National Security Agency. Bridges looked over at Adriana and then spoke.

"What else my friend…is this the former roommate of Michael Myers?"

"Your damn right it is, NSA hasn't heard from him in five days. They knew, at least his friends knew he planned a trip to New York and that's it. We're sure he's the roommate."

Adriana looked down at her hands, she felt a moment of deep sadness, then she spoke as Bridges waited. "Will the wife of James Allen be told…or do we have to keep it to ourselves until this entire mess is resolved?"

Bridges looked over at Tom and then answered her question which he knew she already expected, although, she wanted to hear it from either men. "Adriana, we can't tell the woman a thing, if we do, we'll place her and of course ourselves in danger. We don't know exactly who we're dealing with."

"Then with Allen dead, it's next to impossible to locate the tapes? Adriana inquired as she stared into space.

Bridges took in a deep breath as to sigh, then he answered her. "It depends on many things, but for now we have to maintain a cool deliberate pace without allowing distractions."

Bridges explained to Tom the need for the tapes and what they may contain.

Tom offered assistance should they need it. He went on to explain that Allen's wife was taken her husband's absence better than one can expect, although explained the information came from a contact at NSA.

Mulling over in his mind, Bridges thought that the trip to New York by Allen would coincide with Michael's return from Tel Aviv. "A trip to New York would fit into Michael returning from Tel Aviv, and the unused AMTRAK tickets."

Adriana thought privately that Richard is a quick thinker and became apprehensive to say too much in fear she may reveal her ignorance in matters of simple investigative procedures. She decided to ask a question disregarding her thought. "If Michael works undercover for the FBI on the terrorist investigations, then how does Allen fit in, I'm assuming from the photographs that he's in no way a Middle Eastern descendant?"

Quick to answer, Tom agreed and explained that James Allen was not an Arab of any form and explained that he was born and raised in the Baltimore area. The father was military and his mother was an RN and worked over at the Bethesda Naval Medical Center. An only child, James Allen attended Georgetown University with Michael Myers, as Tom elaborated from information received from the investigators

"He was employed at NSA at the same time Michael Myers went to work at the Treasury Department during the Reagan administration."

Bridges went over the events, from Tel Aviv to New York. "Michael told us that he would take the AMTRAK from New York to Baltimore so as to visit his girlfriend. Allen meeting him in New York doesn't compute no matter how you slice it, unless Allen had communications that Michael needed before he returned to Baltimore. If this were the case, then they drove back…or planned to drive from New York to Baltimore. The shooting of Allen had to occur somewhere on the way to Baltimore and Michael has knowledge."

Tom agreed that it sounded plausible.

Adriana carefully listened then added to the scenario. "We thought it was strange that Michael would take a train from New York instead of flying to Washington-Baltimore National even though he wanted to stop in Baltimore to visit his girlfriend. By the way, I met her at the funeral this morning. She's a pleasant young woman, I learned she teaches over at the University of Maryland."

Tom expressed himself using pointed language. “This entire mess smells of shit. Pardon me Ms. Myers.”

Adriana smiled and provided Tom with a glance that waived censorship of language. Then she spoke out in total agreement.

Bridges added to the conversation, reminding them Michael, as an informant for the Bureau and the information he provide during the Pollard case may have put him in harms way. As Bridges reviewed details of evidence with Tom and Adriana, he pointed to a cover-up, and admitted it was difficult to put both men together in New York other than as friends. He went on to agree there was more they needed in order to make an intelligent deduction.

Tom Moore cautioned them that if he reopened the investigation, it certainly would place them in a dangerous situation. He did offer to help by providing resources and approach the entire situation with extreme caution.

Sitting back, looking at the overhead fan which he thought was strange in view of the building being air conditioned, Bridges suggested that looking for Michael would be like looking for a needle in a hay stack, although he was certain he was still alive. “The FBI knows a great deal, but wouldn’t dare disclose a thing. I need to talk to my friends at Langley.”

Tom then strongly suggested they talk to Allen’s wife without revealing he was dead. A tedious task that should be accomplished with the utmost caution. “Do you both have the stomach for this sort of thing?”

Bridges knew exactly what Tom was suggesting. The question couldn’t be answered until they actually confronted the situation and spoke to Michael’s girlfriend and then to the wife of James Allen. Again with sincerity, Tom offered his help in anyway he could.

As Adriana and Bridges left the Metro Police Building, they agreed to go over to the University and locate Michael’s girlfriend. It was getting late and hoped they were in time to locate and talk to her.

At the University of Maryland, students were coming and going. As Bridges and Adriana entered the administration building, they noticed the first office they came to was the office of admissions. Bridges allowed Adriana to inquire as to how they may find Joanne Walker. The older woman at the counter directed them to the art department and indicated doubt if Ms. Walker was present at school, and went on to explain she attended a funeral of a friend and she may have taken the remainder of the day off.

Adriana seemed familiar with the campus and located the Art Department with little difficulty. Inside the building, they inquired about Joanne Walker, immediately they were informed by what they believed was a student. The young lady directed them to the office. As they approached the doorway, Joanne Walker recognized Adriana and came from behind the desk to greet her and to meet Richard Bridges, whom Adriana introduced as a family friend, and left it at that without further explanation.

They were offered a seat and during conversation learned that Michael planned to visit her upon his return trip from Amman. She continued by explaining how shocked she was to learn of Michael's death. Bridges inquired if she knew James Allen. The immediate response was they were good friends and have been since before they married. Adriana noticed that Joanne was still dressed in the black outfit she wore to the funeral that morning.

Her attitude was not as they expected, almost as she knew the truth. She provided Adriana with her home telephone number and address. As both women talked about irrelevant things, Bridges couldn't help thinking that in addition to her beauty, the young woman was intelligent and presented herself well. He looked around the office and discovered she enjoyed collecting German made figures made of painted purslane. On the wall next to the book case was an oil painting of an American bald-eagle, perfectly done allowing the viewer to experience a sensation that the eagle was alive. The light shining on the canvas provided a three dimension illusion. Bridges was impressed and from where he was sitting he was able to determine the painting was done by Joanne. He didn't hesitate complementing her.

Adriana explained that Michael was her brother in law and that Michael's brother was killed in an auto accident ten years ago. The young woman was aware of Adriana and that Michael often spoke of her and his late brother.

Bridges assumed a semi-professional attitude with Joanne now that he could see she wasn't depressed and emotional. He strongly suspected she may have knowledge of the body in the casket and it wasn't Michael. He requested the telephone number and address of the Allens. With little hesitation, Joanne wrote the address and phone number on a piece of paper and handed it to Bridges as their eyes met and her hand touched his. Adriana didn't see the delicate incident. Bridges interpretation wasn't flirting, but an invitation to talk to her in private. He thought it was mysterious although clairvoyant and decided to return on a later day to have the private discussion.

With permission to use the phone, Adriana called Mrs. Allen and asked if she could visit her after talking to Joanne Walker. Directions to the Allen house were provided by Joanne. On the way over to the Allen's home, not far from the university, Adriana shared with Bridges her impression of Joanne Walker and the impression she received while talking to James Allen's wife over the phone.

"I like Joanne, she's bright but I'm sure you felt as I did, she wasn't that upset over Michael's death. I almost believe she knows he's still alive. On the phone with Mrs. Allen, she was immediately receptive to us visiting her. Richard, what do think of that?"

Bridges thought about it for a what seemed a minute, then he agreed with Adriana's impression of Joanne Walker. He almost shared the telepathic experience he had with her, then thought better. He was curious, although it would have to wait until another day.

They arrived at the group of older townhouses in the Germantown area. Bridges couldn't help noticing the area was well kept, streets clean and the houses appeared well cared for. At the address, Adriana rang the door bell and was greeted by a young woman in her late twenties or maybe early thirties. She was attractive, long dark almost black hair, she was dressed in an outfit that she may have worn to Michael's funeral. Adriana doesn't remember seeing her there, however there were many people and she could have been present and not noticed unless you were looking for her. They were seated in the small living room, years ago referred to as the parlor. Mrs. Allen invited them to have some tea. Adriana accepted, Bridges declined. As both woman got acquainted as woman do, Bridges looked around the living room at familiar items most people have in their homes. He noticed a framed photograph of James Allen with a baby. He waited until Adriana took a breather and asked if they had children. Immediately she proudly replied they had one daughter two years old asleep upstairs and she was pregnant expecting their second child in six months.

Mrs. Allen served tea and fresh baked banana nut-bread with cream cheese, a favorite in that part of the country. As Adriana put a spoon of sugar into her tea, she asked the pointed question. "Mrs. Allen…what do you know about Michael's and James' activity with the government."

She replied first by asking them to call her Chris, her real first name is Christina and her maiden name Rizzo, she came from a traditional Italian family, born on a farm near Rochester, New Hampshire. "To answer the question, nothing. My husband works for the National Security Agency, he's been there since completing college. His specific job over there wasn't known, although from time to time he leaves for a few days, no more than two or three, then returns and I see some extra money in our savings account, I suspect he deposits it. I asked him once about the money. He didn't get mad, he never becomes angry, although he was stern and insisted it wasn't illegal money and that they would report it on their income tax, which he has done for the past two years."

Chris continued to explain that she works over at the State Department, assigned to the Central American desk. When Bridges heard that, his brain went into high gear. Adriana informed her that she worked the same desk ten years ago. Chris explained that her bottom line job was working with government contractors. During Adriana's second cup of tea, she managed to learn that Chris met her husband while attending college and that's where she also met Michael.

Bridges cut to the chase. "Where is your husband?"

Chris lowered her head, then looked up and explained she didn't know. She explained that he has been gone for over five days and friends in his office were concerned as to his whereabouts. "I'm worried, I know he took the train to New York to meet Michael, I haven't heard anything since. He usually calls me at work or at home. He and Michael often go up to New Jersey and New York together, some kind of business. This time he didn't take his tools, I noticed them in the hall closet."

Adriana noticed Chris was becoming upset, she thought they should back off, she had to ask another question about tape recordings. "Chris have you seen your husband with audio tapes, did he bring any home?"

"Yes, he said that if Michael asked for them to let him have them, I know he put them in our safe deposit box at the bank. My husband is a communication specialist, he's always messing with tapes. He has a workshop in the basement where he takes information from reel to reel tapes and puts them on cassettes. Why do you ask, is James in some kind of trouble?"

Adriana responded quickly. "We don't think so. We met Michael in Tel Aviv and he informed us that your husband had certain tape recordings that may be of interest to us." Adriana wrote her telephone number on a White House business card and gave it to Chris.

Chris immediately thanked her. "Since you're family and Michael isn't here…I'll get the tapes out of the safe deposit box tomorrow when I pickup my daughter at the day care center."

Bridges thought this was too easy, there had to be a hitch, the woman is calm and not aware of the contents of the tapes and she isn't showing any signs of being worried about her missing husband. He thought maybe there's something she knows that isn't obvious. Adriana asked if she was familiar with the contents of the tapes. Chris answered without blinking an eye that the tapes contained Spanish speaking and that she doesn't understand Spanish, she was unaware what the tapes were about. "My husband speaks Spanish like a native, he also speaks several Arabic dialogues."

Bridges perked up. The connection between the woman's husband and Michael's undercover assignment is becoming obvious. He looked at Adriana who kept herself under control. “How well does your husband speak Arabic?”

“Very well I’m told…as you know Michael’s friends were from Jordan and other Mid-=Eastern countries. They were always trying to trick James when ever he spoke their language. I understand they never were able to catch him off guard and often complemented him on knowing the Arab language.”

As Adriana finished her tea, Bridges mentioned they had to return to DC and he expressed appreciation for talking to them. Adriana agreed to meet with Chris the following day and reminded her to call her before they met. The purpose of the meeting was to obtain the tapes. As they were leaving, Chris complemented Adriana and that she had always wanted to meet her ever she learned Michael was her brother in law. They said goodbye.

It was getting dark and Adriana got on the interstate I-95 headed for DC and to the restaurant where Bridges left his car. As they traveled, the traffic was heavy. They agreed they made some progress and hoped there wouldn’t be a hitch with obtaining the tapes. Bridges reminded Adriana he had to contact Tom Moore to inform him that the tapes were located and he had to return to his farm to catch up on some personal business.

This disappointed Adriana, however she thought there would be other times they would spend social time together and reminded herself it was a long day and she was tired. She promised to call Bridges when she heard from Chris and suggested he should be with her when Chris provides the tapes.

Adriana drove up to the entrance to restaurant allowing Bridges to get out of her car and have the valet bring his car around. Before Adriana drove off, she assured Bridges that she would call him later that evening before she went to bed. As she drove away, bridges noticed a car pull out behind her. Adriana drove fast and the chase car seemed to have problems keeping up to her. It was obvious the car was government and he noticed a woman driving and a man in the front passenger seat. He wanted to call her and warn her but he didn’t have her cellular number, then he remembered it was listed on her business card. Bridges quickly entered the restaurant and called Adriana from the pay phone at the entrance. After two rings, she answered. Bridges alerted her that she was being followed. She laughed and thanked him. She explained that the car was from the Secret Service watching over her. Bridges wasn't certain it was Secret Service and felt strongly that it was FBI, although he didn't share his thoughts with her. Again he said goodbye and felt foolish for calling.

It was getting late, Bridges decided to call Tom as soon as he arrived home. He entered his old renovated farm house. The house had been remodled by his wife over three years ago. The kitchen was large with and cooking island that contained a range and indoor barbaque. The dining area was furnished with French Provincial, something Bridges late wife loved. The smell of food reminded him his was hungry. Jennifer prepared dinner and became obvious that she was proud of the meat-loaf she made with mashed potatoes and a tossed green salad. Bridges remembered William and beth were away.

Before he sat down to have dinner with Jennifer, he made the call to Tom. During conversation he informed him they located the tapes and more than likely the tapes would be in his hands tomorrow. Tom seemed aloof to the news although cautioned Bridges that it sounds too simple

Bridges agreed, although he related details of their meeting with Chris, James Allen's wife. "Tommy, we have to listen to the tapes first before we can do anything else. I think your investigative file contains something we may have over looked. The fact remains that the killers left the unused AMTRAK tickets in the suit pocket on purpose. This fact alone suggests Michael purchased the ticket when he arrived at JFK, clearly dated and in his name. He had definite plans to travel to Baltimore, alone, the reason his friend James Allen met him I suspect was maybe to warn him concerning an important matter or that he was in danger. I don't mean to say James Allen was killed by mistake, and then maybe he was." I would imagine, those responsible knew them both. Michael being the valuable one, James Allen had collateral knowledge of the terrorist activities or, and I hesitate, clairvoyant knowledge of the assassination plot. Then again Allen's death may not have been in anyway connected to the plot."

Tom listened and remained distant. With caution, reminded Bridges they were on the phone even though the lines were clean. Bridges agreed and assured Tom they would meet the following day.

After dinner Bridges did a few chores around the farm. He thought of the excitement in Jennifer's voice when he gave her the gold engraved invitation to visit with Princes Alia in Amman. He smiled to himself and went about his business. William, his caretaker and Beth were away for a few days taking care of personal business.

As Bridges removed bailed hay from the loft, Jennifer came out to the barn to inform her father that he had a phone call and that the caller was a woman. "She said her name was Adriana?"

Bridges smiled at the way Jennifer said 'Adriana' as though she was jealous. He answered the call on the extension in the barn. Adriana informed him that she was planning to meet Chris Allen tomorrow at noon. For some reason this was sooner than he thought until Adriana explained Chris had a doctors appointment and wanted to provide the items before her appointment. Adriana suggested she meet with Chris alone, to Bridges, it sounded harmless at first, unless a third party knew of the meeting between the two woman. Bridges was apprehensive although agreed with Adriana's suggestion. He informed her that she could locate him either at the farm or at Tom's office and provided the telephone numbers in the event she didn't have them.

The following morning, Jennifer woke her father before she left for he classes at Georgetown. She reminded him to check the colt before he left the farm and reminded him the caretaker was off for a few a days. Bridges immediately got out of bed before Jennifer left. She avoided looking at her father, and immediately inquired who 'Adriana' was. Bridges quickly explained that she's a friend and reminded Jennifer that her sister is married to the King of Jordan. Jennifer apologized in a sarcastic tone and then realized that she was the woman in the photographs her father took when he visited Jordan. Jennifer gave her father an artificial smile then left the farm in her Jeep. Bridges suddenly realized his daughter was jealous of another woman, something he thought was normal, he hoped. He returned to the main house to phone Tom at police headquarters. The woman officer that answered put him through to Tom's secretary. She informed Bridges that 'Captain Moore' was in conference with the Chief. Bridges left a message for him to return the call and left his number.

Most of the morning, Bridges puttered around the barn and spent most of the time in his study. As he sifted though papers on his desk, he found two written messages from old associates that left the Agency the same time he did. The messages were taken by Jennifer and were inconsequential. He dialed one of the numbers, the message machine answered and he left a simple message that he returned the call. Both messages were from two former members of the Office of Security, he thought. At first he didn't think much about them calling during his absence, then he wondered what they wanted to discuss.

His curiosity was tempered when he thought maybe both men were looking for part-time work, knowing he has attracted USAID contracts since leaving the Agency.

As he sat back in his chair, he thought that anyone from the Office of Security, short of the Deputy Director of Administration, may have difficulty getting work in the security world because of their reputation as being in-house finks. As he thought, he remembered that Billy-Ray was from the Office of Communications, maybe they had something concerning Billy-Ray they wanted to share with him. Just then the phone rang. It was Adriana, she reported receiving a telephone call from Chris Allen. "The woman sounded sincerely upset although she assured me that she was able to obtain the tapes from the safe-deposit box, but then she informed me that she discovered a mysterious twenty-thousand dollars in her account. The money was electronically deposited this morning and the source unknown. She checked with the bank officials and they reassured her the transaction was legitimate and the deposit originated from the Chase Manhattan Bank, New York. It was sent by persons unknown and the transaction number was traced to a non-customer of the bank. No names available.".

Bridges smiled to himself and didn't immediately share his suspicions with Adriana right away. He asked her what she thought, and she acted dumfounded. "It sounds familiar but I'll reserve my opinions, then he decided to lay it on the line. He explained that it sounded government and who ever sent the money knew James Allen was dead.". "Richard what now?". "Get the tapes, it's my hunch she'll continue to receive cash deposits equaling her husbands's annual salary for an indefinite period. CIA or FBI procedures is my guess. If it's either of them, or maybe ATF, the money will continue until she remarries."

"When will she know her husband is dead?"

"No telling...she'll figure it out as the money continues and her husband doesn't return."

"Those cold bastards, the money isn't going to heal Chris' feeling...ever."

"You're right, but the money will allow her to live a normal life without her husband, not taken into account her feelings. I agree it's cold, but what would you do...tell her, apologize, and allow her to collect the life insurance policy, at the same time leading her to believe her husband died as a hero in the line of duty for the United States without compensation. This way, she'll become accustomed to the money and later, much later, she will be informed by some government lacky. Besides, how do they explain her husband being in Michael's casket?"

"Do we want to know more?"

"Adriana, I'm not sure...more might hurt us, or more may help us, it all depends why an NSA employee died. I'm almost afraid to find out, especially if his death is connected to our project."

"Richard...I'm on my way over to meet Chris, she'll provide them with the tapes, then what?"

"Let's meet at my place and listen to them."

Adriana agreed and explained that she would have to go to the White House before they met at the farm. Bridges indicated he understood her reasons and went about his business. He felt comfortable sitting in his favorite chair and experiencing the quiet with the exception to the wind blowing, causing the old farm house to creak. He could hear the horses in the barn, although it wasn't an alarming sound, it was their way of communicating with each other. He dozed off while sitting behind his nineteenth century desk. The phone rang, waking him, at first he seemed disoriented. He answered, it was Adriana informing him that she would be at his place, although she needed directions. Bridges provided the easiest direction he could after repeating them at least three times.

While waiting for Adriana, his daughter came into the house sounding alarmed. He immediately asked what was wrong. "Daddy, I was followed again, I was able to get the license number of the car and the description of the man. He's a student at the school, I've seen him on campus, he looks at me strange and gives me the creeps."

Without hesitation, Bridges called Tom and passed on the information concerning the incident with his daughter. Tom reassured Bridges they would get right on it and that he would see to it that the young man won't bother Jennifer again. Jennifer felt better, although she knew most of the Arab students liked blond girls, they were obsessed with them.

Adriana called to inform Bridges that she had the tapes and completed her business at the White House. She would be at the farm in thirty minutes providing the traffic wasn't too-heavy. As Bridges hung the phone up, hew noticed his message machine light was blinking. He hadn't noticed it before. He played the message. Pleasantly, he was surprised it was Charlie calling from the Israeli Embassy. The message was simple, he was to return Charlie's call at the embassy. He immediately called the Israeli Embassy and requested to speak to Charles Goldberg. The receptionist informed Bridges that no one by that name was there. Immediately Bridges recalled Charlie's Israeli name, he then requested to speak to David Halim. Charlie answered in a cheerful voice. "How the hell are you Richard?"

Bridges was taken back with him being able to talk to Charlie after the Commander made a big thing out of them not being in contact with each other while in the DC area.

"I'm great Charlie, why the change in plans?"

"The plans are not changed, just modified because I discovered you need our help. Is your phone clean?"

"I'm not sure, I feel certain. I had it checked by the Metropolitan Police a few days ago. They're checking it daily, I hope. What's up?"

"I like to talk to you about several things, and we must maintain confidential relations by alkl means."

Bridges sensed that Charlie ment not to shyare the information with Adriana. "You're more then welcome to come to the farm, Adriana will be here in a few minutes. She's agreed to stay for dinner, I'd like you to come."

"I need to talk to you alone, not in the presence of Adriana. We have some interesting information, but we will talk later. I can tell you the cash in the woman's account is from us, well not exactly the Israeli Government. Can we meet at the embassy at ten in the morning, just you and me? Please don't tell Adriana about the meeting

"I'll be there my friend, ten…sharp."

Adriana arrived, she had a strange look on her face. Bridges offered her a scotch, she accepted and then explained that the tapes were blank. "After I left the White House I decided to play the tapes on my car tape deck." She went on to explain the tapes were blank. Bridges suggested they attempt to play them on his tape-player, discovering also the tapes were blank. It was his guess the tapes were new and never used. Bridges looked at her, and then thought about Charlie wanting to meet with him alone. He was suspicious. Adriana interrupted his thought by asking if he received any additional information since last they spoke. It was obvious that Bridges was upset over the blank tapes. "When you received the tapes from Chris, where did you keep them?"

"In my purse, I didn't let it out of my sight the entire time I was at the White House. I was only there less than thirty minutes. I had a brief conversation with Heidi and agreed to return to the office in a day or so and that I would call her and let her know for sure. She thinks I was stressed out, that's the reason I went on my trip. The tapes were always with me, even when I went to the rest room."

"What the hell is going on? Was Chris in a strange mood when she gave you the tapes, with the exception of finding that money in her bank account?"

"No, other than she was puzzled over the money situation."

Bridges thought he would change the subject and told Adriana about his daughter being stalked by an Arab kid at the university.

"Richard do you think it's serious?"

"I don't know, I turned it over to Tom's office, hopefully he nip it before it gets out of hand. Jennifer complained that the kid followed her to her part time job over at the State Department annex. It's serious enough to scare my daughter, she's not easy to scare."

They went into the kitchen from the warm comfortable family room. The temperature outside was dropping, fall was in the air. The time of the year Bridges liked. Adriana helped Jennifer with the dinner. They seemed to get along good. Bridges looked at them together and knew certain that Jennifer missed her mother very much. For the moment she was enjoying the company of another woman. Jennifer spoke of her new baby-colt and the plans she had for him. He would soon turn true black and his coat would shine. Adriana seemed interested, although Bridges knew she had many other things on her mind.

After dinner, Adriana decided to leave. She promised to call Bridges the following afternoon. He walked her to her car. She asked again what his thoughts were concerning the blank tapes. Bridges wanted to stall her until he had a chance to talk to Charlie in the morning. After Adriana got into her car, he reached down to kiss her. She then drove off.

As Bridges entered the house, the phone rang. It was Adriana calling from her car. "Richard I'm sorry I wasn't much company tonight, I share your disappointment over the tapes. Please forgive me for not being good company, you know we'll resolve this thing. She said goodnight. Bridges was concerned as to why Charlie wanted to meet alone.

Bridges arrived at the Israeli Embassy before ten. Charlie was at the receptionists desk when he entered the main entrance. Charlie greeted him with a warm brotherly welcome. They had coffee in a private office. Charlie led the conversation by informing him that they believed Adriana has a separate agenda. "I don't mean to imply she want's the President assassinated, although it is well know throughout the intelligence community that she doesn't like him and she hates the First Lady, even though she works for her. We strongly suggest you be cautious until you're convinced she's not plotting to kill the President or anyone else. If she's plotting, she's using you to point out her mistakes without you knowing. But I don't want to sound alarming about her, she is still our friend and many people in high places respect her."

Bridges sat quiet, listening to Charlie. He looked around the scarcely furnished office and thought it was hostelry set up for Charlie's use as long as he was at the embassy. "How good is your information?"

"The information is only speculation, no evidence, at least that would fly in the face of justice. But she certainly driven. What's your thoughts?"

"I have none, I have been suspicions, they come and go. Nothing tangible. I want to trust her, but I hesitate, even before you mentioned it. An example yesterday she retrieved tapes from Chris Allen's wife, a totally different story. She was successful in obtaining two tapes but they turned out blank." Bridges noticed a silly look come over Charlie's face as he spoke. He knew Charlie wanted to interrupt him, so he took a breather.

"Richard, we got the tapes…matter of fact we know of James Allen and his wife. The money she found in her account today was from us. We know all about the disappearance of Michael Myers. Listen, Michael and James were working for us, the CIA as well as the FBI.

The FBI has used both men for the domestic terrorist activities. Those idiots lost control of the situation and that's the reason why James Allen is dead. They cooked up the idea to put Allen in the casket and call him Michael Myers. We agreed to help the widow after we met with your people. I don't know when she'll be told about her husband, maybe never if Michael Myers shows up dead. The money comes from your government. The woman can't collect the life insurance on her husband until his death is verified, this can be done but it won't because of Michael Myers. We think he's out of the country, then he may be hiding out in New York or New Jersey. Some planners think he's being used as a bargaining chip for things to come. We can say for sure the communications between him and the FBI is severed.

"What the hell is going on Charlie?"

"Your guess is as good as mine. I can tell you that your friend Billy-Ray, has been taken care of, he's over. It was learned that he and a renegade Mossad agent were dealing weapons with the Iraqis. I'm sure as I sit here talking, upon his return to the Middle East, Billy Ray will get killed in the line of duty, the poor bastard."

Ignoring the last comment by Charlie, Bridges didn't want to know, he changed the subject "You mentioned the tapes?"

"Let's listen to them, I'll have a Spanish translator help us. I must admit the President's wife speaks damn good Spanish and Adriana does as well."

Both men entered a sound proof room designed for communication work. The room had a low-dropped overhead and two-way mirrors on two of the walls. In the room there were monitors and stop-action recorders. Charlie arranged for a Spanish translator to meet them in the sound room. As the first tape was turned on, Bridges noticed there were count down signals authenticating the tape that was being played was recorded by NSA. The Spanish translator informed both men that the woman identified as Heidi has proposed a proposition with the Spanish speaking woman assuring her automatic citizenship and a large sum of American money if she's successful in the proposed project. Most of which was translated amounted to a promise of citizenship for the woman and her daughter with certain provisoes, although the project had to be completed before the turkey was cooked.

Immediately, Bridges looked over at Charlie and commented. "It sounds like Thanksgiving is the dead-line."

Charlie smiled and then agreed. The translator explained that both woman were speaking about small children and the Spanish speaking woman spoke of her daughter as being an infant. Bridges had met the woman's daughter and she was at least ten-eleven years old. Right away Bridges thought the conversation was cryptic, understood only by both woman. The remainder of the tape between Heidi and the Spanish speaking woman discussed cooking receipts that are unique to Central America.

The tape recording that contained Adriana's conversation with the same woman involved an agreement to meet Los Angeles. No mention of money or specific dates. Adriana agreed to meet with the woman in Los Angeles as soon as she received direction from Heidi. Adriana sounded excited to meet the woman. As the tape continued, there was a blank spot. The translator looked at Charlie for approval to shut the recorder off. Charlie shook his head NO. The tape arrived at a point where there were other recorded calls. One in particular was Adriana talking to the White House travel office making reservation for her trip to Amman. Then another blank spot…in a few seconds appeared Heidi's voice talking to an older man. Charlie had the call traced to Reno, Nevada. Their conversation didn't amount to much, however Charlie learned the man was a 'money' broker. In simple terms, the man provided illicit untrascable amounts of cash. They replayed the part again and discovered Heidi spoke of numbers. The only deduction was that the numbers represented dollars. Charlie allowed the tape to continue until Spanish speaking conversations between Heidi and the same woman in El Salvador, although the conversation involved the woman's trip to Los Angeles. The woman protested having to stay with relatives in South Central Los Angeles. Heidi sounded as though she was at the mercy of the woman when she consented to arrangements for the woman and her daughter to stay with people in the Brentwood area of Los Angeles. The woman immediately protested again…clearly refusing to do domestic work.

Heidi became aggressive and insisted she had to do something to prevent people from getting suspicious. The woman settled down when she understood, and then agreed with Heidi's suggestion, the tape went blank. as it was allowed to play further, there were sounds of calls made, although no connection. Charlie had the dialed numbers traced to a wealthy couple in West Los Angeles, the Brentwood area. A day later, according to the date signals on the tape recording, Heidi managed to reach the woman in Brentwood. The conversation was innocent. Heidi requested her friend Julia to hire a domestic and allow her to live at her home with her nine year old daughter. The woman at first hesitated, then agreed to hire Rosa Carrea Gonzales as a domestic. The rest of the conversation amounted to old-friend conversation, nothing of any consequence. The last call on the tape was a call to Immigration Nationalization Services. Heidi spoke to the Director and strongly suggested he process papers allowing Rosa Carrea Gonzales and her daughter Maria to become citizens in record time. The tone of voice indicated the director attempted to protest, Heidi wouldn't allow it or even hear him protest. She then provided the necessary information the Director would need to expedite the woman and her daughter's papers. Once completed, she directed the approved papers to be sent to her by courier

After the translator left the room, Bridges sighed and commented. "The only thing we have is a violation of the immigration laws, and that's a joke in any-ones eyes. And then Adriana, I doubt that she's involved in a plot to assassinate the President. I think she means what she said, but I must admit, she's over her head in many ways. I'll continue to be captious." Charlie smiled, as he nodded his head. "You could be right, maybe we're too hasty in our assessment of her by the tapes, after all, the information came from a translator. Let' not lose sight of the fact that Adriana still believes Heidi had something to do with her husband's death some ten years ago."

Bridges reminded Charlie about the 'money-man' on the tape. "That's a lead Charlie, but with the mumble-jumble talking to a suspected money laundry man, doesn't say an assassination is in the winds…it only suggests heidi is attempting to obtain untracable funds, maybe to finance her husband's re-election campaign. Do you think there are other tapes out there?"

Charlie always being cautious, smiled and informed Bridges that he read his mind. "Judging from the date signals on the tapes…there must be other tapes out there, but where?"

As Bridges thought, the only place is at the Allen house, he recalled that Chris mentioned that her husband often worked in the basement of their townhouse, transforming reel-to-reel tapes to cassettes. "Charlie, the Allen house…how can we convince Chris to allow us access to her husband's workshop. If she knew he was dead, she may agree, thinking we're looking for her husband's killers. What's your thought?"

"Richard…you don't want to know what I'm thinking…because it's against the law.".Bridges was grateful for Charlie obtaining the tapes. "By the way, you never mentioned how you came-by the tapes?"

"Again Richard…it's a secret." Then he smiled like a cat that swallowed a mouse.

Charlie provided a copy of the tapes and agreed to get back with Bridges later that day. Bridges decided to go over to Tom's office and review the photographs that were taken at Michael's funeral.

Both men sat in one of the interview room away from the busy traffic in police headquarters. As they examined the photographs that had been enlarged to 11 X 14, Tom was able to identify several of the woman as employees at the Treasury Department and wives of members of his Kwainis Club. Bridges was quick to point out that most in attendance were woman, the only men that were present were possibly FBI and relatives. The Bureau people stuck out like sore thumbs. Bridges was able to locate Adriana standing next to Michael's mother and father. Chris Allen was there and Bridges couldn't find Michael's girlfriend, Joanne Walker in the photographs. He thought it was peculiar and then remembered the telepathic incident he experienced with her. Bridges immediately called Adriana and asked if she remembered seeing Joanne Walker at the funeral. Adriana explained that she was at the house after the funeral and didn't recall seeing her at grave-side. To satisfy Adriana, Bridges informed her that he and Tom were reviewing the photos taken at the funeral. This seemed to appease her, although he recalled she initially objected to the idea.

With Tom's permission, Bridges made another call. When he asked to speak to Justice Castilli, he looked over at Tom and winked. Tom smiled and recalled they were all in the Corps together. Bridges was unsuccessful in talking to Paul Castilli and left a message for him to return his call at his home that evening. As soon as Bridges hung the phone up, Tom commented. "What the hell are to calling Paul for, there's not much he can do since he became a member of the Supreme

Court. I hear he's changed since Reagan appointed him God, he doesn't have time for us old friends."

Bridges smiled, then responded. "He'll have time for me…damn it, I need to consult him on various thinks. Besides I heard after his wife died, he briefly dated Adriana. When he hears I'm her beau he'll be willing to talk to me out of curiosity. I've socialized with him before he was appointed to the high-court, he's okay, still thinks he's a ladies man. Adriana assured me they were never intimate.

Tom expressed his dislike for members of the Supreme Court. "It didn't matter what political party they came from, they still politic as though their jobs were on the line, and we know they're there for life. Some of those Godly decisions they make scare hell out of me."

Even though Bridges agreed, he didn't add to Tom's comments. "Tommy, I need your help on this project hopefully you won't back out…I don't mean actually back out, I mean simply object to who we may have to deal with in order to prevent the assassination of the President."

"Richard…damn it, you know me…I'll be with you until the end, so help me. It's just that a cop is dirt beneath their feet, that's my feelings and I can't change them."

"Look at you Tommy, you're a Captain in charge of the most important division in this department, what else do you want…the chief's job?"

"Hell no…I wouldn't take that job if it was forced on me. You know the first time you came over from Langley to help us was ten years ago. Do you remember?". "I sure do…it involved one of your trusted narcotic enforcement officers that went bad…the poor bastard, but i recall you resented the information because you took a liken to the youngster, I recall he came from a nice quiet black family over in Baltimore. He was a good cop until he was bitten by dope. I didn't know if you resented me because I was CIA or I told you something you didn't want to know."

"It was both…but it reacquainted us as friends…didn't it?"

"Damn straight my friend."

As both men went over the rest of the funeral photos, Bridges noticed a man-figure near a tree in the distance. He pointed to the image and Tom agreed that it appeared the figure had been watching the funeral from a distance. Bridges then committed himself. "I recognize the man…can your lab people improve on the image at the same time enlarge it to at least 4 x 5."

They waited for the lab to produce the enlargement of the male figure in the distance. In thirty minutes the lab technician returned with several copies of the figure. Bridges looked at the image and made his statement. "Tommy my man…that's Michael Myers in the distance. So help me it is. Well my friend, it's true that a photograph is worth a thousand words. When I was assigned to OIA, the aerial photos of Castro's Missiles were clear to me. The Office of Imagery Analysis did a hell of a job back then. When I was there, things were antiquated, none of this computer photography. I'm sure they can improve on the image of Michael, could I borrow the negatives?"

The conversation turned to the tape that were provided by the Israelis. Tom clearly understood what procedure they went through to obtain the tape and commented it was out of his jurisdiction and he didn't care, as long as they got the tapes.

Bridges had to leave and thanked Tom for the help. As he was leaving, Tom remembered to tell Bridges that the Arab that was stalking his daughter is on his way back to Iran. Bridges smiled. "Jennifer will be happy to about it, thanks my friend, I owe you one."

"Richard is was our pleasure…have a good weekend…any plans?"

I'd like to see Paul first then Sunday Adriana is coming over to the farm. We plan to take ride in the countryside with the horses. She doesn't know I have the tapes, I have to tell her, I'm sure she'll want to listen to them."

CHAPTER 8
GOOD ADVICE

Bridges maneuvered his Jeep Cherokee methodically around golf carts as he made his way up the drive of Chevy Chase Country Club. Meeting at seven was the Judge's idea since he was scheduled to tee off at ten with a foursome made up of members of the Maryland Delegation. Bridges was thirty minutes early. Even back in the Corps, Paul Castilli had taken great pride in being punctual. And he expected everyone else to do the same.

The early morning air was chilly and a gentle wind blew autumn's leaves in swirls around Bridges' feet as he made his way to the clubhouse.

"Christ, I haven't seen you since Bill Casey's funeral." Bridges remarked when he found Paul waiting for him inside

"I should've guessed you'd already be here." They had both known Casey for years before he became the Director of the Central Intelligence Agency.

"It's good to see you, Richard…how the hell have you been?" Paul asked.

"Good. Very good, Paul"

The Judge led the way to a table overlooking the first hole where they ordered breakfast and caught up on Marine Corps gossip. They chatted like old friends who hadn't seen each other in quite some time.

But Bridges knew his Marine Corps buddy too well. Well enough to know he was about to bust at the seems with curiosity. Bridges seemed to take some personal enjoyment out of making the Judge wait for just the right moment before he announced why he wanted to see him. Like some game he might have played with Paul in the Corps.

After breakfast, Paul escorted Bridges to a private room reserved for club members, only. A place where card games were played and conversations considered sacred.

"So—Richard, you should be enjoying life a little easier now that you've left the Agency, or is that the problem?" Paul asked.

Bridges was sure he detected a sarcastic tone in the question.

"I couldn't be happier, Paul. Jennifer's about to finish at Georgetown and finish her graduate studies at Yale. She's grown into a beautiful young woman. Her mother would have been proud of her."

The Judge started to fidget and looked at his watch. Bridges knew he better get to the point. Maybe the Country Club wasn't the right place to discuss this particular topic, but it would have to do. Afterall, since they served in the same battalion in Viet Nam and Quantico, they had many conversations in strange places.

"I've heard you've been seeing Adriana Myers. She's a good woman—well respected. Beautiful, too. But then once a Marine always a Marine, right Richard?" The Judge laughed.

Bridges didn't find the comment humorous and made no comment.

"I'm not sure where to begin. It's complicated and extremely confidential. I need your cooperation and your word you won't reveal anything we discuss."

"Of course." The smile vanished from Paul's face as he suddenly realized that whatever brought Bridges to see him was of monumentous importance. He sat on the edge of his chair, slightly forward, elbows resting on his knees with his hands clasped together.

"Yes—I'm seeing Adriana, but it didn't start out that way. We met in the Middle East during my last contract. Later, I found out we had mutual friends at the Mossad. She came to me. Said she needed my help. At first, I didn't trust her, but then I found out she wasn't bullshitting me." Bridges paused for a moment. His face drawn and sober. He wondered how the Judge would handle what he was about to tell him.

"You've got my word. Anything you say will not leave this room." Paul promised.

"There's a plot to assassinate the President."

"Christ!" Paul whispered out-loud. "But why tell me? You should tell the FBI boys or the Agency."

"Get serious, Paul. Who the hell can anyone trust? There's powerful people involved in this. And if we break this open, well, prosecuting them is going to be…well, I don't need to spell it out for you?"

"Don't give me any names, at least right now." Paul warned. Personally, he didn't like the President, wasn't even qualified to clerk in his office, he thought. But this…this was heavy.

"You'll be surprised! There's an offshoot machine out there who's decided they can't use this President. He's inept…the worst." Bridges was composed as he unraveled the details to his old friend.

Paul listened as Bridges explained his theory on the assassination. Paul already knew about a movement to change the Constitution with as little public attention as possible. The media loved their antics, made good press. And this administration was saturated with incompetent, corrupt, and immoral individuals. But Paul already knew this.

"The Country's changing, Paul, and not for the better. Even the police aren't allowed to use the confessions obtained from criminal suspects. You sit on the highest bench in the land and you're hands are tied. I'm telling you, there's an offshoot machine with a long range plan and it doesn't include this President." Bridges didn't want to sound like some radical or extremist. He just wanted to make a point, but how much was the Judge hearing?

"You have an impeccable reputation, Richard, don't get too carried away. I realize it's difficult to trust anyone these days, but…"

"Thanks for the vote of confidence, Paul."

"Tell me, how does Adriana Myers fit into all this?"

"Adriana came to me and revealed what's going on. You know, of course, she works for the President's wife."

"Now there's a thorn in my ass..." The Judge stopped short of saying another word. He looked into Bridges' eyes. "You're not trying to tell me that she...or members of the President's staff..." Paul choked.

"I need your advice."

"Stay out of it—that's my advice. This is deep shit as we used to say in the Corps."

"You know me better than that, Paul." Bridges snapped back.

"Yes, I'm quite aware of your sense of duty to the American people. You've always been a patriot, Richard."

"That's what Tom Moore said."

"What the hell's Moore got to do with this?" The Judge asked with an element of surprise at the mention of Moore's name.

"He's the only one I trust outside of the Mossad." He knew he shouldn't have mentioned Tom. It was too late now. He remembered how the Judge recommended Moore for the Silver Star when they served in Viet Nam. But even then, they were never good friends. Tom's platoon got into a fire-fight with a company of NVA troops. Paul was the platoon leader and Tom had filled in as the platoon sergeant.

"I hear Tom's a big cop now with Metropolitan Police. Special Investigation Unit, right?" The Judge said sarcastically.

The comment angered Bridges but he didn't react.

"Moore was a sergeant in my unit. Da Nang in sixty-six. Seems like a hundred years ago."

"You recommended him for the Silver Star. Besides, he's been a friend to me and I need him as a contact. I can depend on him."

There was a sinister laugh from the Judge.

"I haven't been to the Agency since I returned from Tel Aviv." Bridges said, trying to get back to the topic.

"Stay away!" The Judge warned. "At least with this shit."

"I would like to see you—tomorrow afternoon—my home. We'll have an early dinner, and I'll give you some advice."

"Alright." Bridges said.

"Anything else?"

"No"

"Good. Now, maybe I can get on with my golfing?"

"Paul, what about Adriana? I mean, I want to trust her but…"

The Judge stood up and shook Bridges' hand, "See you tomorrow."

Glancing over his right shoulder, Bridges put the Jeep Cherokee in reverse but waited for a golfer to pass. He couldn't help but wonder why the Judge ignored his comment on Adriana. Suddenly, he focused on the elusive figure passing behind the Cherokee. It someone he recognized from the agency, the one who was assigned to Central America with him.

Bridges waved and tooted the horn. No response. He felt foolish until he remembered that when an agent leaves the Agency—he never existed, which he felt was bullshit.

He maneuvered the Cherokee down the club drive unable to avoid a shower of gold leaves as they fell from the trees. He wondered about Adriana. It was time to have a serious talk with her.

He was almost to the Beltway when he spotted Adriana's black Mercedes SL on the other side of the highway. At least it looked like Adriana's car. There were only a few like it in the area. Probably wasn't her, he thought.

Within a short time, he arrived at his farm. Bridges shut the Cherokee's ignition off and reached for his briefcase in the back seat. Through the rear window, he could see Jennifer and one of her friends down at the barn. It was the right decision to keep the horses after his wife died, he knew that now. Every time a new foal was born it was a miracle beyond explanation. And, it kept both Bridges and Jennifer busy.

He went directly to his study and called Tom Moore.

"Just thinking of you, Richard. From the looks of the weather, we're going to have snow for 'turkey day'." Tom commented.

"Yes…you're right. It looks that way, doesn't it." Bridges understood…before Thanksgiving, that's when it would happen.

Bridges told Tom of his meeting with Justice Castilli and that they would meet for dinner the next day.

"Figures." Tom commented.

"I spotted Adriana's car on the highway out near Chevy Chase Country Club. I'd like to know what the hell she's up to."

"You sure?" Tom inquired.

"Not too many cars like hers around". Bridges said. "By the way, any news for me?"

"No. Been too busy with administration shit." Tom could sense Bridges' mistrust for Adriana and his disappointment with Justice Castilli.

"How about breakfast Monday morning?"

"Sounds good, Tommy. Have a good weekend and get some rest, you may need it."

Bridges made a few calls to friends at the Agency. Nothing important, just small talk about changes at the Langley and McLean offices. He knew he might need the help of some of these guys and just wanted to keep in touch.

Reluctantly, he dialed Adriana's number.

"Hello, this is Adriana..." the machine echoed.

"Hell." Bridges said outloud. He left a message to call him, then settled back in the deep leather chair and looked out over the farm land from the window behind his desk. He liked the view. It was peaceful. Just fields of farm land and the trees in all their glorious color, for as far as the eye could see. He fell asleep.

Suddenly the phone rang.

"Hello."

"I'm returning your call." Adriana said.

"Thanks," he said, hoping she couldn't tell he had been napping, "I thought I saw you out by Chevy Chase Country Club this morning."

"You played golf without me?" Adriana laughed

"No. I had a breakfast meeting."

"Family business." Adriana didn't elaborate.

So it was her. The sharp tone of her voice made him wonder. Maybe there was some other reason she was in Maryland.

"Actually, I met Paul Castilli for breakfast before his round of golf."

"Productive, I hope".

"Yes. Invited me to dinner tomorrow at his house. Wants to talk privately. He thinks there's something between us?" Bridges said, as if he were asking a question.

Adriana laughed. "Paul and I go back a long way, before Reagan appointed him to the Supreme Court. And he's a great guy to have around during election time. I hope he's doing better. He was pretty devastated after his wife died."

"He's pretty shook over this information. Maybe more for his own hide than anything else."

"Are we still on for a ride through the Virginia countryside?" Adriana asked.

"You bet. Thought we'd have a breakfast first."

"I can hardly wait. Even bought some new pants."

Bridges laughed to himself. All women must be the same, he thought.

"Wonderful. Is six thirty too early?"

"No. I've had trouble sleeping and I'm sure I'll be awake anyway."

Bridges went to the barn to see what the girls were up to. Somehow, he wasn't surprised to see them still grooming and playing with the new colt. He told Jennifer about Adriana's visit the next morning and asked her to see that "Fire" was lunged out and the saddles were ready. The mare could be a handful at times, and he didn't want Adriana to get the wrong impression of Arabian horses.

"You know, the hair on that horse is going to fall out if you brush him anymore." He teased. The girls laughed and assured him they would get everything ready so all he and Adriana had to do was saddle up and leave.

"Don't worry, Dad. And I'll make dinner when I'm done." She shouted after him.

He went back to his study with the latest copy of the Washington Times and settled in behind his desk. There on the third page was an article about the body found at Union Station. He began to get angry. Why Tom hadn't told him, he wondered. Why did he have to read it in the paper? He picked up the phone and dialed Tom Moore's residence.

Tom's wife answered and quickly excused herself to get Tom.

"Richard, what can I do for you?" Tom asked.

"I just read the paper. What's this about having a suspect, and why didn't you tell me?" There was hostility in Bridges' voice.

"It's bullshit, Richard. Some asshole walked into the station and confessed. The sonofabitch just needed a place to sleep for the night. You know the press has access to the booking blotter and the shit-heads ran with a story."

"Sorry, I should've known."

"Calm down, Richard, you know I would've let you know if it was anything. By the way, I got the funeral photos after I spoke to you."

"What-cha-got?"

"Well, the lab people figured the distance from the grave site to the tree where we think Myers was standing, was about one hundred feet. Of course you know that camera had about a three hundred millimeter lens on it. It's a wonder no one recognized him standing there."

"Thanks, Tom. I think I should have a chat with Adriana in the morning—including these photos."

Before hanging up, Tom reminded Bridges about having dinner one night. His wife was looking forward to it.

Bridges returned to the paper. In the Society Section, there was a small article about Adriana Myers returning from a vacation in Amman, Jordan. Bridges smiled to himself as he wondered why the press hadn't printed that the two of them were having an affair. Afterall, they seemed to love that type of stuff.

Bridges finished his shower. He could smell bacon coming from the kitchen. He quickly put on his khaki riding breeches, white turtleneck and a spruce green pullover sweater, a birthday gift from Jennifer.

"Well, good morning ladies." He said, surprised to find Adriana had arrived and pitched in to help Jennifer with breakfast. In fact, she was on her second cup of coffee.

"Hello. We were wondering about you." Adriana said as she smiled softly.

"Is there a cup of coffee for an old farm hand?" He teased.

Adriana poured the coffee and was about to hand it to him when he leaned over and kissed her on her lips. She was surprised at the overt move, especially with Jennifer in the room. And when Jennifer turned slight and caught her about to return the kiss, Adriana blushed. Bridges winked at her and took the coffee and sat down.

"It's a good day for a ride." He tried to make light of the embarrassing moment, but found himself intrigued that Adriana could get flustered so easily.

There was a distinct chill in the morning air and snow clouds hovered overhead. Adriana struggled to hold her horse down to walk. Finally, she let her spirited mount canter hoping it would relieve the some of the horses energy. Bridges followed. There was a clump of trees about a mile over the hill. It would be a good place to dismount and give the horses a rest. And, it would be a good time to ask Adriana some questions.

"I think I need a rest." Adriana said as she jumped off her horse and tethered her to a branch. "Fire is in better shape than I am." She laughed

Bridges smiled and dismounted. He was a bit out of breath himself but hated to admit it. He found a spot on an old fallen log and sat down. Adriana joined him.

"Adriana…" He began.

"It's beautiful out here. Makes you forget the city and all your problems, doesn't it?" She was looking off at the hills rich with colors of red and gold, and there was the sound of a pheasant calling her mate. For the first time, Bridges saw her really relaxed. He hated to bring up business.

"Adriana, I need to discuss something important."

Instantly, her smile faded. She looked into Bridges' eyes as if waiting for him to continue.

"You're holding back. Maybe acting independent of me. I sense it. You haven't been honest with me, not even about the woman from El Salvador." Bridges was sick that he had to confront her this way. She was so beautiful, he thought, and he had to ruin her morning by talking business. But how else could he clear the air?

Adriana looked away and it was several minutes before she spoke.

"You're very perceptive, Richard." She said still not looking at him.

"I'm sure the woman from El Salvador and one of her friends are the ones who will assassinate the President."

But Bridges already knew this. What he didn't know was that there would be a second party involved. He waited and didn't say anything. Maybe Adriana was stalling.

"As I was driving over this morning, I knew I had to tell you. At first, I couldn't be sure."

"Sure? Sure of what? Bridges asked.

"These people in El Salvador were part of the death-squad. They'll do anything for money—anything. They're not afraid of dying, and that scares me."

There was a long silence.

"Anything else?" Bridges asked.

"After I returned from my trip, Heidi was different—distant. She took her calls in private where I couldn't hear, or told the party she would call back."

"You thought this was strange?" Bridges asked again.

"Yes, of course. Heidi never hid anything from me before, not even the calls from El Salvador. And she knows I speak Spanish." Adriana paused. "She's not speaking to the President, you know. They don't eat together or sleep together."

"Can't say I blame the old chap." Bridges laughed.

"I had hoped that incompetent bastard would've been impeached before someone blew him away. And Heidi, well…the bitch thinks she ought to be the president. It's all I can do to stay in the same room with her." Adriana's voice trembled as she spoke.

Bridges sat quietly and allowed Adriana release her bitterness.

"A few days ago they had a heated argument. The story buzzed by the staff is that Heidi threw a priceless vase, at the President. One from the Lincoln collection. Unfortunately, it missed him and shattered in a million pieces."

"And how do you know this woman from El Salvador will be the assassin?" Bridges asked.

"I flew to Los Angeles. Gave the woman cash and arranged for her to return to El Salvador without her daughter. I put it together from the things you've told me. Of course I have to do what Heidi asks."

Bridges was satisfied the explanation. He told her about Michael being in the photos at the funeral.

"Michael…at the funeral? Are you sure." Adriana seemed surprised.

Bridges explained the photos and promised to show them to her when they returned to the house.

A slight rain fell as the sun went behind the clouds as the two mounted their horses for the ride back to the farm. Adriana nudged the grey mare into a lope leaving Bridges behind.

"You better put a blanket on that horse and walk her down." Bridges growled when he got back to the barn minutes after Adriana.

Jennifer observed from an upstairs window and quickly put on a jacket to help Adriana.

Later, in Bridges' study, Adriana promised not to keep anything from him again. She pushed him back in his chair, leaned over and gently kissed his mouth. He held her close returned the kiss.

"Adriana—the photos…"

"Hell with the photos." And she kissed him again.

"You're going to get us into trouble, Lady." He whispered in her ear.

"Oh, I hope so." She whispered back.

Bridges reached for envelope containing the photos on the desk and Adriana got to her feet. He handed it to her.

"Where?" She asked unable to find the image.

Bridges pointed to a figure in the distance next to a tree.

"I don't think…" She paused as she examined the photo.

"Look at the blowup." He handed her another photo.

"And—look at this one. We have a more refined image."

"My God, Richard, you're right." Adriana sat for a long time starring at the photos. Her thoughts were full of all the events up until now. What did all this mean, she wondered.

It was later when Adriana used Jennifer's room to shower and change clothes. Bridges remained in his study to phone the Agency.

"Please connect me to Jerry Thompson." Bridges asked the receptionist. He went through two more people before getting through.

"Gerald Thompson!" The voice announced.

"Mister…T, Jerry, it's Richard."

"Hey, I was wonderin' when you would get around to calling' me. Word has it you're so involved with Adriana Myers that you don't have time for any of your friends."

"News travels fast." Bridges joked. "How are things over there?" Bridges asked.

"Good, now that we've exposed the mole. Those ass-holes in the Office of Security almost caused us the case. Shit, they had enough evidence to nail him long ago, just drug their asses. And if that wasn't enough, those FBI bastards bullshitted us about having the guy under surveillance for a year. Don't get me started. What can I do for you?"

"You guys are hiring?" Bridges asked.

"Don't tell me you're looking for work?" Jerry teased.

"No, no. Just have a friend in mind."

"Actually, we're cutting back. The only active program we have involved the college group you started before you left. It's a good deal for a kid to work here at 'Tech Services' while they complete graduate school. Why the interest?"

"I met a young American woman with dual citizenship. Works for the Mossad but she's returning to the States to graduate school. Looking for a career job."

"Should've known there was a woman involved." Jerry teased.

"Just an acquaintance." The thought that he was some kind of Romeo was getting on Bridges' nerves.

"The dual citizenship might be a little tricky. We'll take it one step at a time. What about a polygraph? Could she pass with the clowns in security?"

"She'd do fine. Comes from a good family, father's a prominent lawyer in California." "I'll personally take care of her."

"Thanks." Bridges said.

"What about Jennifer? Think she might be interested in the program?"

Bridges didn't answer and wondered whether or not to level with Jerry.

"What's on your mind, Richard? I know you too well old buddy."

"I need advice. I'd like to meet with you—unofficially, that is."

"Sure, just say when."

"Late Monday afternoon—your office?"

"Good. Security's tight ever since the shooting incident. Park in VIP, and if any of those security cops fuck with ya, let me know. It'll be good seeing you."

"See you Monday." Bridges penciled the appointment in his book.

It was exactly four when Bridges pulled up in front of Justice Castilli's home. It was almost dark and he found himself jumping puddles left by the afternoons storm to reach the front door.

"Richard, get in here before you float away." The Judge had a spirited tone to his voice, quite unlike his mood the day before. He took Bridge's coat and hung it on the hall-tree.

"If it comes down any harder, we'll have to get the boat out." He laughed and led the way to a sitting room. Two oversized leather chairs flanked each side of a leather sofa set right in the middle of the room. An afghan draped neatly across the seat of one chair made a perfect resting spot for the big black Persian cat who occupied it. A miniature law library, Bridges thought.

"Thought any more about our discussion yesterday?" Bridges asked getting right to the point.

"It's had me so God damn upset." The Judge growled as he poured his favorite premium single malt scotch into two etched crystal glasses.

"Just what exactly is the relationship between you and Adriana?"

"Adriana followed me to Israel. When we met and she gained my trust, she told me about the plot to assassinate the President. Why, just this morning she told me who she suspected as being the assassin."

"No, no!" The Judge snapped. "Don't give me any names, yet. Just brief me."

"For God's sake, Paul, I can't explain this without mentioning names. That is the entire point. Put your position aside for a moment. Trust me—anything we discuss is strictly confidential. Christ, you were a hell of a prosecutor when you served as U.S. Attorney, and no one objected to you when you were a Federal Judge. You can't play it safe anymore. I'm laying this at your feet and you can't ignore it. Let's get down and dirty."

"Okay, okay, just a little cautious. You understand Richard. Now, if you want advice from me, I need all the facts—don't hold back. Another scotch?"

Bridges accepted the offer. He looked at the pictures on the wall while Paul poured the drinks. There was a lot of Marine Corps memorabilia and photos of Paul with his platoon in Vietnam. He found a picture of he and Paul standing next to an armed personnel carrier. It had belonged to the Engineer Battalion where they stayed when they were on stand-down after spending days in the field. He couldn't help notice the frame box containing Paul's medals and rank insignias. His Marine Corps emblems from his dress blues were even framed. It was a comfortable room, obviously Paul's cat thought so.

"Lots of memories." Bridges said as he took the scotch from Paul. "I remember when your platoon was pinned down with NVA fire and we went in and rescued you."

There was a silence in the room and for a moment, their thoughts were synchronized as they remembered those lost in that awful war. Bridges' eyes filled.

"We lost a lot." Paul said. "I only pray to God we learned from it."

Bridges wanted to change the subject. He often wondered how anyone involved in that war handled their memories. Did they put them on a wall like Paul, or away in a box. His way was to put all mementos and pictures away, only to be looked at when he felt strong enough to handle the pain that surfaced. But how do you live in a room surrounded by pictures of lost friends, boys barely old enough to leave home. They were gone.

"They're gone, Paul, thousands of them. And for what? Some God damn political game, I know that now. We should've won that war. Bridges' voice was bitter

"You're right. Heaven help the boys under this President's command."

"And here we are, tryin' to save his fuckin' ass."

"Yes, but if he's blown away, history will change and I'm not sure it will be for the good of this country. That's why we have to stop this attempt." The Judge urged.

Bridges sipped his scotch and began to unravel the assassination attempt as he saw it. He told Paul about the woman from El Salvador and that he was sure she was a member of a death squad. When things got hot in El Salvador, she came to the United States with her daughter to live with relatives in Los Angeles. Then he told him about Adriana and how she gave the woman a large sum of cash. And about Michael Myers who was found dead at Union Station, and the twist of events that followed. Fingerprints had verified the body belonged to that of James Allen.

"Slow down, Richard. Did you say that Adriana Myers hired the assassin?"

"She was directed to give a certain amount of cash to the woman but thought it was for some project Heidi Shepard was involved with."

"Jesus." The Judge mumbled.

"This is where I'm having problems. I have a tape recording made by NSA or actually, James Allen. It is of Heidi, Adriana and the woman from El Salvador, and they are speaking Spanish. Let me tell you what I suspect."

"Go on, Richard, I'm listening."

"Adriana uncovered the plot. While dealing with the woman, she got an idea to assemble her own plot, by blowing away either the First Lady whom she hates, or either both of them. That would leave the seat vacant for the Vice President who would probably be impeached before raising his right h and. If this scenario is correct, we have members of Congress who will need to be dealt with in open court or tried as criminals. And they'll be several others asked to resign without any benefits."

"Where are the tapes now?" The Judge asked.

"The originals are safe at the Israeli Embassy. The tape of Heidi Shepard talking to the woman in el Salvador is not that incriminating, and nothing Adriana said can be interpreted as criminal in nature. These tapes were made by accident. Seems some of the numbers at the

White House were to be changed and a few people assigned to the communication section from NSA were involved. James Allen was one of those people. He didn't know what he had until he listened to the tapes. Allen knew Adriana was related to Michael Myers, that's why he made copies then destroyed the reel-to-reel tapes."

"Any Republicans in the Congress involved?"

"That's the odd part. They're all from the President's own party."

"I see why you've been so uptight."

"If anyone on the Hill is involved, I'm going to find out about it. I need your advice."

"I need some time to think this through, to figure out options. I can't just be shooting from the hip on this one. If anything happened to the President, I want to be prepared. They'll be asking my advice on how to handle the conspirators. You understand.?"

"Of course."

"I can't give you any quick answers. It'll appear you're trying to overthrow the Government. Besides, they'll be the media to contend with."

"I didn't come here tonight expecting you to have all the answers. Take some time to think about this...but not too much time."

Bridges returned home much later. It was good that he lived not far from Justice Castilli. After a lasagna dinner, they downed two bottles of Italian wine, a gift to Paul.

Several messages had been left while he was out. A couple from Adriana, someone looking to buy an Arabian horse, and another inviting him to a dinner party. He called Adriana and she asked him to call her the next day at the White House. The other calls could wait, and he said goodnight to Jennifer who was still up and working on a research paper for school.

Early the next morning Bridges met Tom for breakfast at a favorite restaurant near his office.

"How it go with Paul last night?" Tom asked.

"He needs time to think this over before giving any advice. Said he'll get back to me in a day or two."

"In the old days, he'd have told you what to do right then and there." Tom laughed. "But, with his position I can see he has to be more cautious. Off the record, did he say what he thought?"

"No. He's too cautious. Paul's a brilliant guy and I can't remember him ever being wrong about anything." Bridges said. "With the exception of one thing."

The waitress cleared away their breakfast dishes and filled their coffee cups again.

"Richard…" Tom paused.

"What is it?" Bridges asked somewhat puzzled.

"I think Allen's death had something to do with the World Trade Center bombing or…."

"Or what?" Bridges asked impatiently.

"Or he knew too much about the plot to assassinate the President. I'm convinced the tapes are the connection. The fucken FBI's responsible for the body switch—I'm sure of it. They're screw-in'g with us…with-holding' information and other shit. I'm gonna have to put some pressure on the bastards." Tom's voice quivered with anger. He had hated the FBI for years. This hadn't been the only situation where the Bureau refused to work with Tom's Department. He was tired of the games—the incompetency. But most of all…their corrupt ways of doing things.

"You're right—they'll give you shit only when they no longer need it. Remember the CIA mole…the Ames case? The Bureau told the press they had Ames under surveillance for two years…pure bullshit, my friend."

"The bastards don't know we matched fingerprints. We've led them down the path thinking they have us bullshitted into believing the body was Myers. I might be able to use it as leverage."

"Hoover may have been a faggot, but he had things jumping."

Bridges used Tom's cellular phone to call Adriana at the White House as she directed. The White House operator put him through to her without hesitation. Adriana explained she had something interesting to discuss and they agreed to meet at the farm later in the day, after his meeting with Jerry Thompson. There was no reaction from Adriana, no questions about Jerry Thompson, and they said goodbye. After walking Tom to his office, Bridges went home. There were calls to return before his meeting with Thompson.

It was two fortyfive when Bridges arrived at CIA Headquarters, passing through the gate without incidence and parking in the VIP lot as suggested. Bridges went in the entrance, as he had done so many times in the past. He remembered his first day on the job, but this time, for some reason, he was apprehensive. He smiled at the very attractive black woman who passed him. She stopped.

"Do I know you, Sir?" She asked.

"No, not really. I used to work here. I'm here for a meeting with Jerry Thompson…Technical Services."

"Jerry's my boss." She said with a smile. Then she assisted him in obtaining a visitor's pass and directed him to a reception area where an older woman sat behind a desk. She informed him that Mr. Thompson was on the phone and asked him to have a seat.

Within moments, Jerry Thompson appeared. Bridges stood and shook hands with his old friend then went to Jerry's office where the older woman shut the door after they went inside.

"It's good to see you, Richard. Have a seat and tell me what's on your mind." Jerry motioned to a chair in front of his desk.

"I need advice. Strictly confidential." Bridges stated, feeling somewhat uncomfortable at having to repeat the situation. But he needed help.

"Something's got you uptight, man. Relax. We'vechanged a little since your days. Security's still tight, but the office isn't bugged." Jerry chuckled trying to make Bridges more comfortable.

Taking a deep breath, "What if I told you about a plot to assassinate the President. What if the persons behind it were members of Congress and the instigator was the First Lady. And what if I told you there was an agenda to tamper with the Constitution, to change it without the people ever being aware of what hit them. And last, what if I told you this shit is already in motion" Bridges looked directly at Jerry waiting for his reaction.

Jerry smiled from behind the large desk. He didn't seemed surprised. On the contrary, his reaction almost disappointed Bridges.

"And what if I told you, Richard, that crap like that has cycled around Washington ever since that poor excuse for a President took office."

"I realize what you're saying. But Jerry, this is happening—I'm in the middle of it, trying to prevent from happening."

"Off the record…let it happen. I hope he gets his ass blown away. But on the record…you better come in here with some pretty strong factual evidence. I know you're wondering who you can trust. And the answer, my friend, is I don't know. Who the hell can be trusted with this?"

Bridges sat back in the leather chair and stared at his long time friend…

CHAPTER 9
THE IDENTITY

Adriana glanced down at the clock on the dash as she turned down the road leading to Bridges' farm. It was six thirty and she was pleased in spite of the weather, she made it in good time. The rhythm of the windshield wipers had long since drowned out the sound of the radio and Adriana was involved with her thoughts to keep her company. She shook her head in disgust as she though how some of the staff members sought refuge in her office earlier that day. One by one, they came to her with their complaints of how an arrogant Heidi had come through the office bellowing out orders and how she deliberately humiliated two women in the presence of White House correspondents. Heidi had a way of making you hate her right from the start.

Suddenly, Adriana's Mercedes hit a rut. A gush of water momentarily blinded her as the wipers worked at full force trying to rid themselves of the muddy mess. She could hear her heart pounding, tapping the brakes gently, a little at a time. The rain was intense and for a moment, she even wondered if she was on the right road. Then, just ahead, she spotted the column of bricks housing the mailbox. On top was a tan sign with dark green letters that read 'Bridlewood Farms, Breeders of Arabian Horses'. It had been one of Bridges' summer projects to take down the old mailbox and make a column of bricks to house the box. He designed the sign himself and made locally. Adriana teased him about going to work as a handy man if all else failed. She laughed to herself as she remembered. She turned down the drive still tapping the brakes lightly. There, only a few feet beyond the brick column, her headlights caught glimpse of a parked car. She didn't notice if anyone was inside but the fact that it was there startled her. She wondered if someone had lost their way. On a night like this it would have been easy. Adriana thought.

Adriana drove past that part of the drive which made a half circle in front of the house then wound its way back to the road. Instead, she parked behind the house, close to the barn where the lights were on. After tightening the belt of her London Fog rain coat, she snapped open her umbrella. Each puddle created its own challenge and she dodged them one at a time until she reached the barn door.

"Hello—Jennifer? Are you in here?" She hollered. Soft nickers and whinnies echoed in answer. Then silence except for the perpetual chomping of the horses feasting on their alfalfa.

Dodging the puddles, she made her way to the back door of the house, trying not to get any wetter than she already was. The rain was blowing sideways and she struggled with the umbrella. Now only a few feet from the back door of the house, she looked up and noticed a shimmer of light coming from the car parked on the road. She paused for a moment and watched. There was an elusive figure behind the wheel. She shivered—but not from the cold.

She knocked on the door—harder, all the while calling Jennifer's name. Her heart pounded. Why didn't they answer?

"Adriana!" Jennifer opened the door a little surprised anyone would have gone clear around to the back of the house. "Come in, come in, you're getting soaked." She said as she reached out and took hold of Adriana's arm trying to hurry her inside.

Adriana explained the light in the barn and how she thought Jennifer had been out there. The girl took her coat and umbrella and hung them neatly on an old hall tree perched in a corner of the back porch. Obviously put there to hold things you throw on in a hurry when the weather was inclimate or if you were going to be working with the horses. She couldn't help notice the contrast of her London Fog next to the stable jackets already hanging there. It was an innocent mistake, one she probably wouldn't have made if her mother was still alive to teach her proper etiquette. She smiled to herself deciding not to say anything, and followed Jennifer to the family room. The fire was warm against Adriana's cold hands and she rubbed them together briskly to get the feeling back in them.

"I thought I heard voices out here." Bridges said as he appeared from his study. "Adriana, how 'bout something to warm you?"

"Scotch please. Single malt...Dalwhinne if you have it—and make it a double...thank you, Richard."

"I think I like a lady who knows her scotch." Bridges teased.

Jennifer excused herself to return to her room where she was working on a paper for one of her classes. Bridges handed Adriana a beautifully etched crystal glass containing the spirit then settled in a leather monstrosity he called 'his' chair which he had strategically placed next to the nineteenth century fireplace he had rebuilt out of field stones used by the original owners over a hundred years ago.

He was obviously proud of the old farm house with its history dating over two hundred years because he made it habit of telling everyone who came to visit. He was especially proud that he had rebuilt much of the sagging structure adding all modern day conveniences. The barn had been no exception and was actually his first project after moving to the place some ten years ago. The family room contained two overstuffed sofas facing each other in front of the fireplace. And there were photographs of Bridges and Jennifer everywhere, recent pictures probably taken on some of their vacations together. One wall was completely dedicated to the horses—trophies, ribbons, pictures. There were pictures of horses alone, horses with Jennifer and Bridges, Jennifer riding. It was their passion and she understood. Adriana put her hands closer to the flames still trying to take away the chill.

"Are you alright?" Bridges asked.

"Rough day." She answered. I had more than enough complaints about Heidi—I hit a bad rut in the road—and then got paranoid over the car parked down the drive out front..." She hardly finished when Bridges got up and made his way to the back door grabbing a jacket off the old hall tree as he fled out the door. Habit she supposed and she followed him

"Secret Service come with you?"

"No, they notified me first." Adriana said trying to hold her umbrella over the two of them.

She pointed to where she saw the car but Bridges couldn't see anything. Whoever it was, was gone.

"Let's hope some poor bastard just lost his way." Bridges said as he ushered Adriana back into the house.

The car incident was not mentioned again but Bridges couldn't help wondering if someone was watching them.

"You had something to tell me." Bridges asked.

"Yes. I received an interesting call this morning." Adriana got closer to the fire. "From an old friend in Los Angeles. We attended law school then worked at the State Department together. He wanted me to know that Rosa Carrea Gonzales was back in L.A., living with an aunt in South Central LA near USC. But I don't believe it."

"You don't believe it?" Bridges asked, not quite sure of what she meant. He wanted to ask more about Adriana's friend but decided it wasn't the right moment.

"She's back too soon—maybe she's ready to move on the project."

If this was true, Bridges knew there wasn't enough time to formulate a plan to foil the assassination. He carefully watched Adriana, searching for any sign that she was concocting information. It was second nature to him, always looking for omissions or some tell tale sign the person wasn't truthful. That's what he had been trained to do.

Adriana was different. He wanted to trust her—he had to trust her if they were going to work together. But it was more than that—he was interested in her. And the fact that she might have a suitor angered him.

"Your 'friend' knows about Rosa?" Bridges asked with a level of cynicism. The mere mention of a 'friend' irritated Bridges and he tried to conceal his feelings from her.

Adriana smiled and seemed to recognized a trace of jealously. "He likes Latino women, Richard. He took a date to a Latin Club in South

East LA and she introduced him to Rosa. Everyone seems to know her, you know."

"Uh huh." Was all Bridges could muster.

Adriana explained that her friend hadn't recognized the Rosa at first. At least not until their conversation centered around the American Embassy in San Salvador and then he remembered that she worked for her own government.

"During my last trip to Los Angeles, I met with Rosa in my hotel. Later, my friend came to take me to dinner as Rosa was leaving. He invited her to join us but she declined." Bridges listened carefully and let Adriana do all the talking.

"During dinner, I mentioned I had business with Rosa and that she was returning to El Salvador to work on a project for the First Lady. He wasn't interested. I don't think he cares what the hell President Banks does."

"Why's that?" Bridges soberly asked.

Adriana laughed. "He's a right wing conservative straight from the Barry Goldwater mold. I think you would like him." Bridges again laughed.

"Then why call you to discuss this woman?" It wasn't making sense to Bridges.

"He needed an excuse to call." Adriana explained. "There was a time I had to keep our relationship in line. I was married to Bill and going to law school. I wasn't about to get involved…"

Bridges understood why men could be attracted to Adriana. He wondered why she didn't call him by name. He even wondered if he knew the poor bastard from his Embassy days in San Salvador.

Bridges thoughts were on Rosa again. He would go to Los Angeles himself, tracing every move Rosa made. Adriana should stay behind, close to Heidi and monitor the President's movements and plans.

His would locate Rosa and renew his acquaintance with her. Of course she would remember he worked for the Agency but he would just have to convince her that he was retired. But even so, she was bound to be suspicious.

Bridges never spoke of being retired…to anyone. It made him feel old, like some old shoe tossed in a corner only to be replaced with a newer version. He was considered.young for retirement but the time he had vested included his military time and twenty years had gone by fast. Besides, Jennifer needed him closer to home and was going through a bad time since her mother died. She was going to attend graduate school and needed the security of having her father home. He actually made more money contracting for the Agency and other government organizations and spent more time home.

"I'll put you in contact with Dean Simmons." Adriana said.

"Who?"

"Dean Simmons…my friend. You'll get along fine with him as long as you don't compete for the same woman."

Her comment amused Bridges and he was quite sure she meant to do just that. Adriana was beautiful, even mysterious. Before getting involved with her there was one thing he needed to do first.

"Before Rosa returned to El Salvador the first time, Heidi made arrangements for her to stay with friends in Brentwood—a Bill and Ellen Compton, high rollers who contributed to her husband's campaign. It was Heidi's idea. She wanted to control Rosa—allow her to live with a little style. Heidi told me Rosa hated living with her aunt in South Central LA. Too many immigrants and gang activity."

Bridges smiled. "According to demographics, there's more people from El Salvador living in Los Angeles than in the entire country."

His comment went unnoticed and he felt odd about telling Adriana about LA. Of course she would know those things, he thought. It was then that he noticed Adriana was caught up in her own thoughts. She had been reluctant to stay behind in DC. What Bridges didn't realize was that she didn't want him to be away for two or three days.

"Dean's a likable guy. Knows his way around the town." Adriana laughed. Bridges looked at Adriana wondering if there was some hidden meaning or joke that he didn't get.

"He has a habit of falling in love with every woman he meets."

Bridges' just smiled, his thoughts were of his trip. He needed Adriana to be aware of the President's trips around the country and his speaking engagements. If the Rosa Carrea Gonzales was the ruthless assassin he remembered, she would take him out in a gathering of Latino people where she wouldn't be noticed.

Adriana was quite, sitting close to the fire. The little flames danced about as if their only job was to cast a spell on her. Her mood seemed to change and it bothered Bridges. He wondered if there was something else she needed to tell him. No...he was being paranoid, he thought.

"Now that you're here, you can translate those tapes." He said remembering the tapes Charlie gave him. He made a comparison of Adriana's translation and that of the translator at the Israeli Embassy. Her Spanish was superb and the translation the same. She was probably better at translating than the translator the Israelis used at the Embassy.

Bridges had some understanding of the Spanish language although from time to time he got his verb tense mixed up, but he knew when she wasn't being completely honest.

Afterwards, Bridges outlined his trip. He would leave on Thursday afternoon and return to Washington no later than Sunday evening. That should be enough time, he thought. He would try and create a 'chance' meeting with Rosa without getting her spooked. If that didn't work out, he could spend his time getting to know this Dean fella and do a little snooping around. And if that failed, there were always his friends at LAPD and the Sheriff's Department who might be helpful.

"What does Rosa do for these friends of Heidi's?" He asked.

"Domestic help." Adriana replied.

Bridges tried to remember the woman he knew as Rosa. She had worked with his team in Honduras. What the team didn't know was that she was part of a secret 'hit squad' against the guerrillas at night. He remembered she was shrewd, cunning, and exceptionally perceptive—even ten years ago. The more he thought about it, the more he realized any chance meeting would be out of the question. The most he could hope for was to follow out her movements

"Is there some connection to your nick name, 'The Highwayman'?" Adriana playfully asked.

Bridges tried to avoid answering. He caught a glimpse of Adriana's green eyes sparkling as she teased him. She seemed to be enjoying this little guessing game about the name, and it was then that he decided not to tell her how his team members in Central America had goaded him. The whole name thing was silly, and he could see that Adriana was getting annoyed by not being let in on the story behind it.

As a matter of fact, he vaguely remembered it being the name he used for communication purposes when he and his team were stranded in Honduras. The rains had been heavy and there was the fear of guerrilla forces in the jungle locating them. He used the name to communicate with the chopper pilots who were trying to get a fix on his location. They didn't have the sophisticated signal equipment needed at the time of the rescue choppers.

"She's a professional, alright. But I wouldn't put her in the category of being a trained assassin." Bridges said.

Adriana remembered the crash course Bridges gave her on political assassinations and figured that was what he meant.

"Rosa has experience shooting her political adversaries…her target, like a hit and run assault. But she doesn't have the experience of plotting, planning and executing her target by laying and waiting."

"Is she good?" Adriana asked.

"Damn good. Especially with a 9mm Beretta. But with a long barrel sniper's rifle, I'm not so sure." Bridges recalled. "Of course that was several years ago in El Salvador. She may have been specifically trained by now. Which reminds me, I need to make a contact in San Salvador and find out before going to Los Angeles."

The Rosa Carrea Gonzalez, Bridges remembered was charming and persuasive, but underneath she was callous and very calculating. At age twenty-nine, the beautiful dark haired beauty had gruesomely killed several hundred people either by blade or gun. She could act quickly taking out her target, then vanish without a trace before anyone knew what had happened. She had volunteered for Bridges' team, gathering intelligence data on the guerrilla factions who used Honduras as their safe haven. A job she did well.

For awhile Bridges convinced himself that Rosa mighteven be glad to see him after all these years. She might really believe their meeting was by chance. He remembered the greedy side of Rosa, always opting to work alone keeping the entire payoffs as her own. She had few passions that he knew of other than her daughter who meant everything to her, and a voracious appetite for money.

"Do you think she's working alone?" Bridges asked in a still moment.

"What?" Adriana hadn't been listening. She was wondering how well Bridges knew this woman and if he had ever been intimate with her. She even wondered who fathered the little girl.

"Adriana, if you're going to help me, I need your ideas." Bridges scolded.

"Did you go to bed with her?" Adriana finally asked. She hadn't really meant to ask, only think it, but the words slipped out.

Women, he never would be able to figure them out. Now he realized why her mood changed ever since he mentioned he was leaving for Los Angeles.

"Well, were you?" Adriana pressed for an answer.

"Absolutely not. " Bridges replied. Rosa had given him the come on a few times but he had always managed to handle the situation without threatening the program. He wasn't about to tell Adriana though.

"My wife and I lived in San Salvador. Every few months she'd return to Virginia to take care of business on the other place, the other farm." Bridges sort of let it go with that remark.

Adriana wished she hadn't asked about such silly school girl nonsense and she felt embarrassed. Besides, what Bridges did in the past was his business just as hers was. She also realized that she cared for him for more than he knew and she wanted to be prepared for any future contacts with Rosa.

It was late in the afternoon when Bridges arrived at Los Angeles International Airport, often referred to as LAX. All the way he had thought about Adriana. Of course she cared for him. Why else would she have asked questions about his past relationship with Rosa? The amusing part was his growing feelings for her. There were times when he wondered how he could care for anyone again. His friends had told him that in time he would find someone else but he hadn't given it much thought, not until now.

He gathered his brief case from under the seat in front of him and was jolted somewhat as the plane came to a stop at the gate. He smiled at the United Airlines attendants as they wished him a pleasant day and he hoped it would be.

Once he was inside the Tom Bradley Terminal named after the former black mayor of Los Angeles and a retired LAPD Lieutenant , he looked around for Dean. Adriana said that he was conservative looking whatever that was supposed to tell him.

Bridges waited in front of the gate where he had arrived. That was the plan. Everyone else headed for the baggage claim area. He hadn't waited more than five minutes when he suddenly turned around and found himself face to face with a tall conservatively dressed man. Even though it was a tan poplin suit, it was obviously a 'Brooks Brother'

"Are you Richard Bridges?" He asked. He sported a deep tan and Bridges wondered if he played tennis every day. He seemed Adriana's age although it was hard to tell because of his blond hair. But as you looked closer, you could see the gray at his temples. Bridges finally decided he was probably older than Adriana.

"Yes, I'm Richard Bridges. And you must be Dean Simmons." They shook hands and Bridges was glad to see that his hand shake matched his size, a strong grip with feeling and sincerity. It was an instant friendship and they chatted like old friends who had not seen each other for a long time, as they left the terminal.

Although Dean had made arrangements for Bridges to stay at the Hyatt Hotel, he did invite him to stay with him at his condo in Marina Del Rey. He would be comfortable and have his own room and phone, but Bridges politely declined the offer. He would be in and out several times, maybe in the middle of the night, and he didn't want to disturb Dean. Besides, although they were getting along very well, and he wanted to keep his business private.

LAX had changed since Bridges was last there several years before but then he only stopped over for a few hours while making a connecting flight. They crossed the street into the parking structure and Bridges wasn't at all surprised to find that Dean drove a dark grey

Mercedes sedan with a license plate which read 'Dean 1'. The only liberal thing about Dean that he was able to recognize.

While they drove to the hotel, Dean Simmons talked on and on about the Embassy in San Salvador. His assignment had ended the year before Bridges arrived and they had many mutual acquaintances in common. Bridges became surprised when they shared the same opinions about the Embassy crew, even the Ambassador. Evidently, Dean was a political officer and felt it had been a joke because all political decisions were made by the Military Attache and, of course, the Ambassador. Bridges knew exactly what he meant.

Dean maneuvered up the drive and stopped in front of the lobby. A bell boy appeared to help with the luggage.

"My calendar is clear this week and you're welcome to use my office." It was a generous offer from Dean and Bridges wondered how much he knew about the project.

"Do you have time for a drink?" Bridges asked.

"Sure. Meet you in the lounge." Dean handed the keys to the valet who was eagerly waiting to get behind the wheel. Bridges checked in and was a little surprised that he already had a message waiting for him. It was from Adriana, 'Please call tonight'. A pleasure he thought. He left his brief case on the bed and put his one over stuffed suitcase on the fold-out in the closet, then left to meet Dean in the lounge.

He spotted Dean at a table in the corner not alone, but in the company of an attractive Hispanic woman. The young woman was wearing a business suit and had a briefcase with her. He wondered if he should interrupt.

"Richard...I'd like you to meet Maria Collins." Dean said as he stood to make the introduction.

He extended his hand and took the woman's fragile hand in his. The last name didn't fit since she wasn't wearing a wedding ring. He wondered if it was a married name.

"Nice to meet you, Richard." Her English was perfect but with a slight Spanish accent. Bridges pulled out a chair next to Maria while Dean ordered a round of drinks. There had been no mention of anyone joining them and Bridges found himself being cautiously suspicious

The young woman put Bridges at ease by explaining that she was originally from Costa Rica and attended school in San Salvador. She had a law practice in Dean's building, specializing in immigration law.

Bridges felt relieved with this information and tried to answer Maria's questions about Washington DC. The city had always intrigued her, as she told him. Her older sister lived in Virginia and operated a business assisting immigrants in processing their citizenship papers and green cards. Then she laughed softly about the green cards no longer being green. She had a wit about her, a friendliness that seemed to soothe all suspicions.

It was amusing how Dean insinuated that he and Bridges had been longtime friends. He wondered what kind of a game Dean was playing and not knowing the rules, he was beginning to feel uneasy. Maria was curious about what Bridges did for a living and before he answered, he glanced at Dean for some signal on how to answer but didn't see any.

"I have a farm. My daughter and I raise Arabian horses." That was a safe comment, he thought.

Maria was fascinated and urged him to explain every detail about horses and farm life. For awhile, even Dean appeared interested. It was sometime during his explanation of how he and Jennifer lived alone on the farm that he felt Maria's hand on his knee. Maybe an accident, he thought, but then she put her hand on his knee again and this time she left it there.

By now, Bridges felt the heat in his face and he could only hope it wasn't noticeable. As inconspicuous as he could, he reached under the table to remove the warm frail piece of anatomy when he felt her press a small card into the palm of his hand. As soon as he grasped it the young woman removed her hand. He was sure Dean hadn't caught the action and carefully placed the small card in his pocket.

Maria Collins left her drink untouched and graciously excused herself. She had another appointment to keep she had said. Bridges picked up on her words. Had she meant this was a 'meeting'? She shook hands with Bridges again and wished him well on his stay in Los Angeles. He watched her walk toward the lobby then vanish through the doors.

"Maria was my date that Saturday night." Dean explained.

"I'm sorry?" Bridges pretended to be unaware of what Dean was talking about.

"Adriana explained a little about Rosa. Maria was with me. In fact, Adriana has asked me to stay with you, you know, assist you while you're here."

Why had Adriana taken it upon herself to involve Dean, he wondered? It angered him, no, it made him down right mad. After-all, she knew he preferred to work alone, going and coming in complete obscurity. She could jeopardize the whole project and cost the President his life. The gesture was probably well intended but gracefully declined and Dean let it go.

"Maria gave you a card." It was a statement of fact and Bridges knew there was no use trying to hide it. Christ—what were the rules to this game he was in. He didn't even know what was on the damn card and here Dean was telling him he saw the whole thing. Was he that obvious? Maybe he was just getting too old for this anymore.

Dean didn't wait for an answer. Maria had been married to an American, he explained. She kept the name because it made business easier or at least that's what she thought. She had connections within the Latino community from Los Angeles clear down to San Diego. In fact, Maria would be Dean's date Saturday night when Bridges would accompany them as they hit as many Latino clubs as it took to find Rosa. There it was the whole damn plan regurgitated back in his face. Of course this is what he had planned to do in the first place, but he was supposed to be in control, not Adriana.

Dean seemed to sense the moment and placed a hand on Bridges' shoulder as they left the lounge. "I'm sure Adriana was just trying to help…it's alright, you can trust us." He said

Bridges waited with Dean while the valet retrieved 'Dean car.' Dean had other business but would be back to get Bridges at six thirty. He knew of a quaint little Italian place in Marina del Rey where they could dine in private.

Back in his room, Bridges looked at the card Maria gave him. It was her business card and on the back she wrote her home phone number. He put it in his wallet with the idea he would call her later in the evening.

Bridges called Captain Jim Matthews of the Los Angeles Police Department. A young woman said he was off duty and not scheduled to return until tomorrow. He left a message then dialed another friend at the Sheriff's office who wasn't in either. With only a few days to spend in Los Angeles, timing would be important.

He was unpacking and mentally going over everything he wanted to accomplish during his stay, when the phone rang. Jim Matthews had picked up his messages and returned the call immediately.

"Won't be necessary." Matthews said when Bridges asked him to do a background check on William and Ellen Compton.

Bridges thought it was strange for Matthews to say that. Or, maybe it was just the tone of his voice that bothered him.

"Okay, I'll bite." Bridges said with a certain amount of sarcasms to his old friend. "Why not?"

There was a long pause. Bridges was uneasy and started to squirm in his seat.

"The Comptons are my in-laws…I'm married to their oldest daughter. Now you tell me why you wanna know?" Matthews said coldly.

Bridges was stunned, almost speechless. He needed to explain in a hurry, before Jim started to get his feathers ruffled more than they already were.

"Actually, well…I'm interested in Rosa Carrea Gonzales who may be working for them."

Matthews laughed. "Bill and Ellen are good people. Not too conservative, but what the hell."

Bridges was glad to hear to hear Matthews laugh. He didn't want to complicate matters and decided to approach matters slowly.

"Jim…it's Rosa Carrea Gonzales who I'm actually interested in. Do you know her?"

"Rosey? Sure, she's a hell-of-a sweetheart. Worked in El Salvador as some kinda government investigator. Why you asking, Rich?"

Bridges was glad to know that at least they were talking about the same woman.

"I knew her when I was in San Salvador…at the Embassy."

Convinced Bridges was only trying to look up an old friend, Matthews changed his tone. Even offered to help get a message to her.

"Better I surprise her." Bridges said trying to steer Matthews clear of getting in the way. There was something about the way Bridges spoke that finally gave Matthews the clue that whatever was going on was CIA business. What Matthews didn't know was that Bridges was retired from the CIA.

"I get it." Matthews said thinking that he really did.

"Yeah, better we don't say anything to her."

Thinking he was really helping, Matthews offered more. "Ya know, Rich, she's been using our range. Made arrangements myself for her to go up to the Academy whenever she wants. I hear she's a hell of a shot."

"What kind of weapons?" Bridges asked.

"I hear she's deadly with a 9mm Beretta. I've even been up there when she's sighting in on a single shot Ruger 380 with a scope. She's a dead eye and has quite a little following at the range. Best woman I ever saw. My father-in-law, Bill, asked me to check out the rifle. Rosa said it was a gift from some people back east. It's solid…not on anyone's stolen list."

"She's not a domestic at your in-laws home?" Bridges asked.

"Hell, no. She's no domestic, not that lady. Too pretty, and what a body. Bill's letting her live at the house with her daughter…it's a favor to some political connection. She house sits when the folks are in Italy. My father-in-law's in the Italian furniture business."

"How long has that been, Jim?" Bridges asked, pushing for more information.

"She comes and goes. If the folks need her and she's in San Salvador, she'll return in a day or two. They love her. Why you asking?"

Bridges knew he was stimulating Jim's curiosity. It was risky to pursue the questions any farther. But, there was one more he had to ask.

"When did she return to California…this last time?"

"A week ago. You have something to share with me, Richard?"

Matthews was suspicious.

"Hey, lets have lunch tomorrow." Bridges asked diplomatically changing the subject.

"You spooks are all alike." Matthews laughed.

They agreed to meet at noon the next day. The Hyatt was fine and convenient since there restaurant downstairs next to the lounge. Bridges hung the phone up and broke out in a cold sweat. He rubbed the moist palms of his hands on his shirt. What were the chances, one in a million maybe that a friend of his would have an inside track to his target. Incredible, he thought, and he laughed at the thought of telling Adriana. Then again, he wouldn't tell her. He would be better off letting her think he was a master detective. Maybe one day he would let her in on the coincidence.

Bridges showered, slipped on a pair of khaki slacks then checked his messages again. He was hoping Adriana would call before he left. At any rate, he had enough time to make a call to another friend, a former CIA agent who was now living in the Mission Viejo area. The friend retired a short time before Bridges. The message machine came on announcing their absence and Bridges left the usual message that he was staying at the Hyatt for a few days and could he please call as soon he received the message. He sat on the edge of the bed for a moment. It was Friday night and most people either hadn't arrived home, or were taking their time about getting there. Traffic would be bad and he tried not to expect that anyone would be returning his call this evening. He tried to call Adriana one more time but only got the machine again. Christ, was everybody out except him?

He thought again about Rosa. If she is permitted to use the police firing range and it turns out she's an assassin…the thought of LAPD looking like a bunch of 'keystone kops' was amusing. He couldn't tip his hand to Jim because he might curtail Rosa's use of the firing range and she would be suspicious. Especially if she were to accidentally run into Bridges this weekend. He thought about the date Dean set up for him on Saturday night. What a bundle of energy and she was probably hell in court. And what a looker…He laughed a little out loud at the thought.

Just then the phone rang interrupting his thought.

"I just got home." Adriana sounded out of breath. She was returning his several calls and she told him that there was also a message from the Honorable Paul Castilli. "What do you make of that?" She asked.

"I don't know." He paused for a long moment and thought only of her. "I miss you."

"I miss you, too." Adriana said it without hesitation. Until now, she had protected her feelings. She had known many men since her husband died, and escorted around town by the city's most eligible bachelors. Mostly social functions and there had been little romance. But Richard was different. She listened patiently as he told her about every detail of his trip. He had been angry at her earlier but he could set that aside for now. The only contact he was able to make so far had been with Jim and the details of that he kept to himself, for now. Dean had turned out to be a hell-of-a guy and they were getting along very well. Adriana was pleased, but then everyone liked Dean.

There was a knock on Bridges room door and he put the receiver down to answer it. She resented the interruption and strained to hear what was happening in the background.

"Adriana—I'll call you after dinner." Then he hung up leaving to her imagination the reason. A bell hop brought him a message that his rental car had been delivered and the guy needed his signature on the agreement.

Bridges appeared through the revolving doors of the lobby right at six thirty and found Dean waiting in 'Dean 1'. It was amazing how clean most Californians kept their cars, like they were their ultra egos or something like that. Dean promised an outstanding dinner and they headed for the marina. The sun appeared as a large orange ball and was about to set into a brown layer of smog. Dean said it was just fog and thought it was a beautiful. But Brides reminded him fog wasn't brown and Dean said something about they had to pretend because California wasn't like it used to be. Dean turned and looked at Bridges when he said it and the two smiled at each other in agreement.

From the looks of the parking lot, Charlie Browns already had quite a crowd and a famished Bridges anticipated a long wait. He was mildly amused when a deeply tanned hostess approached Dean and said his table was waiting. Bridges followed as they were escorted to a table overlooking the marina. It appeared to be the best table in the house. Dean teased the young woman and seemed to be getting a kind of chauvinistic charge out making her giggle. She reminded Bridges of Becky. Maybe it was her long blond hair or her laugh, or maybe it was the deep tan that covered her body that made him think of Becky. He wondered about her in Tel Aviv. Probably keeping everyone on their toes. He smiled to himself at the thought of her.

"Something to drink—Sir?" Bridges looked up. Two blue eyes looked directly into his and they were surrounded by a mass of dark curls which fell down her back. One rather large and long strand cascaded over her shoulder almost covering the name tag 'Tanya'.

"Well Tanya, how 'bout a Kamikaze?"

She didn't say anything, just wrote down his order and kept on smiling. He figured her father was a well known dentist because the young woman's teeth were perfect.

Bridges was intrigued watching Dean indulge in painful deliberation over what to order. Finally, he ordered his usual—T and T.

"Well, it's true...California has the most beautiful girls." He included Becky as a private thought and Dean just smiled and nodded.

The view of the marina was spectacular. Flood lights from under the restaurant's pilings lit the docks and Bridges watched a gathering of seagulls hover above, taking time only to land for their share of scraps being tossed from the kitchen. A large sail boat maneuvered into it's slip and he watched as the captain tied and anchored the vessel. It bobbed in soft unison with miniature swells but in contrast to the other yachts already in their place. The spellbinding events were intimately familiar as he remembered Bodega Bay.

Once a year he and his wife would fly to San Francisco, spend a few days on a shopping spree then rent a car. They would head north sixty miles to Petuluma and from there cross the farmland to the quaint little fishing village. Bridges had a friend in the agency who owned a house on the hill overlooking the bay. It was always completely stocked although no one lived in it year round. It was mainly rented to fellow agents and their families.

He reminisced the long leisurely strolls along the beach watching sandpipers search for food—breathing the salt air and holding hands. In the distance, the rhythmic sound of the coast guard beacon could be heard signaling the fishing boats entering the channel. And occasionally one could see a wind suffer cutting across the bay holding onto some brightly colored sail. But that was a life time ago and suddenly he was aware Dean was speaking to him.

"Richard—everything alright?" Dean asked.

"So when were you in El Salvador last?" Bridges asked getting back to reality and the project.

"Quite awhile ago. But Costa Rica's where I'd like to be."

"They've got some pretty women..." Bridges joked.

"My thoughts precisely." They both laughed and then there was a long moment of silence until Dean spoke again.

"Adriana's an incredible woman. But then I've always had a weakness for intelligent women." He paused. "I guess I never really had the time to pursue her."

Bridges thought the remark was odd. According to Adriana, Dean chased her for a long time but she had no interest in him, at least not a romantic one. It was uncomfortable talking about Adriana with another man. Perhaps because of his feelings for her.

"Adriana seems more than just an admirer of yours."

Bridges wasn't sure if it was a statement or a question. "Let's just say the feelings are mutual and let it go at that." He knew Dean was trying to draw him out about their relationship and he wanted it clear with Dean. It was—and his new friend decided to change the subject.

"Adriana mentioned you thought it best if you had a 'chance' meeting with Rosa. So—I arranged a date for you tomorrow night. I thought we'd go to the Latin disco. There's a good chance she'll be there…the best I can do. Hope you don't mind if Marie Collins is your date. I thought she would be perfect for you."

Bridges laughed. "I don't know if I can handle her."

Dean knew exactly what he meant and smiled. He gave Bridges his address in Century City, the South Tower and they agreed to meet after lunch the following day after Bridges pointed out that he was meeting with a friend from LAPD at the hotel.

***

Richard Bridges read the Los Angeles Times and sipped his coffee. Room service brought up a tray of fresh fruit and a muffin but for some reason he wasn't hungry. A woman on a local news channel was talking about some shooting the night before in South Central L.A. It appeared gang related but police were skeptical. He turned the page of the paper and sipped his coffee then heard '…Jose Carrea Gonzales, the victim, age forty-five…' He quickly turned up the sound trying not to miss another word.

"Shit." The anchorwoman was going on about the weather. The story had to be in the paper. Bridges quickly turned the pages until he found it. There it was in black and white and he tore it out being careful not to rip away any part of the story. The name wasn't all that common and he was sure it had to be a relative of Rosa's. He folded the article and neatly stuck it in his wallet for safe keeping. Why, he wasn't quite sure yet, but his best bet was to check it out with Jim Matthews when they met for lunch.

During his conversation with Adriana last night, she informed him she had the President's itinerary and travel list for the next several weeks. The dates were not firm because of some foreign policy negotiations with Israel and the President may have to make a trip to Europe. But on the list was a trip to San Diego with a stop in San Francisco before going on to the mid-west. It was a trip that had to be made before the end of the year and it was already October.

He recalled a conversation on the tape between Rosa and Heidi and that Heidi mentioned something about before Thanksgiving. If that was their time table, he had a little under two months to work. Then again, that seemed to be a deadline. It could take place at any time.

Adriana would have to monitor his every move so they had enough time to reach any given location if they had to. He didn't know exactly why, but intuition told him that any attempt on the President's life would happen in Washington, maybe while attending church or on one of his phony jogging sessions in the morning.

The hotel restaurant was crowded and as Bridges made his way to the hostess, he was glad to see Jim Matthews was already waiting for him and had even successfully bribed the hostess into letting them have the next available table. That was just like Jim, he thought.

No sooner had they ordered lunch, than a distressed Matthews spoke.

"Richard, what the hell is going on with Rosa?" He didn't wait for an answer. "I know you too well and you just don't ask questions about someone unless there's a reason. If it's CIA stuff…I'll understand. It's the in-laws I'm worried about."

When Matthews finished, Bridges didn't quite know what to say. Damn if he told Jim, and damn if he didn't.

"Rosa worked on an intelligence team with me in El Salvador. You know, Jim, I just didn't want to alert the bone heads at the FBI. I only need to check on her, that's all. You understand?"

Matthews wasn't sure if he understood or not but saw no reason not to believe Bridges. He softened his tone and listened while Bridges explained that he didn't want anyone to alert her that he was checking on her because she might leave and return to El Salvador. As far as the Compton's were concerned, he didn't think they were in any danger.

"I read in the paper your Robbery-Homicide Division is investigating a shooting last night. I suspect it's a relative of Rosa's—same last name."

"Checked it out…no relationship." A whisper of huffiness still lingered in Matthews' voice and Bridges wasn't sure if he was telling him the truth. He decided not to pursue it any further for now. If Matthews knew Rosa was a member of some El Salvador hit squad, he'd come apart.

"Our concern is the trips she's making back and forth to Central America and who's sponsoring the trips."

"She's got money. My father-in-law did some investing for her and I know she has accounts at Bank of America and the Dresdner Bank downtown on Figuroa."

Bridges knew that for someone who was in charge of the Organized Crime and Intelligence Divisions, Jim Matthews should have more of a handle on her. He should have account numbers and the name of her financier.

"Don't shit me, Jim." Bridges didn't want to be patronized. "Where's she getting the money."

"I'm not shitting ya buddy. My father-in-law said she invested an initial fifty grand on several stock options which he suggested to her. He thinks she's got about a hundred grand in both banks. Besides, Rosa's told me she also sold some property in El Salvador and Costa Rica. If you're going to tell me it's drug money…"

"No, not exactly." Bridges interrupted. "But it would have to be some pretty expensive real estate. The market's not the same as here, ya know."

A disconcerted Matthews suspected Bridges was holding back on him. "Everything was fine until you blew into town, Richard. But if it will help, I can find out how much is in her Bank of America account, but the German bank…out of the question. You know we can't get into that one."

"Okay, find out what you can. I'd appreciate it." Bridges was satisfied he had stimulated some concern but neither did he want Matthews to overreact and tip his hand. Rosa would spook and he didn't want that. It would be good if he could see her shoot at the range but time wasn't on his side.

Jim Matthews finished his lunch and explained to Bridges that Rosa can use the range at will. All she has to do is contact a woman officer in his division and the officer sets up the time. He could check on this and get back to Bridges later in the day.

***

About a half hour after Bridges returned to his room, Matthews called from his car phone. Rosa was scheduled to use the range early Saturday morning. Matthews would make arrangements for him to observe from inside the Range Masters observation tower and because of it's tinted windows Rosa would be unable to see anyone watching her. The trip was going smooth so far, and he was glad for that. But the situation with Matthews bothered him. He could control Matthews if he were in the circle.

"When are your in-laws planning to leave the country again?" He asked.

"Monday, as a matter of fact."

That was good news and it would make it that much easier. No doubt he would shit his pants when Bridges finally told him what was going on, especially since Matthews authorized Rosa's use of the police department's shooting range.

After speaking to Matthews, Bridges called Dean's office for directions. It was easy the young woman told him making sure he parked in the underground parking. They were in the South Tower.

Bridges smiled at the young woman's reference to 'easy' as he headed out the parking lot of the hotel. He took the San Diego 405 freeway north to the Santa Monica Boulevard exit. He passed the Federal Building where he worked briefly several years ago. He made a right turn onto Avenue Of The Stars driving past the Century Plaza Hotel. Then left on Empyrean Way. A sign marked directions to underground parking for the towers. He rode the elevator to the nineteenth floor like the woman had instructed.

"You must be Mr. Bridges." The young receptionist said. She was handsomely dressed in a navy dress and not a hair out of place and Bridges was impressed with her style. She knew right away who he was. As he was about to be seated, Dean appeared and escorted him down a corridor of cubicles. In each one sat a secretary with her own desk and computer and each worked for a different attorney Dean explained. It was typical of a large law firm and Bridges was awed by its sophistication.

Dean's office was nonetheless impressive. Large, very bright and surrounded with windows offering a sweeping view of the city. He took a seat in one of the overstuffed chairs in front of Dean's desk, which was nothing more than a massive piece of glass. Behind it stood an ornately carved credenza with a few books and several file folders on it. Bridges wondered where the client files were but then decided they were probably housed in some obscure place. There were two sofas in the corner of the room separated by a glass top table. Dean showed him the large screen television behind a picture above them.

At that moment, a young secretary, probably Dean's, showed up and offered Bridges a drink of his choice. Iced tea would be fine he told her and she shut the door behind her promising to return in minutes.

"I would like you to meet me at the Police Academy in the morning…say seven?" Bridges asked in a sober tone.

"Of course." Dean said it without hesitation and knew instantly whatever it was, was important.

Convinced they were alone, Bridges leveled with him. "We have reason to believe someone will attempt to assassinate the President."

Momentarily speechless, Dean struggled to hold back any political comments in light of the serious subject matter. He listened carefully as Bridges explained the part Rosa played, being careful not to mention the First Lady

"They'd make a martyr out of the sonofabitch…like Kennedy." Dean finally said. "I only hope the Republicans aren't involved."

"No. On the contrary, his own people."

Dean laughed.

Just then the young woman returned with tea and informed Dean he had a meeting with a client but the conference room was available. Bridges was left alone to use Dean's office as his own. He would be about forty-five minutes, and then he left with file in his hand.

Bridges reached across the glass top desk pulling the phone towards him. He would have sat in Dean's chair but felt uneasy and didn't want to appear too assuming.

He opened his briefcase and took out his list of contacts in the Los Angeles area. He dialed the Oceanside number of Tim Young, a retired Master Gunnery Sergeant, and an old buddy who just happened to be an expert sniper during the Vietnam War. Tim had been in charge of the Sniper School at Camp Pendleton and would know which weapons a sniper might use at long distance, or at less than five-hundred yards.

He was disappointed when a young woman informed him her father now worked for the Oceanside Post Office and wouldn't return until after five that evening. She would have him return the call at the hotel.

Bridges put the phone down and realized he had to trust Jim Matthews. After-all, he had worked criminal intelligence at LAPD for several years and was as trustworthy as they come. The only problem was his in-laws, but they were leaving the country Monday. Bridges phoned Matthews and even though they had just had lunch together, a baffled Matthews agreed to meet at Dean's office within the hour.

"You're shittin' me." Matthews said looking at Dean and Bridges. He just sat there shaking his head in disbelief.

"I have to insist on complete secrecy." Bridges said after telling him everything except the part about Heidi.

Matthews was still shaking his head and made it clear that he'd have to inform his boss if his assistance went any further. It was something he felt compelled to say. But he understood too well, that because of Bridges' sensitive position and the nature of business, he was now drawn into a very small circle and bound by its secrecy at all costs. Matthews left, reminding Bridges that he would pick him up at six in the morning.

"He's apprehensive." Dean pointed out.

"He's also the best in criminal intelligence. It's his wife's parents...he's worried about their safety."

Dean finally put the whole thing together. "What a coincidence. I mean a suspected assassin playing housekeeper to your in-laws." He mused the thought to himself.

"I never imagined this. What luck."

Dean left the office once again and Bridges decided to try calling Tim Young once again. Looking at his watch, he figured he should be home by now.

"Tim, Richard Bridges here. Do you remember me?"

"Captain, you old son-of-a-bitch. Of course. How the hell are you? Still working for the spooks?"

"Retired. And drop the Captain shit. It's been twenty years since Da Nang." Bridges took on a more serious tone and proceeded to quiz Tim on weapons. There was a change in Tim's voice and a long pause after Bridges finished.

"What's the problem, Tim, can't talk?" He asked.

There was no answer.

"Tim? You there buddy?" Bridges tried again to break the silence.

"Sorry, you're asking the wrong guy." It was the somber way Tim said this that made Bridges realize something awful was coming.

"What's the problem, Tim?" Bridges asked in such a gentle way that almost compelled an answer.

"Few years ago…I uhh…I uhh accidently shot a kid…a little girl…an accident." He went silent again.

"Want to talk about it?" He asked softly, almost at a loss for the right thing to say himself.

"Not much to talk about," Tim said.

Bridges listened. The poor bastard broke down and was telling him how he had just installed a scope on his friend's rifle. The guy was some deputy sheriff, at that. Tim figured he must have got caught up talking to the guy and he thought the gun was unloaded.

Bridges pursued the outcome and the poor bastard with his broken words was barely able to explain that he was arrested but not charged. Why, he didn't know. From there, his life had gone downhill. There wasn't any way he could help Bridges and he just sort of hung up.

"Poor bastard…" Bridges whispered out-loud. He leaned back in the chair and thought about Tim's situation and wondered how any man could live with himself after such a thing. He glanced at the wall in front of him and noticed a Yale Law School graduation photograph. Adriana was in the front row. She was extraordinary beautiful even then and for a brief second he wished he was holding her right now.

There were other things on the wall, too. It was like something out of 'This Is Your Life, Dean'. He must have framed every certificate he ever earned and Bridges seemed a little disappointed when he didn't find a little league picture of Dean, too. He smiled at the thought and was sure he had seen everything hanging up there but another picture caught his eye. It was a photograph of the Embassy staff in San Salvador. Why, even Billy Ray was in the group.

The Agency had a policy about participating in photographs…you didn't, that simple. It was similar to their policy about using last names. You never did. He was always referred to as Richard B. and it was that way at Langley, too. The only exception would be covert operatives who used full names.

"Richard, you have a call from Adriana on line three." Dean said as he opened the door finding Bridges studying the picture. Dean gestured to a phone on a table in the corner.

"Hello, there." He said.

"Perhaps I'm intruding on your day, Richard, but Paul has invited us to dinner…a birthday party of sort for another Justice. It's a must. I'm sure he's up to something."

"You're not intruding. Paul's just playing a little politics…just a little insurance policy in case this project presents a difficult problem for the high court."

"I'll call Paul and tell him we'll be there."

With Dean sitting only a few feet away, Bridges let Adriana do most of the talking. It wasn't that he didn't trust Dean, but more that he had to keep most of the details of this project to himself. Adriana rambled on about the Banks spending the weekend at Camp David and how Heidi had invited her to go along. Of course she declined making some excuse about working. She knew the asshole would put a move on her if Heidi was ever out of sight.

Bridges promised to call her later night even though it would be late, maybe almost morning, by the time he got in.

"I miss you." And she hung up. She knew he missed her too, but by the way Richard spoke to her, she knew someone was probably in the room, probably Dean.

***

Bridges returned to his hotel and handed a message at the front desk, 'Dinner tonight? Jim'. Matthews seemed disappointed when Bridges phoned to beg off. More than likely Jim had wanted him to meet his in-laws. He showered

It was a little before nine when Dean used his car phone to call Bridges. He was just pulling into the hotel parking lot and would meet him in the lounge for a drink. They could wait for Maria Collins there.

Dean ordered a second round of drinks about the same time Maria arrived. She slid an around Bridges from behind and when he turned, she kissed him.

"Are you taken for the evening?" She playfully asked.

"I am now." Bridges stood up to greeted the young woman who was standing behind him dressed in a slinky black dress. In fact, everything was black, shoes, stockings and handbag. She was very seductive and perfect for the part she would play. He pulled out the chair next to him and Maria joined them.

"You're not acting much like a Judge, Marie." Dean joked.

"What do you mean…a judge?" Bridges asked.

"Marie is on the Governor's list to be appointed to the bench next time around." Dean said reaching in his coat pocket and pulling out a sheet of paper.

Maria, who apparently didn't know about it, was ecstatic over the news. "Who else?" She asked hardly able to control herself as she reached over and took the paper from Dean.

"Dean…"

But before Maria could go on about the two of them being on the list, Dean stopped her and said he planned to turn the appointment down. It wasn't good economics.

Inside the Club Bahia, on Sunset, the band played some little number which blasted the speakers. Maria pointed to a table farthest from the speakers. She excused herself after they ordered a round of drinks.

I ran into Rosa's girlfriend in the powder room." She said when she returned. She reminded Dean it was the same one who was with Rosa the last time they were there. For some reason the girlfriend told Maria that Rosa wasn't feeling well and couldn't come tonight. Why she told Maria wasn't quite clear.

Disappointed at the news, Bridges suggested they wait for awhile then leave and get something to eat. There was a large group of Latinos sitting at the next table carrying on louder than usual. Bridges understood enough Spanish to understand the tone and slurs were directed at him. He went to the restroom and when he returned, one of the women at the table stood up in front of him and asked him to dance. He reluctantly accepted and followed the young woman to the dance floor. She spoke to him in Spanish as they danced and said she was from El Salvador. She seemed to know he was looking for Rosa and implied they were old school chums. He pretended he wasn't sure of what she was talking about and just smiled. Afterwards, he escorted her back to her table. There was an uneasiness about the whole matter and Bridges could feel the eyes of her friends as they looked him over.

"We better leave." Dean said catching the whole incident. He pulled a twenty from his wallet and tossed it on the table then took Maria's arm as she stood and grabbed her purse.

"Yep—let's get out of here." Bridges said getting the feeling they were not welcome. The woman followed pushed her way in front of him asking them to join her friends at their table. She smelled of booze and he gently pushed her aside with a polite 'no thank you' in Spanish. He was careful to avoid eye contact with the men at the table. She repeated her request only louder.

As Dean and Maria led the way through the crowd Bridges followed. The music was blasting from all directions and he could still hear the woman yelling something about her friends not being good enough for him and then she screamed obscenities. Bridges caught glimpse of a heavy set Mexican in a tuxedo forcibly escort the woman away. Probably the club manager, he thought.

Outside, the valet waited while Dean fumbled for the parking ticket which he finally found.

"Hey maaannn...you sonofa-beecha, you offended my seester." Bridges turned and saw two Hispanic youths in baggy black pants and white t-shirts approaching him. One of them, the taller of the two, staggered closer to Bridges just as the valet brought Maria's car around. Dean quickly put Maria into the passenger seat then hurried around the other side handing the valet a tip as he slipped behind the wheel. Bridges reached for the handle of the rear door but by now he could smell the heavy stench of beer and cigarettes and could feel the young hood behind him. Instinctively, he stepped aside as the man swung falling flat on his face. Bridges could still hear the crowd laughing as Dean drove off.

After stopping for quick bite to eat, Dean drove Bridges to the hotel where 'Dean was left earlier. Maria hung onto Bridges' arm as they watched Dean pull away

"Wanna buy a new judge a drink?" Maria pressed her breast into his shoulder and moved her hand across his chest sliding it down to his belt buckle. Her fingers found his zipper and when she felt him, it seemed to excite her even more. Bridges quickly took both of her hands in his, turned her around and helped her back into her car. Mustering his best diplomacy he explained he had a busy day coming up and to drive carefully.

"Okay, but you must promise to call me before you leave town."

"I promise." He said waving goodbye to her.

Back in his room Bridges phoned Adriana as he promised, as he was about to hang up when she answered.

"Richard, you okay…call me in the morning." She was barely awake and Bridges agreed to call the next day and explain what had happened.

***

After a couple hours of sleep, Bridges sipped on a fresh cup of coffee brought to him by a bubbly little thing down in the hotel coffee shop. He had just popped two aspirin when Jim Matthews arrived looking well rested and ready to go.

"Boy am I hungry." Matthews said as he jested the waitress to bring him a cup of the hot brew and take their order. He seemed so caught up in his own world that he hardly noticed Bridges' drawn out look from being up most of the night and it was probably just as well since Bridges had decided not to mention any part of the incident.

Afterwards, they drove to the Police Academy stopping first at the administrative office. It would be better if Bridges stayed with the range master during shooting exercises and since he was already there, Matthews decided he would fire his monthly requirement

While they waited, Bridges got acquainted with the range master who, to his surprise, was born and raised in Silversprings, Maryland. He just happened to be a former Marine.

At seventy-thirty sharp, a Hispanic woman signed in to shoot. The range master used the loud speaker to assign her a target.

"Who is she?" Bridges asked.

"Rosa something or other…former police officer from El Salvador and the best shot at the range. Puts the officers to shame."

Bridges watched as planned. The woman had gone over and said something funny to Matthews then returned to her assigned target. She loaded the 9mm Beretta, waited for the safety officer's word, then hit the black ring fifteen out of fifteen times.

"Amazing." Commented the range master. Just then the door of the observation tower opened and an officer came in with the sign-in log sheet. The woman had signed in as Rosa Carrera.

Bridges couldn't take his eyes off the signature. He looked at the woman again, then once more. Something was wrong. He would have to bring Matthews into his confidence.

Afterwards, Matthews came to the observation tower. He could take Bridges down to the snack shop and introduce him to Rosa. Bridges was confused but agreed.

Bridges spoke in Spanish and shook the woman's hand. She laughed and said something about hoping her English would be as good as his because was going to be a citizen soon.

Matthews looked on and for a few minutes, thought Bridges was hiding the fact that the two had known each other several years before in El Salvador.

"I understand you were a police officer in El Salvador?" Bridges asked in Spanish.

The woman gave a puzzled look directed at Matthews before she answered. "No. I've never been a police officer like you know one to be. I worked for a special investigative unit for my government is all."

Bridges had known all the women assigned to the unit. Perhaps she was recruited after he returned to the States, he thought.

"When were you a member of SIU?" He asked.

"Have you ever been in my country?" The woman asked. She had figured that he must have spent some time there because of the questions he was asking.

Bridges explained he had spent time working at the Embassy, then thought it was a good idea to get off the subject. From the look in the woman's eyes, it was obvious she wasn't going to let the matter drop.

"Rosa is quite a shot." Matthews had sensed the strain.

"She sure is. Best shot out there this morning." Bridges tried to flatter the woman and somehow it worked because the comment brought a smile to her face.

It was late in the morning and the woman made an excuse she had to leave. She kissed Matthews on the cheek then picked up her tote and said goodbye.

Bridges watched with sudden disbelief as the petite young woman put her things into her car and sped off. "She's not the same one!" He said it softly as if thinking out loud.

"What did you say?" Matthews wasn't sure what Bridges said but from the look on his face, there was reason to be confused.

Bridges drew him deeper into the plot and explained the woman who just left was not the Rosa Carrea Gonzales he knew in San Salvador. That Rosa would have been older, brawny and spoke excellent English; not like the pretty, young woman who just left. Matthews drove Bridges back to his hotel neither one speaking. It had been a long morning Bridges felt drained. He hadn't expected this turn of events. Over and over in his mind he wondered about the young woman and if there was just some coincidence she had the same name. Worn by his own thoughts, he dialed Adriana's number.

Damn it…the answering machine picked up the call and he was about to hang up without leaving a message when suddenly she came on.

"Richard." She sounded out of breath. "I was just loading my clubs in the car and barely heard the phone…"

"Describe the woman you met in Los Angeles." She sensed his urgency and quickly described the woman she knew as Rosa. Her description was the same as the woman he met on the range.

"What is it, Richard? What's wrong?"

"I'm not sure. I'll have to make a few calls to San Salvador." He quickly terminated the call but not before making sure Adriana took her cellular phone with her. For Christsakes, if she was going to be on the golf course with God knows who, at least she could keep a phone with her in case he needed her. He'd been harsh with her but maybe that was because he sensed she deliberately neglected to tell him who she was playing golf with. He hadn't given her a chance, he thought.

He sat in the chair next to the bed for a few moments collecting his thoughts and overcoming a feeling of frustration until he realized it wasn't about Rosa—it was about Adriana.

He dialed the Embassy in San Salvador and asked for the security chief.

"Terry Holden." A familiar voice said.

"The Highwayman here."

"Richard Bridges, you old sonofabitch. How the hell are you? You in town?"

"No, matter of fact, I'm not." Bridges was relieved that the head of security turned out to be someone he knew. Terry Holden had been part of a rescue team who flew into Honduras to pick him up after being left and stranded. Terry explained that he had just returned from an assignment in the Middle East and requested the new Embassy in San Salvador.

"You'd love it." Terry said, explaining that the Ambassador was an easy guy to work for.

"The stupid sonofabitch was appointed by the President." There was a thunderous laugh and Bridges got the picture.

"So, how can I help yeh?" The sober tone of Terry's voice indicated it was time to get serious.

"Terry…I need some information on a woman who worked for SIU several years ago-name ID Rosa Carrea or Rosa Carrea Gonzales. One of those caught up in the hit squad in 1989…remember?"

"Yeh, yeh, I remember. The Goddamn woman and her partner were ambushed…killed by a couple of factions in an incident near the coffee plantation next to where they built the new Embassy. Why do you ask?"

Bridges explained the woman he met earlier at the LAPD pistol range and how he wondered why she used Rosa's name.

"Congratulations, Richard, you've just met Carmen Veralis. From what we know, she's assumed the identity of Rosa Carrea. What we don't know is, why? She worked for SIU until the last election. When the AID money was cut back, she left. Pops up in San Salvador every now and then.

"I'll be damned." Bridges said.

"I suggest you call the Station Chief or the AID people if you need anything."

Terry Holden had been helpful and Bridges told him so before hanging up. He remembered the enthusiasm and the thrill of the old Agency days and the thought of it made him more determined than ever to stop this plot.

Richard phoned Adriana but not on the cellular; he left a message on her home phone to meet him at the farm Sunday night when he returned.

CHAPTER 10
LESSON LEARNED

The drive from the Dullas Airport seemed long. Sunday afternoon traffic was heavy as Bridges thought of his recent trip to Los Angeles. His thoughts of his Marine Corps friend Tim Young and the trouble he had over a foolish shooting accident. The poor guy, he thought went through Vietnam with a minor wounds and he remembered when ever Tim spoke of retirement from the Marine Corps, his plans were to open a NRA regulation indoor and outdoor firing range for the public. After Bridges left the Marine Corps he encouraged Tim to become a police officer or move to Washington area and work for the Agency. The Agency always needs people with good military skills, of course to the public, a sniper wasn't one of the skills, at least to the Senate Committee over-looking activities of the intelligence community.

It started to rain, which distracted Bridges from his train of thought. He finally arrived at his farm and felt good to drive up to the old house he and his late wife completely renovated and to hear the horses nickering in the barn when they heard him drive up. Adriana's Mercedes was parked next to Jennifer's green Jeep. For some reason it appeared natural to see the both vehicles parked there. He pulled the Cherokee next to the barn and walked to the back door of the house. While entering, he could smell a fire in the fireplace and laughter coming from the family room.

Bridges stuck his head in the doorway of the family room where Adriana and Jennifer were sitting sipping tea and having an old fashion gab-fest as most woman do. Jennifer immediately got up and hugged her father. Adriana seemed reserved and allowed for Bridges to freshen up before she expressed her feelings. In a few minutes, Bridges returned to the room as Jennifer announced she had to feed the horses. Adriana got up from her chair as Jennifer left the room, she gave Bridges a hug and allowed him to kiss her on the mouth. A short but appreciated kiss by Adriana. She smelled fresh and sweet, he thought. He didn't want to let her go…but thought for now, he would.

They sat across from each other as Bridges put a log on the fire to keep the chill from the room. Adriana was dressed in a black knit sweater that complemented her grey worsted-wool slacks. Around her neck she wore a gold chain and cross. Her face was fresh looking and her lipstick was slight-pink that accented her small mouth. Her hair was combed back from her ears and Bridges could see single pearl earrings in her small pierced ears. Jennifer appeared as though she had been riding and was still in her tan 'Harry-Halls'and green colored sweatshirt that read something complementary to the Arabian breed.

Bridges poured himself a cognac after Adriana declined the offer. He made himself comfortable in the chair and smiled at Adriana as if to say he was happy to see her.

Adriana started the conversation by asking the first question. "Richard I'm glad you're back…what happened that made you cut the trip short or ar least return earlier?"

Bridges didn't know where he should start, so he decided to start from the beginning and worked his way to the point that the Rosa he met, wasn't the same person he knew in El Salvador several years before, she's dead. "The woman I met, is beautiful, younger, and it seems she assumed Rosa Carrea's identity, for what reason I don't know yet. You described her as the person you met. Captain Matthews of the Los Angeles Police Department provided me a her photograph."

Bridges produced the black and white photo and Adriana confirmed it was the same person she visited in Los Angeles before her trip to Jordan.

Adriana provided a list of the President's travel agenda prepared by the secretary to the President's and approved by the White House chief of staff. Often there are two prepared agendas, one coded to distinguish between them both in case there was a leak from the White House before a formal announcement was made. This procedure has been set up by the President's Secret Service security detail. "The only breach of security, is from the First Lady who is careless as to what agenda will be followed and refused to follow security plans. They have complained but it does no good." Adriana explained.

Bridges studied the agenda, the visit to Los Angeles in a week is his focus. At this point, Bridges informed Adriana that Rosa has the privilege of using the LAPD firing range to sharpen up her skills. He didn't recall telling her over the phone while still in LA. Adriana couldn't believe what she was hearing and asked Bridges what could be done. "Nothing…if we arranged for the termination of her shooting privileges, she'd become suspicious."

Bridges had a plan, a plan he didn't want to discuss with Adriana because it may confuse her at this time. He was explicit when he informed her that they had to go to Los Angeles a day before the President's visit. He noticed that the agenda called for the President to speak to the Hispanic and Afro-American communities in the South Central part of the city. To the people on the ground, sleeves rolled up, tie loosened, something he got from the Kennedy era, Bridges thought as he read details of the agenda. This brought a smile to his face as he glanced over at Adriana. She clearly understood and also smiled.

Bridges spoke in a convincing tone, although he didn't expect Adriana would disagree. "I think the hit on the President will be in Los Angeles next week, what do you think?" Bridges looked over at Adriana as he sipped the cognac.

"I don't think so…it's too damn easy for us to guess…I think it will happen in San Diego."

Bridges was taken back with Adriana until he realized she had an advantage by access to the President's detailed agenda. He smiled, then took another sip of the cognac, he asked Adriana to disclose what else she knew. She grinned in a teasing way…then responded. "The trip to

LA will be tight security, the Secret Service expects trouble, why I don't know. The San Diego trip will be lay-back including golf and social events. The Secret Service guys are looking forward to San Diego."

Bridges felt maybe Adriana had something. He hadn't talked to Paul and was looking for his advice. There were no messages from him and he wondered why.

Jennifer returned to the room and remembered not telling her father that Judge Castilli called while he was away and she just forgot to tell him. Bridges thought that it wasn't like Jennifer to neglect to write down messages. "Thanks Jennifer...you read my mind, I was wondering about not hearing from the Judge." Adriana reminded Bridges that she accepted Paul's invitation to attend a dinner party. She insisted they should attend. Bridges thought she was starting to sound like a wife. He smiled over the thought. Adriana inquired as to his smile and Bridges shared his thought with her. Adriana acted serious, hearing Bridges make the comment that she was sounding like a wife. This was the last thing she wanted to sound like, especially at this point in their relationship. "Richard...what else did you find out?"

Bridges was hesitant to say much, although he explained about the name Rosa. "Her real name is Carmen Veralis, as I said she assumed Rosa Carrea's identity, she's at least five years younger. Her daughter is only five. I was told that the real Rosa, the one I worked with in Honduras is dead, caught up in an ambush by the Armed Propagander Team (APT), a known guerrilla force in retaliation of killing the nuns and priests during 1989. "Then why has she assumed her identity?"

"I can only guess...and my guess is freedom of movement, to and from El Salvador. There's another reason, but I haven't found it yet."

The telephone rang, Bridges excused himself to answer it in the study. It was Paul Castilli asking him to visit with that evening. He made a point that Bridges should be alone. Bridges was anxious to meet with him, although he felt that meeting the good judge alone would upset Adriana. He agreed to the meeting at the judge's home in an hour, that would be eight-thirty.

He returned to Adriana in the cozy family room and explained the circumstances. She wasn't upset in the least. Bridges suggested they have a quick dinner and Adriana could wait for him to return from his meeting with Paul.

After steak and a tossed green salad, Jennifer's favorite, Adriana helped Jennifer clean up and Bridges left for Paul's home. It wasn't far, as the crow flies, however overland he would have to drive around to the farm roads in the rain.

Bridges arrived at Paul's as the rain was letting up. He was greeted at the front door by the housekeeper. A pleasant black woman that had been with Paul before his wife died. She escorted Bridges to Paul's study and closed the door behind them. She returned with a tray of coffee and a bottle of cognac as Bridges was seated.

Bridges spoke first. "Paul…thank you for getting back to me on the subject we discussed. I'm anxious to hear your advice."

As Paul assumed a voice of authority, he looked up at the photographs of Vietnam. Both men pictured with their platoons after a vicious fire-fight with a Battalion of North Vietnamese regulars. Their casualties were light. Bridges immediately sensed he was going to be on the receiving end of a lecture. He couldn't help feeling angry, although he would allow Paul to have his way.

"Richard, remember that day?" As he pointed to the photograph. "It was the toughest day of my life and I'm sure it was yours. The situation you present to me from a legal stand point is hard to digest, however as a friend, I'm strongly suggesting you drop any idea to foil this event of history that may takes its course."

Bridges in protest, forgetting Paul was a legal mind. "But Paul."

"I know what you're about to say…we don't need another assassination that will turn this stumbling bum into a historical hero. I hear you my friend. This was thought through and through, I don't want you to even share any of this with the FBI or anyone else. Drop it and get on with other things that'll please you. Marry Adriana or something."

Bridges looked into the man's grey-blue eyes that once were bright blue, he couldn't believe what he was hearing from his friend. To argue the point would be a waste of time, Paul's mind was made up. Bridges asked Paul a compromising question. "If it go's down, someone takes the President out, what well you do?"

"I'll attend the funeral and pretend to comfort the widow. Maybe swear-in the new President. If you're asking me about having prior knowledge, I never spoke to anyone including you about an assassination. Our conversations never took place. Is that clear my Richard?"

Bridges sat back in his chair. He couldn't believe his ears. The only person that he expected strong advice from just told him to put his head in the sand and let it happen. Bridges thought Paul wasn't the same person he once knew and thought he wasn't the same person in the photograph. "Paul why…why are you telling me this, why can't you just give your blessing because of your position with the Supreme Court, why are you telling me to look the other way?"

"Because my friend, it has to be this way. The no good sonofabitch has disgraced the office of the President, he's brought disgrace to our country. As I said before, he isn't qualified to clerk for me, let alone be my President."

As Bridges was about to make a comment, Paul suggested he leave and forget they had the conversation.

Bridges sat in his car thinking for a few minutes. He thought maybe Paul was part of the plot. He knew now that he couldn't go to anyone in the Senate or House, or for that matter the FBI or even the Secret Service. For the first time since arriving in DC many years ago, he felt as an outsider, an outsider of the happenings inside the beltway. It was a distant feeling, something he never wanted to experience.

The moon was shining over the wet meadows as Bridges drove the unpaved roads and every time he hit a pot hole he thought what Paul said. Upon arrival at home, he noticed Adriana asleep on the couch in the family room. The barn lights were off which suggested Jennifer was in bed. The lights at William's house were dim and he presumed they were in bed or were getting ready for bed.

As he entered the room, Adriana woke, sat up and provided a strained smile. She came to reality and sensed Bridges was upset and angry. "What's wrong Richard?"

"Paul...told me to look the other way and let history take its course."

Adriana commented as she stretched her arms. "I always though Paul was a gutless bastard...I never said it...but when I was looking for you before I went to Jordan, I spoke to him. He couldn't outright praise you or damn you. He's a middle of the roader, has he always been that way?"

"I don't know. When we were in the Marine Corps he never demonstrated this attitude, then again he got most of his platoon killed one day. Maybe he did and I didn't pick up on it. He won't even acknowledge that we spoke."

Bridges suggested Adriana stay for the night. She could sleep in the guest room. Adriana gladly accepted the invitation and explained she had to get up early and return to her townhouse to change clothes for work.

Bridges couldn't sleep, he tossed and turned and on two or three occasions wanted to call Tom, but thought better. He finally fell asleep after thought of Adriana sleeping in the next room.

The following morning, Bridges woke and heard Jennifer and Adriana talking in the kitchen. He quickly put on some clothes and entered the kitchen. Both of them cheerfully greeted him.

Bridges sipping coffee at Tom More's office, he gave him the entire picture. Tom thought that Paul Castilli lost his nerve or never had balls when they were in Nam. Tom asked about the contents of the tapes he obtained and what Adriana's reactions had been. Bridges admitted he may be too hard on her and his mistrust is misdirected. Tom strongly suggested he and Adriana go over to Baltimore and talk to Michael Meyers' girlfriend and the wife of James Allen, what's her name?"

"You mean Christine Allen, James Allen's wife?"

"Ya...maybe you missed something." Tom directed as though Bridges was one of his detectives.

Bridges agreed, however Adriana was working over at the White House and he didn't think she could get away this afternoon. Tom offered one of his female detectives. Bridges hesitated and then accepted the offer after he called Adriana. She didn't see any problem and indicated she couldn't talk at the moment. Tom assigned Officer Kerri Jackson to work with Bridges. She was young, about twenty-nine, maybe younger. Articulate and a neat dresser.

After lunch, Bridges and Officer Jackson drove over to the Baltimore side, Germantown. Their first stop was the University of Maryland. Bridges agreed maybe Michael's girlfriend had more information that would help them in piecing the case together and determine if there was a connection to the plot to assassinate the President. When they arrived at her office, they were told Professor Joanne Walker is on sabbatical and left the previous day. Date of return wasn't known. Bridges glanced into the office and noticed the woman's personal items had been removed, as though she left and wasn't returning. Officer Jackson dressed in plain clothes and not knowing exactly what they were looking for, except she knew Bridges wanted to interview a member of the faculty. She was quick to notice Professor Walker's name had been removed from the posted list at the entrance. Bridges thought the observation was a good one and he decided they go over to visit Christine Allen. He looked at his watch and noticed that she may not be home yet, but decided to go by the house. When they arrived, Bridges noticed a government car parked in front. He decided to park up the street and observe who entered the car. They were in luck, two men, obviously FBI Agents were leaving the Allen house. Bridges recognized one of the agents as Jim Connolly, a person he knew was assigned to terrorist activities and Bridges recalled when the agent was in New York, he neglected to notify the New York Police Department concerning a possible bombing at the National Trade Center. It was common knowledge he lied when he reported that he alerted the police. He was later transferred to DC after the Trade Center explosion. The other person may have been a new FBI agent fresh out of the academy.

Bridges allowed them to pull away from the curb and leave the neighborhood before he and Officer Jackson knocked on Christine's door.

Christine answered the door. Once she recognized Bridges, she smiled and immediately invited him and officer Jackson into the house.

Bridges introduced Kerri Jackson as his assistant and deliberately omitted that she was a police detective from Metropolitan Police. He didn't want to alarm her. Christine immediately asked about Adriana, Bridges explained she was detained at the White House and sent her regards.

It was obvious the child was not in the house as Christine explained she sent her to the grandparents in New Hampshire. As they were seated in the living room, Christine didn't hesitate telling Bridges that two FBI Agents were there and wanted to talk to her husband. A tears came to her eyes when she mentioned her husband, Jim Allen. "They said they were searching for Jim and wanted to know if I had any idea where was. I don't think they believed me…to be honest Mr. Bridges, I think my husband is dead. Don't ask me why I feel that way, but I'm certain he's dead."

Bridges tried to comfort her but her mind was made up. He didn't think it was his place to tell her, but maybe it would be better coming from him and Adriana, another day.

Kerri Jackson sat quiet, not knowing a thing about the situation. She knew the woman was pregnant and she gathered the husband was missing. Bridges deliberately didn't provide details to the detective.

"Did you tell the FBI anything about the tapes?"

"No and they didn't ask."

"Good…how are you…can we help in some way?"

I'm fine except my husband is missing…that's all." Tears again rolled down her cheeks.

Christine asked Bridges what he knew about the money being placed in her account. Bridges pretended he didn't know, and suggested she use he money as though it came from her husband's salary. Christine informed Bridges that another deposit was made and she was told by a girlfriend who's an attorney it was alright to use the money.

"Chris…we were over to the University to talk to Joanne, she's not there, what do you know about that?"

"Mr. Bridges…she left yesterday for New Jersey she isn't coming back to Maryland. Why she would go to New Jersey is beyond me.

She's not from there and has no family there that I know about. She told me she'd call and let me know where she's staying."

Bridges asked Chris about her job and was told she should take time off and she would remain on the payroll. This didn't surprise Bridges and when he was told by Chris that none of her husband's friends visited her, he then knew there had to be a concerted effort by those in government to cover-up James Allen's disappearance. Bridges wanted to tell Chris what he knew, but didn't think he would until Adriana was present. As they were leaving, Chris offered to call Bridges when Joanne checked in with her. Bridges reassured her that if she needed anything, not to hesitate to call Adriana or himself. Bridges didn't know if Chris was safe living alone and whether or not a terrorist group would harm her.

Bridges noticed a stack of mail on the dining-room table. With his aging eyes, he managed to notice the top envelope had a New Jersey post-mark, although no visible return address. The house seemed clean and freshly wall-papered. The china cabinet contained expensive looking china and nick-knacks Bridges guessed was from Germany and Italy. The carpet looked clean and probably a few months old. The old home was cozy and big enough for a young couple and a child. The front door was of solid oak and had recently been refinished, the windows were spotless. Drapes nearly hung and complemented the room. Chris impulsively hugged Bridges as a lonesome girl hugging her father. She smiled at Officer Jackson and shook her had as she and Bridges walked out the door. As a last thought, Bridges suggested Chris call him should the FBI Agents return. This made Chris feel comfortable and thanked Bridges with another hug.

While Detective Jackson drove them back to Police Headquarters, she smiled and looked over at Bridges who was deep in thought. She smiled again and boldly commented that he was a comfort to be around and complemented him in making Mrs. Allen feel comfortable. Bridges didn't know if the young officer was flirting with him or she was sincere in her remarks. He, for some reason felt as he did when ever he was alone with Becky.

As Bridges smiled and thought Officer Jackson was an attractive black woman with class. He wondered why she would be a police officer in DC when there were other jobs in Washington that she could qualify for and not place herself in harms way. He then asked. The young woman explained her father retired from the DC Metro Police and she was planning to work for one of the Federal Agencies when she finished a graduate program.

They arrived at the Station. Bridges thanked her for the help. She smiled and offered herself anytime he needed her. Bridges didn't know what she meant, then smiled when he realized she was flirting again.

In Tom's office, Bridges thanked him for loaning the officer to him. Tom smiled and knew that Kerri Jackson flirted with him. "She likes older men I'm told."

"Tom, I don't need complications now in my life, but she is an attractive woman." Then he dropped the subject. Bridges went over what he learned from Mrs. Allen, which wasn't much, he contended. "She explained that Michael Meyers' girlfriend, Joanne Walker left the Baltimore area and she is believed to be in New Jersey."

Tom perked up and reminded Bridges that criminal intelligence reported that 'Jersey' is the hot-bed of the terrorist groups. "Maybe she heard from Michael and went up there to be with him."

Bridges thought Tom read his mind. "If that were the case, then she may have told Christine Allen that her husband was dead, or words that gave Chris the impression her husband Jim was dead. When I met with her, she at first was cheerful then she became frightened when she spoke of her missing husband. A natural reaction. The two FBI suits didn't help things by paying her a visit under the guise that they were investigating the whereabouts of her husband, when those dip-shits know that he's in Michael's Meyers' grave."

Tom sat and toyed with the thoughts of Chris already knowing her husband was dead. He thought maybe she should be placed in protective custody in the event those responsible for her husbands death want to use her for what ever reason. He shared this thought with Bridges.

Bridges revealed that he noticed unopened mail sittingon Chris Allen's table. "I noticed the top envelop was post-marked 'NJ' although the city couldn't be distinguished."

"If the woman left Baltimore yesterday and drove to New Jersey, I'm certain a letter mailed to Chris could have arrived today from the southern part of the state. Richard, I think you and Adriana should pay the woman another visit, or maybe just Adriana run by there and find out. But then again you should be there. What do you have to loose?" Tom Moore advised Bridges and provided a strong suggestion.Bridges thought before he spoke. "Something I didn't mention, Chris sent her two year old daughter to her parents home in New Hampshire, at the same time she is off work with pay, what does she do all day?"

"Good question Richard...that's why you and Adriana have to return this evening and talk to her. As I said before, the motive for killing the Allen kid is either he knew too much about Madam Heidi's relationship with the woman in Central America or its got something to do with terrorist activity, remember, the Allen kid worked for NSA, they got their ears on suspected terrorist groups operating in the states, don't forget."

Adriana agreed to revisit Chris Allen. Bridges called Chris from Adriana's townhouse. She was receptive to them visiting her and sounded peculiar by comparison to his earlier conversation with her. Bridges didn't want to spook her and bring it to her attention, he thought better and saved it for when they met.

***

They arrived at Chris Allen's townhouse close to eight, it started to rain again and the street was vacant other than for the residence cars parked curbside. Bridges had difficulty locating a parking space near the house. He and Adriana had to walk a block down to the Allen house after Bridges parked his Cherokee in a tight spot.

They arrived at the house and noticed no lights were on. Bridges rung the bell and moments later, Chris answered and invited them in. Seated in the living room, Bridges led off by asking if Chris heard from Joanne Walker.

Chris surprisingly answered YES and went on to explain she received a short letter and then a telephone call. "Joanne is in New Jersey with friends…I didn't know she had friends there."

Bridges suspected she knew more. "What else Chris?"

"I don't know, I don't understand…Joanne is with Michael? What's going on…?"

Adriana comforted Chris as she explained that she learned Michael was not dead. She then asked the dreaded question. "Where is my husband…is he dead?"

Bridges stood, looked down at her as Adriana held her close, then he informed Chris her husband was dead and was buried in Michael's grave.

The woman screamed out of control and broke into tears. Her scream was loud enough to be heard by neighbors.

Adriana reasoned with her that there was an explanation to the entire mess and was successful on calming her down. The telephone rang, Bridges suggested Adriana answer it. When Adriana lifted the receiver to say hello…the line went dead. They asked to see the letter from Joanne. It was simple explaining she had to leave Baltimore and that she would call to explain. Signed ~Jo~…

As Chris settled down and she was under emotional control, Adriana proceeded to explain what little she knew concerning terrorist activity involving Michael and possibly he husband. Bridges filled in the blanks and safeguarded what he and Adriana were working on. The woman couldn't handle any more, she needed basic facts about why her husband was dead and buried in another person's grave.

The telephone range again, Bridges pointed to Chris to answer it…the caller was Joanne. The conversation was a brief explanation as to why she left and she was with Michael. She confirmed that James was killed and buried in Michael's grave. As she listened, she looked up at Bridges and received a nod as to tell Joanne that he and Adriana were in the house with her. Once Joanne heard she had company, found a reason to terminate the phone call and promised to contact her the following day. Before Chris could ask for a phone number, the line went dead, obvious Joanne hung up. Bridges check caller ID and it noted NONE.

Adriana suggested Chris move in with her until the mess was sorted out. Bridges agreed and informed Chris that the DC Metro Police wanted to talk to her about her husband and explained they already knew of her husband's death.

She was assured by Adriana that she would be alright and that Richard would be with her when she met with the police.

The following morning, Bridges met Adriana and Chris and they proceeded to Metro Police Headquarters. They were escorted to Captain Moore's office and were seated. Tom smiled at Adriana as she introduced Chris to him. After the introduction, Adriana explained she had a meeting at the White House and she would be late if she didn't leave.

During the meeting, Tom explained the entire situation to Chris and deliberately left out anything to do with Bridges and Adriana's project. She started crying as she did most of the night while she was with Adriana. She was told that the correction of the burial site wouldn't be made until they were finished with the investigation. Tom went on to explain that he had reason to suspect James was killed by Middle-Eastern terrorists. This wasn't confirmed thus far, however it was the best information to provide the grieving widow of James Allen. After the meeting, Bridges agreed to drive Chris over to townhouse to gather more of her personal belongings she needed while she was staying with Adriana.

They arrived at the house just before the noon hour. Bridges parked the Cherokee in front of the row similar decorated townhouses. He was able to distinguish the Allen house from the others by the small religious shrine of the blessed mother inside the small wrought-iron fenced yard.

Chris put the key into the lock of the front door, she immediately realized the door wasn't locked. Bridges entered first after Chris informed him the door was unlocked. He suggested she stay outside, however Chris insisted she follow Bridges into the house. Inside, they discovered that someone ransacked the house looking for something

Bridges suspected was the tapes. Chris appeared overwhelmed by the destruction that had been made. She started to cry when she discovered her china and nick-nacks were damaged by the search. The couches in the loving room were torn at the seems, when the searcher could have un-zippered the seat covers. Upstairs in her bedroom the closet containing hers and James' clothes were thrown around. The place was beyond repair.

Bridges suggested Chris make a formal report to the police and provide them a statement when they arrived. He cautioned her not to reveal anything concerning suspected terrorist activity.

Before the Baltimore Police arrived, Bridges went down to the basement. For some reason the intruders neglected the basement or found what they were looking for in the living quarters. He noticed the elaborate recording set-up on neatly constructed benches and various recording editing devices. He returned to Chris who was in her bedroom crying while gathering some clothes and personal items. Bridges asked her a question. "Chris, what do you suspect they were looking for?"

"I don't know Mr. Bridges…I don't know, maybe tapes or something that belonged to James. Bridges informed her that nothing seem to be bothered in the basement. Chris in a crying state asked if the large metal locker in the basement had been forced open. Before Bridges answered, he didn't recall seeing a metal locker when he was down there. They both returned to the basement and discovered the metal locker was missing.

"Chris what did James keep in the box?"

"I don't know, but he always kept it locked, either from me or who ever came to visit him. Often he would entertain friends in the basement while he was working or playing around with the recording equipment." By now Chris' sadness turned to anger.

Two uniformed officers arrived, one was a woman officer that expressed sincere concern when she interviewed Chris, the male officer looked around and pretended to know what he was doing. He went to the basement, Bridges followed. The Officer suggested to Bridges that it probably was kids that committed the burglary. Bridges didn't disagree but thought the officer out of his league and shouldn't make statements as he did. After the woman officer completed her interview of Chris, she thanked her and both officers left advising Chris that she could get a copy of the report next week so she could forward it to her insurance company. The statement alone caused Chris to cry again. Bridges thought that both of them were a sorry bunch, however they often respond to residential burglary calls that are committed by gang members or neighbor kids.

After the officers left, Chris informed Bridges that they haven't had a burglary call in this neighborhood in two years, according to the woman officer. "What will I do Mr. Bridges?"

"The first thing is stop calling me Mr. Bridges, my first name is Richard, I prefer you call me that." Bridges thought maybe he was to harsh with her, but she looked up at him with her tear stained face, smiled and hugged him.

"Chris you have to clean things up, put the place back in shape. Don't through anything away, what is damaged and you don't want or need, put in boxes. While living with Adriana, you may want to come by the house once and awhile, in the day time. Where is your car?"

"It's in the garage at the rear of the house, we have to go to the alley in order to get there."

Bridges drove Chris through the alley that separated the houses between streets, they found her garage and she managed to remove her white Ford Mustang and followed Bridges over to Adriana's townhouse. Once inside Bridges called Adriana at the White House.

"Hello Richard what's new, or shouldn't I ask?"

"Nothing that can't wait until I see your smiling face, just thought I'd check in. How about you?"

"I need to get together with you…the word around here is that we are getting married, so if you hear that news, it came from here. Seriously, we need to talk."

"Early dinner okay?"

"Richard I'm leaving now, I have some small items to pick up at the store and I'll be there…tell Chris to make herself at home."

Bridges planned to go over to see Tom and then return. He left Chris alone at Adriana's Townhouse, he walked to his Cherokee parked curbside in front of the house and noticed the leaves had fallen on his car during the short time he was inside Adriana's house.

The street was slick from the recent rain. As he unlocked his car door, he noticed a young man standing across the street staring at him. He stood up straight to get a better look and realized the face was familiar, but couldn't place it. He decided to be neighborly and wave at the man. This caused him to cross the street and approach Bridges. As he approached, he extended his hand in a gesture to shake. A that moment, a single gun shot echoed a cracked sound and the man dropped to the pavement in front of Bridges. Bridges looked around while in the crouched position. He wished he was armed, he felt defenseless. Bridges crouched down in case the shooter wanted to take him out. He noticed an old looking grey colored VW speed away from the curb. Bridges noticed New Jersey license, although he couldn't interpret the numbers because of the poor lighting from the over cast sky.

Bridges attended to the man and discovered he didn't know him after all, although he was Middle Easterner, Iranian or Jordanian, he couldn't tell. Bridges searched the man's pockets after he discovered he was dead. He had no identification on him and his clothes were not American made.

By then, various people came out of the townhouses and came to his aid. One man informed Bridges that he already called the Para-Medics and the Police. Shortly, the Virginia State Police arrived at the same time the Para-Medics. Bridges provided a statement and was allowed to leave. He returned to Adriana's house and discovered Chris was afraid to open the door until she was certain it was Bridges. She let him in and he immediately called Tom More and related details of the incident. Tom assured Bridges that he'll get two of his detectives to assist the Virginia Police and determine as much information as possible.

***

Adriana arrived home as Bridges was hanging the phone up. She was anxious to know why the police and Para-Medics were out front. Bridges quickly filled her in and she sat down, kicked off her shoes and seemed speechless. Chris came out of the bathroom when Adriana started to talk. She didn't care if Chris was there, she had to get it off her chest.

"That fucken…Heidi is sick…I mean it…she thinks she's running the country." Adriana took a deep breath, Richard thought she was going to blow a gasket. "She got into an argument over a stupid thing with the President, the Secret Service knew better to interfere…she couldn't get her way and picked up a small lamp and threw it at him…in front of the aids and Security. I tried to calm her down…she listens to me most of the time…this time she accused me of fucking her husband, can you believe that, that slime ball?"

"Then what?" Bridges asked with disgust.

"When she cooled off…she apologized to me…I mean she almost got on her knees to tell me she didn't mean what she said. I thought she was going to hug me or kiss me when she begged me not to resign."

Chris sensed that Bridges and Adriana had business to discuss. It was early evening and she left to go over to her office to get some personal things at the State Department. Before she left, Bridges assured her she would be alright…the man that was shot was a target and not just anybody. Chris now seemed calm, but they both knew she was twisting inside over the news of her husband's death.

Bridges immediately filled Adriana in on the details of Chris' house being ransacked and a metal locker stolen

"I think the burglary may have a connection to our project, the persons that ransacked the house were looking for tapes, unless James Allen had tapes of terrorist activities."

Adriana expressed she needed a stiff drink. She fixed herself a double shot of bourbon, 'Wild-Turkey' and water. She took it in two gulps. Then poured another and sat down allowing her skirt to go up to reveal more of her legs and her black lace pants. She didn't seem to care, although if it turned Bridges on, it was just what she needed, she thought. He looked with a certain amount of curiosity then looked away. Adriana became aware Bridges looked and she repositioned herself on the couch by uncrossing her legs and then slowly crossing them again. By that time Bridges fixed himself a drink, he decided to have the same as Adriana, although he drank it in a civilized fashion.

The telephone rang twice before Adriana got off the couch to answered. It was Tom Moore asking to speak to Richard after he jokingly flirted with Adriana.

"If your not sitting, you better Richard…the poor bastard that was attempting to make contact with you was on the FBI's list of terrorist that are based in New Jersey."

"How the hell were you able to find out?"

"He's been printed, they run it through the bureau and bingo…it came up with a full profile. I wonder why he was attempting to make contact with you?"

"Beats me…he looked familiar, however, when I got up close, I realized I never met him before."

"I got some more good shit for you…in the trunk of an abandoned Hertz rental car, parked down the street from Adriana's place, they found a metal box about the size of the locker boxes we had in the Corps. The sonofabitch contained all sorts and sizes of recorded tapes. Get this…James Allen's name is all over the contents, either his initials or his name. It seems, the poor dead bastard burglarized Chris Allen's house, one thing…he couldn't have carried the box alone, it was too damn heavy. The car was rented in the dead guys real name, or at least the name we have, one of those Arab names I have difficulty pronouncing.

"Tommy, I'd like the poor bastards profile, but I'm interested to know more about the shooting…what caliber and type of gun?"

Tom was quick to inform Bridges about the gun. "I can tell you this much…it was a thirty caliber, maybe the rifle was bolt action, like the old Springfield, we can't be sure. Our lab boys will be over there with the State Crime Lab people to search the firing point. Can you at least tell me where the shot came from?"

"Not very well…it came from a roof on the north side of the street. Not far…you have to remember the echo distorted the sound. It was a single crack…that's it. The man was down before I realized what happened. Scared the hell out of me. What a helpless feeling…I didn't have a gun to protect myself."

"I'll be over with the lab people…you can show them where you think the shot came from…I'll get another chance to see that sweet woman." Tom chuckled at his own comment.

Adriana answered the door. By that time she changed into a grey jogging suit with the zipper drawn down slightly exposing her cleavage. Her reception of Tom was more than he expected, she gave him a peck on the mouth in her greeting. His Irish face became flush and hoped Bridges didn't notice.

Outside with the Lab Technician and Tom's people, they searched the townhouses Bridges thought the shot had been fired from. They came up with nothing. Bridges suggested they check several more, further away from the location the victim had been shot. Tom with a ceratin amount of hesitation along with the lab people, agreed and they searched several houses about 300 hundred yards away. Up in the garret of the last house that was vacated, they discovered an expended 30 caliber cartridge, and two Wrigley gum wrappers. Preliminary opinions agreed that the shot was fired through a small opening in the attic lugered vent.

The house hadn't been empty long, maybe two-three days at the most. The crime scene team felt satisfied their search was a success. Photographs and prints taken along with the usual requirements in the preservation of a crime scene.

"You know Richard…I thought 300 yards away was too far to look, I only agreed with you because we used to fire on the range from two-to-three hundred yards with the M-1 and later M-14"

"Tom you forget we also had to qualify from the five-hundred yard line…remember?" Bridges pointed out, then made a bold comment. The—16 wasn't bad either."

"The shooter was an American…Tom, it wasn't a 'sand-niger' they can't shoot for shit no matter how much training they had. The Israeli are the exception.

Tom took Bridges word for it and talked to the State Lab Supervisor. The supervisor agreed with Bridges, which hurt Tom's feeling because he hadn't been up on the information.

They returned to Adriana's townhouse. Inside Adriana made some appetizers and both men had a drink. The conversation was about the project and they all went over the events as they happened. They agreed the shooter wasn't from the Middle-East.

Bridges ruled out Agency or anyone else from government. "It may have been a renegade agent from here or Israel doing it for money. Remember, the VW was registered in New Jersey. Chris' friend Joanne Walker left for New Jersey…we think Michael is there, and criminal intelligence tells us the terrorist groups assemble there, around the Clifton area, easy access to New York. But then maybe, just maybe…if it's connected to us and our project…perhaps the shooter was hired by…you know who Adriana."

Bridges thought of Tim Young and thought he should tell Tom about is misfortune. When Tom heard, he became emotional, they bunked together during stand-down, which was often because of the politicians were running the Vietnam war during their tour. Their activities were limited to search and destroy missions, they all thought was a joke. Tim was the only one that got action when ever he went out. He'd tie himself to a tree and did what he did best, shooting…he was the Corps best sniper. He didn't brag too much, but the stories that came back to the states about collecting VC ears was true when Tim had a kill. When he knew it was safe, Tim went over to the VC body and cut the ears off. He kept them in a jar he got from a Navy Corpsman at the hospital ship docked in Da Nang

Bridges remembered and protected Tim from the Battalion Commander who issued an order that 'no body parts' would be collected. The ears kept Tim lucid even though it appeared barbaric.

Tom had to leave, it was obvious he was still upset about his Vietnam buddy Tim Young and the misfortune he had. He didn't want to think about him anymore. As Tom was leaving, both Adriana and Bridges went to the door, Adriana hugged him and Bridges shock his hand, and made one more comment. "Remember…the sniper's choice was a 30 caliber Springfield bolt action."

Tom looked away, then responded as a cop. "I hear ya…Richard…I hear ya…we're looking for a Springfield no doubt, maybe not…Oswald used that piece of shit he bought from a mail house. It did the job and then some."

Chris pulled up as Tom was getting in his car. She took the parking space he vacated. When she entered Adriana noticed she had been crying and suggested they talk. Bridges decided to leave and return to his farm. He hadn't spent much time with Jennifer, certainly she as a young woman had problems she may want to discuss with her good-old.father.

***

At home, Bridges discovered Jennifer in the barn with the horses. She was in the first stall with the black colt and when Bridges approached, she was startled. At the same time was glad to see her father. They talked about trivial things and Bridges sensed she was lonesome. He thought it was a good time to talk about her trip to Jordan. Jennifer agreed she would leave during the Thanksgiving break. She was due to graduate in June and then grad-school.

She seemed to perk up when the plans seemed solid and she would visit Princes Lia in Amman. She would be the envy of the American Arabian horse world, especially those in her age group she competes against during the Nationals every year. Bridges assured her he would make the arrangements first thing in the morning and Adriana paved the way with the Princes. Jennifer cheered up and the news made her feel great. As she kissed and hugged her father, the black-colt walked between them appearing as though he wanted in-on-the affectionate moment.

No sooner Bridges entered the house, the phone rang. He looked at his watch and discovered it was nine-thirty. "Bridges here…oh hello Adriana…what's the matter, you feel down."

Adriana was down but could figure the reason. "I managed to calm Chris down and after she went to bed, I felt this lonesome feeling. Then I thought maybe that bullet was meant for you."

"I'm sure it wasn't…I'm ceratin the target was the Arab. But I will admit if the shooter didn't know his stuff…I could have been the mark. We were about to shake hands, that's how close we were. Enough Adriana…we have to determine if the incidents are connected to our project.

By the way, will you arrange for Jennifer to visit the palace and Princes Lia…right after Thanksgiving?"

Early the following day, Bridges phoned Dean in Los Angeles. Then he called Captain Matthews at LAPD. He wanted to inform Dean that he and Adriana would be there the first of next week and needed some confidential information pertaining to the President's visit from Matthews. What Bridges wanted Mathews to do was run record checks on a few people he was concerned with. He furnished the information and inquired about Rosa Carrea. Mathews informed him that everything was statuesque which satisfied Bridges and he termination the call…

CHAPTER 11
THE SURPRISE

The flight was fifteen minutes behind schedule and that meant they had to circle until the LAX tower gave then clearance to land on the busy runways. This upset Adriana for some reason other than she didn't like to fly. Bridges sensed there was something wrong and inquired, she replied that it was personal. He hadn't seen her act this way, and recalled she was excited to make the trip to Los Angeles and would be glad when the project came to an end, no matter what the out-come. The plan was to set up an observation position after locating Rosa and placed her under constant surveillance.

LAPD Captain Matthews met them at the United Airlines gate and drove them to the Hyatt hotel on Aviation Boulevard

Later, they were committed to attend a meeting at LAPD to exchange information without bringing attention to the project. Captain Matthews, as Commander of the Organized Crime and Intelligence Division, often referred to OCID, assured them he had things under control. The men assigned to the detail didn't have a clue as to a possible assassination attempt on the President's life. They were assigned to assist the Secret Service as they did on previous visits. The traffic from LAX to the hotel was heavy, although they didn't have to travel far.

Dean made reservation for them at the and left a message he would see them both later. Matthews received cellular phone call from the surveillance team. They reluctantly informed him that Rosa Carrea gave them the slip. The message upset the plans from the get-go. If they couldn't find the suspected assassin, then the entire plan would be a wash. Bridges, once hearing the news maintained his cool, although Adriana demonstrated her anger causing embarrassment to Bridges. She soon settled down when she discovered both men were not attempting to calm her. All Richard did was shake his head which seemed to work calming Adriana.

"What went wrong?" Bridges asked to gain knowledge and to settle Adriana's concern.

"From what they reported, she gave them the slip sometime during the hours of darkness. Her 'Beamer' is gone and they put out an all points…to just locate…not to approach the woman, and to keep her under surveillance."

Matthews stated with confidence and assurance, Rosa would be located before the President speaks the following day.

Adriana apologized to both men as they arrived at the Hyatt. Bridges smiled as he looked out the window of the car and privately thought she was experiencing PMS, although he knew better. There was something else bugging her and he didn't have the faintest idea what it was. He further thought it might be her last incident with the President's wife.

After registering, they went over to the office of OCID over on Georgia Street, not far from the hotel. In the conference room, Captain Matthews introduced them, Adriana as the First Lady's assistant and Bridges, most of the men knew him and believed he was with the Agency.

The routine was discussed as to deployment of uniformed police officers as security in and around the location the President planned to speak. The officers in attendance at the meeting were older officers and Bridges knew they were close to retirement. The only woman present was a detective from Internal Affairs Division. Bridges didn't quite understand her position, although she was an attractive Hispanic that spoke fluent Spanish.

They all received a security kit which included a color coded street map and locations of communication points. The intelligence report estimated three-four thousand Hispanics the first day, and the estimated number Afro-Americans the following day. The speaking platform was built ten-feet off the street and all vehicle traffic will be diverted at least a mile around the center of activity. The reason for separating the two ethnic groups was to avoid trouble, although no doubt there would be fighting and disruption in the crowds.

LAPD Aviation Division would be on standby with two helicopters on top of adjacent buildings away from the location, although in constant communication with the Command and Communication Post at the center of the attraction. Two SWAT Teams were assigned standby inside adjacent buildings and should be out of sight from the public, although on alert.

Para-medic units were scheduled to be on location that allowed to transport injured away from the activity center and easy access to hospitals.

Bridges thought for a moment that Federal law enforcement agencies had different communication codes, especially the FBI. LAPD used a code similar to other Police Departments' TEN-CODE but unique to the department. The exercise of providing security for the President had in the past been successful with little or no communication screw-ups, this shouldn't be any different. He thought about mentioning it to the group, then decided not to, in fear of sounding behind the times.

Captain Mathews announced that the FBI would be available for assistance. The group of seasoned detectives were entertained by the comment and laughed in harmony. Adriana seemed to be coming around after she became acquainted with the Hispanic woman officer. Bridges was happy to see Adriana had a smile on her face when the officers laughed and the woman officer leaned over and spoke to her.

While they were taking a break, a call came in from the Chief's office announcing that the President's advance detail wanted to change the plans and allow for Hispanic and Blacks to attend his presentation together. Also there would be one presentation because the President was anxious to attend the planned session in San Diego. Adriana spoke up and said “Golf” and the room full of detectives broke out in a roar. Bridges was happy to see her come back to earth and play the game.

Before they left the Georgia Street office, a call came in from the California Highway Patrol reporting the suspect car was parked outside the Del Mar Hotel in Oceanside, a hundred miles away in San Diego County and across from the Marine Corps Base, Camp Pendleton. This information was not appreciated by the detectives because in every VIP detail, suspects are placed under surveillance until after the scheduled incident.

Bridges was assured by Matthews that Oceanside Police Department had the suspect under surveillance. This sounded alright, however why was Rosa on her way to San Diego and not using the Los Angeles visit as a dress rehearsal. He shared his thought with Adriana and Matthews. They needed a positive identification of the woman and the assurance that the Oceanside situation wasn't a diversion. Mathews made arrangements for a photographer to take the woman's picture, however, this was a chance and the Oceanside Chief was uncertain his people would be able to unless she came out of the hotel, although they would try without blowing the surveillance.

Thirty minutes latter, an enlarged Polaroid photo of the woman came over the FAX. Matthews confirmed the photo resembled Rosa Carrea, the same woman that lived with his wife's parents. Adriana was happy to hear the news and by this times forgot her troubles and was a team player again. A second FAX photograph came in depicting the woman meeting with a white-male, estimated age, forty plus. The face wasn't clear although his entire body was in plain view. Bridges looked at the photo and remained silent. Adriana thought it was peculiar for Bridges not to make a comment. She left it alone until later. Adriana was beginning to read Bridges in a telepathic manner.

They returned to the hotel with Matthews and met Dean for dinner. The meeting between them seemed anxious. Bridges dismissed the feeling although after dinner and away from Dean and Adriana, he asked for the photos that came over the FAX.

Matthews readily produced the photos and Bridges examined the one with the male subject. He asked Matthews his opinion concerning the photo. "What do make of the male-figure with Rosa?"

"Not much…they look as though they're conducting business, nothing hanky-panky, just business I would guess."

"Do you see anything else?"

Matthews looked again and quickly responded. "The guy is a mail-man, see his pants with the stripe and the light shirt, maybe blue stripe and his pants grey. Are you telling me he's delivering a letter or package to her?"

Bridges smiled before he answered. "I don't know, but your observation agreed with my own."

Dean and Adriana finished their conversation and walked over to them. She had a broad smile on her face and thanked Captain Matthews for his assistance. Dean had to leave and said goodnight. The plan was to meet Matthews at seven in the morning at his office for an additional briefing

Bridges escorted Adriana to her room that was on the fourth floor and Bridges' room was on the fifth. He said good night, although he wanted to talk to Adriana, but thought maybe it wasn't the right time.

***

The following morning, Bridges was surprised that no one was at Captain Matthews office besides his secretary and a file clerk.

Adriana was curious as well and didn't hesitate to ask where his detectives where.

Matthews smiled and explained they were in place at the location of the President's speech. "We will be in contact with them later in the morning. Adriana, I hope you like coffee and donuts, that's all I have to offer."

Adriana smiled in a flirting manner and accepted the coffee and a plain cake-donut. She was dressed in her black jumpsuit allowing the slightest exposure of her cleavage.

Captain Matthews noticed and expressed his curiosity as to why the 'First Lady' wasn't making the trip. Adriana answered in a satirical manner. "Because she has more important things to do."

Bridges hoped Adriana would n't say anymore about Heidi, if she did, it might cause Matthews to be curious beyond what he's been told about the project. A call came in from Oceanside Police Department. They reported Rosa's car was still parked in the same spot. They hadn't seen her since she entered her room after receiving what may have been mail from the mail carrier the previous night. They managed to secure the adjacent room to hers, although there wasn't a sign of life inside. Bridges knew she gave them the slip. At seven in the morning, Rosa would be up and about and she would be expected to leave for her final destination which may be San Diego.

Twenty minutes later, Matthews received a call from the Oceanside Police Department surveillance team confirming the suspect-woman was inside room 122, or at least they heard her talking to someone over the phone. Matthews requested they monitor her calls and record them if possible. The surveillance officer in charge informed Matthews they were attempting to accomplish monitoring of the phone at this time. The first call that had been monitored was to her daughter in Los Angeles. Rosa spoke to her daughter who was being cared for by a neighbor in Brentwood, a domestic Rosa knew and who worked for one of the movie stars, which one, wasn't known at this time, although would be learned if necessary, they had the phone number and address.

Matthews suggested they go over the map of where the President would be speaking. Adriana reminded them that the President would not be in a suite, rather a light-blue shirt and tie, sleeves rolled up and top button of his shirt unbuttoned, necktie flaccid. "His Secret Service security closest to him, attempted to get him to wear a vest, the President refused…end of topic. The President is a wimp…he doesn't think an ethnic would assassinate him, this provides for a false sense of security."

Matthews agreed as he used an excuse to look at Adriana and admire her beauty. She enjoyed the attention and Bridges thought maybe that was the reason she was in a fowl mood because she wasn't receiving the attention she thought she deserved. Then he thought he was being unfair, she may have a legitimate reason and was certain Adriana would fill him in later.

They went over the map of Exposition Park where the President would be speaking that afternoon at noon. The suggestion was to use the Coliseum which would allow for a better control of the crowds. The President declined in the event they couldn't fill the Coliseum it would appear to the news media as though he threw a party and no one came. The location next to the museum was the choice. His advance team selected the Los Angeles Museum of Natural Sciences as the back-drop for the presentation. Bridges spoke out. "What a nice place for an afternoon assassination. There's residential buildings around the park, perfect for a trained sniper to use and get away without being caught, especially if the assassin was black or Hispanic."

Matthews smiled at Bridges' comment and shared with them some traffic problems in the area. "The Harbor Freeway was spiting-distance from the location. Our helicopters can't be as close as I want them and the SWAT Teams are going to be changed instead of inside buildings, they'll be inside borrowed moving vans parked close by. We will place a third SWAT team on the various roofs overlooking the park. Our command center is on the USC Campus across facing the park. No traffic permitted on Exposition, Vermont and Martin Luther King Boulevards with the exception of law enforcement and medical units.

Adriana appeared impressed with the plan even though there were problems with the President subscribing to security recommendations. "The presentation is designed for fifty-five minutes, it's my bet he'll turn it into two hours."

Mathews commented. "We're prepared and expect it, also when he's done, a military chopper will land and pick him up, this alone will force the crowds away from the speaking platform. We expect the worse besides what you guys expect."

Bridges felt, with Rosa being in San Diego, she may not be around for a dress rehearsal she doesn't know the second day has been canceled and that maybe the day she plans to take the President out. He shared his thoughts with Adriana and Matthews. Adriana again expressed her opinion that the assassination attempt would be in San Diego, maybe on the golf-course. This was the first time Bridges heard

Adriana mention the event may go-down on the golf-course. He didn't let it show that he was surprised.

At the Command-Communication Post on USC Campus, Adriana and Bridges sat inside a mobile-home being used to direct security for the President. FBI and Secret Service agents were in and out of the mobile unit using the phones and checking maps, drinking coffee and smiling at Adriana whom they thought was familiar but didn't know who she was

Bridges suggested he walk over to the speaking platform and Adriana agreed to stay in the Command Center until he returned. They had a good two hours until the President arrived by helicopter and Matthews sent one his men to make sure the landing-pad was clear and enough officers around to provide security.

The people started to arrive. Many brought lunches and of course their favorite beverage. It was a chance for many to see a live-president and didn't care what he said or for that matter, promised. Bridges approached the landing-pad and was challenged by two police officers. He reached into his shirt pocket and attached an ID badge to his coat. The red-colored badge alerted the officers that he was someone important, but they didn't know who. The color code wasn't known to anyone until six that morning, therefore Rosa couldn't know unless she had inside knowledge. Bridges walked over to the platform, inspected the construction and climbed the stairs and looked around the podium. City communication employees wearing yellow ID badges were checking the equipment.

As Bridges looked over to where the crowds were assembling, he looked past them to various two and three level houses about 300 yards away. He thought the locations were perfect for a sniper. He was able to distinguish various SWAT team members on the roofs or top floor windows, every-other-house. He returned to the Command Post. Adriana was busy talking to the Hispanic officer they met at OCID the previous day.

The woman was dressed in civilian clothes, jeans, white blouse and a brown tweed sport coat. As she talked to Adriana, she removed her coat, exposing a brown leather shoulder holster and a short 9mm

Beretta along with her LAPD badge clipped to her belt. The top button of her blouse revealed her beauty of the curve of her breasts and protruding nipples. Besides her looks, there appeared a certain sexual-attraction with her wearing the holster and Beretta. The woman was about thirty to thirty-five. She sounded intelligent and Adriana was getting along with her

Bridges was impressed as she smiled when she glanced over at him, and continued her conversation with Adriana. It was getting close to the noon hour and the arrival of the President by helicopter.

Matthews was on the phone when he learned the President would be an estimated thirty-minutes late. This alone created a problem for uniformed police officers that are responsible for controlling the crowed.

The agent in charge of the Secret Service entered the Command Post, he immediately recognized Adriana and questioned her reason for being there. Adriana, slightly embarrassed, responded, forcing the agent to back off. "I'm doing your job "Jack" I was sent by the First Lady to keep an eye on the Prez...making sure he doesn't stray."

Bridges smiled at Adriana's comment and her ability to handle people, especially when they challenge her. The CP was so crowded no one else heard the brief tiff between the agent and Adriana. Shortly after, a call came in from Heidi, she spoke to Adriana, praising her for the way she handled the Secret Service agent. News travels fast she thought. Evidently the agent checked it out and Heidi jumped all over his shit. No sooner she hung the phone up, the agent offered his apology. The Hispanic officer smiled and looked the other way.

Adriana and the officer left the CP and walked over to the platform. They were both challenged by uniformed officers until they produced their pass-cards that had been on beaded chains around their necks. The bright green pass around Officer Quinn's neck signified 'law enforcement' and the red pass around Adriana's neck identified her as VIP.

Officer Quinn was stopped by a uniformed Hispanic officer who knew Officer Quinn at the Academy. Adriana was introduced to the officer as a member of the Washington Security Team. He knew better because of the VIP red-badge.

Upon their return to the CP, Captain Matthews commented that he was glad Officer Quinn had returned and had a specific job for her. "Elvia, I'd like you to interpret the Spanish in this tape recording of a telephone conversation. Adriana and the officer went over to the next smaller mobile-home and used the recording equipment. She handed Adriana a head set and placed one on her own head. They heard a conversation in Spanish whom Adriana recognized as Rosa Carrea talking Spanish to another woman. The summary of the conversation amounted to the unidentified woman giving Rosa permission to use a Condo that belonged to her boss. The boss was out of the country and Officer Quinn and Adriana smiled at each other when they learned the Condo was over-looking a golf course. Adriana, as she removed the head-phones, indicating the information had to be related to Bridges. Officer Quinn didn't understand, she thought their suspect was taking advantage of a friendship and was planning a brief vacation without having to pay for lodging.

Bridges met Adriana and Officer Quinn as he was stepping out of the CP trailer. He sensed excitement in her voice as she proceeded to tell him of the discovery. Bridges smiled and commented. "I guess you're right, the attempt will go down at the Golf Course in San Diego, as you predicted. What does the President's agenda call for…what golf course and when will he be there?"

Officer Quinn realized they were talking about something she wasn't privileged to and entered the CP.

The President's helicopter arrived and he got out and climbed the erected platform. The crowd cheered as he raised his arms in recognition of them. Security was tight and Bridges knew that no one person could stop an assassin bent of taking the President out, at least two-three hundred yards away. Because they had a handle on Rosa Carrea, they didn't let their guard down. The President's speech went on without a hitch. The crowd had mixed feelings, many cheers and just as many expressions of disapproval. Several attending the function were arrested for being drunk and fighting. After the President gave his

55 minute speech that lasted an hour and a half, he left by helicopter. The crowd cleared, a body of a young black woman was found, she had been shot in the back by a small caliber gun. Bridges thought there was a similarity in the way James Allen was killed. Small caliber at close range through the back and lodged in the heart, very little blood.

They had two days to prepare for the San Diego event. Bridges rented a car and they drove to San Diego County, stopping in Oceanside to visit with the Chief of Police

Bridges thanked the Chief and his men for the assistance and learned something surprising. He felt certain it was a coincidence and decided not to share the information with Adriana, at least not at this time.

Before they left Oceanside, Bridges phoned his old friend, Tim Young. The daughter answered the phone and once she learned Bridges was in Vietnam with her father, she informed him that her father hadn't been home for two days and she didn't know where to find him. Bridges learned from the daughter that Tim was drinking again and often missed work. The daughter sounded intelligent, maybe in her late teens, or older. She further added that her father sometimes hangs-out at the del-Mar Staff-NCO-Club, at the Marine Corps Base. This was a lead, if Tim wasn't there maybe someone may know his whereabouts. Adriana seemed confused, she wondered why it was important to locate Tim Young. She decided to ask. "What's the urgency in locating your friend, Tim Young?"

Bridges felt helpless, he had to locate Tim for several reasons. He didn't know if he should share the reasons with Adriana. He then decided to answer her question. "He was a Sniper in Vietnam, he also was in charge of the Marine Corps Sniper School before he retired. I'd like to consult him on a few things before we go after Rosa…or who ever." He felt uncomfortable fragmenting his reasons. She seemed satisfied and spoke of how professional the Chief of Police at Oceanside Police Department was in rendering assistance.

Bridges dialed the information operator at the Marine Base. The cellular phone on the rental was handy. The operator provided Bridges the Club phone number at Camp Del Mar. Immediately he dialed, the phone rang several times before someone answered. “Hi I’m Richard Bridges, may I speak to the manager?”

The young woman must be a Marine. “Yes Sir…I’ll get him…one minute Sir.”

Shortly a voice came on the phone. “Sergeant Cummings Sir.”

“Sergeant I’m trying to locate a retired Master-Gunnery Sergeant who spends a lot of time at your club, his name is…” Before Bridges could finish, the Club Manager provided Tim Young’s name.

“Sarge…can you tell me where I can find him, I was in Nam with him, it’s important that I reach him.”

“Sir…he was here last night with one of his woman, but I don’t know where he is now, maybe at the Post Office in Oceanside, that’s where he works…or pretends to work.”

Bridges didn’t know what the Sergeant meant, but he let it go. “Does he frequent the club…often?”

“He sure does, I’ll bet he’ll be here tonight.”

Bridges thanked the Sergeant and said goodbye. Adriana sitting in the front passenger seat of the rental car was busy reading the Los Angeles Times she picked up at the news-stand. She read out-loud the media’s opinion concerning the President’s visit and how the people in attendance appreciated the presentation on maintaining the Affirmative Action Program. “There’s a photograph of us with Captain Matthews, although the newspaper only mentions we were part of the security…no names.”

Bridges was glad the newspaper didn’t mention names, and unhappy with the photo in the paper and couldn’t remember when it was taken.

Bridges suggested they continue to San Diego, check into the hotel and meet with the San Diego Sheriff’s Department people. The plan was to work with them as they did in Los Angeles. He didn’t want to make a big deal out of meeting with his friend Tim, at least for now.

Bridges thought he would return to Oceanside later that evening after their meeting and locate Tim. At that time, if Adriana wanted to take the sixty mile trip, he would explain the urgency of finding and talking to him. If she didn’t feel up to taking the ride back up the coast, he didn't know if he would share the information. He thought about Tim, he's getting up in age, maybe fifty-two or three. The poor bastard was good at what he did in Vietnam. He was awarded a Silver-Star and two Bronze Stars for valor. Two Purple Hearts for wounds. Bridges recalled Tim didn't want to accept the Purple Heart Medals because his wounds were superficial by his interpretation, however, he caught an AK-47 round through the arm inches from his flack jacket and the second wound was a pungee-stick through the left foot, leaving him with a slight limp.

After they checked into the Mir Mar Hotel, they went over to the Sheriff's Department. They were not as organized as LAPD when came to VIP details and having it all-together for the President's visit. The Secret Service advance team attended the meeting, two of them came down from LA. They both knew Adriana and made it known they did, although totally ignored Bridges

It was getting late and they all agreed to meet early the next morning. Adriana wanted to return to the hotel and catch up in her sleep. Bridges, as planned headed up the coast after he phoned Tim's house and learned from the daughter that he had been there and left after changing clothes. The daughter forgot to tell her father that Bridges called, which Bridges was happy to hear. She also learned that he would be going to San Diego the following day to meet some friends for a golf game.

Bridges arrived at the Marine Base, Camp Del Mar location. He reminisced to himself that it didn't seem almost twenty years since he left Camp Pendleton for Vietnam. He was a inexperienced platoon leader, just made first-lieutenant with a precedence number senior to Paul Castilli. In those days, a Marine Officer made Captain based on performance and of course the precedence. This pissed off Paul when Bridges made Captain before him. Bridges now thought the bastard is a Supreme Court Justice. He wondered how many Marines knew that Paul was in the Corps. He then thought, why should they know…they didn't care.

At the Staff-NCO-Club, Bridges was met at the door by a young woman, about thirty plus. She had to be a Woman Marine in the way she challenged him at the door. Bridges smiled and was polite when he explained he was in search of his long lost buddy, Tim Young. The woman relaxed and informed Bridges the 'old-gunny' was at the bar telling his Vietnam stories.

As Bridges approached the bar, he couldn't help thinking Tim aged fast. He looked older than he was. It was obvious he was drunk and chain smoking as he told two sergeants listening, a tale of the Vietnam War experience. The two sergeants were babies when we were in Nam, It did Tim good to get it all out, he needed respect since the accidental shooting of the young girl. Bridges ordered a draft beer with a whiskey shooter. The bartender immediately said 'Yes-Sir' knowing Bridges was a civilian and had business there. The two sergeants listening to Tim, glanced over when the bartender demonstrated respect for Bridges. Tim didn't turn around to see. Bridges sat on the bar stool and listened as Tim told a true story about Vietnam, he knew it was true because he was with Tim the day it happened. Bridges waited for Tim to finish, then he said hello. Tim whirled around, almost in a fighting position and recognized Bridges. He didn't smile…just sat there and stared. Then got off the barstool and came to attention, in his intoxicated state…saluted Bridges. The two sergeants didn't know what to do, they sat there and watched Tim cry like a kid as he embraced his old platoon leader. Seeing that they wanted to talk, the two sergeants left.

"What the fuck you doing here…Lieutenant?"

Bridges made light of it and answered the question with a question. "That's what I want to know Tim, why aren't you home taken it easy like most retired Marines?"

Tim wasn't as drunk as Bridges first thought. He became serious and told Bridges that he had to do one more deed for his country. Bridges didn't like what he was hearing. Both men moved to a booth and Bridges insisted they have coffee.

"What the hell are you talking about, what's this about?" Bridges suspected but didn't even want to whisper his thoughts.

"I got my last job to…Lieutenant…I mean Captain, we got problems and I have to do my last mission before I die." Bridges interrupted and suggested he hit the head and wash his face with cold water, he'll go with him. Tim agreed and both men walked to the men's head. Bridges noticed Tim limping more than he remembered.

They returned to the table and had their coffee. Bridges wanted to hear what Tim was involved in, he knew but didn't understand how he got involved. He'd hoped Adriana was there to mellow the situation, but he had to wing-it himself. Tim put his head down in his hands. "The shooting of the kid ruined me and my life…everything was great and I had my plans for the shooting ranges, then I made the stupid mistake by doing a favor for a friend by installing a scope on his rifle."

Bridges had to get to the bottom of the mess before it went down. "Tim, how do you know a woman from San Salvador that go's by the name 'Rosa Carrea', where in the hell did you meet her?"

As the club started filling up with Marines and their dates, and the music was playing, Bridges didn't think it was a good place to talk. He suggested they leave. As they sat in the rental car Bridges reminded Tim of the question. He didn't respond at first, then he replied. "I don't know any woman from San Salvador or any other place in Central America."

Bridges pulled the photos out of a folder he had in the back seat of the rental car. At first Tim denied the photo was him, he did admit the male figure was a mail-carrier. Then he admitted that it was him. "All I was doing is delivering a package to her, never saw the lady before, so help me."

"Bull-shit Tim, bull shit…the meeting was planned and you know it. According to your daughter you hadn't been home in two days, where the hell were you?"

Tim sat in silence—then answered. "I was up in LA."

"What were you doing in LA?" Bridges snapped back.

"Fuck-you Capen…fuck you, I don't have to tell you a fuchen thing."

"I damn well know it Tim, but if this so called mission go's any further than right now, you're history my friend. They'll lock your ass up forever. Now what's up in LA?"

"I went up to look at things."

The fragmented answer caused Bridges anger. "What things...damn it...what the hell are you saying?"

"I went up to look around for the Spanish chick, I saw you with the cops and decided to head back to Oceanside, that's it."

"Are you aware she's an assassin, planning of taking the President out?" Bridges shouted at Tim, then settled down.

"Ya...I know...that piece of shit they call a President needs to be buried."

Bridges wanted to agree with him but rather, explained that if the President was taken-out, he would become a hero because he was assassinated while in office."

Tim agreed, but attempted to explain. "There's nothing I can do to stop it...the wheels are in motion, the sonofabitch is going down. If I sat here all night, he'd still be killed. I can't stop it. The only part I had was providing the ammo...that's it...oh I gave her some lessons, she gave me intimate feelings...not to mention fresh clean one-hundred dollar bills, too many for what little I did, it just happened that way."

Bridges was disgusted, he noticed Tim was sobering up, he suggested they have some food and talk some more. After a brief stop at Denny's coffee-shop, they returned to the car where Bridges tried to make good sense. "Tim, what we did in Vietnam will be wasted if you continue helping this woman...it's not political for her...she's a paid assassin, no more. She cares less about what we may feel about this President, as long as she get's her purse filled, she'll do the job. You should know that."

"It's too late Captain...it's too late...the wheels are in motion."

The attitude alone angered Bridges. "What do you mean...the wheels are in motion? We can stop it if you help?"

"That's if I help, I don't think I can...Captain."

Bridges suggested Tim go to San Diego with him and further discuss the situation. Tim refused, although invited Bridges to his home.

When they arrived, the lights were out in the house. Upon entering, the telephone rang, Tim ignored it and allowed the recorder to pick-up the message. It was from Rosa Carrea instructing Tim to call her as soon as he was able to. "Fuck-it, I'll call her when ever I want."

Tim was sober now and made more coffee for them. Bridges thought by bringing up Vietnam again, Tim would mellow and change his mind. It didn't work, matter of fact by reminding him about Vietnam made him worse. Bridges pleaded with Tim for at least his daughter's sake. He brought up the daughter because while in the kitchen Bridges read a not from the daughter informing her father where she was and signed it with 'love', this gave Bridges the impression the daughter loved her father but couldn't reason with him.

"How old is your daughter…?

"She'll be twenty soon…she attends college and wants to be a FBI agent, can you beat that…her father wants to pop the Prez and she wants to be a cop. This is shit, she's a good person…she has a boyfriend, but good old dad comes first."

Bridges felt that he didn't have enough information that would assist in foiling the assassination. He wanted help, but then who ever assisted, would be all over him for not reporting what he had when first learned from Adriana the President was a target. If Adriana was with him, he doubted what good she's be. It was getting late. He had to get some further information. "When's it going down?"

"Day after tomorrow…while he's playing golf."

This information shocked Bridges, he didn't think Tim would give him that much. "What else?"

"On the ninth-hole or near it, the hole that's nearest the condominiums. I don't know which one, but I'll know tomorrow."

"Why can't we stop it?"

"Because she's all set and ready to go. When I meet her tomorrow, I give her a new ten-power scope. She has the ammo…it will go through a house without loosing speed.I gave her only three-rounds. I wish I had them in Nam, but they're my special order-ammo, I packed them myself. It has to be a head shot or at least, the heart. She's good…I've seen her shoot, I'd say the best. The only time she smiles is when she's in bed, she's a hard body…she knows what to do. Pretty woman…have you seen her?"

Bridges was pissed, he had to convince Tim not to assist her in any other way. "How'd she find you?"

"Easy…a gunny at the embassy in San Salvador told her about me, he was one of the Marines assigned there. She called me one day and came down to see me, we spent the weekend together and I liked what she said, then I bought into it. I've been with her about ten times since then, not all work, plenty of play."

Bridges thought he should bate Tim. "You know the President is playing golf tomorrow as well, why isn't tomorrow a target day?"

"It is…she'll be there…but it'll be a dry run. She can't do shit without the new scope. I don't care how good she is, the new scope at 300 yards will but the shot exactly where she aims. Oh, she could take him down at that distance, but the chance of hitting him at the right moment is questionable. She's using a bolt action—single shot, 308. Three rounds, that's it. She plans to use one and only one round."

Bridges couldn't help thinking that maybe Tim wanted to help by laying out the plans, but then maybe not. He hasn't said much more about where exactly she would, he claimed he wouldn't know until tomorrow. "Tim…if you backed out, what then?

"She'll try anyway, then look for me, that is if she got away. Her escape plan is perfect."

Bridges tried again. "How perfect?

"Perfect…but can't tell…can't tell and don't know until tomorrow, but the plan is great."

Bridges tried again without blowing it. "I can see one option Tim, that is you take her out…that's it."

"Are you shitting, if I took her out then what? No way."

"Meet me tomorrow in San Diego at the Oceanside Motel?"

"Not going to do it Captain, can't do it. Besides you're as illegal as I am. As a spook, you can't operate in the US…I know you're not representing the law, if you were I'd be under arrest, am I right.?"

Bridges didn't have to answer…Tim had him and he was running out of steam. He decided to return to his hotel in San Diego. In the morning, attend the meeting at the sheriff's office. His only hope to foil the assassination attempt was to cancel the golf game. Then he would have to give a reason. “Take care Tim, hopefully after I leave, you’ll come to your senses and change your mind about assassinating the President even though we may agree he’s a total incompetent.”

Bridges returned to the hotel and didn’t bother to check in with Adriana. His mind was full of all sorts of things concerning Tim Young, the woman, Rosa Carrea, the location where the assassination attempt would go down. He finally fell asleep…

CHAPTER 12
THE TANGLE

The sunrise shining through the tinted windows enough to provide a pleasant affect as Adriana and Bridges enjoyed an early morning breakfast at the Hyatt Regency Hotel, San Diego.

Adriana was anxious to hear if Bridges discovered anything new concerning their project. Adriana hasn't been herself lately and her not going on the trip up the coast to visit Tim Young isn't her at all, Bridges thought. He wanted to answer her question, although he didn't know where to start without her getting the impression of concealing other information that led to his reasons for meeting Tim. He decided to start from the surveillance photos depicting Rosa, subject number-one, and an unidentified male dressed in a mail carriers uniform. Adriana at first had difficulty understanding the connection until Bridges explained that he suspected the male figure in the photo may be his Marine Corps buddy known to him as an expert sniper.

"If the photo was of Rosa and just a mailman, it was innocent…but if it was Tim Young…BINGO, it had a connection."

Adriana sat and thought maybe Bridges didn't want to share the information, for some reason that wasn't clear. She decided to challenge it. "Richard, are you protecting your Marine buddy?"

Bridges hesitated, then answered. "I guess you can say I am, at least until I knew for sure if he was involved."

Adriana smiled, expecting to hear more. Bridges sat there sipping his coffee as the waiter served their breakfast.

"Well…are you going to tell me?"

Bridges smiled, then answered. "Tell you what?"

"Damn it…is your Marine buddy involved?"

Bridges still toying with how he should answer, responded. "I'm not sure yet…I do know he made the ammo for her…our friend Rosa."

"Then he is involved?"

"I didn't say that…he knows where and when it will go down, he doesn't know exactly where the shot will be fired from. I have to meet him and determine that information after the meeting this morning at the sheriff's office."

"Richard you sound doubtful…is he going to cooperate, or do I sense your friend is screwed up and can't make up his mind."

"You hit it on the head…I don't want him arrested if he helps us. If he doesn't, then I may take him out myself, sort of taking him out of his misery. The poor bastard hasn't recovered from the accidental shooting of a young girl several years ago." Bridges had mixed emotions as to Tim showing up at the hotel. If he didn't, then he was compelled to lay the entire situation on the lap of the local law enforcement community and Secret Service. He didn't want to do that. He wanted Tim to wake up and smell-the-coffee. Come forward, provide the information and then fade into the sunset, stay out of it. Bridges felt, even though he had an obligation to report Tim's involvement, even if he backed out of it, he wanted to protect him, but he had to help taking the assassin out.

The meeting at the Sheriff's Office went very much as the meeting at LAPD. They were provided maps and communication locations color coded. Bridges was satisfied when the briefing officer assured them the condominiums were covered and SWAT teams would be in place. Today there would be a golf game, but the President has agreed to stay away for personal reasons. Adriana nudged Bridges when she heard the announcement and whispered. "I wonder what 'bimbo' would it be today, maybe he'll try boys for a change." The officer sitting next to her laughed at the comment.

After the meeting they socialized with the ranking officers in attendance, and of course a call was received from your-highness the First-Lady. Adriana assured her things were under control as usual. Adriana thought she was really asking if the bastard was with a 'bimbo' as usual when she wasn't along on the trip.

They returned to the hotel. Bridges checked his messages. There was a message from Tim requesting he call him at a local number. This caused Bridges to feel relieved. He dialed the number and discovered it was the NCO Club at the Marine Corps Recruit Depot. Bridges asked for Tim Young…the pause was for longer than a moment…then Bridges asked to speak to Gunny Young. The woman at the other end then understood and asked Bridges to hold

"Young here.".?

"Tim…Richard here, what's up?

"I don't know, I haven't met with her yet, we were suppose to meet by now, but I got to thinking about what you said…then I haven't decided yet, give me an hour, maybe two…I'll call you at the hotel…okay?"

"We are at the Hyatt, Ya, but I should meet with you first, before you go over to see her?"

"Hell no…she'd spot you as a spook, you know that."

"I'm dressed in blue-jeans and a western shirt, oh ya…western boots, the uniform of the day, will it do?"

"Richard, I respect you, I have always…but I got to go-it alone…I'll make up my mind." The phone went dead and then a dial tone. Bridges felt like the kid that dropped the ice-cream from the cone.

Adriana was again anxious to hear. Bridges couldn't help feeling down over this mess. Why couldn't it be simple…Rosa being the lone assassin, the cops bag her and that's it. The project would be over. He had to think it out, if Tim doesn't call back, then he had to inform at least the Sheriff's people and leave the Secret Service out of it, they would over-react anyway you look at it.

From his hotel room, Bridges called Tom Moore in Washington. He brought Tom up to speed. He hesitated telling Tom about their old buddy Tim Young. Tom remembered Tim Young from Vietnam and was surprised to hear of his involvement. Tom informed Bridges that he was certain James Allen's death was not connected to their project and the FBI is moving in on the group in New Jersey. "You recall Joanne Walker, Michael's girlfriend, well she turned out to be an informant for the Bureau. She confirmed Michael was alive but she hadn't met with him yet. The shooting of James Allen was simple…he had recordings of telephone calls the terrorist group made concerning the Trade Center bombing and other potential places in the United States ear-marked for destruction."

Bridges expressed relief after hearing what Tom had to say. They ended the call as Bridges reminded him they were still on for dinner when he and Adriana returned to Washington. "How does Filomena's sound?"

"Great…a bit over priced for a pasta house, but it will be a pleasure seeing who's screwing around with who around town…that's the place."

No sooner Bridges hung the phone up, he received a call. It was from Tim. "Captain…I haven't made up my mind yet…but Condo two-two-four may be worth looking at." He was drunk and slurred his words. Bridges insisted he come to the hotel and sleep it off. Tim became indignant over the accusation that Bridges suggested he was drunk. Immediately Tim hung up. This frustrated Bridges, at least he knew where the assassin would be when she fired the fatal shot, unless he stopped her. Then he recalled the number being two-two-four, or did Tim say two-four. He sat and thought what he should do and decided to contact Adriana. Dressed in casual clothes, they drove up to La Costa Country Club and looked around. They went through the security gate without being challenged. Bridges figured the security was for after dark. There were condominiums overlooking the tennis courts and golf course. Bridges smiled at the attractive young woman on their way to play tennis as he drove around to the main club house. He suggested they have a drink and reminded Adriana that bartenders have a wealth of information.

Inside the Clubhouse, Adriana noticed a directory of residences and started looking for Condo 224. When it was located, they both realized it wasn't the right address simply the building didn't face the golf course. Bridges suggested Adriana locate Condo 24. She found it on the directory without hesitation. It must be the one because the building over-looked the golf course and was an estimated two-hundred yards from the 9th hole. The directory wasn't to scale but an estimate was good enough. They finished their drinks and drove up to Condo 24. Bridges drove past and parked a distance from the Condo. As they walked down, they met an older couple that said hello and thought they knew Adriana and Bridges.

Bridges together with Adriana walked along the narrow curved parkway in front of the Condominiums facing the golf course. Without the benefit of the unit number, estimated where twenty-four was. They stopped and Bridges looked in the direction of the ninth-hole. He agreed with the original estimation that it was two-hundred yards away. This satisfied him and decided to leave. To add reality to their presence, Adriana grabbed Bridges arm and leaned her head against him as they walked close to the Condo that was to be used for the assassination the following morning

Adriana felt comfortable and didn't want to discontinue play-acting. Bridges sensed it and encouraged her to continue. As they arrived at their car that was illegally parked, a woman security officer was placing a notice on the windshield. She noticed what she thought were a romantic couple walk to the car, she immediately withdrew the notice and wished them a pleasant afternoon.

On the return trip to downtown San Diego, Adriana produced several brochures and a map of the country club area including the Condominium believed Rosa Carrea was planning to use to snuff the President out. "Too bad we don't have time for a golf game, I haven't played since I met you, Richard."

A smile came over Bridges face, he felt frisky, he wanted to tell Adriana he hadn't played or more specifically had a woman since he met Adriana, but contained himself. Adriana got the drift of things when she caught the smile

"Not my fault Richard."

He knew what she meant and knew she wanted them both to forget the world and enjoy each other. The project was almost over, maybe they could build a relationship. They arrived at the Hyatt, the valet parked the car as they entered through the side entrance. Adriana reminded Bridges they had a meeting with the Secret Service and Sheriff's people at five-in the morning. It was still early, they hadn't had dinner and agreed to meet in the hotel restaurant in an hour. Bridges escorted Adriana to her room, as she inserted the card to unlock the door, Bridges turned to leave. Adriana quickly asked him into the room, he was in need of a shower. He hesitated. I"d like to, but I need to shower."

Adriana smiled in the certain way that Bridges became to like. It wasn't a smile that was phony like flight-attendants use, it was a smile informing him that she had a secret. Bridges reconsidered after Adriana revealed she had a small bottle of cognac.

Adriana noticed her message light was on. She ignored them until she served Bridges a double blast of cognac in a water glass. She sat on the edge of the bed while she wrote the messages on a hotel pad. Bridges sat back and enjoyed the cognac, the glass didn't matter at this point. He glanced at Adriana as she spoke on the phone and stretched her arm and expanded her chest, revealing breasts concealed under the casual pale blue polo-shirt. He became stimulated and followed her moves as she hung the phone up. Adriana became apologetic when she explained she had several messages, one she had to return at once, Heidi's lap-dog secretary. The remainder could wait.

Adriana moved to the desk next to the window, sat down, kicked her sandals off and got into a comfortable position, one foot on the seat as Bridges watched her moves and she dialed assistance to call the White House. The phone was answered on the other end by the secretary, when she recognized Adriana, she whispered Heidi was pissed. This didn't bother Adriana and requested to speak to your highness. Heidi informed Adriana that the President isn't staying at the Mayor's home, they moved up to the country club, this surprised Adriana and assured madam First Lady she would check it out.

Immediately, Adriana called the Secret Service on cellular phone, once making contact she learned that the President wanted to stay at the country-club, and the agent knew without deep discussion, that Robert Banks, the President of the United Stares was meeting a "bimbo" there. At that moment, she knew why Heidi was angry. It wasn't the other woman, it was his disgraceful attitude. Adriana agreed. She smiled and informed Bridges the President was tucked into a Condo at the country-club, with a "bimbo" and that they had to find out which one. The Secret Service had things under control, as many times before. This information alerted Bridges, immediately he suggested they contact the Agent in Charge and inform him there may be an attempt on the President's life, tonight. "That will cause them to double the guard and make the poor bastard nervous to the point he couldn't get it up." They both laughed.

Adriana contacted the Agent in Charge and told him of an anonymous call indicating the threat. That's all they needed to hear. The last call Adriana made was to the Sheriff's office and spoke to a Captain she met earlier. He confirmed the meeting would be at five-thirty at the same place. The golf game would be when the-Prez got out of bed, and informed Adriana they already received a threat. As she hung the phone up, she smiled and repeated the information to Bridges. He laughed and poured another cognac.

Adriana started removing her clothes in front of Bridges. He couldn't at first figure if this was a game or she was serious. He sat and watched as she smiled and beckoned him to come to her. Immediately, Bridges got up and slowly walked over until his body was touching her. By that time she was down to her french cut panties and bra. With a soft kiss, she inserted her tongue slightly into his mouth. He didn't resist in the least. He unfastened her bra from behind, she quickly removed her panties as Bridges slowly walked them both to the bed. Starving for Bridges affection, opened her mouth and kissed him as he awkwardly removed his pants. He knew she would be an aggressive lover, he didn't mind. The phone rang as they lay there, Bridges cradling her in his arms. She reached for the phone as Bridges lay there and admired her body and well shaped breasts.

The call was from the Sheriff's office informing Adriana the meeting was changed to five in the morning and would be held at country-club. That meant they had to leave the hotel by four. Adriana thanked the caller and hung the phone up. She rolled over facing Bridges and suggested they shower if they hopped to have dinner. Adriana regulated the shower-water temperature and they both got in. It seemed Adriana couldn't get enough of Bridges and she felt the feeling was mutual. He was a bit shy in his own way, although, happy they became intimate before their return trip to Washington.

Bridges couldn't return to his room after dinner. One reason was that Adriana wouldn't allow him to, the other was he didn't want to. They experienced one-another again and Adriana wasn't inhibited in the least. Bridges felt himself and proceeded to please her in every way he knew. Bridges glanced at the clock and discovered and discovered it was past one…they had a short time for sleep. He called the desk to determine if he had messages. One the clerk informed him. "Call Mr. Young when you returned."

Bridges immediately dial the local number provided by the clerk. The phone rang at least five times before it was answered. It was Tim, he of course had been drinking but didn't sound too far gone, Bridges realized. "Captain…I'm out, I'm out of the game…I told her I was out and she blew her top…fuck her…get her ass, I understand what you said, you're right, we can't make this bum a hero. Bridges thanked Tim and asked again what the Condo number was.

"It's 24…Twenty-four, the place you went to, I had you in my sights. She'll be on the balcony of the Condo, she's been snapping in all day, even when you love birds were there. She didn't see you…too busy snapping-in, see you Captain, good luck." The phone went dead.

Bridges had an eerie feeling, to think Tim had them in his sights. Then he recalled that most snipers used spotters, that's what he was doing for Rosa this morning when they were at the Condo.

At four-forty five Bridges and Adriana arrived at the country-club. A private conference room was set up as the CP and communications center. They were informed that the President's golf game would start ten and the plan was they would play the entire course of 18 holes and lunch well be set up at the club-house. The entire course is closed to the public and members. It was six-thirty when the meeting was over. A Secret Service agent that knew Adriana at the White House came over to their table as they were having breakfast. Adriana deliberately didn't introduce the agent because she wanted to discourage him from joining them. After he left, she informed Bridges that the Agent has been trying to date her ever since she arrived at the White House. Bridges smiled and admired Adriana on how she defused the situation. After breakfast, they drove around to Condo twenty-four.

It was still dark as the sun was rising. Bridges decided they shouldn't get out of the car. They noticed a four-some of golfers on the course, they were at the ninth hole. Bridges drove over to one of the Secret Service agents and he and Adriana were informed the four-some would finish before the President's group played. Bridges decided to get a better look and parked down from the Condo. He thought of his obligation to report what he knew, then he would have to hand Tim Young over, something he didn't want to do. He had to think about how he alone could foil the assassination without making a scene and bringing the woman down. In the trunk of the car, Bridges removed a 9mm Beretta he borrowed from the San Diego Sheriff's Office.r. He tucked the gun into his belt and removed his golf shirt from his pants.

Adriana agreed to stay in the car and observe. Bridges walked over to the Condo and spotted a woman jogger in the distance. He turned away from her and returned to the car. Immediately, Adriana saw what Bridges observed. The jogger was none other than Rosa Carrea. She was dressed in an expensive jogging suite and listening to maybe music on the walkman as she intently jogged as a dedicated runner.

They were sure she didn't see them as she jogged by. When she was out of sight, Bridges thought he would try to enter the Condo while Rosa was out jogging. He managed to open the sliding glass door facing the golf course and quietly entered. Above the door was the balcony. The place was furnished and decorated by a professional he noticed. He looked carefully around the rooms until he discovered a hispanic woman sleeping in the room next to the master bedroom. She was about forty-plus, probably the housekeeper and a friend of Rosa.

He managed to go inside the master bedroom crawling on his hands and knees. He managed to make it to the balcony. On the balcony floor was a matt and nothing else. Bridges hastily searched the room and entered the walk-in closet. He searched for a rifle and ammo. He found a sniper scope, US Government issue. Nothing else. He was running out of time, she would return soon and he didn't want to be discovered. He thought for a brief second that he would conceal himself in one of the closets in another bedroom.

Bridges was desperate, he thought he should have enlisted the aid of the Secret Service, then he was glad he didn't. As he sat on the floor memorizing the lay-out of the Condo, her heard a door open and close. He was stuck now, he thought. The person spoke Spanish and was calling to the woman in the other room. In the closet, Bridges positioned himself back in the dark corner, he left the door slightly open so as to hear. The voice was not of a young woman, it was probably another domestic help visiting her friend in the other room. Bridges heard what sounded like a shower and conversation between the women. Shortly they both left the Condo and Bridges felt comfortable deciding to remain inside the dark closet.

With the little light coming in through the crack, he noticed it was almost nine. He didn't want Adriana to sit in the car and wished he hadn't left her alone. Then he thought she'd figure it out and make contact with the Secret Service Agent that had the hots for her, at least he hoped so. Minutes felt like hours, he heard the front door open and a person climbing the stairs. He was certain it was Rosa. He peaked out the crack of the sliding closet door, it was Rosa. She had removed her clothes and was nude planing to shower. He thought, what a cool-bitch she is. Shower before the kill and leave after as though nothing happened. He heard the water turned off and observed her walk with a white towel wrapped around her. Bridges could hear her getting dressed then he heard a familiar sound. The sound of a bolt of a rifle being worked. He heard her open the sliding glass door to the balcony. Then he couldn't hear a thing, what now he thought. He could wait until she got in position to fire and shoot her from behind. He didn't know if this was what he should do. He now listened, and he could hear her open the door again and enter the large bathroom. He heard her take a piss and thought she was human after all. The flush of the water startled him as he crept from the closet to get a better look at her. He had the Beretta 9mm in his right hand, as he slowly crawled to a vantage point. He could see her bare feet, she was in the prone position lying on the matt facing the golf course.

He edged himself further into the wide hallway. He couldn't believe what he saw. The woman was in the nude, the rifle was next to her. She was masturbating with her eyes closed. A sight that no-one would believe. As she increased her pleasure, he could hear her make sounds of pleasure. When she finished, she licked her fingers, then rolled over on her stomach, spread her legs wide and started practicing taking aim.

Bridges glanced at his watch. It was just ten, if they started on time it would be at least an hour before they arrived at the tee-off for the ninth-hole. He sat in the closet and went over his plan. Remembering Tim informed him that Rosa planned to shoot the President as he positioned himself to take a driving stroke. His back would be facing the Condo.

Bridges had to protect Tim no matter what. The poor bastard had a string of bad luck, starting with the wife and then accidentally shooting the young girl, and know he felt that he lowered himself by becoming a mail-carrier. As he sat and contemplated, he heard the door downstairs open and slam shut, then sound of someone running up the stairs. It was Tim, he approached Rosa from behind. She didn't move. In a shouting voice he told her he wouldn't spot for her. She indicated in English that it wasn't necessary, never lifting her head to face him. Bridges felt good that Tim wasn't leading him on. As he turned to leave, he threw three-rounds on the matt. She thanked him coldly and Tim left. The woman sat up, with her tongue, licked the rounds then she rubbed them up and down on her vagina. Bridges caught the image as he positioned himself after Tim left.

This was the strangest thing he ever witnessed. He guessed the masturbation session was for relaxation and the licking and rubbing the rounds was, imagined, good luck.

Bridges formulated a plan. He would shoot the woman at the time she loaded one round into the rifle, never mind trying to subdue her. He could see Rosa get tense, she locked her legs in position, her feet and ankles flat. The rifle pointed in the direction of the ninth hole, although he couldn't see. She slowly picked up a round that had been lined up. She licked it again and inserted into the chamber of the Remington 308 equipped with the ten-powered scope. He then thought he had to take her out before she got a round off. She relaxed and lay on her side. She closed her eyes for a minute, then she took up the position of aiming. Now was the time, Bridges quietly got to his knees, aimed, cradling his Beretta with both hands, pointed at the woman that lay eight feet before him, just then, a crack sounded, the sound of a rifle shot, the woman's head fell to her arm and blood sprayed all over the sliding glass door. The single round went though her head and lodged in the stucco above the door frame. Cautiously Bridges moved up to the body and assured himself she was dead.

It was over, Bridges thought. He knew who ever shot Rosa Carrea or what ever her true name was, had to make peace with himself and this was his way of repenting.

Bridges was in a daze when the Secret Service Agents and Sheriff Deputies arrived. He sat there half hearing them as they asked for details. He could hear Adriana as he sat propped against the door jam to the master bedroom suite. She got down on her knees and hugged him. She didn't care who was watching. Bridges smiled at her when she gave him a sweet kiss. He suddenly realized that the Secret Service Agents and the Sheriff's people all thought Bridges shot the would-be assassin.

The senior agent gave the President's thanks to Bridges. He had to explain but with the commotion, he couldn't get a word with them, until a uniformed woman deputy sheriff formally interviewed him. The Secret Service Agents had the good sense to clear the Condo and section off the scene. Once the law enforcement authorities learned that Bridges didn't shoot the assassin, they started asking questions as to how he knew the assassin would be at the particular Condo. Bridges provided a simple answer that he had a hunch and observed the traffic of Hispanic people entering the Condo that caused him suspicion.

Then the final question was asked. If Bridges didn't shoot the woman, then who did. Bridges explained. He planned to shoot her, but the woman slumped at the same time he heard the sound of a rifle being fired. The shot hit her in the head passing through and lodged into the stucco above the door frame. The woman was hit as she took aim at the target, I would imagine, the President, he repeated.

As the deputies covered the woman's body with a sheet, the Secret Service Agent in Charge expressed an interest in interviewing Bridges. Adriana superseded and assured them he would be available later. She didn't necessary mean later before they left La Costa.

No sooner Adriana convinced the Secret Service to interview Bridges later, one of the agents handed Adriana a cellular phone. It was the First Lady. As she said hello, Adriana smiled and winked at Bridges. "Mrs. Banks the President is fine, the assassin was killed, your husband is safe. I'll return to Washington tomorrow." Adriana was happy to be able to twist the words into Heidi's back as she would a knife: "The President is Fine." The Secret Service had already briefed Heidi, but for some reason she had to her it from Adriana.

Bridges thought of Tim as he and Adriana walked to their car. The curious neighbors gathered around the building. He heard several mention 'somebody tried to kill the President' this caused a smile to his face and thought, if they only knew. No sooner Bridges sat behind the wheel, Adriana kissed him and told him she loved him from the moment they met at the Allenby Bridge.

They kissed again as Bridges used the cellular phone and dialed his home number in Virginia. He had to let Jennifer know he was alright. His daughter spontaneously asked about Adriana. Jennifer informed her father that she thought Adriana was in love with him. Ignoring Jennifer's comment, Bridges smiled as he said goodbye and assured her he would be home the next day. Bridges contacted the Sheriff's Captain in charge of the security and returned the Beretta.

As they left the entrance to the La Costa Country Club they headed north on Interstate highway 405. Bridges informed Adriana that he had to meet with Tim in Oceanside.

Adriana agreed as she acted like a bride on her honeymoon. Bridges knew it and was happy that maybe he found someone to not only fill the void since his wife died, someone that he could share the better part of his life with.

In less than thirty minutes, they arrived in Oceanside. Bridges drove into a gas station to fill the car up and take a whiz. Adriana remained in the car as the car phone rang, Adriana picked the receiver up discovered it was the Secret Service Agent that knew her at the White House. He wanted to talk to both Bridges and Adriana concerning the attempt on the President's life. Adriana laughed as she explained they were on their way to Los Angeles. "If you'd like to talk to us, we should be in Los Angeles this evening and plan to return to Washington the following morning."

This didn't settle too well with the agent. Adriana didn't care and she didn't hesitate to tell him, although informed him they would be staying at the Hyatt near LAX that evening. Bridges returned to the car as Adriana was terminating the call. As he got back in the car, he noticed a smile on Andriana's face and hesitated to ask.

"What did you do?"

"Nothing…the President's security people are looking for us and I told them we would be in Los Angles if they wanted to talk to us. They didn't like it, the hell with them."

"I'm sure they want to know how I knew about the woman in Condo 24. I've got to locate Tim before I talk with them." Bridges grabbed the car-phone and dialed Tim Young's home number. The phone rang four times before it was answered. "Hello…Tim here."

"Tim…Rich here, be over your place in a few minutes, stay there, I need to talk to you, damn it."

Tim was reluctant, then he agreed if Bridges was alone. Bridges informed him of his lady friend and that it was important that she be present.

Sitting in Tim's family room. Adriana looked at the many photos he had framed and hung on the wall of he and his Marine Corps buddies. In one photo, she recognized Paul Castilli and Bridges standing together with Tim holding what she suspect was a North Vietnamese flag. They all had cigars in their mouths and looked skinny and needed a bath, she thought. On the wall next to the fireplace, was a large framed awards display of Tim's medals he was awarded for heroism in Vietnam. She felt sad that the man who won the medals had been reduced to a disoriented man over a foolish accident that could have been avoided had he practiced the rules he knew and lived by, up until the incident.

Both men were seated across from each other holding a bottle of beer and talking about nothing of importance until Bridges explained who Adriana was and that they both had reason to believe the First Lady hired the Hispanic woman to take the President out.

Tim looked at Adriana and offered his apology concerning not wanting her to be present during the meeting. She smiled briefly as indicating she understood and allowed Tim to hug her. They sat together and Adriana also accepted the beer Tim offered.

Bridges assured Tim he wouldn't be contacted by anyone from law enforcement over the shooting. His identity will remain a secret unless there was something he didn't know. Tim looked at Adriana and looked into Bridges eyes.

"Are you suggesting that you think I capped the Spanish chic…captain?"

"Yes…didn't you?"

"Hell no…I saw her and went to the Condo to tell her I wasn't in on the deal, then I left the Condo and returned to Oceanside."

"I know that much Tim, I was in one of the closets when you came in and gave her the three-rounds, I heard you tell her that you were out, but if you didn't shoot her, then who did?"

"You were there? Then you saw what a nut she was, she loves to shoot in the nude. She got a thrill out of it she said, maybe a sexual high. To answer the question, I don't know. You'll find that the round that killed her didn't come from me. You were there…did the round stay in her or go through her and lodge in the wall or something?"

"It went through her and hit the wall above the door frame."

"Then damn it, my rounds enter and blow-up inside, why would I not use my own rounds?"

Adriana listening intently, answered. "To make it look like someone else did it."

"You're a smart woman…but that isn't the case…a master as I am, wants to make sure his target dies the second the round hits. No chance of the target recovering and telling wild tales."

Bridges looked at Adriana then spoke. "You're right Tim and if you have a hint as to who did it, we got to know."

"I don't think the person was from here…I mean the local area. When the news announced the assassin was killed by a single shot to the head, I was at the club having my liquid breakfast. I have to inspect the round in order to tell you anything."

Adriana interrupted and offered something that may be the case. "Maybe Heidi changed her mind and hired someone else to take out the woman…Rosa."

Tim anxiously answered. "Couldn't have…no one knew the plan except you guys, myself and of course the woman. You guys didn't learn about the time until that morning…although you knew the day before where the woman would fire from and where the target would be. I realize I'm the likely suspect…so help me, it wasn't me."

Bridges didn't know if he wanted to believe Tim, if they were alone maybe he would tell a different story. As Tim went to the kitchen for another beer, Bridges suggested Adriana leave the room or go to the car and get something and take her time returning. As Adriana went out the front door, Tim's daughter was arriving and she said hello to Adriana. The young woman was petite, long blond hair and sparkling blue eyes. She in no resembled her father. Adriana briefly explained that her father was talking about a serious matter and didn't want us woman in there." The daughter became serious and objected to what Adriana said and went storming into the house. She knew better to interrupt her father while he was talking to Bridges, but she felt that what she had to say was more important. She entered the family-room as her father was finishing the conversation with Bridges. She insisted she talk to him privately. They went into the kitchen and the daughter informed him that the FBI was looking for him. Tim smiled and told the daughter not to worry and asked not to be disturbed. Tim's daughter was worried and added that the FBI agents would return shortly. Tim calmed her down and quickly persuaded her to go outside until he finished talking to Mr. Bridges. She smiled when she realized her father was with Bridges. Evidently she didn't hear Adriana when she tried to explain. While both women were standing next to the rental-car, an official looking car arrived. Tim's daughter became nervous as Adriana recognized the driver as a Secrets Service agent. "What are you guys doing here." That was the question they were going to ask but thought better. Adriana insisted the two agents leave and they will get together later. Adriana wondered why they were there. She decided to ask. "What business do you have with Tim Young?"

The agent that knew Adriana replied. "Tim Young is known to us as an expert on sniping and we heard he was the person to consult."

This comment alone relieved Adriana and explained Tim Young was busy talking to Richard, and led them into the house. She felt things were clear and knew Bridges heard them talking at the front door.

The Secrets Service Agents addressed Tim with obvious respect as though they had made contact with him in the past. Tim was eager to talk to them and insisted they all go out to his workshop in the garage. Adriana wanted to listen but thought she should talk to Tim's daughter, maybe she may let something slip that may shed light on who shot and killed the hispanic assassin.

The senior agent handed Tim the round dug out of the stucco above the balcony door of the Condo. Right away he identified the round as ball-ammo, military type, maybe Winchester, more than likely extended range 308, it came from about 160 to 170 grain, factory pack. "Nothing special, you can buy them anywhere, K-mart included. The pack is designed for hunting deer, nothing bigger. We packed our own rounds used in Vietnam. Hollow point or hollow with nitroglycerin center, it would blow up inside the target. They're a lot of fun to make."

The information provided seemed to satisfy the Secret Service Agents. They left after saying a special goodbye to Adriana. Bridges thought the agents would once again question him concerning his knowledge of the Hispanic woman, although it was knowledge among the agents, Bridges was with the Agency.

Back to Tim, Bridges questioned him as to how he managed to get on grounds of La Costa, especially since the President would be visiting. Tim smiled and provided his answer.

"I have friend's that drive vendor trucks, a piece of cake…as far as climbing the hill where the Condos are, I'm still in shape my friend, I walked. Now if you really want to know, I stayed over night in the Condo.

The contingency plan was to stay put until the excitement was over, Rosa had her car parked up the street. She was a crazy bitch, who would ever believe that a woman assassin shot without clothes on."

Adriana sat in silence after Tim's daughter left. She heard most of what Tim said and became interested in how Tim was able to move around the residential area without being stopped by the Sheriff's people or La Costa security. "Tim did anyone stop you last night or today before the incident?"

"Nope…after I left the Condo this morning…I walked down the road and did my thing."

Adriana knew the last statement Tim made was a lie, at least she thought it was. She sat in the car and saw no-one other than Rosa jogging. "When you left the Condo, what door did you use?"

"The front, the one facing the street, why?"

"I was in the car, spoke to several Secret Service people and police officers, but never saw you."

Tim thought for a minute, then answered. "Oh wait, I left the Condo by the sliding glass doors over-looking the golf course."

Bridges thought that could be true, although he wasn't in a position to see. He thought maybe Adriana was on to something and Tim knew it. "Without a security pass, such as the one we wore…how in the hell did you get around?"

"No problem, I guess I better stop shiting you two, Ms. Meyers is a smart one…I took the parameter around the golf course, behind the dog-wood trees that line the golf-course. Then I walked the street like anyone else and was never stopped."

Bridges felt his friend had been playing with them…he thought that if Tim left the way he said, then he either shot the woman from a distance of 150 yards, where the trees are growing on the side of the hill. What about the rifle and his prints. "Cut the shit Tim…really I don't need you to confess, you blew her away and saved me the task, but if I'm to help you, damn it…then explain where the rifle is and why you used such inferior ammo?"

Adriana got up from her seat as Bridges paused, she located the bathroom off the hall. Bridges took advantage of her absence. "Tim, quit fucking with me…fill me in."

Tim slowly answered after he took the last swig from his bottle of beer. "I did not shoot that bitch, so help me Captain."

Then who did?"

"The truth, I think it was the FBI or Secret Service.

They found out about her, how I don't know, and took her out. With a ten-powered scope, firing from the trees, of course knowing the target location, squeezed the round off, plain and simple."

"Tim, they're going to trace the two un-used rounds found at the scene, to you."

"No they won't…if you're talking about prints, I doubt it. If you remember, when I handed the three-rounds to her, I had latex gloves on. I polished the jackets of the rounds when I made them yesterday and placed them in my cigarette package wrapped in a small silicone rag cut from a new one and discarded the remainder by burning."

Adriana hesitated to return to the family room. She looked around the house and discovered it was an expensive neighborhood, the house was worth three-hundred thousand on today's market. It was neat, clean and decorated. It had to be the daughters responsibility. The bathroom she used was spotless, fresh towels as though company had been expected. No dishes in the sink and the Spanish tile-floor was clean and taken care of as a woman would do, but there's no woman, just the daughter. She could have kept it up, but Adriana now doubted it. She then walked into the laundry room. The washer-dryer were clean and no evidence of soap residue around the washer. Although, Tim is a former Marine, maybe he is the one that keeps it spotless, then she decided it wasn't Tim, it was probably one of the Hispanic woman that does domestic cleaning. At that very moment, the back door to the kitchen opened, it startled Adriana as will as the woman entering. She was Hispanic, maybe Mexican, forty-five or older. She looked vaguely familiar. Adriana apologized to the woman and in Spanish the woman did like wise. She was surprised Adriana spoke native Spanish which caused a smile on the woman's face. The woman introduced herself as 'Lupi' and didn't hesitate in Spanish to ask if Adriana was Tim's lady-friend.

Evidently, Tim heard the woman enter from the back door and came into the large kitchen to greet her. Bridges followed out of curiosity. Instantly, Bridges recognized the woman as the one asleep in the guest room of the Condo. She was a friend of Rosa and obviously arrange for Rosa to use the Condo without knowing why. If Tim slept with Rosa, then the woman would know. Tim sensed that Bridges recognized the woman. Immediately he had the woman verify that he stayed in the Condo with Rosa the previous night.

Bridges didn't believe Tim, he was certain he shot the woman. Both men returned to the family room after they got a beer from the refrigerator. Adriana continued her tour of the house, keeping an ear to the conversation in the family room. She came upon the daughter's room, Adriana was impressed, bed made and everything in place. The girl's bathroom was clean and fresh towel hung on the racks. The master bedroom was a mess with clothes thrown over a chair. The bed didn't appear as though it had been slept in. If it had then the person made it. Adriana doubted it.

In the corner of the large room was an oak-gun cabinet. It was obviously empty. She remembered that Tim didn't own guns anymore since accidently shooting the young girl. In the corner was a container of undelivered mail. This embarrassed Adriana, for what reason she didn't know. It appeared as though he walked off the job in a hurry. Maybe to meet Rosa in San Diego or some other reason.

Adriana returned to the family room where she over-heard Tim once again deny shooting Rosa. Bridges glanced over at her with a digusting look on his face and made his last attempt to convince Tim to reveal what he knew.

"Tim…I can not help you if the wall tumbles on your head over this incident, I can help you right now. After I leave here and return to Washimngton, you are on your own plain and simple."

Adriana added to what Bridges. "Tim, Richard means what he said…we together can help if you shot the woman, that's if you tell us now, if not then there isn't a thing left for us to do."

Bridges watched Tim while Adriana was talking. He thought for a moment he was going to fess-up, but then he continued to deny it.

***

While driving from Oceanside to Los Angeles, Bridges didn't say much until they came to a traffic bottle neck as the traffic from I-5 intersected the I-405 in the vicinity of El Toro and the Marine Corps Air Station, the base Bridges remembered he and Paul Castilli along with their platoons flew from, El Toro en route to Vietnam.

The thought brought back a disastrous memory that the C-130 taking off before them, crashed into the foothills killing countless Marines. Bridges' flight was canceled for two days and they were used as security at the crash sight. He recalled bodies thrown all over the hillside. He related the experience to Adriana as she listened with tears in her eyes. She insisted he change the subject.

As they increased speed, Adriana remarked about the sweet smell of orange blossoms. It reminded Bridges of the smell of tear-gas. "By the way, where were you when Rosa was shot?"

She busted into laughter. "I was with the Secrets Service at the ninth hole…you should have seen the President when the Secrets Service Agent jumped on top of him when they heard the shot. It was funny seeing that lubofshit struggling to get out from under the agent, it was a laugh. Why do you ask?"

Bridges smiled. "Just checking, making sure you didn't snuff Rosa, I don't want to over-look anything." He laughed again as Adriana sat closer and touched his neck and played with his greying hair as he drive.

***

The hotel was crowded with people in formal are, evidently there was a special event going on. Bridges was surprised to find they had reservations. Adriana thought it had to be Dean. As they boarded the elevator, Captain Matthews was right behind them. He didn't say anything to them until he caught Adriana's eye. "Little lady…are you alone, if so…you can be my date."

Adriana looked up and discovered it was Matthews dressed in a black tuxedo and black tie. She managed to hug him as Bridges worked his way over to them in the elevator

The elevator stopped at the sixth floor and all three walked to the room. Inside, Adriana ordered a bottle of Dom and four glasses.

Matthews had a smile on his face when he congratulated Bridges on a job well done. Bridges reluctantly accepted the complement but asked what Matthews was talking about.

"We hear you took her out, you know Rosa, you were right, she was the assassin. Bridges looked at Adriana as she walked over to the door to let the service in. She smiled and hunched her shoulders as to say, she didn't know.

"What are you saying, the word's out that you took her out without any help from the Secret Service and San Diego Sheriff's people." Matthews spoke with admiration and he was pleased to know Bridges.

"Who's saying I took her out?"

"The FeeBee's, you know the FBI, they don't usually give complements to anyone except themselves."

Bridges was not going to accept any complement for the kill, they got the story wrong.

"You've got to get the straight scoop from the Secret Service."

"Rich…they say the same thing, what's the matter, you shy…I'd like to hear how you did it."

Before Bridges could answer, Adriana asked Matthews is he would like to invite his wife up for some Champagne, he announced that she went to Italy with her parents.

Bridges replied. "How the hell do I know…I didn't do it."

"What do you mean…we have an Intell-report indicating praise that Richard Thomas Bridges, a former member of the Central Intelligence Agency saved the President's life by shooting the would be assassin with a single shot to the head."

"That's bull-shit, I didn't do a fucken thing to take her out, I was there in the building in the ready, with intension of shooting her, but I didn't. Someone fired a rifle from a distance of…I would say 150 yards, single shot to her head. I was ten, maybe twenty feet from her when she took it in the head. The round went right through her and lodged into the wall."

Matthews became serious. "Our copy of the report says she was killed with a 9mm from a Beretta, a hand gun."

Adriana didn't know what to say. She decided to call the First Lady. After her brief conversation, she returned to the conversation with a long face and confirmed what Matthews had been saying. "The President wants to present you with the civilian medal for valor in saving his life. They're planning a dinner in your honor…Richard."

Bridges, in a fit of rage, threw his champagne glass against the wall, causing glass to splinter all over Adriana jumped back and stepped on Matthews toes. She laughed out loud and then started crying. "I'm sorry…I'm sorry, all the work and energy we put into this, they twist the facts to protect some asshole in the FBI or Secret Service, or who ever shot her, Richard didn't do it, I don't care what that fuckern report says. But then…Richard you were alone in the house with her. There is no one to refute the report, except us, but then we'll have to reveal we had advance knowledge and accuse the First Lady of plotting to kill her husband, who in their right mind will believe it."

Bridges apologize to Matthews and put his arm around Adriana. She cuddled close to him as she sniffed and held back her tears. Matthews took out his handkerchief from his pocket and offered it to Adriana, she accepted and dried her eyes.

Matthews had to return to his group of retired LAPD officers. "This was the night we award the medal of valor to a deserving officer that put their life on the line. Tonight I'm sorry to say, posthumously."

Matthews left after he and Bridges shook hands and he hugged Adriana. Bridges promised to call him the next time he was in Los Angeles.

Adriana poured them another glass of champagne, not in celebration, rather to cleanse their palate for a long night of love making.

***

Adriana slept on the plane while Bridges read and stewed over corruption in government. He didn't know how he was going to back out of the presentation and the fan fair at the White House. He was angry, Adriana knew it and was helpless as to what they should do.

CHAPTER 13
DEBAUCHERY

It was raining with some determination when Bridges arrived at the District of Columbia Police Headquarters. Captain Tom Moore completed his morning duties, part of which was making his superiors happy.

Bridges sat in front of Tom's desk as a young petite woman of African decent served them coffee. She smiled at Bridges as she set his coffee down next to him and left the office exaggerating her steps, producing an attractive appearance for most horny old men. Tom spoke louder over the sound of rain hitting the window. "Richard, you're a hero, at least with the Democrats. Why the face, you'll get to dine at the White House and shake the man's hand as he pins the medal on you. What's wrong with that?"

I'll tell you what's wrong, somebody snuffed the woman and reported I did. I'm telling you, I didn't take her ass out, almost…but didn't. I can't refute anything, if I try, we will look like fools, at the least. We knew about this assassination attempt but didn't report it. How's that going to play in the press…we should have reported what we knew, but didn't trust anyone in Government. Then if we reveal that her-highness the First Lady set it up, who will believe us. The fucken FBI is behind this in some way, how, I don't know."

Tom smiled and suggested Bridges relax and take a few deep breaths. "When I first heard, I thought you did it…simply, you snuffed the woman. But the more I thought about it, it wasn't your style, meaning, you'd do it without them knowing, plain and simple."

Bridges looked at Tom and pleaded for help in this mess. "Tom I can't stand up there in front of the American people and receive that medal…it's bull shit, you know it, they know it…not so sure the President knows it, but your highness Heidi Jefferson Shepard damn well knows it. She foiled her own plot, damn it…I'm sure. You remember Tim Young in our outfit in Nam, I mentioned him when I called you, he was our sniper in the Company, I strongly suspect he was the trigger man…but now I'm not sure. I'll bet it was one of Sam Evens boys from their flaky Hostage Rescue Team, I may be wrong…or I'm right, what's the connection to Heidi Banks?"

"Evens was appointed by the President, he was a judge in Virginia before the appointed as FBI Director. No dirt on him that I know of, but there was talk about Heidi and him. Nothing that could sell newspapers. The guy is young unmarried, never was…and a hell of a golfer. That sums it up. The field agents think he's a candy-ass and he's afraid of Congress, he may as well be, I don't know."

"Another subject my friend…who killed the kid, James Allen?" Bridges aggressively asked, wanting to change the subject but still felt the connection between the project and the Allen shooting.

"I'm certain the Allen kid wasn't snuffed by an Arabs, it's too clean…besides they don't shoot people, they blow them up, isn't that what you guys at Langley say?"

"As far as I know, but then using a 22 long at close distance, had to be surgical…someone knew exactly where to place the round in order for it to hit the heart. It wasn't Arab I agree…maybe the motive was to protect terrorist activities, but the shooter was an American or even an Israeli, now that's' a thought. When I say Israeli, I mean a rouge agent, or former agent." "Do you think there's a connection between the shooting of James Allen and this woman, Rosa Carrea?"

"Well, the only way I can connect them is through skill, nothing else. Both surgical shootings. I'll bet the shooter is a paid member of the National Rifle Association." Bridges thought he'd be funny and both men laughed well knowing it may be true.

Bridges didn't sleep very well after the trip to California and both he and Adriana agreed they should go to their own places. At Bridges farm house there was at least ten-messages on his answer-machine. He didn't recall from who, but he should get back to the house and do some work. Tom seemed disappointed that he wouldn't go to his favorite place for breakfast. They said goodbye and agreed to dinner at Filomena's Friday night.

***

The rain seemed to let up until Bridges got to the parkway. The traffic was bad and he had a near collision when attempting to make a lane change. The wind-shield wipers were worn and left water streaks as they worked back and forth. The situation made it difficult, but Bridges managed. He finally arrived at the exit to his farm. He glanced in the rear view mirror. He immediately thought someone was following him but couldn't distinguish the type car because it was raining hard. He'd hoped it wasn't Adriana because he wasn't in the mood to go over the situation again.

Bridges was relieved when the car turned off and he was convinced he wasn't being followed. He became angry with himself for becoming paranoid. Finally he arrived at the farm, the dirt road was muddy and when ever it rained, he promised himself time after time that he would do something to prevent the road from becoming so muddy.

At the house Bridges discovered Jennifer was gone, probably at school and William was out in the barn. He didn't know where the housekeeper was but it didn't matter. Sitting behind his desk he hit the button to listen to his messages. The first message was from Charlie requesting he call him at the Israeli Embassy, nothing urgent. He shut the machine off and dialed the embassy number. When he asked for Charlie, a peculiar feeling came over him. The receptionist put him on hold, which is annoyed him. Shortly, she returned and requested Bridges to state his business. Bridges replied that he was returning David Halim's earlier call to him. He was asked to hold again. A man's voice answered this time, he identified himself as Victor Levine. He spoke in American-English and asked who was calling. Bridges, loosing patience, replied sarcasticly. "Richard Bridges, I'd like to speak to David Halim, you know, Charlie."

"What organization sir?"

"No organization, I'm returning Charlie's call…we are friends, please put me through, damn it."

The phone went dead. Bridges hit the redial button and the receptionist answered, announcing the Israeli Embassy.

"Mamn…may I speak to the Vice-Conciliate?" The receptionist placed him on hold, shortly the Vice Conciliate's secretary came on the phone asking how she could help. Bridges asked for David Halim. There was silence for a few seconds, then the young woman explained that Mr. Halim had an accident. Bridges, demanded to know the details. The woman in a soft voice as though she didn't want anyone to hear, stated Mr. Halim passed away. Bridges couldn't believe what he just heard, he impatiently demanded details and the woman politely explained that she didn't have the authority to relate any further information and hung up.

Bridges phoned Tom at Metro Police. Once he came on the phone, Bridges requested any and all information concerning the death of an Israeli Diplomat David Halim. Tom promised to call him at the house with the information. Ten minutes past, the phone rang. "Rich…the only Israeli listed as deceased was a Charles Goldberg."

"That's him…what's the scoop, how'd he die?"

"The usual…shot in the back with a 9mm, why?

"Mossad, and a good friend." Bridges was dismayed, he couldn't speak. He then said something to Tom that wasn't audible. Tom asked him to repeat himself. "He was my good friend, I hadn't known him long, but we became brothers in a short period of time. Where's the body?"

"The Israelis have it, they picked it up two days ago and I guess they flew him back to Israel. I'm sorry Rich…we don't have a clue as to who was responsible. Funny thing, Mr. Goldberg had duel citizenship and was born in Philadelphia."

"Tommy…I knew all that, he was a prince of a man, and a hell of a intelligence agent. What's the name of the Israeli official the body was released to?"

"It says, Shulman, Rebecca Shulman."

Bridges smiled to himself and wasn't surprised that Becky was in town, he wondered why she hadn't called him, then again it may be on the message machine. "What do make of it Tommy?"

"Not a drive-by, nothing like that, I think it was a professional hit. He was shot someplace else and his body dumped at the entrance to the Israeli Embassy three days ago."

"Tom please call the Israeli Embassy and determine if their agent, Becky Shulman is there or did she accompany the body to Israel, use a little official muscle, I'd appreciate it."

Tom called the embassy and after identifying himself, learned that Ms. Shulman is at the embassy, however she wasn't available. When Bridges heard that Becky was there he wonderedif Charlie's body was at some mortuary in and around DC.

"How can we determine if the body is still here?"

"I'll call the mortuary that transported the body to and find out. After the call, Tom related the information that the body was transported to a mortuary in Philadelphia.

Bridges instantly remarked. "They've buried him in Philadelphia probably next to his parents. I know his sister lives in California, where I don't know. It's unimportant right now. I can't believe he's dead, this guy was full of life, we hit it off the minute he met me at the airport in Tel Aviv."

"I think there's a connection Tommy, I think there is a connection with the project, the attempt on the President's life and the death of James Allen…but where I don't know."

"We can start from what is available…the 9mm taken from your friend, the mud on his shoes and clothes, the fact his wallet was in his pocket. The wallet contained cash, two hundred American and some Sheckles in small amounts. Credit cards and the ordinary items we men would keep in our wallets. Nothing that identified him as an Israeli official, but they knew him right away."

"Funny thing Tommy…he didn't want me to contact him at the embassy or be seen in and around DC together, that wasn't by his choice, it came from his boss, the head of the Mossad. I know he came to DC for some confidential business, what I don't know, however, I do know he had done a favor for the CIA Station Chief in Tel Aviv, may be a connection. You mentioned something about Michael's girlfriend surfacing in New Jersey and she confirmed Michael was alive although she hadn't seen him yet, what was that all about. It seems to me this all went down around the same time."

Tom sat back and explained. "Joanne Walker contacted the Allen woman, you know Christine Allen, the one staying over at Adriana's, well from conversations between the women, it sounded as though there wasn't a connection between your project and the terrorist activity the FBI has under surveillance."

"What do you now think, my friend?"

"I have to admit it's suspicious. Tom shuffled his papers as though he had something else he wanted to discuss. Bridges sensed it, and allowed Tom to bring it up.

"The shooting of the Arab over in Georgetown has given us a fit. There have other murders to investigate but the Arab community is demanding information. The round that killed the guy was a 308…isn't that the same as what killed the hispanic woman in California. Now that the authorities…FBI and Secrets Service are claiming…you killed her with a 9mm, then I guess there can't be a comparison made?"

"There may be a possibility Tom, I'll call some people in California including Tim Young, maybe, just maybe someone has that round they dug out of the stucco wall. I don't know the condition it's in, but I'll try." Bridges went on to inform Tom of the incident at Tim's home, Secret Service Agents came by with the expended round for Tim to check. "He told me after the agents left about the 308 rounds he made for the Hispanic woman. I saw with my eyes…the three rounds Tim made for her…those stupid bastards didn't follow through to determine where the rounds came from."

"Those bastards wanted to give me praise for snuffing the woman…and nothing else. A fucken conveyance, they didn't have to beat the bushes for the shooter. To my knowledge they never searched for a gun. That's why I'm convinced the government did it. They would like to blame it on the CIA or the entire intelligence community, and I'm the next best thing. This is the message to the people that domestic intelligence exists. Do you see my drift Tom, they make me the hero…never the less the press will…no doubt mention I'm former Agency."

Tom smiled before he answered and agreed with Bridges, although, cautioned him that anyone else would think he flipped his mind with his analog and allegation made against the First Lady of the land. A tongue in cheek remark.

Bridges clearly understood. He had to find a way out of the predicament. "Maybe Adriana had an idea on how I can get out of this mess…she works for Heidi, just maybe she picked up some information that can be used. I'll bet the President's ratings are up over the news that he was a target for an assassination. The sorry bastard. I got to get together with Adriana today, keep in touch."

Bridges finally checked his messages, the voice of Charlie made him feel sad and at the same time, angry. The second call came from Becky alerting him that she was in the DC area on official business, she requested they get together. The other messages were from old retired Agency friends calling to compliment him on foiling the assassination.

As he sat in his favorite chair in the family room with a small fire in the fireplace, he could hear the rain beat up against the windows and the horses in the barn whinnying, to him, was pleasant sound. The phone rang, interrupting the silence. He answered it in the family room. He was happy to hear Adriana's voice. "Hi sweet,…what's new over at the palace?"

"I'm not at work, I'm home sitting here with Chris Allen. She just informed me that the Arab that was killed in front of my place, she knew him and he was a friend of her husband's. She doesn't recall his name, but her husband called him Jon, some of the others called him Jonny."

"Adriana, has Chris heard from Joanne again?"

"I'm told no...but she did receive a letter from her with a post-mark Clifton, New Jersey. Chris has her telephone on call-forwarding and she now receives her calls here. Do you want to talk to her?"

"Yes and no...I want to talk to her in person and not over the phone."

Bridges gathered himself, put on some rain gear and drove over to Adriana's place in the down pour. The weather was getting colder and he thought maybe they would have snow for Thanksgiving. In no time, he arrived in Geargetown and the street where Adriana's townhouse was. In spite of the rain, the street provided a soft refection of the row of townhouses in the wet street. He felt annoyed when he had to park down the street and walk in the rain to Adriana's place. While walking up the steps, he glanced down the street in the direction where the Arab was shot. He couldn't help wonder if the shot was meant for him, then he shook it off and agreed to himself that who ever killed the Arab, knew who he was shooting at. Adriana came to the door dressed in a casual jogging suit and her hair pulled back off her face and behind her small ears that Bridges admired.

Once inside the warm house, he could smell the sweet smell of cooking and didn't recall if Adriana was a cook of any accomplishment. "Smells good, what is it?"

Adriana smiled and informed Bridges she was making a pot of old fashion stew. Bridges sat next to the fire after he shed his rain gear. Adriana immediately served him his favorite, cognac. Chris came down the stairs and was pleased to see Bridges as she walked over and hugged him. She appeared larger than he remembered and wondered when her baby was due.

As they all sat around the fire Chris reiterated receiving a letter from Joanne Walker informing her that Michael was alive although she hadn't met with him, only spoke with for a brief time over the phone. She was in New Jersey although didn't provide an address, although the post-mark indicated Clifton. The date was blurred and she couldn't make it out. She went on to say that she hadn't checked her mail at her place in two days and expected she had another letter from Chris with more details and possibly had information concerning Michael. Chris sensed that Adriana and Bridges wanted to talk, therefore she announced she would return after checking the mail at her place.

After Chris left, Adriana invited Bridges to have lunch with her and she made them both tuna salad sandwiches. As she prepared the lunch, she explained the reason she hadn't gone to the White House. Her reason was plain and simple, she didn't feel like it. She had called Heidi and left a message with her dippy secretary. As they were enjoying their lunch the phone rang, it was Heidi, she insisted Adriana be at the White House at two, she had an important matter to discuss and a special project for her.

Adriana hung up and called her a 'bitch' after agreeing to be there as Bridges knew what she was thinking. "The project is over…I'm going to resign from my job."

Bridges calmly suggested she shouldn't just yet and explained he needed her help in avoiding the fan-fair of receiving the phony award from the President. Adriana looked up at Bridges as she thought of something that could turn the dinner and presentation of the medal around. He dare not share her thoughts for fear he wouldn't approve, although he was desperate

"Richard, I think it would be a blast with you receiving the medal from the President and the dinner party, mostly made up of Heidi's financial supporters and responsible for financing the Rosa Carrea venture." She smiled sheepishly.

"Bull shit, I will not do it, not for anything or anyone. Do you have any ideas?"

"A few…but I won't share them with you, at least at this time…trust me, it will be a duzzy.

Bridges wasn't sure what that meant and decided to drop the subject and went on to tell Adriana about Charlie's death. Adriana was startled and shed a tear and went about clearing the long dinning room table they used for lunch.

After returning from the kitchen, she inquired as to what happened and Bridges shared his suspicions with her. Adriana agreed and appeared sincerely broken up at the news of Charlie's death. "What now…when did it happen?"

"It happened when we were in San Diego, I received a call from Charlie on the message machine. He wanted me to return his call, when I did, that's when I learned he was dead. They wouldn't give me details, I had to get Tom Moore to provide specifics. He was shot elsewhere and his body dumped at the Israeli Embassy over on Embassy Drive., I can't recall the name of the street, Oh wait, International Drive, I think North West." Richard smiled and pleased he remembered the address. " I understand Becky is in town, she received the body and I'm guessing Charlie's been buried next to his parents in the vicinity of Philadelphia."

"Have you spoke to Becky?"

"No, I've returned her call but I'm told she's there, but wasn't able to take my call. The Israelis can be idiosyncratic at times, but I'm sure if Becky knew I called, she'd speak to me. I guess she didn't call you?"

"No but I've received hang-up calls if that means anything?"

As they became intimate in their conversation, Adriana realized she had been summonsed to the White House by her-highness Heidi. She dressed in a simple black dress and jacket. When she put her light green raincoat on she looked like a different person. Bridges walked her to her car after Adriana wrote a note to Chris. After she pulled away from the curb, Bridges walked up the street to his Jeep Cherokee, as he unlocked the door he suddenly realized he hadn't locked them and was annoyed at himself for being so neglectful. As he got behind the steering wheel after removing his rain gear, he noticed the glove compartment was open, papers and maps on the floor and the sun-visors down, it seemed someone was looking for something. He didn't like what he felt, there's nothing in the car that would interest a thief other than the radio, besides he thought, they would have stolen the entire vehicle. It was something to do with the project he was sure. But what, he thought. As he pulled away from the curb, he realized his tire was flat. At that moment, his extra sense kicked in, he was being set up for the kill, he thought. He didn't have a gun with him and remembered he removed the small 25 automatic Beretta from under the seat before he left for Los Angeles. His mind was working fast, he couldn't think what he could use as a weapon in the event they, who ever ambushed him when he got out of the car. Then he recalled the Arab being taken out by a sniper, maybe this was the same thing they had planned for him. In a calm moment, he thought of driving the car with a flat, but then he didn't know if one tire was flat or two. He'd hoped it was one, he could make a run until arriving at a safe place or at least a filling station. Then he thought maybe it wasn't a set up at all, it was his imagination running wild. This wasn't like Bridges to panic, he recalled his many situations while in other countries that placed him in danger…he maintained his cool. By now he started the engine against his better judgement, who ever, could have placed a car-bomb under the hood, but he took the chance. The car was purring as he noticed a car approaching, it was Chris returning with her mail. She noticed Bridges car and realized he had a flat tire, she stopped next to him. He rolled the window down and didn't want to frighten her but he did tell her to unlock the passenger door and remain there.

"Chris I'm going to slide over and get into your car…stay put…I'll explain after…when I'm in your car, drive like hell out of the neighborhood. Chris was becoming anxious although suddenly realized that Bridges was in some kind of danger. She did what he said. They drove off down the street until they arrived at a filling station. Bridges went to the phone booth and called Tom Moore. Arrangements were made to have the bomb detail and a SWAT Team meet him near Adriana's place.

The bomb team examined with caution Bridges Cherokee approaching it with canniness while the officer activated the robot, opened the hood and discovered what they were looking for. A bomb device that should have gone off the minute Bridges turned the ignition switch. Luck was with him, it didn't.

After removing the bomb, Tom Moore who arrived later, instructed the team to tow Bridges' car to the yard and check the vehicle for prints and anything else that may be important.

Chris was distressed, a woman officer consoled her inside Adriana's Townhouse. Bridges and Tom returned to Metro Police

Headquarters after they determined Chris would be alright.

The bomb team leader met them and explained the device was made of parts manufactured in France except for the wire, which no doubt made in the US. Photographs of the device revealed it was the same type and design used by the Arabs throughout Europe and the Middleeast. The reason it didn't go off was hastier installation and the wire became detached and wasn't making a connection when Bridges started the Cherokee. This brought a chill to Bridges although he attempted to conceal his emotions. From Tom's office Bridges telephoned his daughter and directed her to take some clothes and stay with a girlfriend over the weekend. She was reluctant to leave the horses alone until Bridges assured her the horses would be cared for and not to worry.

After talking to Jennifer and feeling she would be safe, Bridges dialed Adriana's townhouse. He was glad to learn she was home.

She explained that Heidi didn't have anything special for her to do and once she discovered it was a ploy to get her to the White House. She returned to her townhouse in total disgust. Bridges filled her in on the details and credited Chris with saving his life. Adriana heard most of the details from Chris.

The ploy Heidi used to get Adriana to return to the White House provided Bridges suspicion that the attempt on his life was ordered by Heidi, he had no doubt. He thought that Heidi wanted to get Adriana away from the house well knowing Bridges was there, and ordered his demise. That would mean if Bridges was terminated, then Adriana would have no corroboration, maybe if necessary terminate her as well. For some reason Heidi didn't want to do that, but Bridges wasn't sure

They agreed to meet for breakfast early in the morning at the Embassy Row Hotel. From there Bridges planned to meet with Tom while Adriana went over to the White House.

***

Five-thirty in the morning the phone rang. Bridges at first thought he was dreaming and finally said 'hello' immediately he recognized the caller was Tom. "What's up Tom?" As he sat up and put his feet on the cold floor. Tom without hesitation informed him that the Park Police found a body of an Arab in Teddy Roosevelt Park next to the monument. "The poor bastard was shot with a 22 long, the same surgical shooting as James Allen…I wouldn't be surprised to learn it was the same people involved. Now get this my friend…fingerprints on the unexploded bomb, yup…they matched the dead man. The Arab was Iraqi attending Georgetown University, we traced it through INS where his 'green-card' was issued."

"Seems the bodies are stacking up, as long as it isn't my body." Bridges agreed to meet with Tom later that morning, after he met Adriana for breakfast. Tom was invited to join them at the Embassy Row Hotel. "Hell no…that place is too rich for my blood. Thanks anyway, see you later, I'll have the photo of the dead Arab by then

It was Friday and Bridges remembered to remind Adriana they had a dinner date with Tom and his wife Alice. They were to meet at Filomena's at eight and Bridges neglected to make reservation. He thought maybe Adriana could pull some strings and get them in.

Adriana was waiting for Bridges in the hotel lobby. She hugged him and then provided a soft kiss on the mouth avoiding to mess up her lip-stick. Once seated in the restaurant, Bridges quietly informed Adriana of the body of his assailant being discovered at TR Park. For some reason Adriana wasn't surprised and repeated that 'the bitch' was behind it.

After Bridges reminded her they had a dinner date, she assured him the dinner reservations would be taken care of. "I'm looking forward to the dinner and meeting one of my fans, according to Tom."

As they were leaving the hotel…Bridges heard a woman's voice calling 'Richard' from near the elevators. They both turned and were surprised to see Becky dressed in a dark women's business suite currying a black brief case.

As she approached them she hugged and touched cheeks with Adriana, and kissed Bridges on the mouth. This surprised Bridges and Adriana ignored the kiss and expressed a sincere concern for her. Becky explained briefly about Charlie, when she did, tears came to her eyes. People from various country origin passed them and looked at

Becky as though she was being reprimanded in public by Bridges and Adriana. They agreed to meet over the weekend when both learned Becky planned to leave for California the following Monday. Bridges provided Becky directions to his farm once he learned Becky had access to a car.

Adriana became excited over the possibility of preparing dinner for them, which Bridges welcomed. Becky explained that she accompanied Charlie's body to Philadelphia and that he was buried next to his parents. "It was sad, most of his family is gone, I was one of three people there, one was his sister that flew in from California. The other was the Israeli Emissary and his military aid. I'll miss him Richard, I loved him like a brother, so help me I did. When I came over from the Kibbutz and entered training for the Mossad, Charlie took me under his wing. He never married, but he would have made a good Jewish husband and the father of children. His love for Israel was strong. Commander Risken decided he should be buried next to his parents. Everyone at the Country-Club send their regards. You remember the training agent that was assigned to you, well he completed the program and was assigned to Central America. He asked for it, after all his hero suggested it."

Adriana spoke. "Richard is a hero to many…even me."The statement was made to alert Becky that Bridges was hers.

It didn't matter to Becky, but she decided to behave herself. Adriana had to get over to the White House and hated to leave Bridges alone with her, she decided to chance it and explained she had to go and made sure she kissed Bridges on the mouth. After Adriana was out of sight, Becky remarked. "I guess you two are together now…now what, getting married?"

Bridges smiled at Becky and thought she was still up to her tricks, he answered. "We recently got to know each other…socially. She's honest and pleasant woman…might add…she likes you as one woman to another."

"I guess I missed out again."

Bridges avoided answering and went right to asking about Charlie again. "What is the Israelis doing about Charlie's death?"

"They can't depend on the local police or even the FBI, so they are investigating themselves. I heard as recent as last night, they had a good lead."

"Anything you care to share with me?"

"Richard my office wants to share it with you...they know there would be an attempt on your life...that's what Charlie wanted to pass on to you. I heard that you almost bought-it yesterday, with a bomb in your car."

"Becky...you heard a lot...where did the Israeli Government learn about the incident?"

"I'm not sure...but they have people inside the terrorist groups, I think in New Jersey."

"Then you heard about the situation with Michael?"

"Can we go somewhere and talk...I don't think standing in front of the United Nations of people is wise."

Bridges looked around and realized Becky was right. He walked her over to a lounge away from the traffic of people. Becky suggested they go to her room and immediately Bridges admitted the rooms are all bugged. He smiled, causing Becky to return the smile. They sat across from one another, separated by a small French Provincial cocktail table. The hotel was completely decorated with French Provincial, eighteenth century. Hanging on the walls were paintings of various Statesmen from other countries and an exhibition painting of Ben Franklin, the same image used on the one-hundred dollar bill. Most of the hotel guests were visiting from other countries. Few Americans were present in and around the restaurant and gift shops. As sound of people passing settled down, Becky revealed to Bridges that the Israeli Government is working with the FBI on domestic intelligence and Michael Myers is working undercover. "The death of his friend was a misfortune and capitalized on when it was necessary."

"Then who killed the young man...James Allen?"

"It was the terrorist...they knew Allen had recordings in his custody that could blow the lid off their operation in the US. They didn't actually kill him, only arranged for his death by hiring a former American weapons expert, who we don't know. As you may know,

Allen was surgically shot, placed in the right spot to lodge into the heart. This guy is good, the shooter that is."

Immediately Bridges thought of Tim Young. He didn't want to share the information with the Israelis at this time, especially now that Charlie was dead. He then dismissed the idea that Tim was the shooter.

"From what my friends at the Police Department are saying, the shooter was good, am I to assume the FBI and Israelis arranged for it to look like Michael was dead so they could put him deeper into the groups activities. Doesn't make sense, why?"

Becky shrugged her shoulder as she crossed and uncrossed her legs slowly allowing Bridges to take a peak up her mini shirt. It was obvious and Bridges knew it, he deliberately didn't look but it would have been a natural reaction. Becky sensed that he avoided peaking and smiled at him then continued with the information.

"It makes seance if the bastards that arranged for the Allen shooting and the FBI and Israelis wanted a perfect cover for Michael, kill him off...make it known...then but the real Michael undercover. That's what is happening."

"What do you know about a woman named Joanne Walker, she had been an associate professor at the University of Maryland and recently moved to New Jersey, she was or is Michael's girlfriend?"

"Nothing much other than a liberal and an Arab sympathizer, she spoke out in public against the Persian Gulf War, so did some of the liberal Congressmen. But we think the woman knows a bit more than she would allow us to think. We think she's got Michael bullshitted."

"She's a friend of the dead man's wife, Chris Allen."

"That's a ploy as we see it...she's using her. We heard the woman is pregnant and is staying with Adriana."

"Well...well...take the girls, excuse me...take the woman out of the desert and she becomes a true spook."

Becky smiled and blushed at the remark. She appeared more mature and spoke with some authority Bridges thought. "Then again Becky, who shot Charlie?"

"That's what I want to know, we don't think it was the same people that tried to take you out. We have two-maybe three situations here. By the way, we didn't believe the bullshit that you the assassin down. That wasn't your kind of gig. We had a good laugh when the news broke and reported the attempt on the President's life and praised you."

"Oh but it almost was my gig, like it or not…I was inside the Condo when the hispanic woman set up for the kill. I had her in my sights when someone took her out from a distance, got any ideas?"

"Why do you think we would have any idea? Becky smiled as though she had a secret and wasn't going to say.

"Then give me a hint."

"I can say this, it wasn't the FBI or any of the Government people, but I can say…it was a friend."

"Did Charlie know?"

"Charlie set it up Richard."

"Say no more…but then his death is connected, isn't it?"

"I'm certain of it." Becky puckered her lips subconsciously and looked down. Staring into space she remarked. "Poor Charlie…he was a Prince. Those bastards killed him, we have to find out who exactly."

"Becky are you on your way over to the embassy, if you are I'll give you a ride. I have to meet with the local police concerning several things including Charlie's death."

"Thanks Richard…I'd rather walk, see you tomorrow at you place, is it difficult to find? I have a rental car but to be honest, this is my second trip to Washington, the first time was when I was in high school."

"Just follow the directions, if you get lost call me."

Becky and Bridges parted company and Bridges had his car brought around by the valet. As he pulled away he could see Becky walking carrying a brief case. He smiled to himself and was happy she matured enough to handle the death of Charlie.

Arriving at Metro-Police, an officer took Bridges loaned car and parked it, recognizing the car was department property.

While seated across from Tom, Richard Bridges informed him as to the information he recently received unofficially from the Mossad. "They took the Hispanic chic out…they have a handle on Michael Myers, and they have the girlfriend under surveillance, she's not to be trusted…she's using Chris Allen, if not Michael. The Arabs arranged for Allen's death although hired a former military weapons expert, could be anybody."

"Our old Nam buddy, Tim Young?"

"Could be…but don't think so."

"Can we call him and pick his brain?"

Bridges figured the time difference and determined it was past seven in California. "We can call him just before he leaves for work."

Bridges located Tim's phone number and punched the number in, after two rings Tim answered. He sounded as though the call woke him. Once he realized it was Bridges, it was almost like he was standing at attention. "Tim, sorry if I woke you, I need a question or two answered."

"Fire away Captain."

"Who uses 22 long to take a target down?"

Silence on the other end, then Tim spoke. "Why do you ask?"

"To be honest Tom Moore, you remember him in our outfit…well he's investigating a few cases where 22 long was used."

"Well Skippa…if it was used like a professional hit, then it had to be close almost touching the target and surgically placed for the kill. Don't get me wrong…it can also be used at a distance, not far but far enough."

"My question was…who uses?"

"Bad people…bad ones…mean people…well your people, or shouldn't I say this over the phone?"

"Go ahead."

"Israelis…I mean the dudes that went south and tasted money."

"Who else?"

"I taught a class at Quantico, I should say…I taught several agents that were going to be used as instructors, you know from the Hostage Rescue Team, I spent a week on surgical-sighting and targets…it wasn't deer hunting practice, it was close range back shots and long range head shots. Skippa…the public doesn't know about this, so help me."

"Have you ever used 22 long and the procedures you mentioned?"

"Hell no…the closest was in Nam…besides I know this is going to make me look bad, but I invented the procedure and taught to the Special Investiagtive Unit in El Salvador, but those people cant shoot to save their asses."

"Have you ever been hired for any special weapons details where the tool of 22 long was required?"

"Shit Skippa…I'm just a mail man…if I had I wouldn't be here in Oceanside…I would be living in style in La Jolla. Are you hiring me?"

"Last question Tim…have you trained anyone…one on one with the use of the 22 long, I mean recently?"

"Ya…around this time last year…he paid me by the hour plus my costs, but he wanted training with long-rifles also, 30 plus."

"Got a name?"

"Nope…I got one better."

"Well…he used to be a member of Her Majesty's the Queen's Marines…I like to say that."

"Are you sure or was he filling you with bull-shit?"

"Skippa…he's straight…he's a car salesman up in Orange County…get this, he sells Mercedes and he drove an BMW."

"What did he say was the reason he wanted to learn the trade?"

"Never gave me one…Christmas was coming and I needed the bucks. Besides I don't care what he uses the training for, I might add…he's a hell-of-a-shot."

"Description, can you describe him?" Bridges was pushing Tim and expected him to shut down any minute.

"What's this about you being the hero Skippa after you interrogated me, I mean…you took the bitch out and wanted me to tell you I did it…what the fuck was that about?"

Bridges didn't want to get into a conversation over the incident and thought maybe Tim was going through a stall. "Nothing Tim, they needed a hero when I couldn't give them you."

"Bull shit, the dude is around six, one-eighty, light hair, almost white—reddish face, not from the sun, you know the kind, slow in his speech and doesn't have a thick British accent. He lives in Newport Beach and works at a Mercedes dealership there, I think he's got something to do with finance, not sales. He paid me cash, big bills and I helped him find some rifles for him. I worked over one of those AR-Sevens for him…you know, handles a 22 long and the pistol model and a Ruger 308 single shot. Nice guy, loved the ladies. Drank like a fish.

"Could you find him if you had to?"

"Maybe…he called me, I never called him. The information I gave you came from our drinking sessions at the Staff-Club."

"Tim…would you come to Washington, all expenses paid, if we needed you?"

"Hell no, why?"

"We may need you, it's for God and Country."

"Ya…bullshit, let me know I have to make arrangements.".

After the call to Tim, Tom Moore played the recording of the call for Bridges. They both came to the same conclusion that Tim wasn't the shooter, but he certainly was getting a reputation as the person that's training them.

Tom put one of his men on locating the Englishman in California. Newport Beach Police Department was helpful in locating the man and was quick to report he disappeared, hasn't been seen in over a week. He left his Condo and job without notice. Name, at least on the Sales License was Dale Gibson, age forty five. Became a citizen of the US five years ago and his Social Security number matched the name. Property records checked out that he owns the Condo right-out, clear. A view of Newport Beach. Three hundred thousand dollar value. Paid off in two months ago. No wife or children.

…

CHAPTER 14
THE FINAL TRUTH

Friday night the crowd at the Filomena Ristorante was chaotic and the wait for a table for four was well over two hours. Bridges and Adriana arrived shortly after Tom and his wife Alice. They were standing near the corner of the entrance when they arrived. It was obvious they hadn't been there long. Tom introduced Adriana to Alice and immediately Adriana excused herself and walked over to the tall attractive looking young man with a well trimmed black mustache dressed in a tux obviously Italian and related to the owners no doubt. She briefly spoke to the young man who thought Adriana was special and signaled for his uncle. Shortly, a short middle aged man also dressed in a tux, with a wide smile, spoke to Adriana and in less than a minute they were seated at a booth in the rear of the restaurant.

Immediately a waiter arrived to take their order for drinks. No sooner the waiter left, a grey haired man came over to Adriana and rudely started talking to her as though she owed him gratitude. Adriana seemed embarrassed, that doesn't happen too often. She deliberately avoided introducing the man to Tom and his wife and of course, Richard.

Bridges knew the man and whispered to Alice that he was a lobbyist and served one term as a Democrat in the House. Tom acknowledged he also knew the 'lush' and suggested he would call the manager to have him removed. Adriana overheard part of what Tom said and signaled she didn't want a scene. Shortly, the man took the hint and left after he kissed and hugged her. No sooner the drinks were served, another man came to the table, Senator Philip Carlson from the great State of Maryland. Bridges seemed annoyed and attempted to get Adriana's attention. Adriana seemed to understand and was experiencing difficulty with the Senator. Bridges sipped his scotch and got up at which point, Adriana introduced Bridges as her fiancee. The Senator went through the motion of shaking Bridges' hand as he looked around, and returned to talking to Adriana. The situation was getting heated, Bridges impulsively wanted to knock the Senator on his ass, but thought better. Other restaurant patrons noticed the Senator getting loud with Adriana. She maintained her patience.

The manager came over and informed Adriana she had a phone call. Bridges walked with her to the front of the restaurant and realized there wasn't a call. She was summonsed to break up the incident with the Senator.

Both returned to their table and discovered two bottles of Dom Pereom chilling in buckets. Adriana immediately wanted to know where the champagne came from. Tom smiled and explained the owner sent them over and came over to explain that his son adored Adriana and was sorry for the incident. At the same time the restaurant owner noticed Adriana returned to the table, he came over and apologized and didn't miss a chance to tell Adriana that his seventeen year old son was in love with her. They laughed over the comment as Adriana asked to meet the young man.

The antipasto was served by the son who introduced himself as Enzo. He produced a smile for Adriana as he served her first. She returned the smile and spoke in what little Italian she knew, sounding more Spanish. The young man again smiled and spoke to her in what little English he knew, as Adriana extended her hand, the young man hissed it as he blushed. Adriana was flattered as he summonsed the Wine Captain over to pour the Champaign.

It was obvious the young man was beaming as he left the table and went about serving other customers. Alice, Tom's wife was entertained with the happenings and commented to Adriana that she knew of her popularity and was excited to meet her. Tom and Bridges talked and reminisced about the Marine Corps days. Both men avoided talking about business although Bridges confirmed Tim Young's arrival at Reagan, Monday.

Tom assured Bridges he will take care of Tim Young and assigned two Detectives to meet him at the terminal.

"Hope it doesn't shit his skivies." Bridges remarked as he smiled over the image of two detectives meeting Tim at the terminal.

The two women hit it off famously. During conversation with Alice, Adriana kept playing with Bridges leg. He didn't mind but it caused a distraction while he was talking to Tom

The entre was served by the owner's son. He was still beaming over Adriana. Alice and Adriana commented that they ate too much Italian bread with the antipasto and didn't think they could eat their entre. Both men looked at each other and ignored the comment. Bridges and Tom had Lingiuni and clams with a strong garlic influence. The women both were served eggplant parmesan with angle-hair pasta as a side dish.

Light conversation and enjoyment of the dinner until Bridges noticed that their waiter was being man-handled by a large built man in a dark suit. He was pushing the young man toward the door. The owner wasn't around, or at least didn't witness the incident. Bridges and Tom excused themselves and went over to the restaurant entrance to discover the young man was outside on the ground, as though he was knocked down.

Tom quickly examined the young man and discovered he had a head injury although conscious. Shortly, the para-medics arrived and treated the young man. By then the boys father came out of the restaurant and informed Tom that someone locked him in a closet.

While returning to the restaurant, walking around the small crowd that assembled, Tom remarked to Bridges in a whisper that the incident was over drugs, nothing more.

By the time they returned to the table the food was cold and the owner came over to apologize to them. The discission to leave was made by Adriana after the owner refused to allow them to pay for their meals.

At Tom and Alice's home, brandy was served and both women sat in the kitchen sipping coffee. Bridges looked up at Tom's trophy wall similar to the one at Paul Castilli's home. The same photo of them after a patrol and ambush by VC was taken and in the photo was Tim. Bridges didn't remember seeing him before. He pointed out the likeness of Tim to Tom and at that moment he recalled Sergeant Tim Young was a hell-of-a-Marine. The Vietnam experience was vivid in their minds, after thirty some years, it was scary to an outsider to hear them carry on about what they did and how their comrades died in a useless war. All that was learned, never to allow us to get involved again without a true military objective not influenced by members of Congress that cared only about being re-elected.

***

The rain stopped and at the farm Adriana was glad to hear they had the house to themselves. Jennifer was over at a girlfriends and was to return in the morning. She thought she could get to know Bridges more in his own bed. Adriana suggested they shower together, insisting it would save water. Bridges smiled and didn't protest.

The following morning, Bridges woke to the smell of Bacon and quickly got out of bed to discover Adriana preparing breakfast. He slightly kissed her on the neck and then the lips well knowing he had the taste of garlic in his mouth even though he brushed his teeth. Adriana knew it because she was having the same problem and smiled as their minds met.

Later that morning Jennifer returned home as Adriana was leaving. She promised to return to prepare dinner for when Becky arrived. Jennifer looked at her father with approval and knew Adriana stayed the night. Bridges smiled and put his arm around her as they walked into the century old house.

Becky arrived that afternoon around four. She was glad to learn Adriana hadn't arrived yet. Bridges was in the barn when Jennifer entered with Becky. Bridges sincerely was happy to see her and assumed they introduced themselves

As Bridges accomplished some small tasks, William brought in a folding chair for Becky to sit on and left to finish his choirs of mending a fence section that came down in the rain.

"Richard, you seem different in this environment, I mean you look rested and at home in this barn. I love your horses and Jennifer is exactly as you described."

"Thanks Becky, what now, are you done with the Mossad?"

"You can say that…I'm bitter over Charlie's death and I don't think I'll ever get over it so help me. It took a big chunk out of my feelings. It's hard to explain."

"It doesn't need explaining, although his memory will remain forever in my mind. What's the plans?"

"You know, gradate school…maybe Yale…I think I'll be a lawyer, but not criminal law like my dad, but something like Adriana, you know. The Virginia countryside is heaven, I'll have to return to California and make a life for myself. You won't have me and I can see you and Adriana are close, to say the least."

Bridges ignored her last comment and continued the light conversation with Becky, showing her around the farm until Adriana arrived. With her, was Chris Allen. Bridges thought she grew overnight. She was taken her pregnancy well not mentioning the death of her husband. They all entered the house and were seated in the family room where Bridges lit a fire. Adriana took charge and opened a fresh bottle of California wine, Cabernet Sauvignon, Robert Mondavi, 1978. Bridges commented on the wine and said it was the best. "Where did you find it Adriana?"

Adriana looked over the top of her glass and quietly explained it came from the Richard's wine closet. Bridges laughed and suggested one needs a permit to enter the closet let alone open a favorite bottle of Cabinet.

Chris was quiet and didn't say much, although drank a good portion of her wine. Adriana excused herself and she and Jennifer prepared prime-rib roast with trimmings. By then it was almost seven. In the family room Becky looked around and discovered photographs of Bridges and his wife and Jennifer as a young girl. Other photographs were of Bridges and his friends, taken in Vietnam. Chris sensing maybe they wanted to talk, left the room and entered the kitchen to help out with the dinner. Becky sat across from Bridges as the fire cracked and sparked in the century old fireplace. She seemed as though Charlie's death matured her and she sounded to Bridges, more responsible. She did flirt with him, although not as overt as she had in Tel Aviv.

Dinner was served just as the phone rang. It was Tom confirming that the body found in Teddy Roosevelt Park was who they thought is was. The man was Iraqi, Tom explained and when he learned that Bridges was just sitting down to have dinner, he excused himself and indicted they would talk later.

Another bottle of Cabernet was served, this time Bridges selected the year and it certainly wasn't...1978. The conversation at the dinner table involved the old farm house and what had to be done to renovate it to its present form. Adriana along with Becky praised the beauty of the house. The hard wood floors were without mares and scratches and the molding around the doors were natural, although Bridges explained the original frames had been painted by the authentic owners with home-brewed white paint as the rest of the house. The hard wood floors were not in place and were obtained from another house built in the thirties. The wood was all refinished. Bridges boasted how well his housekeeper Tilly kept the place up.

Dinner was over, Adriana and Jennifer cleaned up with the help of Chris. Becky had a cognac with Richard in the family room. He invited her into his study where Becky provided him her parents address in California. It was getting late and she had to return to the hotel and get ready for her trip to California in the morning. As she was putting on a coat, Adriana entered the study to bid her good luck and a safe trip. In addition, Adriana provided an invitation to Becky to visit her when she returns to Washington. Bridges requested her obtain Charlie's sister's address in California.

Bridges commented that Becky seemed to have matured as she drove down the dirt road heading for the beltway.

Adriana left shortly after. Bridges returned to the house, Jennifer had already gone to bed. He thought he should call Tom, then decided against it, he felt there was more he wanted to say when he called. It could wait until the morning. As he sat in his study with the lights dim, he thought about calling Becky to offer to take her to Reagan Airport in the morning. He dialed the hotel number, 202 285-1600 after looking it up. The desk clerk answered and Bridges asked for Becky Shulman's room. Shortly, Becky answered. Becky was excited to hear Bridges' voice. He offered to take her to the airport. Becky accepted then had to decline because of unfinished business at the Israeli Embassy. She thanked Bridges and reminded him that she often thinks about him and only wished they could be lovers. This took Bridges by surprise, at least after he commented to Adriana noticing the seriousness of her attitude displayed when she was at his home earlier that day.

Bridges said goodbye and promised to look her up when he was in California again or in the event she attended Yale, he would make a point to visit her.

***

The brightness Sunday morning added a certain cleansed look after it had rained all night. The trees were bright with red and golden colors. The evergreen trees were deep green and it made the countryside a picture never to forget.

Adriana arrived early and was out in the barn with Jennifer. Bridges dressed after shaving and showering. He noticed his mustache was quickly turning grey. He didn't like what he saw, but then he was pleased, it made him appear distinguished. He smiled as he dressed in jeans and a flannel shirt and of course his favorite riding boots that had been recently polished by William. As he entered the barn he over heard Jennifer and Adriana talking and didn't want to give the impression he was listening in on their conversation, although he did hear Jennifer say something about missing her menstrual period. Both women changed the subject when they noticed Bridges.

"Hi Richard, I had a golf game at the club but begged out of it because I wanted to be here with you two."

Bridges knew that was true but also knew the subject was changed in fear that he may have over-heard them talking about a problem

Jennifer thought she had. “Adriana…you didn’t have to cancel, we could have gotten together later, after your game.”

An official looking car came up the muddy dirt road. Bridges was embarrassed when he discovered it was Tom Moore. As Tom parked and got out of the car, he also was dressed in jeans, a plaid shirt and boots. He reached into the car to get his jacket when he discovered it was cold. He had a five shot Chiefs Special snub nose S&W 38 on his belt. As he approached the barn he yelled to Bridges that he should put a road in. “The damn mud is up to your ass.”

Both men laughed as Tom said hello and hugged Jennifer and shook Adriana’s hand. Adriana felt slighted and remarked. “Where’s my hug Tom?”

“Adriana, ever since I saw you in action at Filomena’s the other night, I thought I had to have permission to hug you.” At that moment Adriana hugged him and Tom kissed her on the cheek. “I knew you were a powerful woman around Washington, didn’t know you were that powerful, I mean if you can get us a table at Filomena’s without a wait, you are a powerful person.” This brought a smile to Adriana’s face and Jennifer didn’t have the slightest clue as to what Tom meant.

Bridges briefly thought of what he over heard between his daughter and Adriana. He wondered if Adriana would fill him in, then he decided he wouldn’t ask. But if Jennifer was in trouble, pregnant, he wanted to help in some way, but to his thinking an abortion was out of the question. He then thought, to his knowledge, Jennifer wasn’t seeing anyone, why should she be pregnant. It had to wait until later. Tom and Bridges entered the house leaving Jennifer and Adriana in the barn. Maybe they’ll go trail riding and Jennifer could finish confiding in Adriana.

In the family room, Tom sat in one of the wing-back chairs next to the fireplace. Bridges placed a small log on the already burning fire. He served coffee then Tom spoke after taking a sip of the coffee. “Richard…do you ever miss the Marine Corps days, I mean if you stayed in you would have been a colonel or maybe even a General, ever think about that?”

"I've though about it, but I couldn't stay, I had too many things to do after Vietnam. What about you, you would have been Sergeant-major or a crusty o'l Warrant Officer, you know, a Marine Gunner as we used to call them."

"No, I had the same feeling after Vietnam, I wanted to be a Cop ever since I saw my uncle 'Tom' in uniform back in Boston. I got the education and could have been an FBI Agent, you know I couldn't handle the bullshit Hoover gave them, now the Bureau has changed, for the worse by comparison to the Hoover days. Say what you want about Hoover, he had many people bullshitted and ran a tight ship.

"You did well Tom, I'm sure once you retire, you'll be fine."

"Forget it, I'm not retiring my friend, never, I'm going to die a Cop."

"What's Alice say?"

"She's with me, now that I'm Captain."

"Did she enjoy Adriana the other night?"

"She was fascinated with her."

"How about you Tommy, what do you think about her?"

"She's top drawer...first class...the best, I would say you're lucky...you and her are perfect."

As the men had small talk, Jennifer was in the barn explaining to Adriana that she went to a party when her father and Adriana were in Israel. She met a guy that she thought at the time was cute. She had too much to drink and found herself in bed with him. Adriana asked if she though he forced her, at which point Jennifer indicated that it was mutual. Adriana insisted she had to tell her father, but first she suggested having a doctor check it out and determine for sure if she was pregnant.

"Adriana...we're against abortion...I will break his heart if he knew I terminated a pregnancy."

I'm not suggesting an abortion, all I'm saying is first determine if you're pregnant, if you are...discuss it with your father in the same way you talked to me. Together you both will determine what should be done, I'm not for abortion either. If you're not pregnant, then no need to discuss it with your father."

Adriana felt flattered that Jennifer would discuss such a discreet topic with her. It seemed Jennifer felt better after the talk and decided to take Adriana's suggestion

.Both women saddled two horses and rode into the country side. The tress were bright with the changing leafs, the horses were alive and wanted to go. As both women rode at a slow pace away from the farm house, Adriana pointed to a strange object in the distance next to a large tree. As they approached the object, they discovered it was a camp sight that someone recently abandoned. They dismounted and Adriana entered the two man tent that had been poorly camouflaged. She discovered at least two people had been there. Two sleeping bags and rations that the military uses for long range patrols. The equipment was government issue, although anyone can buy the equipment at an Army-Navy store. Jennifer assured Adriana there shouldn't be anyone on the property and she was certain her father didn't grant anyone authorization to camp there.

Adriana being inquisitive, checked around and discovered radio equipment and monitoring devices she wasn't familiar with. She decided to take the equipment and return to the farm house.

After wrapping the equipment in a rain cover for one of the sleeping bags, both women mounted the horses and rode toward the barn at a fast pace. Upon arrival, Jennifer ran into the house and alerted her father and Tom as the findings. Both men went to the barn and agreed, the radio and monitoring equipment isn't sold at any Army-Navy store. It had to be government, maybe FBI, or NSA. Bridges didn't rule out CIA.

Bridges and Tom jumped into Jennifer's Jeep and drove out to the camp sight. By the time they arrived the other equipment was gone and the only thing left was the mountain tent. They searched the area and discovered that the surveillance team had been in place for at least two days. One of them was a smoker. They collected the tent and returned to the farm house. Bridges contacted an old friend recently retired from NSA. He inquired as to inventory control on monitoring equipment. The friend without hesitation informed Bridges the equipment is tightly controlled and each unit had its own diary-log as to maintenance and use by date and serial number. Bridges thanked his friend and returned to discussing the situation with Tom.

"From the looks of this equipment, the farm house was under surveillance by someone in government. I didn't want to think it was Agency, matter of fact they are low on the list. But with this Heidi thing, its got to be NSA or those knuckle heads…the FBI."

Tom agreed with Bridges and called his office to determine if any of the items had been reported missing from any of the government installations in and around Washington. In less than five-minutes, Tom received a call that the described units were reported stolen from Fort Monroe. Tom immediately contacted the Army CID at Fort Monroe. He was patched through to the residence of the Special Agent in Charge who informed him the items were reported missing from NSA two weeks ago. The FBI has taken jurisdiction of the investigation. "Bingo, NSA reported the items missing or stolen Tom related.

"It doesn't mean NSA is behind this…only means they reported the equipment missing, could be FBI using the equipment. It could be someone other than government was conducting a surveillance." Bridges expounded, although he knew down deep, it was the Bureau and Heidi Banks is behind it.

Tom picked up the cadence and spelled out his suspicions that the Bureau was being used by Heidi. "Then what we're saying is the equipment was stolen and with permission of the Director of NSA, the equipment was used by members of the Bureau to keep an eye on your comings and goings. I don't like this myself Richard, and I'm sure you are not jived over it."

"Tommy, I'm so fucken glad I left the Agency when I did, the politics that's controlling the Agency is now beyond belief, the Bureau and NSA is no different. When this idiot President appoints a shoe salesman to be the Director of the CIA, things have to run sour. Now what do you think those assholes learned from spiking my house?"

"Probably nothing, except your private moments with Adriana, maybe that's it. The First Lady wants to get her kicks by listening to you and Adriana get it on."

Bridges didn't respond. He thought if he shared the thought with Adriana, she'd pull Heidi's hairs out of her cunt, one by one. "Now where do we go?" Bridges asked well knowing that the dinner and presentation was scheduled at the White House for friday evening. A trepidation no doubt. Both men went over the body count and attempted to relate each incident to either terrorist activity or the plot to assassinate the President. They both realized an attempt may still be made on the President's life even though the Secret Service doubled there efforts in safeguarding the President.

The latest casualty was the Arab found in TR Park, the one that's believed to have planted the bomb in Bridges' Jeep Cherokee.

As both men discussed the various incidents, the phone rang. Bridges picked it up and answered as always. The caller was male and in a low and duskiest voice, informed Bridges his daughter Jennifer was pregnant by a nigger. The phone went dead.

Bridges sat back in his chair and looked over at Tom. A look of puzzlement was obvious to him. "What's wrong?"

"The bastard said Jennifer was pregnant, it was by a black person and she's arranging for an abortion."

"Slow down Richard...slow down, I suggest nothing other than talking to Adriana first...if there is a situation, Jennifer may have trusted Adriana, however, I don't think Adriana will violate a trust unless you explain receiving the call."

"Good idea Tom, I shouldn't jump to conclusions, its harassing that's all I'm sure. But to talk about my daughter, I see Red...God damn it...those fucken bastards.

The two women entered the house, Jennifer went to her bathroom to take a shower. Adriana helped herself to a glass of orange juice and sat with Tom and Bridges next to the fire. She sensed there was something wrong. She looked over at Bridges and with a look, invited him to open up and tell her what's going on. "Are you upset about the camp-sight?"

"Yes...damn it, but I just received an anonymous caller informing me that Jennifer was pregnant, and that her lover was black."

Adriana held her look, not daring to change her expression for fear she may violate Jennifer's trust. "Did the caller say anything else?"

"No…but I think it's some asshole attempting to harass me."

At that moment, Adriana thought about the conversation she had with Jennifer in the barn, then they went for a ride and discovered the camp-sight. She immediately believed the surveillance team heard the conversation and decided to pull Bridges chain. She couldn't share her thoughts with him until she knew for sure if Jennifer was or was not pregnant.

The sound of the shower water was turned off. Adriana suggested they discontinue the conversation concerning the call and Jennifer. Both men agreed.

As Tom was leaving Jennifer reappeared to say good bye. Bridges walked him out to his car. While inside, Adriana questioned Jennifer about her lover. Jennifer was inquisitive until Adriana was compelled to tell her about the anonymous phone call. Upset and almost crying, Jennifer informed Adriana that the young man was not black and hesitantly informed her, the young man was from Jordan and a student at Georgetown.

Adriana was pleased she was so open with her and thought that when Bridges finds out, if he has to know, he wouldn't object, at least she didn't think so. The situation involving Jennifer reminded Adriana of herself and her late husband.

Early Monday morning, two detectives from Washington Metropolitan Police met Tim Young at the Reagan International Airport American Airlines gates. The terminal was crowded as always and the detectives had a description of Tim, six-feet tall, in his early fifties, although looked younger, dark grey hair, a handle-bar grey mustache about one-hundred seventy bounds, and probably dressed casually.

The flight originating in San Diego arrived and unloaded passengers. No-one fitting the description of Tim got off the plane. One of the detectives consulted the airlines representative and determined that Tim Young had been on the flight. The two officers were embarrassed and had Tim paged. Shortly, Tim approached the detectives, he was unexpectedly dressed in a dark business suite minus the mustache. The detectives greeted him and explained the dilemma.

Tim laughed quietly and walked with the two officers to their car after retrieving his bags and tool chest

***

Early that morning, Adriana drove Chris to the airport where she took a flight to Boston. She planned to stay with her parents in New Hampshire until the baby was born. Her daughter had already been with them and she seemed anxious to see her. Chris started crying as she said goodbye to Adriana, she hoped that the situation with her husband would be determined and she could get on with her life.

After the flight lifted off the runway at Reagan Inernational, Adriana hurried to her car and drove over to the White House. She immediately went to the living quarters where her office was. Heidi met her and insisted they have a conference. Adriana wasn't in the mood for a chat with 'your highness' but she sat down next to Heidi's desk. Heidi looked haggard and had a frown on her face. Adriana thought the woman could be an attractive woman if she wasn't a bitch. Heidi smiled and asked Adriana about her plans.

"Heidi…I don't have any immediate plans, If Bob runs for another term, I'll stay here with you. If not, then maybe I'll return to the State Department, haven't thought that far. I'm seriously dating someone, it may or may not lead to marriage."

"That's what I want to talk to you about…what's his name…Richard something or other?"

"Richard Bridges!"

"Oh yes, that's it, he's a hero for saving the President's life. Wouldn't you know it, someone you're dating is my husband's savior…that's a crook of shit."

"I'm sorry, I don't understand."

"I'll tell you, Richard Bridges was forced to leave the CIA because he was considered incompetent. He was known to have fucked up the programs the United States put in place during the Reagan and Bush administrations. So you see, your lover-boy is not what you think. I'm sorry you had to hear that from me."

Adriana sat still in the chair with her legs crossed and dressed in a dark blue women's suite. Her stockings matched the blue suite and as Heidi talked Adriana's leg began to rock slightly. She impulsively wanted to jump up and smack the woman, but thought better. "Heidi, I don't know where your information came from, but its all wrong. Besides he's good for Bob's campaign if he should seek a second term."

"Of course he'll seek a second term, what makes you think that he won't?"

Adriana paused..."Well, someone tried to kill him when we were in California, they may try again, then what?"

"Then WHAT...if they get him...then I'll run for his seat...that's WHAT."

Adriana wanted to laugh out loud, but felt comfortable hearing her suspicions come out of Heidi's mouth. "Wouldn't people think you set your husband up so you could run for his seat?" Adriana felt bold and waited for Heidi to blow-up.

"The fucken Republicans are the only group that would start that shit."

Adriana couldn't believe she was having this conversation with Heidi. She decided to switch the conversation back to Bridges. "Are you saying I shouldn't get involved with Richard Bridges?"

"You do as you wish...but you could be caught up in a mess if you did become serious with this person, listen I know plenty of people at Langley that would set you straight on him."

Adriana already checked him out every which-way, the Israelis as well...Heidi is up to her tricks again. "But he's good in bed Heidi, he really is."

"Well that may be so...but other than a good fuck, you don't want to continue."

"Am I to assume you don't want me to continue with my relationship with Richard Bridges?"

"You don't have to assume anything, I...don't want you to continue with him."

Adriana knew some point in time she's get around to conversation with Heidi, she decided to pull out the stops and cut to the chase. "Isn't the woman that attempted to assassinate your husband the same person you have been talking to and I gave money to, or am I mistaken?"

The First Lady rocked back in her executive leather chair…looked out the window and looked deep into Adriana's eyes. "Listen, if you whisper to anyone what you just stated, I'm sure you'll be in deep trouble."

"Then am I to assume you want me to resign my job?"

"No…damn it, you know very well the woman your lover killed was the same person you visited in Los Angeles, I might add, gave her a bundle of cash."

Adriana knew Bridges didn't shoot the women, but she wanted to continue playing the game. But the sound of Heidi explaining the bundle of cash was a blackmail. She wanted to smash her right in the face. Adriana was small in comparison to Heidi, her weight was at least twenty-five pounds lighter. If they had a fight, Heidi could over power her but Adriana could hold her own. Then she snapped to her senses and found an excuse to terminate the conversation.

At noon, Adriana informed Heidi's secretary that she was leaving for the day, that if she was needed by the First Lady, she would be home. Before she left the White House Adriana decided to go down to the sub-level and talk to the young men that operate the communication for the White House. One of the young men Adriana knew, he being a Marine, felt compelled to flirt with her every time he saw her. She decided to pick his brain about calls to Central America by the First Lady.

The young Marine sergeant was flattered and informed Adriana that the NSA people took charge of Mrs. Banks lines. This disappointed Adriana, she thanked the sergeant and without anyone seeing, she hugged him and allowed her cheek to touch his. She could feel him tremble and his shave lotion smelled pleasant and fresh. For a brief moment, this excited her. In her mind she believed the Marine would break his ass to get information Adriana wanted. She smiled to herself and lectured that she was a bad girl. A smile came over her face as she walked to the exit of the White House. One of the young press-assistants thought she was smiling at him.

Adriana decided not to go home. She remembered that Bridges was with Tom, she impulsively went directly over to Metropolitan Police Headquarters. She hated to enter the building from the front, especially dressed with a short shirt. The young officers overtly flirt with her and she wasn't in the mood. At the front desk she asked for Captain Moore. In a matter of seconds she was escorted by a young women officer to Tom's office. Both Bridges and Tom were glad to see her. "I put Chris on a plane to Boston this morning. She'll be better off with her parents until the baby arrives."

Tom contacted his counter-part at Baltimore Police Department and used his influence to get them to keep a watch for Chris Allen's townhouse. It was past the noon hour and Tom suggested lunch, Adriana impulsively accepted and all three left in Tom's car as Adriana suggested the Peasant Restaurant over on Pennsylvania Avenue. "I need a pepper-upper and to see some people that are alive, instead of that bitch at the White House. She's got everyone bullshitted."

Bridges detected Adriana had to unload something, so he came out and asked. "What happened?"

"Glad you asked Richard, but do you know that 'bitch' tried to bad mouth you…she even suggested you were fired form the Agency. She also made reference to you be incompetent, that's why they let you go. At the same time she knows damn well you didn't take the Salvadorian woman out."

Bridges glanced over at Tom, and then looked back at Adriana in the back seat. "Adriana, she doesn't know…it wasn't her choice to take the woman out…it was a favor to us by the Israelis."

Silence…then Adriana spoke. "You mean Charlie arranged for it?"

"That's exactly what I mean."

Tom was surprised Bridges hadn't discussed it with him, he continued to drive and listen.

"But who…was it someone they hired?"

"No…someone fresh from Tel Aviv, clean and simple."

"Do we know him or now should I say her?"

"No…doesn't make any difference…but why was Charlie killed, it had to have a relationship."

Tom entered the conversation. "Maybe…just maybe…the First Lady arranged for it. That's my hunch."

Bridges then asked Tom a question involving the investigation. "I know the Israelis are conducting their own investigation, but what have your guys come up with?"

"Nothing, except we think the single round came from a 9mm Beretta, Parabellum. Now we know just about every government agency including the military uses the Beretta, with exception to the FBI, they went to a 10 mm. But that doesn't rule them out. We believe Charlie Goldberg was killed because of what you said Richard or some other reason having to do with Israeli Intelligence. But now you reveal he was involved in taking the Hispanic woman out…that sheds new light on motive. Someone your Highness arranged."

"I agree…she was a complete bitch this morning, now that explains why she bad mouthed you Richard."

"She believes what the Secret Service reported, they know damn well the hispanic woman was shot by a 308, and needed an answer right away, that's why I was made to look like a hero."

Tom looked over at Bridges and smiled as hepulled into a space marked for police parking. The restaurant appeared crowded and no doubt there was a wait. Bridges didn't mind and Tom looked at his watch, shrugged his shoulders and commented that it didn't matter, he was hungry.

No sooner they entered, Adriana was greeted by the manager. He hugged her with a big smile on his face and directed them to a table as those waiting remained behind.

"If nothing else Richard, she'll get you into any restaurant in the District of Columbia."

As they were seated, immediately two women came to their table to say hello to Adriana. She stood and greeted them as Bridges and Tom sat back and smiled as they were entertained. In a few minutes the women left and Adriana returned to the booth with a smile on her face. She quickly explained that the two women also dislike Heidi.

They had a brief lunch made up of house specialty Cobb salad and a glass of wine selected by Bridges. During their meal, Adriana couldn't help touching Bridges under the table. He didn't mind, but hoped no one could see.

"I've got shopping to do here at Gallerie, can you gentleman leave me here and Richard please pick me up at the restaurant around five."

Bridges looked around and remembered that the Mazza Gallerie Peasant was a favorite place for his wife to shop, then he spoke. "Yes of course, see you at five." Adriana kissed him. Tom and Bridges decided to take a ride around the city, no place in particular, just a simple ride to discuss everything that had to do with the body count.

"Tommy what the hell do I do Friday night, I meanI feel like a fool accepting the medal from the President with the world watching?"

"It could be worse...the First Lady could be presenting it to you."

"Damn it Tom, you got me wrong, I mean I don't deserve a medal. I didn't do shit, must admit I almost took her out. But when I heard that fired round...crack...it scared the hell out of me. For a moment I thought I was the target."

While browsing in several of the women's shops, Adriana, by chance, run into a familiar face. He was either a member of the FBI, or someone she met over at Langley. He smiled and greeted her with over whelming gestures. It was almost as though he wanted to kiss her in public. That renewed the acquaintance with the middle aged man, distinguished greying hair and a smile that never left his face, was attractive. He immediately asked about Bridges, after all he recommended him for her special project. He further commented about the incident in California with the President and he finally arrived at asking if Richard Bridges ever told her how he got his nick-name. This comment alerted Adriana and politely answered that Bridges avoided telling her about the nickname. At that moment, they were met by a woman Adriana thought she knew and later discovered it was the man's wife. She was at least fifteen years younger than the man. They exchanged hellos and said goodbye. The man never had a chance to inform her as to what she wanted to know about Bridges nick-name. She made a point to ask and even insisting when they were intimate again.

She thought, as she strolled throughout the mall exchanging hellos with women she thought she knew, or thought knew her. Her thoughts were of Bridges and how he had managed to avoid telling her about a simple intimate part of his life. She became slightly annoyed that he never told her, then she thought maybe it wasn't that important.

Adriana was insistent that she had to buy something to get over her feelings about Heidi. She stopped at an Espresso stand to rest and reflect on things she's experienced since meeting Bridges. As she sipped her coffee, she smiled to herself as to what a wonderful person he was and maybe someday they would marry. Then her thoughts returned to the White House, and the present administration. Being a imperious Republican and working among the liberal thinkers, sometime gave rise to her emotions, but she was proud of herself that she never allowed her own politics to affect her performance and judgement when it came to serious matters.

She located a pay-phone after she completed her espresso. She dialed her home and listened to the messages. The message that most interested her was a call from Jennifer. She sounded cheerful and requested Adriana call her at the farm. Immediately Adriana dialed the number, after three rings Jennifer answered while in the barn. She was excited to tell Adriana that she wasn't pregnant and swore she wouldn't have sex again until she married her prince. Adriana agreed, but thought better. She was happy for Jennifer and that meant they didn't have to bring up the subject with her father.

At four-forty five, Adriana started walking toward the restaurant after she purchased a pair of casual shoes, something one would wear if they were going sailing. As she arrived at the restaurant, Adriana decided she would enter and chat for a minute with the manager. No sooner she entered she was informed that she had a message from Richard Bridges. The message informed her that he would be late by ten-twenty minutes. She didn't mind and decided to have a martini, she didn't care for martinis, but for some reason she felt like one. The bar was empty for that time. The bartender identified himself as being from Jordan. This of course didn't impress her but she wasn't rude. As she sat and sipped her drink, the bartender started hitting on her. He was in his late twenties and bragged that he came from Amman and his family was related to the King of Jordan. She smiled to herself and pretended to be impressed. The bartender thought he was making time with Adriana and continued to tell her about his homeland. She couldn't handle it anymore, she quickly finished her drink and made sure she under tipped him, a message that she wasn't pleased. She waited in the entry way. She glanced at her watch, it was five thirty, this annoyed her, but she maintained her cool.

Bridges finally arrived. She hugged and kissed him as though they hadn't seen each other in a long time. She was certain the bartender could see her reception of Bridges.

They returned to the police department to get Adriana's car and the plan was to meet at the farm. Before she entered her own car, Adriana made Bridges promise to allow her to stay the night. He sounded flattered even though he thought in the back of his mind Jennifer was home and wondered what she would think.

As though she was reading his mind, Adriana responded

"Don't be concerned about Jennifer, she's cool and won't loose respect for her father, believe me." She knew of Jennifer's secret and thought that Jennifer really wouldn't mind.

It was past seven when they arrived at the farm. They could smell cooking and both guessed it was Italian cooking. Bridges suggested it had to be Jennifer cooking because that's all she knows how to prepare. Sure enough it was Jennifer and she made an entire Italian dinner, antipasto, lasagna, meatballs and French bread prepared with garlic butter and apple pie which she admitted Tilly baked

During dinner, Adriana felt playful and asked Jennifer if she knew her father's nickname. Bridges was surprised that Adriana would be so bold to ask Jennifer. It didn't bother him because Jennifer didn't know. Jennifer confirmed what Bridges knew, that was she didn't know and recognized that Adriana was playing with her father's head. She wanted to join in but didn't know at what point she could contribute. She was so happy not to be pregnant and grateful that Adriana was there to talk to.

After dinner Bridges remembered that he failed to check his messages. The one and only message was from the White House. It was one of the staffers making preparations for the dinner and presentation of the medal to Bridges. It was too late to return the call and decided it could wait until the morning.

Jennifer and Adriana went out to the barn after they put the dinner dishes in the dishwasher. Adriana watched as Jennifer put blankets on the horses and noticed the colt was growing fast. They returned to the house and Jennifer decided she would go to bed after a shower. Adriana became excited at the thought of being in bed with Bridges.

During a romantic shower together, Adriana kissed Bridges passionately, he returned the feeling as she relaxed and turned her back to him. she asked him to wash her back. He agreed and at that point she asked about the name 'The Highwayman'

Bridges knew then that he was in a corner…he had to tell her something, not everything, but something that would satisfy her. He thought and thought but couldn't find enough details that allowed him to fabricate the story.

"It's complicated Adriana, they don't call me that anymore."

Please tell me…I need to know, is it bad, or does it have something to do with another woman, what is it?"

"My answer is Yes, and Yes, now that's it."

"Come on, I can handle it Mister Highwayman…" Adriana felt playful but yet she seriously wanted to know.

"Would your feelings be hurt if I didn't tell you?"

"Of course not…but I'd hate you."

"Okay…then hate me. I don't know where to start."

"Start from the beginning." Adriana turned to face Bridges and allowed her hand to touch his wet body and finally his almost erect penis. She played with it for a few seconds as she begged him to tell her.

"That's not fair…you touching me and trying to get me to say something." Bridges didn't know where to start, it was in Central America during his assignment in eighty-eight. It wasn't the right moment he thought and he had to put Adriana off.

Adriana was insistent and continued to tease him until he turned the water off. They both got out of the shower at different ends, meeting in the center of the large tiled bathroom. Bridges handed her an over-sized white towel and made remarks how perfect her body was as she started drying him with the towel. He leaned over to kiss her, she responded to the point of almost touching lips, she quickly turned her face avoiding the kiss. Bridges smiled and knew she was playing with him. Then she got up on her toes and kissed him on the side of his face. Bridges thought that he would explain the name but it wasn't the time. If only he could convince her, he'd feel better.

Adriana dried herself with another towel and managed to the rear of Bridges, grabbed him around the mid-section and hugged him with all her strength. "Richard…I understand, you'll tell me when ever you feel comfortable…but it better be damn soon, it's killing me, the curiosity is."

Both walked in the nude to the dimly lit bedroom and got into bed. Adriana couldn't wait to kiss Bridges passionately. She was starved for his affection and needed him to touch her all over. She couldn't wait any longer as she allowed herself to get on top of him and they became one.

Adriana got up early, showered and left for her Townhoues to change for a days work at the White House. Bridges was surprised to find her gone when he woke. He also discovered Jennifer left for school and he was alone in the house until Tilly came up from the servant's quarters. The small bungalow was originally built to house slaves before the war between the States. When he bought the property, he renovated the house and installed modern plumbing and what else was needed to make it livable for William and Tilly.

Adriana arrived at the White House at nine. For some reason the press-corps was all excited and they were hurrying in and out of the press rooms. She immediately headed for the living quarters and for some reason wasn't curious as to why the excitement. Upon arriving at her office, Heidi greeted her in a pleasant attitude, almost sickening and obviously patronizing. Adriana decided to play the game. She liked working at the White House and doing the project research for Heidi, as long as there wasn't side trips and projects that truly smacked of cold and cruel politics. She thought that her job would be a lot better if a Republican was President.

Heidi immediately informed Adriana the reason for the excitement. "One of the chamber-maids that Bob was fucking was found dead. She was shot while sleeping at her apartment. The press-corps are going nuts over this ridiculous story. None of them know the little tramp was giving Robert some of her private time."

Adriana was taken back with Heidi's attitude. She immediately thought Heidi had the young black woman killed. Adriana recalled the woman and discovered the President and her in the Lincoln bedroom one late afternoon. Adriana assumed her position and started making telephone calls to people connected with Heidi's social welfare projects. When she exhausted the list of names, it was almost lunch time. She decided to have a light lunch in the kitchen with the staff. As she sat at the long table, the young Marine Sergeant entered the kitchen and beamed when he discovered Adriana. He immediately sat across from her and she provided him with a pleasant smile. The sergeant in a soft voice informed her that he had access to what she was looking for. Adriana threw him a simulated kiss which flattered the sergeant.

Bridges worked around the farm and at lunch time Tilly announced that she made stew and he was to come in from the barn for lunch. It sounded good. He thought he should at least contact Paul Castilli and set the record straight. He was surprised that the Judge hadn't called him concerning the news that Bridges allegedly snuffed the Hispanic woman that attempted to assassinate the President. This alone confirmed what Bridges had mentioned when last they met

Bridges dialed the switch-board of the Supreme Court. He couldn't find Paul's private number that rang direct to him. The receptionist put Bridges on hold after he asked for the judge and announced he was calling. Shortly the receptionist informed Bridges that the Judge wasn't available to speak to him. Bridges felt disappointed, and he didn't think of it until later.

Adriana called right after he hung the phone up. She quickly informed him of the black woman's death.

CHAPTER 15
OBLIGATORY

While at the office at Metro Police Headquarters, Tom was seated behind his desk as he spoke to Tim Young. Their conversation was about the Vietnam experience. In the middle of their conversation, Tom remembered he should call Bridges. As he interrupted to place a the call.

During the conversation with Bridges, coffee was brought into the office and Tim helped himself. As Tom hung the phone up, he informed Tim that Bridges would be over shortly

"What's this about…you invented the surgical shooting using the 22 long?"

"Ya…I had to take some classes in physiology…to understand where the round should be placed in order to explode the heart. I didn't invent it, just developed the procedure."

"Sounds wicket." Tom remarked and thought the shootings of both Allen and the Iraqi were the same as Tim described. The procedure was taught to the FBI as well, why he thought…why would a domestic law enforcement agency want to learn about surgical shooting except for investigative purposes. He looked at Tim then asked.

"Did you teach the FBI guys how to use the procedure or how it is done for investigative purposes?"

"How to employ the procedure." Tim remarked without hesitation.

Tom picked the phone up and dialed a friend over at Quantico. The friend had at one time been a member of Washington Metro Police. He was now an instructor at the FBI Academy. A young woman answered the phone and Tom asked for his friend by name. "John Faye here."

"John you old son-of-a-so and so, how are you?"

"Tommy, is that you, I was just thinking about calling you, what's up?"

I'd like to talk about firearms and firing procedures, can you talk now, got the time?"

"Of course…fire away."

"Surgical shooting, who teaches that?" Before John Faye could answer, Tom asked why they use it

"Well, the need to know, that's it…for investigative purposes, why?

"With a 22 long round?"

"Ya…we came up with the procedure resulting from an investigation we conducted last year, why are you interested?

"Well…explain, the Bureau designed the procedure?" Tom smiled at Tim when he asked the question.

"Ya…why do you have something we should have?"

"Not yet, I was reading about it in one of our Memos." Tom knew this was not the truth and hoped John Faye didn't ask for a copy.

"We sent out a bulletin on the subject, that's where your guys got the information."

Tom knew this wasn't true, he couldn't believe John Faye who he weaned as a cop would be engrossed with FBI propaganda.

"Okay John, if I come over, can I get your people to put on a demonstration?"

John Faye responded that he'd need a day to arrange for it. The call was then terminated on a cordial note.

Needless to say, he didn't have to tell Tim what John Faye said. Tim smiled and went on to explain about the classes he provided to the Bureau's Hostage Rescue Team the previous year.

"Do you have any live experiences?"

"No…but the procedure was my creation, thought about it when we were in Nam." Tim went on to explain the students were the instructors at the firearms section

Bridges arrived and was escorted back to Tom,'s office. He shook hands with Tim and welcomed him to Washington.

The three men engaged in conversation about the methods of surgical shooting that Tim created and solicited ideas as to who may be responsible. Tom couldn't help laughing when he informed Bridges that the Bureau claims they developed surgical shooting, I just spoke to one my former officers who's now with the Bureau.

Tom shared the information with Tim concerning the Mecedes Salesman in California.

Tim offered his own ideas. "If the salesman, what's his name…Gibson, ya Dale Gibson…did it, it had to be for a large sum of money, but I don't see him connected to any terrorist activities. But as I said, money is the motivator."

"What's your feelings that the Bureau is claiming your procedure was created by them?" Bridges asked impatiently.

Tom answered for Tim. "Those asshole always bullshit the public. No doubt John Faye believes the Bureau engineered the procedure. He wouldn't set out to lie to me, at least I hope he didn't."

Tim added that he didn't care "One day they will embarrass themselves when they get into a shooting situation as they did in Northern Idaho, then they'll say I designed the procedure."

At that point, Bridges suggested they go over the reasons for the shootings.

"We have Allen dead, and now an Iraqi. The Iraqi attempted to take me out with the car bomb, turns up dead with a single round in the heart. Allen as a NSA employee, has tapes of terrorist activities. Was he a double agent and they took him out, or did they arrange for his assassination to make it easy for Michael Myer to move freely undercover. This is our question gentlemen."

Tom explained that he thought Allen was a pawn in the terrorist activity, using him to assure Michael's success. "This suggests FBI."

Bridges agreed. "Now how does my situation compare?"

Tim Young sitting and listening, not knowing half of what they were saying, came up with an answer. "Same shooter…different contract."

"We thought of that, but who ordered my demise?"

"The First Lady, out of spite." Tom suggested as Tim sat there in amazement over the conversation he heard.

"Gentlemen…I'm just a mailman from Southern California…a retired Marine at most. Listening to you both talk about Washington politics is scaring the hell out of me, even though I've been to hell already."

Bridges smiled at Tim's comment and attempted to convince him there was a simple life inside the beltway.

Tom requested Tim provide a crash-course on surgical shooting and they proceeded to one of the departments class room after Tom invited two his trusted investigators.

The classroom was large enough to handle twenty-five students. Professionally done with green chalk boards and overhead and 35mm projectors. The room was built on tiers and Bridges and Tom along with the investigators sat down front. Tim was in his element teaching his favorite subject. He put a carousal of 35mm slides in the projector after he lowered the screen and flipped to the first slide

The slide depicted a professionally drawn diagram with the human target two hundred meters away from the sniper. Tim explained the basic requirements for taking the target out by aiming for the head. A high caliber rifle is recommended he pointed out as he flicked the switch as the next slide appeared. It listed the weapons of choice and all men were surprised to see the weapon used to assassinate President Kennedy was listed.

When Tim pointed to the weapon, he explained that many so called experts criticized the rifle Oswald used, but then he explained it was successful and went on to explain Oswald had to received special training or instructions from an authority that directed him to shoot for the head. Most layman would have aimed for the body such as in deer hunting. Same thing is true in a military operation, the infantry soldier will fire at the enemy's body, the exception to the rule is the military sniper.

"Surgical shooting dates back to the Revolutionary War although with improvements in weaponry and training."

Tom requested Tim explain close range surgical shooting. The two investigators looked at each other when their boss made the request. Realizing that was the answer they were looking for concerning the Allen investigation and the Iraqi found in Teddy Roosevelt Park. Tim continued.

"The surgical shooting at close range can either be from a short distance from the target, such as in a crowd or from behind almost touching the target while he sat away from the shooter. The weapon of choice in this particular case is an AR-7, either the rifle from a short distance, or the pistol version. Both can be rapidly disassembled and concealed. However, the shooter had to have knowledge of physiology. The shooter has to know where to place the round to the right of the left wing bone allowing the round to penetrate the heart, causing it to explode inside the body."

Bridges sat and listened and allowed Tom to ask questions. "What about the long distance using a higher powered rifle?"

Tim flicked the slide until he came to the profile of a human head.

"In the long distent shot, using the higher powered rifle, a scope must be used, at least 10 powered and the sniper aims just above the ear in a profile shot, probably the best position. In the case of head on, the shot is placed between the eyes. From the rear, this shot is more difficult and is recommended dead-center. If you recall, Oswald almost missed, I'm sure he was aiming for the right profile of Kennedy, just above the ear."

Tom explained that in both cases, the victims, James Allen and the Iraqi, were surgically shot in the back next to the left wing bone. "We have reason to believe the Allen shooting was accomplished while he was asleep. The Iraqi was in a seated position when he met his death. What a wicked way to go."

"Were both, twenty-two caliber?" Tim asked.

"Ya, I forgot that part…think it was the same gun."

Tim flipped through the slides again until he came to the weapons of choice. The AR-7 either pistol or rifle is sold as a survival weapon. All parts are concealed in the butt when it's disassembled, very light. The one with a scope, this can be rapidly removed and placed in a suite pocket."

For the benefit of his men, Tom asked why the heart exploded.

"We don't know, I can only speculate…its close and when the round strikes, it blows in pieces. It's no special ammo, it's standard store bought. In Vietnam I used the 03—Springfield with a scope. I had no need for close range, but it was surgical. The M-14 later was used and after me, I heard from others that civilian rifles were used. But the same thing applied, aim for the head. There are many 22 caliber pistols, some on a heavy frame like the Smith and Western 38, but for some reason, the AR-7 22 long was the choice. If you haven't seen one, it's a crude weapon, nothing to it. It can also be turned into an automatic in no time. No need for automatic during surgical shooting. My endorsement for the AR is based on test results. I have nothing to gain by endorsing it. I know the FBI uses a Remington 308 for long distance. City and County law enforcement agencies use everything from the M-14 to the M-16, and some in between."

After Tim's presentation, the two investigators thanked him and left the classroom. The three men returned to Tom's office and then left for lunch after Bridges called the White House and learned that Adriana was not in and expected to return soon. Bridges thought for sure he spoke to Heidi and she sounded pleasant when he identified himself.

In the presence of Tim, Bridges spoke freely. "The contract was still out there for a hit on the President."

Tom added. "With the Hispanic chic dead…who ever would find another shooter. She wanted him dead and his memory as being assassinated while in office would be the most honorable thing the President could do, at least that's Heidi's thinking."

Tim didn't feel comfortable listening to the conversation. He suggested he get out of the car and walk to the restaurant. Bridges insisted he stay and went on to invite him to dinner and the medal presentation Friday evening. Tim protested by explaining that he didn't own a tux. Tom expressed sarcastic sympathy and suggested he rent one.

"Then what you're saying, another attempt on the President will be made Friday at the dinner." Tom knowingly asked.

"It will be the first time an attempt would be made on any president inside the White House." Bridges strongly suggested was the next move.

Tim sat in amazement and didn't say a thing. He couldn't believe he was hearing the two men he knew in Vietnam talking about an assassination of the President. They both looked at Tim as he sat in silence.

Tom spoke and explained. "This is the life inside the beltway and we invite you to join us Friday. The tuxedo is a minor detail Tim, but if an attempt were to made on the President, we want you there to render assistance."

"If you and the Skippa insists, I'll be there, providing I live that long."

The plain marked police car smelled new and Tim looked out the window as they moved through the traffic. He remembered when he was a boy how he enjoyed when his father bought a new car, the smell was the same. Tim wanted a cigarette although wouldn't dare light up for fear of getting his ass chewed by Tom, his old squad leader in Nam.

At Starbucks coffee house the three men sat at the rear and ordered coffee and breakfast rolls, although it was past the noon hour. The manager, a heavy set older man of obvious Irish decent came over to greet Tom. The older woman waiting on them was obvious the his wife or sister.

"The place looks like hell for a Starbucks but the service was great. I've been coming here since I was a beat-cop." Tom remarked as the old-man walked back behind the counter.

As they sat and ate breakfast, Tim spoke and protested that they didn't need him. Tom wouldn't hear of it and invited Tim to move out of the hotel and stay with him and Alice for the duration of his stay in Washington, and explained that his expenses will be covered by the department.

Bridges smiled as he sipped his second cup of coffee as Tom sounded like he was issuing orders back in the Marine Corps days. Tom remembered Tim retired from the Corps and didn't want to let up on him. They sincerely needed his expertise when it came to surgical shooting and firearms.

Tim declined the invitation to attend the demonstration at the FBI Academy that Tom set up. Bridges agreed that they may get suspicious if anyone were to recognize Tim. The demonstration was set for seven in the morning and Bridges agreed to be there.

***

At the White House, Heidi informed Adriana , Bridges called. Adriana was surprised Heidi gave her the message. She immediately phoned Bridges at the farm and left a message that she would be at his house guest that evening.

Heidi left the office after she announced she would be taking a nap and she didn't want to be disturbed. As soon as she left, Adriana headed for the communication room in the basement of the White House and met the Marine Sergeant as though they were lovers. She hugged him as he gave her a package containing two tape cassettes. Evidently he made them for her.

Adriana returned to the living quarters and accomplished little work. She was anxious to hear the tapes.

At the farm house, Bridges returned the call from the White House to confirm the information and providing the number of people in his party. The aid sounded young and didn't seem confident in his job. Bridges that the entire administration was the same, including the President.

After the call, he listened to Adriana's message again, she invited herself for the night and Bridges felt good about her visit. He was becoming serious about their relationship, although they hadn't spent much intimate time together. As the message play out, Jennifer returned from school and asked her father if she could beg off from the Friday night event at the White House. Bridges wasn't prepared for Jennifer attempting to beg off. He inquired immediately why she didn't want to attend. Jennifer responded that she felt strange about the entire episode and besides she didn't have a dress to wear. Bridges smiled and assured Jennifer that the dress was no problem, Adriana would take her shopping the next day. Jennifer pouted and reluctantly agreed. She went into the kitchen to do what ever college girls do during their relationship with the refrigerator.

Adriana arrived with an over night bag and a pastry box containing a pie. Jennifer helped her by taking the box from her hand and opened it to see what it was. Apple of course, her father's favorite.

After the evening meal, Jennifer went to her room and Adriana and Bridges sat in the family room sipping on cognac. The fire was crackling and the room felt cozy. Adriana felt aggressive and dimmed the room lights and sat on Bridges lap. He hugged her as she put her head on his shoulder like a little girl. They sat there in silence for what seemed thirty-minutes.

Bridges informed her that he thought another attempt on the President's life would be made on Friday evening. Adriana didn't respond, kissed him as she got off of his lap and went to her purse. She recovered a small folded government manila envelope containing two-audio cassettes. The cassettes were unmarked as to side one or two. Bridges immediately came alive when Adriana explained where she obtained the tapes.

The first tape contained several calls by Heidi to various people throughout the country, most of which were in conjunction with donations for the President's re-election committee. One of the calls near the end of the first tape was an British accented man with a soft voice. The dialogue of the conversation was cordial. Heidi never said it, at least not on the tape, but the man accepted the invitation to attend the function Friday evening. Adriana jokingly remarked that the Brit was probably one of Heidi's secret lovers. Bridges remained quiet and didn't respond to Adriana's remarked, although he heard it.

"Run that back…I have to hear the voice again."

As Adriana reversed the tape…she asked Bridges what was so important about the voice, and explained it was a simple Brit talking to Heidi.

"That's it, he's a Brit…Tim Young trained a former British Marine in the fine art of surgical shooting."

"Then you think she has hired him to snuff the President while inside the White House, it will never happen Richard. If he did, the Secret Service will be all over him. Besides how will he get a weapon in?"

"Adriana…that's your job…find out how he could get a weapon into the White House Friday night."

They played the remainder of the tapes and monitored a brief section of the second tape that the same voice was heard. The British speaking man called Heidi to confirm the attire. Heidi insisted they meet when she went to a speaking engagement Thursday afternoon.

"Adriana, that's something else we need to know, where will she be speaking Thursday?"

"That's a piece of cake, I'll consult her calendar or ask her dippy secretary. If the secretary wasn't black, I swear she was blond. The dumbest woman I've ever met."

Nothing of any other significance was heard on the tapes. Bridges asked Adriana how she acquired them.

"Simple…this young Marine Sergeant that works communications has for a long time been flirtatious with me. A hugh and kiss on the cheek went a long way."

"How are you going to turn him off…I mean when you have to?"

"I'll tell him I'm getting married to you."

"That will piss him off, won't it?"

"Well…I know a few people over at Marine Corps Headquarters, I'll arrange for him to be transferred to Hawaii or some other place that he wouldn't mind."

"You got it figured, don't you?"

"Of course."

It was getting late and Bridges called Tom's house. He requested to talk to Tim. When Tim came on the line, Bridges asked if he could recognize Gibson's voice.

With a quick response, Tom answered. "Sure can…he sounds like a whoosh, you know a gay guy, but he's not, believe me."

"When was the last time you saw him?"

"Almost a year ago, around Christmas time last year."

"Could you recognize him now?"

"Of course Skippa…I'd know him anywhere…I spent every weekend with him for two months."

"How did he find you?"

"He run into a retired Colonel where he lives in Newport Beach."

"Someone we know?"

"No one I know,. maybe you officer-type may know him."

"When he first contacted you, what did he ask for?"

"Training…on how to shoot, then he felt comfortable and paid me more for teaching surgical shooting."

"That's it?"

"You got it Skippa…why you asking now?"

"I think…he's our guy."

"No shit Skippa?"

"Let me talk to Tom?"

"Tommy, I think we got our man, not sure, but feel certain."

The contents of the tapes were discussed and Bridges agreed to meet at Tom's office in the morning.

The following morning after Adriana fervidly made love to Bridges. They lay in bed until they heard Jennifer leave for school.

They quickly showered and Adriana left for the White House. Bridges was right behind her as he made his way downtown DC and over to the 300 block of Indiana street on the northwest side, where Police Headquarters is located.

Bridges played the tapes for Tom as Tim listened and insisted the British voice sounded like Gibson. He commented that all Brits sound alike bringing laughter among them.

Bridges insisted they needed to formulate a plan. "Tom we can't share a thing with the Secret Service for fear they would over-react, but at the same time if it goes down in the White House, we can never admit we had advance knowledge, sorry, don't mean to be dishonest."

Tom looked out the window and Tim shrugged his shoulders. The three men remained silent. Tom and Bridges were the same age, Tim three years younger, but for some reason Tim looked the senior of the three. He looked out of place in Washington and he knew it. Although he felt obligated to his Vietnam buddies to assist wherever he could. His greatest apprehension was when he met with Paul Castilli, now a Supreme Court Justice. He recalled that Bridges made Captain before him, yet, Paul's promotion precedence number was senior. He recalled hearing they got into it the day the battalion commander pinned Captain Bars on Bridges. He also remembered Lieutenant Castilli was recommended for the Navy Cross and for some reason the medal was reduced to the Silver Star. The Lieutenant blamed Bridges and said he had something to do with it. Tom reminded Bridges of his apprehension and also reminded him of the medal situation between he and Paul Castilli.

Bridges completely forgot the incident in Vietnam and wondered if Paul Castilli held a grudge. He decided not to comment to Tom's recollection and suggested he stay away from meeting Paul while at the dinner and the ceremony.

Tom smiled as he picked up on Tim's comment.

"Castilli was an asshole then and is now, I don't care how great he thinks he is. We all thought he was a super platoon leader until you made captain before him, then the Navy Cross recommendation reduced to the Silver Star put him in a different frame of mind, he became a big asshole."

Initially Bridges wanted to avoid the conversation. Since Tom commented he added to the story.

"Do you two gentlemen know who recommended Paul for the Navy Cross?"

Tim spoke first. "Ya…the troops."

"You're half right…the troops and himself…what he did was only Bronze Star Medal caliber, but he suggested to the snuffies to recommend him for the Navy Cross."

Tom looked over and commented. "That's a crock-of-shit. Let me tell you how he got the Purple Heart. During a VC B-40 rocket attack, he was at the bunker, you remember, the club…well he cut his thumb during Red-Alert. No one said anything and you remember no big thing was made of the Purple Heart the CO presented to him."

"The troops thought he was a big-ass-hole. He was lucky he didn't get fragged." Tim couldn't resist the remark.

"I reacquainted myself with him when he was a Federal Judge. What ever pissed him off, changed and he and I were real close buds."

"What about this situation with the First Lady and the attempt on the President's life?" Tom jumped back almost sounding angry.

"I couldn't figure it, he was interested in what I had to say, then overnight he did a…180, why I don't know."

"Do you think the good Judge has a finger in this thing, has he ever had a friendship with the Banks?" Tom commented and sounded like the a Cop.

"Who knows…if he is in some way involved, I'm sure it will reveal itself, that is if an attempt is made once again on the President." Bridges wanted to change the subject. He wasn't happy over the situation of Paul turning on him.

The meeting broke up as Bridges had to return to his farm to prepare a proposal for his next government contract and finish an after-action report covering his last contract to Israel. Before he left Tom's office, he called Adriana at the White House. She was happy to hear from him and reminded him of their pleasant moment that morning. Bridges could feel his ears getting red as he looked around the room at Tim and Tom. She again invited herself to spend the night, he didn't resist.

During a brief conversation with William in the barn, William informed Bridges that he and Tilly were planning a trip to visit their only son in the Army stationed in South Carolina. After agreeing to a date, Bridges returned to the house and while sitting behind his restored eighteenth century desk, listened to his messages. One of the messages was from Newport Beach Police Department, in California. He thought that it was peculiar. He glanced at his watched to calculate the West Coast time and dialed the number.

"Detective Peters, please." He asked.

When the detective answered, Bridges identified himself an learned from Detective Peters that Dale Gibson, also known as Dilbert Gibson had been located and was back at his job at the Mercedes dealership. The information was learned earlier that morning. Bridges thanked the detective and wondered how he knew to locate him at his home. He shrugged it off for now and called Tom to relate the news. Tom already knew and asked the Detective to call Bridges with the information.

"Then he won't be here Friday night?" Bridges remarked.

Tom answered. "Don't bet on it, if that voice on the tape was his, he'll be here."

Bridges hoped he wouldn't make an attempt on the President's live. After the phone call to Tom, he sat back on his wing back chair and drifted off to sleep. He was awaken by Jennifer and her girlfriend. They were planning to go for a ride before dinner. Bridges reminded Jennifer that his mare had to get out.

The cloud cover demonstrated the threat of rain. Bridges reminded the girls not to go far into the wooded area. Adriana arrived at the farm. With her she had a cheese cake one of the White House Pastry Chefs gave her. She placed it in the refrigerator and joined Bridges in his study with two snifters of cognac.

Bridges turned to allow Adriana to sit on his lap while they cuddled and sipped their cognac. She kissed him on the neck and nibbled his left ear-lobe. Bridges felt comfortable with her and almost forgot what it was like to have a woman around.

A roast turkey dinner was prepared by Tilly. Bridges was hungry and wondered where Jennifer and her friend was

Adriana walked out to the barn and went to the other end. She opened the small door, allowing her to see past the meadow and over at the trees. It started to rain. She waited. To the right of the large tree where the camp sight had been, she could see the girls walking the horses back. She felt better and returned to the house to inform Bridges the girls were alright and were on there way back. Before they left the study, Bridges kissed Adriana and she returned the kiss, while cuddling up to him. She was happy and pleased with herself.

Adriana remembered to tell Bridges about the shooting of the White House chamber maid. "She was shot by her boyfriend. I thought Heidi arranged for it. If I caught them coming out of the Lincoln bedroom, she was sure to have caught them as well."

Bridges was surprised Tom hadn't told him, then from what Adriana said, the woman was killed in her apartment over in Baltimore.

Wednesday, Tim picked up a tuxedo at the rental shop. One of Tom's woman officers drove him there. He returned to Police Headquarters. Shortly after his arrival, Bridges came in and they went into the classroom just as a group of officers were completing a class.

The three men discussed what they should do at the White House Friday evening. Bridges suggested that if this goes down, and the Brit attempts to take the President out, it would be toward the end of the evening. Maybe when he's in the head taking a piss. Presidents do piss, don't they?"

The men laughed and Bridges suggested Tim not bring attention to himself, meaning the Secret Service. "They'll be shaky as it is. But then, in the White House they may relax their guard."

Tom suggested he and Alice stay with Adriana. "After the medal presentation, people including the press-corps will break and head for the restrooms."

"The President will also break and that will be the time for us to observe the Brit." Bridges suggested.

Tim asked an important question no one brought up. "What if the Brit isn't there or is there and we loose track of him?"

"Then we better find the bastard fast." Tom remarked almost in a panic.

During a silence, Bridges then thought out loud, and spoke. "I can't be the one to take the Brit down if he's there to take the President out. It won't look right, so it's got to be you Tommy along with the Secret Service."

Tom in a brilliant moment, asked a question. "Let's say the Brit is the shooter, kills or wounds the President…the Secret Service catches him…will this bring suspicion on the First Lady?"

"I'm sure she's got it covered…someone else will shoot the Brit and there will be no trace of who invited him to the presentation, not even with the sign in log. Heidi is too smart for that." Bridges pleasingly announced, not out of fondness for her, but to be able to read her moves.

The remainder of the day was inconsequential, Bridges needed to take care of business at his bank and return to the farm. Adriana called, once again to invite herself over for the evening. Bridges didn't mind in the least and looked forward to her spending time with him. In the back of his mind hoped Jennifer wouldn't get tired of her or start resenting her for occupying his time.

Thursday morning, Tom and Bridges met at the FBI National Academy over at Quantico. They were met by Special Agent Faye. The sun wasn't up yet and Bridges remembered as they arrived at the weapons range the many early mornings at the rifle-range when he was in the Corps. Something no former Marine forgets. A week of snapping in and a week for qualifying with their rifles. The M-14 replaced by the M-1 Garand when he was in the Marine Corps.

The FBI demonstration went on as planned and was professionally executed. Bridges was impressed with the agents that acted as assassins and live-like targets. The program went through several possibilities with the exception of close-surgical shooting. The program was no different than what Tim taught at Camp Pendleton during his tenure at the Marine Corps Sniper School.

Bridges whispered to Tom that he was impressed. Tom quietly laughed and expressed himself with a smile. There were other visitors from the public relation program the FBI puts on for the Police and Sheriff's Departments throughout the country including allied countries.

Coffee was provided during the break. Tom and Bridges clustered in a corner away from the others and Bridges couldn't help expressing himself as to why they were not demonstrating the procedures Tim taught the FBI involving close surgical firing. Before Tom could offer his opinion, John Faye came over with a smile on his face. Tom, for no other reason introduced Bridges again. The reason was to stall for time and compose himself over disappointment.

"John, is there more to the program, I'm impressed so far." Tom obviously was patronizing the Agent although he didn't perceive it that way.

The Agent concluded that after the break there would be questions and answer session. Bridges expressed to the Agent that they put on an impressive show, then smiled

The Agent accepted the complement although Bridges didn't mean for it to be complementary to the FBI. ***

Upon return to Metropolitan Police Headquarters, Bridges took possession of his Jeep-Cherokee from the police evidence parking lot. The vehicle was dusty even though it sat out in the rain for several days. As he entered from the driver's side, he noticed fingerprint-powder all over the dash and doors. He smiled at Tom as to say, thanks for the dirty car, although he was happy to have it back. Both men agreed to talk later that day and Bridges returned to the farm.

In his study, Bridges received a call. Thinking it was either Adriana or Tom, answered in a manner of expectation. The caller identified himself as a Secret Service Agent assigned to the President's detail. Bridges became alert and listened to the Agent's request for information concerning Tim Young. Bridges immediately became annoyed and reminded the Agent that Mr. Young was well known to the Service and sighted other agents in California consulting Mr. Young.

"Matter of fact, your boss spoke to Mr. Young right after the attempt on the President's life in California, correct that, your boss consulted Mr. Young on a technical subject. Is there anything else?"

The Agent was taken back with Bridges' attitude and offered an apology for offending him. After they hung up, Bridges called Tom and related his recent experience with a Secret Service Agent from the White House.

"It figures…the left hand doesn't know what the right hand already did." Tom answered with amusement.

Bridges shook his head and agreed to get together later.

There was a break in the weather, the sun was shining enough to warm the air around the farm. Bridges saddled his favorite mare and went for a ride into the countryside. He left his property and rode across his neighbor's land away from their barn and main house. He had an agreement with the neighbor, a retired Naval Captain and former Deputy Director of Defense Intelligence. The agreement allowed him and anyone else from his barn access to the property situated nearer to the forrest and a heavy growth of trees

As he rode, he became deep in thought. He mulled over in his mind the entire situation. There were certain mysterious things about Adriana. He couldn't come up with exactly what, but he knew he was falling in love with her, but felt guilt over his wife's death. He liked the feeling of falling in love, but he had to obtain answers to why he had a certain suspicion about her.

As his ride took him into the wooded area, he became chilly and wished he had enough fore-sight to have worn a heavier jacket. As he rode to the clearing on the opposite side, he discovered what at first looked like a abounded deer. He thought someone shot it and couldn't haul it out

The closer he got he suddenly realized it was the body of a young black woman. She lay on the ground, what seemed the spot she fell at. He dismounted his horse, ground tied it and examined the woman. He immediately discovered she was dead. The condition of the body appeared as though she hadn't been there long. She was dressed in a maids uniform and there wasn't any sign of her identification or a purse. Bridges could see a trickle of blood from the mouth. No other signs were obvious. She was lying on her back, legs bent, arms out-stretched. Her estimated age was early twenties.

Bridges looked around to get his bearings and rode his horse over to the nearest house. Once at the house, he convinced the maid to allow him to use the phone. He first dialed Tom who gave him directions to first call the Virginia State Police. Give them a semblance of the location and return to the body and wait. They would be certain to send a helicopter. Tom agreed to meet him there in a short time.

Upon return to the scene, he at first had difficulty finding the location of the body. His horse seemed to know and resisted direction until Bridges located the body again

Bridges searched around for the dead woman's purse. Nothing in sight. He was tempted to turn the body over, but thought he should wait for the crime scene people.

A Virginia State Police Helicopter arrived and Bridges directed them to a clearing not far from the body. It was reminiscence of Vietnam when a med-a-vac chopper came in to pick-up wounded or dead Marines. Bridges' mare became upset when the chopper landed then she settle down.

Another chopper arrived, he was surprised to discover it contained Tom. Time was with him for lack of anything else to do. It became obvious when the choppers were silenced Tom knew the Virginia State Investigators.

As the crime scene people went to work processing the scene, they determined the woman had been shot in the back from a distance. A large caliber single shot. Bridges was eager to learn if it had been surgical and was not surprised it wasn't.

That evening while Bridges sat in his study, he received a call from Tom.

"The young black woman was shot with a thirty-caliber of some sort and that the most interesting part was she also was a chamber maid at the White House."

You could cut the silence with a dull knife.

"She was studying to become a photographers model." Adriana was in the family room talking to Jennifer.

"This is two for two, days that is." Tom remarked.

"What do you make of it, Tommy?"

"Shit if I know, the other one was a jealous lover, this one, who the hell knows. She rented a room from a white family not far from you. The Virginia State Investigation have nothing on the motives, do we?"

Bridges laughed and agreed. "I'd like to think your highness the first lady ordered it, but I doubt it."

"We can't be too sure."

This surprised Bridges and he went on to inquire as to why he said what he said.

"What's in that Irish mind of yours?"

"Now you're discriminating Rich…I just have a fucken feeling about that bitch."

"I haven't run it past Adriana yet, but then I didn't know it was White House connected. She'll have an answer, I'm certain."

Adriana could hear parts of the conversation and entered the study when she heard her name. She whispered to Bridges, "who is it?"

Bridges…looked up and with a smile…expressed it was Tom.

When the conversation was over, Bridges provided the information to Adriana. She wasn't moved by it in the least. Bridges solicited her opinion and she shrugged her shoulders.

"Another bimbo the President was fucken."

"Well do you believe the First lady ordered the hit?"

"No…at first you would think that, but the bitch wants him dead, not the women…she looks at the women as the President's right hand masturbating himself. She doesn't care who he fucks, as long as he doesn't disgrace the office." Adriana laughed at her own comment

Friday morning Jennifer remembered to turn the clocks back to standard time. This threw Adriana off as she and Bridges showered together after making love. She had a smile on her face the entire time they spent in the shower. Bridges dried her back as he changed the subject.

"What are you going to do with the extra hour you have?"

Adriana looked up at him, dropped her towel and pressed her body against him as they kissed. They stood together in the nude, the early morning sun shining through the opaque window Bridges installed when he renovated the century old home. Nothing mattered at the time. They heard Jennifer moving about and realized she hadn't left for school because of the time change. They both wanted a return match of love making, but Bridges was distracted by the presence of his daughter. Adriana understood and began putting her bra and panties on. Bridges kissed her on the shoulder as she wiped the steamed mirror with a hand towel.

"Richard, I'll be back early." She almost said 'home' but caught herself, she didn't want to be too assuming. She reminded him about his tuxedo. Bridges in a not to caring attitude informed her it was in the closet and hoped it fit

Adriana left at the same time Jennifer pulled away from the farm house. She could see her wave at her from the green Jeep as she drove fast down the muddy rode and turned onto the main road in the direction of Georgetown University.

The weather this time of year was unpredictable. It appeared as thought it would rain and Adriana remembered she had to wear something that evening that would accommodate a rain coat. The even was formal and the only gown that would be suited was her solid black Italian silk gown that fitted tight and would go perfect with the raincoat, although she wanted to wear a fur piece, but didn't dare with all the liberals expected at the presentation that evening. Up ahead as she drove, Adriana thought she noticed Jennifer's Jeep off the side of the rode. The closer she got, she was convinced it was the Jeep. She pulled over and sure enough it was Jennifer with a flat tire waiting for the Auto Club to assist her.

Adriana re-parked her car in front of the Jeep after she learned what the problem was.

"Did you call your father?"

"Thank God for the cellular phone. No I called the Auto Club, they will be here soon."

Adriana insisted she should wait with her as she climbed into the Jeep. Both women sat waiting until the Auto Club tow truck arrived. As the young man changed tires, Adriana learned from Jennifer that her father wore a size 38/32 pant when Adriana asked with the idea she would pick up a rental tuxedo for Bridges in the event his didn't fit.

Bridges went out to the barn and puttered around with the horses. He was impressed with the colt and how he was maturing. William reminded him that he and the wife were leaving on their trip that afternoon. Bridges did forget but pretended he hadn't.

In the farm house Bridges wrote William a check as extra cash for the trip. William was appreciative after he at first refused to take the check.

At lunch, Bridges met with Tom at the favorite eating place Bridges wouldn't take his worst enemy to. Tim joined them and the three discussed what they would do that evening.

"What's the latest on the Brit?" Bridges asked abruptly.

"As recent as two hours ago, he was at his job in California, that doesn't mean he wont be here." Tom explained.

Bridges was afraid of that and hoped it wouldn't be the case. Tim made no contribution to the conversation until they finished lunch which amounted to a hamburger made on s greasy grill and a bowl of canned vegetable soup. The coffee was good.

"If the Brit doesn't show, that doesn't mean an attempt wouldn't go down." Tim added.

"You are right, but who will be the trigger?" Bridges asked although didn't expect an answer.

Tom with a broad smile commented. "The First Lady, who else."

"Oh shit, she wouldn't dare, would she?" Tim asked in an excited tone, revealing a side of him Tom hadn't seen.

Bridges thought Tim's comment was as though he knew the First Lady, but dismissed it as his imagination.

The three men returned to Tom's office. Bridges excused himself and explained he had to visit a friend over at Langley. Tom didn't think much of it until after he left and realized Bridges was up to something. He didn't share his thoughts with Tim and allowed him to sit in on classes the officers were involved with. By observing behind a two-way mirror, he watched a polygraph examination in progress. He wasn't impressed and thought it was boring and decided to go over to the crime lab to talk to the firearms people. Tom provided him with a visitors pass allowing him access to the building.

***

Over at the White House Adriana was in a good mood and noticed that Heidi was feeling the same. They briefly had a conversation about women's clothing and were interrupted by a phone call from Bridges. She looked over at Heidi as she listened and simulated a kiss into the phone receiver when she said goodbye. Heidi went into a mood swing when she realized Bridges was on the other end of the call.

Adriana reminded Heidi she planned to leave before lunch and she would see her at the evening dinner. Before she left the White House she made sure to obtain the guest list for the evening affair and made a point in stopping downstairs to visit with the Marine Sergeant. He thought she needed something else and Adriana mentioned it was a social visit, causing the sergeant to beam with a smile. Adriana learned from the Marine that he volunteered for extra duty when he heard Adriana would be at the reception that evening.

The Marine didn't realize the reception was being held in honor of Adriana's lover. Something that could get out of hand if the young Marine sergeant was infatuated and not used to attention from an attractive woman as Adriana. A problem she'd deal with later, although she wished it wasn't a problem at all.

She then thought maybe it was a good thing she knew the Marine and if things got out of control that evening, he would be on her side, or at least, provide assistance.

CHAPTER 16
THE RECEPTION

Adriana helped Jennifer dress in a sleek black cocktail gown and she planned to wear her mother's fur, but Adriana suggested she not. She explained that it isn't politically correct and there may be the wack-os that forbid the wearing of animal fur as a coat unless it was necessary. In this day and age, no one needed a fur to keep the cruel winter off them. Jennifer gave a smile of understanding and expressed to Adriana, she trusted she was nervous and didn't hide her feelings in the least.

Jennifer revealed to Adriana she once visited the White House when she was seven years old, although she didn't remember the reason.

Before Bridges dressed, he and Adriana looked over the guest list and didn't find the name Gibson anywhere. In addition, Steve Young's name wasn't on the list as well and Bridges was sure he provided the protocol-secretary with Tom and Alice Moore along with Steven Young's names. Tom and Alice had been listed, this caused Bridges to be concerned. Adriana smiled and explained it was typical of the administration to mess things up. Never the less, Bridges called Tom to tell him Steve's name wasn't on the guest list and to make sure Steve carried some form of photo identification. During the brief conversation, Tom disclosed to Bridges that the gun used to kill the black maid was the same gun used kill his friend over at the Israeli Embassy.

"What do you make of it."

Bridges couldn't figure the connection, other than the same gun, same shooter.

"We've got to settle on a pattern of events, all the incidents may have some relevances."

"You got that right my friend, you've hit it."

Adriana assured him that there will be many people there that are not on the guest list.

After the call to Tom, Bridges returned to looking at the guest list. Adriana left the bedroom and in the spaces bathroom Bridges built for his late wife, she was putting on her make up. Bridges noticed she had circle two names on the guest list. This stimulated Bridges' curiosity. As he entered the bathroom, he noticed Adriana attaching a small handgun to her upper inside thigh of her left leg. She didn't attempt to conceal it from Bridges.

"How will you get through the metal detector?"

"I work there, everyone knows me, do you think for one minute anyone on the security detail will subject me to a search or a metal detector."

Bridges didn't like it, he never knew Adriana was into carrying a hand gun. He wanted to examine the gun, but was apprehensive to ask

"Don't you think I should check it before you put your dress on?" Adriana smiled.

"Sure…you can touch it but you better be ready to take all our clothes off and start over again." She smiled.

Adriana smiled again and reached down to remove the small caliber semi-automatic pistol from the holster. With caution she removed the small magazine and handed it to Bridges.

Bridges examined the small Sterling Model 302, it was a twenty-two caliber. He then spoke.

"This couldn't stop a thing."

"At close rang it could." Adriana answered as though she knew and had experience with the pistol.

"Do you carry it often?"

"In DC I do…I know, its against the law, who cares, as long as I can protect myself when I'm not with you."

This entire situation was mind boggling for Bridges. Here he is, a woman he's learned to trust and was falling in love with, plans to carry a concealed weapon into the White House. He recovered from deep thought and put on a mock smile.

They finished dressing and the plan was to go over to Tom's home before they went to the White House. At Tom's they had drinks and for some reason Steve was taciturn, beyond hello. Jennifer felt out of place although stayed close to her father. Tom's wife, tried to comfort her by asking questions about school and her plans for graduate school. Alice remembered that she hadn't seen Jennifer since her mother's funeral, two years ago. Steve, Tom and Bridges were dressed in tuxedos and appeared as though they were uncomfortable, although didn't complain.

Bridges decided to asked Adriana why she circled two names on the guest list, then he thought it may be appropriate to discuss it when they were alone. The plan was for them to ride in the official car with the Tom and Alice.

The traffic was heavy along Interstate 395. The lights over at the Pentagon were bright for a Friday evening. Bridges immediately thought there may be a crises, but then it didn't matter to him anymore. He now was retired and didn't need the burden, or worry. As they traveled across the Arland Williams Bridge heading toward the White House, Adriana directed Tom down 14th Street to an entrance to the White House immediately after passing Pershing Square. The entrance was used by employees and special category persons that worked close to the President. While pulling in, Adriana rolled the rear seat window down and winked at the guard who instantly recognized her. At the direction of Adriana, Tom parked the car. Bridges was impressed with the assuage in entering the White House grounds and how the gate guards waved them through, once they recognized Adriana. Tom smiled and in the glimpse of light, Bridges caught his smirk.

Steve was quiet until he complained about the tuxedo and when he realized he was getting no sympathy, he discontinued his complaining.

The men wore grey top coats over the tuxedos. Steve rented his top coat on the advice of Franc, the proprietor of the rental shop. At first Steve didn't like Frank because he suspected he was gay, but the more he was around him he found Frank amusing if not entertaining and made him laugh in the way he spoke.

Tom removed his shoulder holster and gun and placed it in the glove box in front of where Alice was sitting. Bridges remembered that Adriana was carrying a concealed weapon strapped to her thigh. He admitted privately that it appeared sexy but for a serious note, it was dangerous to carry a hand gun into the White House.

They all walked toward the White House side entrance. Adriana reminded Bridges that the initial presentation would be made in the Oval-Office with the press being present. After the photo-shoot, they would then proceed to the banquet room.

As Adriana walked close to Bridges with her right gloved hand on his arm, she whispered how handsome he was and couldn't wait to get him in bed. Bridges whispered back by asking her if she was going to wear the Sterling to bed with them. Adriana tightened her grip of his arm and they walked in silence. As they walked toward the Oval-Office, pass the press room and the cabinet room, many of the people from the TV and Newspapers wanted to stop Bridges for an interview. Adriana held on to Bridges and suggested they walk faster until they arrived at the President's study adjacent to the Oval-Office. Many of the invited guest knew Adriana and expressed greetings as they walked at a fast pace. While inside the President's Study, a Presidential Aid suggested they wait in the aide-fowler next to the secretary's office. He went on to explain that the press wasn't allowed at that point unless invited, no matter who they thought they were.

Inside the Oval-Office, Bridges was positioned adjacent to the President and both men engaged in small talk about horses. Bridges thought that the aids did their homework concerning his love for horses. Bridges boldly explained that his interest in horses was not any breed of horse, rather the Arabian breed. Showing his ignorance, the President asked Bridges the difference. Bridges smiled and provided a thumb-nail summary of the breed. He added that President Washington rode a grey mare. The President responded by attempting to correct Bridges by saying it had been a white horse President Washington rode. Bridges smiled and decided not to explain. In the Arabian horse world, white horses are called Gray.

Adriana standing to Bridges left, she whispered that the hold up with the presentation was that the First Lady wasn't ready and she would be down to the Oval-Office soon. She then grabbed Brides' arm and realized without a topcoat on, she could feel his masculine arm. The feeling turned her on and she felt excited.

The First Lady arrived, she was dressed in a formal grey and maroon gown. Her hair was up off her ears. Adriana admitted to herself that she appeared attractive. The press-corps was allowed into the Oval Office. They positioned themselves as the President and Bridges faced each other. Tom, Alice and Steve were standing next to the press people. Steve whispered that he had to piss, causing Tom laugh. One of the women from the press looked over at Steve, it was obvious she heard him and gave a disgusting look. Tom smiled even more as the camera and flash units went of. The President provided a brief speech, a portion as to what he planned to say latter after the dinner. He presented the Freedom medal to Bridges and shook his hand. Bridges couldn't help feeling that he was an apprehensive and unsure of himself. The hand shake was like a wet noodle, but Bridges played the game. He couldn't believe he was part of this game the President was playing.

After the presentation, Adriana hugged Bridges as the President attempted to talk to her. She then shook his hand and reminded him that she worked for his wife. He provided a big smile and commented that he would have to make changes in the work force, suggesting that he wanted Adriana to work close to him.

The group broke up and all present tried to interview Bridge. Everyone of them brought up the fact that he was former CIA. Bridges provided a brief statement that he wanted to puke over, but he continued to play along with the entire game. He almost believed the President didn't know the truth. The First Lady grabbed Bridge's arm as they left the Oval Office. Adriana was insulted when they left her behind. She caught up with them while walking from the west-wing of the White House over to the East wing. Bridges didn't know what he should do. He stopped long enough for Adriana to catch up. Heidi gave Adriana a dirty look and continued to the room where the reception dinner was being held. Bridges caught, from the corner of his eye that Tom and Alice were keeping up with them, but suddenly missed Steve. He wondered where he was. Tom was quick to inform him that Steve had an over-whelming desire to go to the rest room. Bridges seemed satisfied with the answer and continued being escorted by Heidi. He thought he looked like a dork with Heidi on his left and Adriana on his right. He then wondered where his daughter was. As he turned his head, he saw that she was smiling as a young-Marine was escorting her.

Immediately he felt angry, but then decided that she was over twenty-one and could handle herself. As they walked into the banquet room, Bridges observed an abundance of attractive young black women dressed as the one he found in the meadow the previous day. He was taken back with the President breaking away from the Secret Service and walked over to flirt with the young women. He could hear Heidi make comment about him that Bridges didn't think he wanted his daughter to hear, not that she hadn't heard already. The young black women circled the President as teenage girls clung to Elvis Presley. Heidi broke loose and walked over to them and ordered the women back to work.

Bridges looked over to the other side of the banquet room and discovered Jennifer talking to one of the women in a maid uniforms. As she spotted her father, she said goodbye to the woman and walked over to her father impatiently explained that the women and her attended Georgetown University together. Bridges was glad to hear that, this could be a lead concerning the dead maid he found in the meadow near his farm. The room filled with people fast. Bridges again was approached by the TV News media. Reporters from the major newspapers were present and he didn't want to tell them a thing, but he knew he had a sense of obligation to answer questions within reason. He should but he was careful not to say something that was fabricated and later contradicted later. He still felt dishonest receiving the medal presented by the President. His impulse was to yell the truth and put this mess aside, but he knew better.

Before he and his party were seated, Supreme Court Justice Paul Castilli approached him. Bridges by then was surrounded by Tom and Steve, both knew the Judge from the Marine Corps days, more specifically, Vietnam.

Steve was first to speak when the Judge approached. Bridges held his breath when he heard Steve's greeting of the Judge.

"Well…I'll be a son-of-a-bitch, Captain Castilli, you haven't changed one bit, except you put on some weight."

There was a brief silence, then the Judge answered.

"Sergeant Young, or is it Gunny?" Castilli's remark was meant to be a put down for Steve but it didn't come out that way.

"Skippa…the last I saw you, you cut your thumb on the O'Club door and wanted a Purple Heart."

"I remember Gunny." Judge answered in a sarcastic manner.

"It's Master-Gunnery Sergeant to you Skippa, excuse me…Judge…your-highness."

Bridges sensed the conversation was getting heated and pointed out to the Judge that Tom and Alice were there. The Judge turned to Tom, shook his hand and exchanged brief hello's. He asked Bridges for a private chat before the dinner was served. Just then, Adriana arrived and Judge Castilli changed the subject and greeted Adriana by hugging and kissing her. This didn't cause Bridges to be concerned, but he now could see what an asshole Castilli was.

The dinner went off as planned. They had a break before the presentation. The President walked over to the nearest restroom without Secret Service protection. He entered the small bathroom and discovered a strange man washing his hands. This took the President by surprise. The room was reserved, for him alone.

Bridges and Tom searched the banquet room for Gibson, he couldn't be found. Steve wasn't around either and Tom needed him to identify Gibson in the crowd. The First Lady came from another restroom on the opposite side of the banquet hall. She was arguing with one of the Secret Service agents and it was obvious to everyone present.

The Agent signaled to another agent as he spoke into the wrist transmitter. Heidi broke away from him and headed right for Bridges and Adriana.

"Oh shit…your highness is heading this way." Tom uttered in a whisper to Adriana.

"I'll handle her…but I hope she hadn't been drinking that hard shit." Adriana snarled.

The First Lady approached Bridges, ignoring everyone else. She grabbed him around the neck and kissed him on the mouth. While kissing, she attempted to insert her tongue. Bridges didn't know what to do. Adriana attempted to get her attention but was unsuccessful. Bridges tried to humor her as best he could. She told him in the presence of everyone that she wanted him to make love to her. Bridges' daughter Jennifer wasn't present, she was over talking to the Marine Sergeant that Adriana previously made friends with.

In the restroom, the man washing his hands spoke to the President. He spoke slow and deliberate. The President had not relieved himself and suggested the man leave the room. A smile came over the man's face as he invited the President to take a piss and that he will wait. The man reached over and locked the door without the President noticing.

The President found it difficult to relieve himself with the stranger watching him. The man spoke again, slow and deliberate.

"Mr. President, I don't like you…but that's not why I'm here."

The President attempted to interrupt the man by threatening him with the Secret Service.

"I don't know who you are, and I don't care if you like me…but I must warn you that by detaining me you are serious trouble."

The man laughed. Mr. President, I'm not the one that is serious trouble…it's you."

"You mean you are here to assassinate me? You'll never get away with it, I'm certain of that."

"Oh Mr. President…to kill you would be my pleasure…but right here would not be sporting."

"Then what is it you want?"

"I want your full attention."

I'm sorry, I have an agenda and they will be looking for me if I don't return."

"Who's they? Certainly not your wife."

"The security, the Secret Service agents."

"Mr. President, after we talk, you'll never see or hear about me again, I'm certain."

"Then what is it...what do you want to talk about?"

"A simple thing." The man displayed a small caliber hand gun he retrieved from under the sink.

The President backed up until he hit the wall of the restroom. His eyes were wide open, he couldn't believe what he saw. It was obvious to the man the President couldn't speak from fear.

"Mr. President...your lovely wife, what's her name, Heidi.well, she hired me to assassinate you tonight." The voice of the man was slow and deliberate. "As far as I'm concerned you are already dead. Bang...I got you." A smile on the strangers's face when he mocked a gun firing.

"Then go ahead and kill me."

"No, I've changed the plan, and the plan of American history as well. If you died in office, you would be a hero, you're no hero, you're a coward Mr. President. You're dead, do you understand?"

"No, I don't, I am history, I am the first black President."

"Then listen, and listen to me with both ears, if you mess up, then you will die a slow death, I promise."

At that moment, a knock on the door interrupted the conversation. It was a Secret Service attempting to find out if the President was alright.

The man instructed the President to acknowledge the knock and explain that he would be right out. The President complied with the man's direction.

"Your wife wants you dead so she could run for President and at the same time make you a hero to the American people...understand?"

"That's ridiculous...Heidi wouldn't dream of it."

"Oh yes she would, she set up the incident in San Diago. Matter of fact, if you don't already know, the person you intend to present a medal to, didn't kill the assassin, your wife made that discussion to have Mr. Bridges the hero at the same time she was angry that you didn't die."

"That's unbelievable…I can't accept that, then who was responsible for killing the assassin?"

"I'll reveal that when you carry-out my instructions."

"What instructions?"

"Not to seek RE-ELECTION."

"What…what do you mean?"

"Go out there, make the presentation…then make the announcement that you will not seek re-election because you plan to resign. Of course the press will want to know why, you will tell them for health and personal reasons, nothing else."

"I can't do that."

"You will do that…do it in the next few minutes.

"But I have to consult my Chief of Staff and others."

The President by now is feeling insecure and sweat beads are popping out all over his face and his upper lip is wet. The strange man stands between him and the door. The President expresses a frown, in an attempt to say something else, he studders. He is experiencing a dry mouth. His tongue wont allow him to speak. The stranger responded immediately

"Fuck your Chief of Staff…this is your call Mr. President. Grow a set of balls and tell the American people that you'll resign. Nixon did, no problem…you'll do it." The stranger wanted to continue insulting the President but thought he'd gone far enough. He felt satisfied with his accomplishments thus far. impulsively, he wanted to shoot him. He knew if he had, the coward would become an instant American hero like JFK.

The stranger slipped the small automatic pistol in the tuxedo pocket. He again washed his hands while the President stood there in silence. The man reminded the President as to what to do.

"If I don't carry out your instructions, then what?"

"You'll die a terrible death…like…your heart will explode inside of your chest, terrible death Mr. President. If you utter one thing to the

Secret Service, you'll suffer as I said."

"You are bluffing me." The President smiled, a nervous smile. The stranger knew he was scared.

"Hide and watch my Dear Mr. President."

"I promise, if you do not follow my directions, you'll be dead in no more than two-days."

"You are serious?" The President put on a frown as a bead of sweat fell from his nose. His upper lip was glistened with sweat.

"Damn straight…it's easy to kill once you've killed before."

A bang on the door again startled the President. He announced he was coming out. The stranger unlocked the door and the President was allowed to leave.

The President once again presented the medal to Richard Bridges for saving his life.

The Secret Service agents assigned to the President reacted to the communication that an attempt would be made on the President's life. They positioned themselves in front of the podium and behind him. This is often a drill, like one would experience a fire drill. It now was obvious they made no attempt to remove the President from the podium.

Tom was familiar with the procedures and as he shook Bridges hand on his way to the table, Steve came from the other side of the room with Adriana and Tom's wife. Jennifer couldn't break away from the Marine Sergeant until she noticed Adriana signal for her to join them.

Bridges inquired as to Gibson's presence. Steve impulsively although in a slow speech as though he had too much to drink, confirmed that Gibson wasn't to be found.

"Well the President is still standing, maybe it wasn't going to go down." Bridges remarked to Tom as Adriana grabbed his left arm. She whispered something into Bridges ear, causing him to smile. Heidi was sitting next to the podium and the President. The Chief of Staff called for the attention. The press wanted to interview Bridges, but they seemed more concerned with the announcement the President was about to make. The President stepped up to the podium again. His face was pale, it was obvious he was shaken and unsure of himself. He signaled for the audience to calm down.

"My Dear friends…as your President." He hesitated, he fished into his coat pocket for notes, the audience started talking, bringing a low roar to the surface. I appreciate your patience." He again hesitated, looked down at the podium and shuffled a piece of paper. During the hesitation, the Chief of Staff motioned with his hands that the audience to simmered down. The only persons standing were Secret Service Agents. "I have an announcement to make." The President hesitated again at the same time shuffled papers again. Steve stood up and slowly walked in the direction of the rest room. Bridges followed him with his eyes and thought that Steve was under the weather or plain drunk. Tom, seated next to Bridges, commented that he admired Steve's temerity. This comment brought a broad smile to Bridges' face. Adriana looked over at them, and with a gentle kick under the table, attracted Bridges attention. She leaned over, and whispered to Bridges. At first she would say something of endearment, that he welcomed. Adriana with a soft and slow whisper, almost to low to appreciate.

"Wait…and you shall hear…the Midnight cry…of Paul Revere." She sat up straight at the same time Bridges looked at her with a puzzled look on his face. He wanted to ask what she meant, but thought better. Tom noticed, but thought Adriana spoke of something romantic. As the President composed himself, he continued at the same time Steve returned from the rest room. Tom thought it was strange that Steve was being escorted back to the table by one of the Secret Service Agents. Upon return to the table, Tom in a whisper, asked Steve if he was alright. He smiled and nodded his head. A look that Tom had seen before. The President started again.

"My dear friends and fellow Americans…you have known me to be a sincere and compassionate person. I…daily…try my very best to govern this great nation…at times it…I must admit it becomes overwhelming to me. As you know, my term is winding down and it is time to get ready for the campaign for my…reelection…I have come to realize that my campaign will be long and hard…I owe it to you, my supporters to announce that I shall…not.seek the nomination of my party and will resign the office of the Presidency."

The President's voice was shaken. He stood there staring over the heads of the audience, he thought as the room full of press corps people roared with mumbles. A few questions from the audience. He then continued. "I can not continue for health reasons, the Vice President will be at my side for the remaining time I will be your President."

The room broke into a roar with questions. Heidi signaled for the Secret Service agent to escort he up to the living quarters. The Chief of Staff announced that a written version of the President's announcement would be provided. With in seconds, the audience clapped and the President left the banquet room.

Adriana smiled, looking very appealing as she stood up in her blue-black low cut gown. Bridges put his arm around her and they walked in the direction of the exit. Tom followed with Jennifer and Alice. Bridges noticed that Steve once again walked toward the rest room.

Bridges smiled at Adriana as if to say…their job was done. There were many questions unanswered and Bridges needed to know. As they walked down the brightly lighted hall, a small number of press corps people attempted to interview Bridges. At least two of them asked if Bridges thought the attempt on the President's life caused him to make the announcement. Bridges refused to comment, although suggested they consult the First Lady. Immediately the comment triggered other questions. Bridges refused to say anything else. By this time, Steve caught up with them. He appeared as though he was now sober and ready to go.

They sat in silence on the return trip to Tom's home. Alice complained about the dinner and the service. Adriana laughed out-loud, causing Alice to also laugh. Jennifer was silent and deep in thought about her trip to Jordan over the Thanksgiving vacation. Bridges broke her silence and asked about the Marine she spoke to. Jennifer remarked that he was charming and friendly.

"He was nice, but all he wanted to talk about was being transferred to Hawaii."

Unknown to Bridges and Jennifer, Adriana arranged for the Marine to entertain Jennifer.

Tom asked the question.

"Why did the President use the reception dinner to make such an announcement?"

Adriana answered. "It was obvious he just made up his mind. Did you watch his lackeys, they were shocked. Heidi didn't stay around to hear anything else."

"I guess you will be in for a rough time in the morning."

"No I don't think so…I quit. Plain and simple."

This surprised Bridges in the darkness of the car, gently grabbed Adriana between the legs through the slit in her gown, instantly was reminded by the presence of a holster. He looked at her profile as the lights from the freeway shined on her. Sensing he was looking at her, she glanced at Steve as he sat in silence until he announced he would return to sunny California the following morning.

At Tom and Alice's house they had a night-cap. Adriana and Bridges sipped at a cognac and Steve a single malt Scotch on the rocks. Steve seemed quiet as they sat around in the family room decorated with photographs of days gone bye. Steve stared at the photograph of himself along with Tom, Bridges and Paul Castilli. He then spoke.

'"I have no use for that sonofabitch." Pointing to Paul Castilli's picture. "I remember that day, that coward bastard…he was the cause of some good men dying for no good reason. Right after you made Captain Skippa and he didn't, he became the biggest asshole."

"Amen" Uttered Tom, and reluctantly, Bridges. He wanted to defend Paul but couldn't find reasons. Adriana smiled at Steve. She got up from her seat next to the stone fireplace and pout her arm around his waist. This was out of character for Adriana. She never spoke as much as ten words to Steve the entire time he was in DC. She acted as though wanted to protect him. For what reason, Bridges couldn't figure.

The conversation turned to the President and his announcement. Adriana smiled and toasted to the President and the most magnificent thing he ever did, announce he would not seek a second term and immediately resign.

Tom asked what everyone thought. Bridges smiled and offered his opinion.

"Seems we had some help from somewhere, isn't that true Adriana?"

"Sounds like it." Adriana looked down into her glass when she spoke.

Tom and Alice looked at each other as Steve downed his Scotch. Jennifer sat in a large over stuffed chair and appeared as though she was about to slip off into a well deserved sleep. She would be leaving for Jordan in a week and her attendance at the reception for her father was over-whelming. Bridges glanced over at her and suggested they leave.

Steve smiled as he shook Bridges hand and invited him to go shooting when he was in the San Diego area. Both men hugged each other.

***

At the farm, Jennifer said goodnight and went directly to bed. Adriana sat in silence waiting for Bridges to ask her questions she wasn't prepared to answer at this time. Bridges suggested they shower together and didn't once ask a question about that evening and the President's announcement. They made love after a warm silent shower. Adriana seemed more relaxed during their love-making. She once again reminded Bridges that he was special and she loved him.

The next morning they heard Jennifer leave for school. The sound of her Jeep woke them. For some reason she raced the engine in a way that it was not like her. Bridges wondered if she was angry or upset about something. Adriana thought maybe it was that she was taking her father away from her.

During breakfast prepared by Adriana, they discussed the night before. Adriana smiled and suggested they exchange ideas but admitted neither had the answers, as though it mattered. Their only reason was to prevent the President from being assassinated. Adriana spoke.

"The sonofabitch is over…he doesn't need to be killed…I'm certain Heidi is stark raven mad right now. If she knew where I was she'd be calling me."

"You mentioned you quit...what then?"

"I quit, but I haven't told her yet...she knows, but I'm sure she'll want me to stay as a friend. The poor bastard of a husband is a lame-duck."

"Don't you mean a lame-dick?" Bridges smiled.

They laughed in harmony as though they had a secret that the other didn't know. The telephone rang. it was Tom.

"What's up Tom?"

"Nothing really, but one of the people that takes care of my car found a small caliber automatic stuffed between the rear seat. It belong to you?" What's the caliber?"

"twenty-two, new looking but I'm sure its at least twenty years old."

"Not mine...keep it, you'll need it for your collection."

Tom thought Bridges' remark wasn't surprising in the least. He answered.

"I thought maybe you'd want it Richard...it may serve as a memento of a celebrated event. I had it checked out, it's clean, no identified owner. I could check it out further but no crime was committed, so the hell with it."

Bridges agreed they should get together that after noon and discuss a few things. Tom informed him that Steve returned to California on the early flight.

"He sure as hell seemed a different man. After the event at the White House, the poor sole clammed up."

Adriana telephoned the White House after Bridges finished his conversation with Tom. Bridges deliberately didn't tell her about Tom finding the gun in his car.

Adriana could be over-heard talking to Heidi. It sounded as thought they were good old friends and were going to meet for lunch. Bridges seemed puzzled, but then thought Adriana was up to one of her tricks. He didn't bother to ask when she returned to the kitchen and had another cup of coffee. She announced she was having lunch with the First Lady. Bridges thought it was cordial and then asked the question.

"Did you tell her you quit?"

"Of course not, it's Saturday and I think I'll just go buy, have lunch with her and then tell her. She suspects, I'm sure."

"Did she mention anything about the President?"

"No…but I'm sure I'll hear when I get there."

Bridges had something on his mind he wanted to discuss with Adriana. He in fact felt in conflict with the situation of the previous evening although he wanted to ask her to accompany Jennifer to Amman. He thought he'd ask later, at least when Jennifer returned from classes. It wasn't as though Jennifer couldn't take care of herself, but the company would be a welcome, besides Adriana was related to the King's wife.

"Adriana, did you loose your gun?"

"No, why do you ask?" Adriana was taken by surprise.

"Tom found a small twenty-two in the back seat of his car."

"Not mine, I have it in my purse."

"Who's gun is it, I mean the one Tom found?"

Bridges didn't believe her, but didn't want to press the issue. He thought he'd take a peak in her purse when she was showering.

"Beats me, thought it was yours, but if you have yours, then who knows."

While Adriana was showering, Bridges discovered the twenty-two Sterling was in her purse. He felt embarrassed after making the discovery.

***

Adriana left for the White House after getting dressed in a casual outfit. After she left, bridges found her hand-gun on the bureau. It was neatly in the holster and a magazine was in place. Again he felt embarrassed for doubting her. He thought about what Tom told him of finding a small caliber hand gun in the car. His mind went in high gear, he thought that he and Adriana sat in the rear seat along with Steve. Immediately he thought Steve left it, on purpose to leave a message. He recalled the attempt on the President at the country club in California. Steve was the suspect until the car salesman was mentioned and of course Steve's convincing story. Then he recalled learning that the Israelis were responsible for killing the woman assassin.

He sat in deep thought. It was raining and the wind slapped a loose shingle on the roof. He hoped it didn't come-off and cause a leak in the ceiling. The horses in the barn sounded above the wind and rain. He looked out the window through the mahogany stained louvered blinds in his study. The lights flickered as the wind became louder and severe. His thoughts were confused, especially now that the President announced that he wouldn't seek a second term. Before the dinner, the President was his arrogant self then later, less than an hour, he made the announcement.

He thought of Adriana, she didn't respond in a manner that would have been expected. After looking at the Bavarian clock on the wall, he decided to call to at home. Alice informed him that Tom went to the office and would return by noon. He immediately called Tom at the office. He sounded preoccupied with something and didn't provide Bridges the impression he wanted to discuss the evening before. Bridges sensed there was someone with him and maybe couldn't talk. Tom promised to call him later, no specific time. He wanted to ask so many questions that he was sure had some connection to the plot to assassinate the President. The Arab found dead in Teddy Roosevelt Park. The two maid, one kissed off as a lover's jealous impulse, the maid found in the field with the same signature of shooting as the Arab. Then there was James Allen…the poor bastard, he thought, the poor soul didn't have a clue, or did he? Then Michael, what the hell is the story and his connection in all this mess. Undercover for the Bureau is one thing, but going under so deep that they, who ever they were, killed his friend to save his ass. Maybe he had it all-wrong, maybe there wasn't a connection between James Allen and Michael.

The more he thought, the more he felt unsure about the entire mess. Funny thing he thought, Heidi Jefferson Banks is a selfish bitch, she has desires for herself, all things that happened pointed to her. But is that true, did she pull the strings and things happened, to include the attempt on his own life with the car-bomb. It sure looks like Heidi, but then maybe not. He surprised himself with the thought. Was he now thinking Adriana is the one that pulled the strings all along, he shook his head and didn't want the thought to linger deep in his mind. Why would she have gone through the trouble of locating him in Tel Aviv.

The phone rang, interrupting his unpleasant thought. it was Tom calling to explain that he had been in the middle of some business and couldn't speak without being inhibited.

"We traced the gun further, it was purchased new in a small town in Idaho, at least five years ago. The person listed is...Walter Schultz. He's dead, we learned that from talking to the local police up there, he retired from the military and would have been sixty when he purchased the gun. No record of being stolen."

"Tommy...why did you follow-up in checking it out?"

"Curiosity...that's all." Tom had another reason, although wasn't prepared to share it with Bridges, at least at this time.

"What can I say...I really thought it belonged to Adriana." This comment didn't surprise Tom in the least, although he decided not to add to it.

During lunch of Caesar-salad and California Chardonnay, Heidi thanked Adriana for her help and with a certain animosity, wished her a happy life with her prince-charming

Adriana looked around the small room Heidi selected for their lunch. The room was once used by Lincoln as a reading room. On the west wall there was a painting of President Lincoln and facing from the east, a painting of a grey stallion that had a resemblance to an Arabian. The furniture was dated and Adriana believed had been present when Lincoln occupied the White House. An old bible lay on a small round table in the corner.

Adriana was surprised the First Lady wasn't upset with her leaving. She sensed Heidi was glad or even relieved. The President would resign in a few days and that it would be over.

Adriana didn't want to get into a deep discussion with Heidi over various things that happened and she was suspected of orchestrating. She decided to leave well enough alone, they would soon be out of the White House and that's really a blessing to the country. The thought of someone attempting to kill Bridges with a car bomb left her cold. She thought it would be better served if she didn't bring it up.

That afternoon, Bridges suggested to Jennifer that Adriana may be a good traveling companion when she made the trip to Jordan. Jennifer was excited with the idea.

"I haven't asked Adriana yet, but I'm sure she will welcome the idea."

"Daddy…it's a good idea…I'd love that."

William and Tilly had left on their trip to visit their son at Fort Jackson, South Carolina.

Jennifer and Adriana agreed to make dinner as Bridges made several phone calls. His first was to Paul Castilli. At first the conversation was cordial until Paul started to degrade Steve Young and what a disgrace he was to the Marine Corps.

"What's wrong Paul…because he didn't kiss your ass and Sir you to death…come on, Steve was a damn good Marine and you know it. I recall you always separated yourself from the troops, that, I always thought was bullshit."

"Yes…he didn't show respect to me, I mean he knew I am a Supreme Court Justice."

"Hold on Paul…you made him feel inferior, yu-know…like shit, he was only reacting you. Besides you blame him for you not getting the Navy Cross and your medal was reduced to the Bronze Star."

"That's not it."

"Well Paul, I think it is it, for Chrise-sake, that was so many fucken years ago." Bridges was getting pissed and remembered how Paul cold be a stubborn bastard.

"We have nothing else to say to each other…Richard."

Bridges waited for Paul to hang up and he did the same. he thought in the shallow corner of his mind that they were never friends…even when they were in Vietnam. He admitted to himself that Steve could be an asshole at times, but didn't think he was out of line at the reception.

He made another call to an old Agency buddy, someone that had access to many things and who was assigned to liaison with the FBI. His request was plain and simple. He wanted information about Michael Myers and who was controlling him.

"If the Agency is in the control, then I will understand. But if the fucken Bureau is…I need to know something about the operation…no violation of and trade secrets. Just weather or not Michael Myers is on our side."

"I can tell you right now, no secrets on this one…this Myers person is a hell-of-a under cover guy…he is working for us…now I didn't say that…but the Bureau wanted to control him and they used the argument that we were not involved in domestic intelligence activities. His friend from NSA was taken out by mistake, by who, I don't know…but I do know the family, yu…know, the wife and children are being cared for. Need I say more?"

"Thanks Chip…I knew I could count on you…we never spoke, I promise."

"You still with that sweetheart, Adriana?"

"Ya…why you asking?"

"I put her on to you."

"Then you're the one that mentioned my nick-name?"

"Not me…it was one of the assholes in the office, someone that never worked with us in El Salvador."

"Thanks again Chip…stay in touch."

Bridges sat behind the desk in the study…he sat in silence until Adriana came in with a martini for him. He smiled at her as he looked up and thought she was an incredible woman. After dinner, they gathered around the fireplace and formulated plans for Adriana and Jennifer to go to Jordan for a week. Jennifer was excited and Bridges thought Adriana was also happy to travel with Jennifer.

After Jennifer showered and went to bed, Adriana poured a cognac for them both and sat in darkness watching the fire. As the fired died down, Adriana suggested they take a hot shower together. He looked at Adriana and thought that she loved her, but didn't know much about who she had been and where she was from. This was a strange thing that he never asked.

"My Adriana…I'm sure I love you."

She cuddled close and kissed Bridges on the mouth. He returned the kiss and then asked a question that came from no where, or did it.

"Where were you born?"

Adriana smiled in the almost darkened room, and answered.

"In the State of Idaho…why…I told you before."

"Just wondered, that's all."

"My dad was in the Air Force for over twenty years. We lived in a small town in Idaho while he was assigned to Fairchild Air Force Base near Spokane, Washington."

"You never told me your maiden name?"

"You never told me why you were called the Highwayman?"

"You first…Adriana."

"Schultz…born as Adriana Marie Schultz."

"Now it's your turn."

"Lets take the shower…and go to bed…I can feel more comfortable telling you there."

Passionately they made love for what seemed an hour. They agreed that it was late and Bridges rolled over on his left side. As Adriana lay on her back in silence…she spoke, "Richard…are you awake? Why do they call you THE HIGHWAYMAN?" No sound, Adriana didn't know if Bridges was asleep or refused to answer